"You remove your hands from me this second!" Kyrstal spit out at Drake.

The handsome Westerner dropped his hands, but leaned in even closer to the Bostonian miss. "Listen, darlin'," he whispered, "either you trust me or you place your life in the hands of that bunch of outlaws over there. The choice is yours, Miss Colbert."

"It's clear you're in cahoots with that gang—" Krystal began, but her words were suddenly cut off by the feel of his lips crushing against hers with an urgency that consumed her spinning mind. His strong arms wrapped around her narrow waist and held her in an imprisoning embrace as his unexpected kiss demanded her complete surrender . . .

Desperado Desire

VERONICA BLAKE

ZEBRA BOOKS
KENSINGTON PUBLISHING CORP.

ZEBRA BOOKS

are published by

Kensington Publishing Corp.
475 Park Avenue South
New York, NY 10016

First printing: April, 1988

Printed in the United States of America

For your understanding, words of encouragement, and most of all, for your unwavering love . . . Thank you with all my love: Jason, Tiffany and Brian.

Prologue

Green River, Wyoming, 1894

Angelina DeGanahl's tiny feet moved across the dark and dusty street with urgency. She was on a mission of desperate salvation. There was not time to wonder why her youngest son was so intent on destroying himself, and the proud name of DeGanahl. First, she had to make sure her eldest son was safe.

Of course, Angelina knew exactly where to go. He was always down here . . . on the wrong side of town. A feeling of despair engulfed her as she hurried past the rowdy saloons and houses of unmistakable repute. Why was this happening to her? She was the daughter of a Spanish Don . . . and the widow of Franklin DeGanahl, a man who had dared to fight for what he believed in and had earned every inch of the respect and honor that he had died with. Even now, she never once regretted her decision to become Frank's wife, and did not ponder over all that she had given up to do so.

Without hesitation she entered the shabby run-down establishment at the end of the narrow street. There was no time to waste. A buxom woman with a large brown mole at the left corner of her mouth

7

confronted the small woman at the entry and demanded that she leave. But Angelina was not deterred and glared up at the blonde trollop without blinking an eye. Realizing the determination of the Mexican lady, the larger woman backed down, and in no time at all was directing the little black-clad figure up to the top of the stairs.

Angelina felt a hard knot well up in her stomach as she rapped her knuckles against the rough wood of the door. Oh, how she hated doing this. Unmistakable noises were emitted from the other side of the door: a bed squeaking, cursing and then a shout. "Go away — Cherry's busy!"

"I must talk to you," Angelina barely managed to choke out in a trembling voice.

Silence was her reply, then more noises, rustling sounds and low murmurings and finally the door swinging open as Angelina's gaze met the broad expanse of a man's furred chest. Her eyes ascended with slow reservation until she looked into the brooding face of her oldest son. Brown tousled hair hung in disarray across his forehead and down past his ears. The bristled growth of several days without a razor covered the area surrounding his scowling mouth, and the pale purple smudges beneath his eyes suggested that he was sorely lacking sleep. Drake DeGanahl's dark olive-colored eyes flashed with annoyance as he finished fastening his breeches and glared down at the tiny woman before him.

"Mother!" he demanded with impatience edging into his voice. "What is the meaning of this?" The irritation he felt began to fade when he noted the strange look on his mother's ashen face. He began to sense that she was not here to lecture him on his lustful pastimes.

Angelina allowed her eyes to travel past her son and

rest briefly on the woman lounging on the bed. Had the brazen creature no shame at all? Angelina wondered to herself. The prostitute made no attempt to hide herself and did not seem to be bothered in the least by the sudden intrusion. She continued to sip on a glass of whiskey while carrying a look of smug indifference upon her hardened face. Her breasts protruded in alert attention, still swollen and taut from their recent fondling, and her legs were spread in a vulgar invitation. The musky smell of recent lovemaking hung heavy in the air and was still evident on the dirty stained sheets that covered the narrow bed.

Angelina swallowed hard and looked away. There was not a moment to waste on this type of trivial distraction, no matter how offensive it was to her. She looked up into her son's questioning face. "Drake, I must speak to you. It is a matter of life and death." Her eyes flickered past him again and then back. "In private," she added in a whisper.

Drake glanced back over his shoulder and felt a feeling of complete disgust flood through his whole being. All at once he became ashamed beyond imagination at the sight that greeted his mother. He quickly pushed her out into the darkened hallway and slammed the door behind them. Since his father's tragic death six months ago, this hell-hole had become his home away from home. But now he was suddenly jolted back to reality, and his sense of decency returned to him with a wave of nausea.

"Drake, you must leave town, tonight!"

His mother's words cut sharply into his thoughts of shame and embarrassment. Drake shook his head and narrowed the thick lashes surrounding his confused gaze.

Angelina did not wait to explain. She shoved a wad

of bills into his hand. "Here is enough money for your provisions and there's not a moment to waste. A lynching party is looking for you and they will not listen to reason if they should find you. Hurry—please!" Her tone grew louder and pleading, the pained expression mirrored in her dark eyes screaming her message of foreboding.

Drake shrugged with a nonchalant gesture. "I have nothing to fear from a lynching party. I've been here for hours. Cherry can vouch for that."

Angelina cringed visably with the thought of her handsome son wasting his days and nights with that wanton woman on the other side of the door. But now was not the time to wonder why he insisted on throwing away his birthright and extensive inheritance on that sort of trash. With her heart breaking like shards of fragile glass, the mother looked up at the face she had gifted with life.

He was a man that made the gentler persuasion melt like ice on a hot summer day, with his slow easy smile and sparkling deep green eyes. No mother could ask for a child who was more perfect to look upon, and Angelina had been blessed with two such sons. But inside, where it was determined what a man would feel and care, the DeGanahl boys were as different as night and day. Angelina could not bear the thought of this son squandering his life away in these filthy shacks of ill repute. She had already given up all hope on her youngest boy.

"Devon did it again. Only this time, he killed a man right here in Green River. There's a group of at least thirty men, crazed with anger, and threatening to hang the first DeGanahl they come across. Please Drake, you must leave . . . Now!"

"Damn," Drake growled with fury clouding his features. His little brother had always been a thorn in

10

his side, but Devon's lastest escapades had become a problem of outlandish proportions. Just last month Devon was accused of shooting a bank teller in Lander, Wyoming. "Who'd he kill this time?"

Angelina drew in a heavy breath. "He was with those men he's been riding with and they tried to hold up the Union Pacific Railroad office, but Sheriff Gardener happened to be passing by and tried to avert the holdup." Drake began to shake his head with dread, knowing what his mother's next words would be.

"Eyewitnesses said Devon shot the Sheriff down in cold blood. And now half the town is up in arms. They're saying Devon did it on purpose, because Dave Gardener just took over your father's job as Sheriff." She reached out a trembling hand and placed it on her son's arm. "I'm begging you Drake, take the money and leave this place. Make something of yourself. You're my last hope. Please don't let me down."

Drake met his mother's sorrowful dark eyes with his own tormented gaze, and he knew immediately that he would do as she asked. Her life was devoted to her sons, and she deserved so much more than the heartache they had given to her in return. Yes, he would leave this town and he would show her that she had not failed as a mother, in spite of his younger brother's efforts to prove otherwise. And someday, Drake vowed, he would return, and when he did, everyone would know that the name of DeGanahl had not become one to look down upon, but rather one that would require respect and honor again . . . just as it had when Franklin DeGanahl had ruled Sweetwater County!

Chapter One

Boston, Massachusetts 1896

Rebecca Colbert was an intelligent woman, though it was her habit to feign ignorance. Her beauty was obvious, so it was not necessary for her to flaunt it. Yet, she had a tendency to do just that. Dressed in fabulous gowns of silk or satin, and draped in shimmering jewels, the sultry blonde always managed to monopolize every male she came in contact with. She possessed a lyrical laugh that made her topaz eyes twinkle like gemstones; so, her numerous men friends always made sure they had a humorous anecdote to quote to her when they competed for her attentions. The elusive Mrs. Colbert appeared to have it all: immense wealth, undeniable beauty, and a natural talent.

Rebecca was an actress in the greatest sense, not only on the stage, where she had achieved great success, but also in her personal life. Her ability to weave a tale brought her sensational performances to life and made her the toast of Boston's high society — and was her downfall in the end.

So, it was with a great sadness that her shocked

friends and devastated daughter gathered at her gravesite on a sunny afternoon in July to pay their last respects. The funeral was elaborate, just as Rebecca had lived out her life. Afterward, the Victorian mansion on Beacon Hill was overflowing with friends of the family and business associates of Rebecca's, not to mention her many devoted fans. She would be missed by all, but especially by her only child.

Krystal Dawn Colbert, a petite young lady garbed in black, was the epitome of sorrow. But unlike her talented mother, Krystal Colbert's feelings were as natural as a spring day in May. She was her mother's daughter in only one aspect . . . she was unnaturally beautiful. The delicate features of her perfect bone structure were encased in magnolia-hued skin, enhanced by large eyes that were the shade of cocoa intermingled with honey, and surrounded by long dark lashes which were gently laced with golden tips. Beneath an abundance of strawberry blonde curls which were always coiffed to reserved perfection was a svelte figure that was a fitting partner for her exquisite beauty. They were inherited traits that Krystal found to be more of a hinderance than an asset, and it was her greatest desire to make something of her life that would not be attributed to her appearance. Rebecca's fondest hope had always been that her daughter would marry into one of the wealthy and prominent families of Boston, but her offspring had a mind of her own.

Krystal Colbert also loved to stand before an audience. Nothing gave her greater pleasure than to look out at the fresh, shining faces before her, knowing that a good deal of their futures rested in her guiding hands. Miss Colbert was a teacher and her only desire was to impart knowledge to the bright and eager children that entered her classroom each day. As prim and proper as her mother was flamboyant and gay, it was Rebecca's worst fear that Krystal would become an old maid school teacher . . . a definite possibility since Krystal found most of the men she met in Boston to be arrogant and boring.

Surrounded by her mother's friends in the lavish house on the Hill, Krystal had never felt so alone. In spite of their completely different lifestyles and goals, Krystal's best friend had been her mother, and now she was gone. Krystal's tear-studded eyes traveled slowly over the parlor, though not really looking at anything or anyone in particular. She was remembering a time from long ago, a cold winter's night when translucent snowflakes fell softly upon the window pane and gentle flames of orange and gold licked out from the hearth to ward off the chill that accompanied the unexpected storm. Wrapped in a heavy patchwork quilt, a little girl with long golden-red curls and twinkling eyes of tawny brown curled up in the comforting arms of her mother and watched the dancing flames beckon to her with their fiery fingers. The woman's soft voice floated to the young girl's attentive ears while the eyes of the child grew wide and excited as the woman told her of the dashing man who had been her father and of a faraway place called the Wild West.

Krystal had not recalled that night for a very long time, and she was surprised that it would be this small memory that would surface now rather than all the fabulous performances her mother had given on the stage. The voices around her all buzzed with those recollections of her mother or of the strange circumstances surrounding Rebecca's death, but Krystal's mind continued to wander back to that wintry eve. What would their lives have been like if her father had lived? As a little girl, John Colbert had been Krystal's

14

ideal hero, and, even now, a man did not exist who could compare with the image she had conceived of this great man. He had been an adventurer who had headed to Virginia City, Nevada, in the early 1860's where he became one of thousands who dug and sweated in the rocky caverns while dreaming of discovering a bonanza. When a traveling theater group arrived in town, a bit of culture and refinement for the rowdy miners, John fell head-over-heels in love with the beautiful blonde actress who headlined the show.

He was wild and brash, everything the young woman did not want in a man. But he was also determined, and before the troupe left town he had won her heart. This was the part Krystal found the most intriguing. A man who could corral a free spirit like her mother must have been quite a man. Since her mother had only spoken of him that one night, and even then had not offered much information, the girl was left to her own imagination as to what he had really been like.

Rebecca had made one point very clear, and that was John's love for his baby daughter. On the morning of Krystal's birth, John had discovered a crystallized gold nugget in his mine on the Comstock Lode. It was his first big find and he was convinced his new daughter had brought him luck, so she was aptly named Krystal Dawn as was his mining stake. But his luck was short lived. When Krystal was a mere two months old, her father was killed in a mining accident and the infant returned to the East with her mother. At least, that was the story her mother had told her.

"Krystal?" Les Macrea touched her arm softly. Traces of tears still lingered in his red-rimmed eyes. He had been Rebecca's lawyer and dearest friend, and was the closest thing Krystal had to a father. Like

15

Krystal, Rebecca's death had left a great void in him that would never be filled again.

Reluctantly Krystal returned to the present, though she would have preferred to remain in the elusive dreams of her childhood. She looked up at the man with a sorrowful gaze. "I'm going to miss her so much, Les."

"I know," he replied in an emotion-choked voice. "We all will. But it's time now, and Rebecca wanted it done immediately." He held out his hand and Krystal placed her small hand in his. She rose and sighed deeply, dreading what was about to take place, since it would only serve to make Rebecca's passing all the more final.

The couple entered the dimly lit study which was filled with mementos of Rebecca's life on the stage: posters of past performances, newspaper clippings framed in glass, and the many tokens of her caring fans. Krystal paused briefly before one of the posters. Her mother's vibrant spirit seemed almost alive on this particular piece of artwork. *A GAME OF CHANCE*, starring Rebecca Colbert, read the caption above the picture of the ravishing blonde woman with the inviting smile resting upon her red lips. This play had been Krystal's favorite. In it, her mother had played a sensuous riverboat gambler, and it was only during her mother's realistic performances that Krystal allowed her normally staunch mind to wander to a more licentious way of life.

Les Macrea pulled out a chair for Krystal and she sat down numbly. Already seated in the room were the four servants that had served the Colbert household and several of Rebecca's dearest friends. Krystal acknowledged them with a slight nod of her head. Obviously they were to be included in her mother's will. And so they were, all receiving generous rewards

16

for their loyalty and devotion. Upon arriving at the clause in the document concerning Krystal, Les asked that the room be cleared with the exception of the girl and himself.

Once they were alone Krystal turned questioning eyes toward him. "It wouldn't have mattered if they had remained. They are—like you—my only family now." She fought back the urge to give in to the threatening tears again when she realized that she was the last Colbert left now that her mother was gone.

"I felt it best to read the rest of it in private. Of course you know that Rebecca's estate all belongs to you now. But there is also a letter that Rebecca wrote to you. She asked that it be given to you after the reading of the will."

He held out a neatly folded paper, but Krystal shied away from it. "Will you read it to me, Les? Please?"

He cleared his throat loudly, his uneasiness evident. He unfolded the paper and started to read. His voice, no longer businesslike, now carried a slight quiver. "My darling Krystal," he began, "since the reading of this letter is obvious proof that I am no longer of this world," and Krystal smiled wistfully; even in death her mother's dramatic nature still prevailed. "I feel I must tell you of a terrible injustice I have done to you. Please try to understand that though my reasons were strictly in a selfish vein, they were only because I love you so very much."

Les drew in a heavy breath and continued as Krystal began to grow very confused and anxious. "Many years ago I told you a story about a man named John Colbert." Krystal's nervous feeling grew in leaps and bounds, her heart suddenly beating very rapidly and unsteadily. Not twenty minutes ago, she had been thinking of that very night. She fidgeted in her seat as she leaned forward to grasp each of Les' next words. "Your father was a miner. His name was John Colbert and our meeting was just as I related it to you. He did discover a huge gold nugget on the day you were born, but everything I told you after that was a lie."

Krystal's stomach felt as if it had just done a complete flip and her breath almost seemed to stop in her chest as Les continued to quote the next line. "Your father did not die when you were two months old and to the best of my knowledge, he is still alive and living in Virginia City, Nevada."

"Good Lord," Krystal whispered. The color drained from her face as the meaning of her mother's words sank into her confused and spinning mind. Her father . . . alive! It had been her greatest wish for most of the twenty years of her life, but now in the face of her mother's death, the news was crushing.

Les moved to her side with concern. "Are you all right, child?" He had watched her grow from a beautiful little girl into a breathtaking young woman of even greater beauty and he also knew she was the strongest-willed person he had ever known. But now she looked as if she had just lost every ounce of that overpowering spirit and Les couldn't help but be worried.

"Is there more?" she queried in a quiet tone, her eyes turned upward to watch Les with unanswered questions running rampant in the depths of those golden-brown pools.

He nodded and straightened. "Yes." Again he cleared his throat and returned his eyes to the paper he held in his shaking hands. "Please try to understand, though I loved John's wild and crazy spirit, I did not love him the way he deserved to be loved. But worse, I could not bear life in that horrible wilder-

18

ness. As soon as I was able to travel after your birth, I stole the money from your father's claim and fled with you in tow."

Krystal gasped, but Les read on. "John's gold discovery was vast and the money I took would not have made the least bit of difference to him. By now, he probably owns most of Virginia City and is the wealthiest man in all of Nevada. You are his legal heir and I have no doubt that he would still love you every bit as much as he did on the day you were born. I know I have done you a great wrong, and I hope you can forgive me, for it was your best interest that was always foremost in my mind. Remember that always, and however you chose to live your life, be happy." Les' voice trailed off and fell silent. Once again Rebecca Colbert had performed superbly and Les found himself wondering how many more surprises she would spring upon them before she could finally rest in peace.

Krystal remained unmoving for a moment as she let the reality settle in her heavy heart. How could she be angry with her mother now? She was not here to defend herself. But still, Krystal found a bit of anger seeping through her veins. She felt cheated that her mother had waited until after her death to tell her of this startling revelation. Krystal Colbert was a fighter, it was not her nature to give in easily to any circumstance, and now she was forced to do just that. She unfolded her tiny frame from the chair and began to move past Les with a stiff stride. He reached out to her but she brushed past him, wanting only to be alone with this added misery.

Unnoticed, she slipped up the wide, carpeted stairway, past the large oil paintings of her mother and herself, a lifetime told in portraits. Her glazed eyes traveled over the rare statues and priceless antiques

19

Rebecca had collected on her worldwide tours. Stolen money had been the basis behind all of Rebecca's wealth. Krystal had never felt so deceived. All this time her father had been alive, and each of them had been robbed. The forgotten feelings of her youth came flooding back . . . The desperate desire to be like her friends and know the comforting feeling of having a complete family. John Colbert's gold had been taken from him, but that seemed unimportant when compared to all the wasted years that had been lost between him and his daughter.

Krystal stood at the threshold of her mother's bedroom. The sweet scent of her mother's lilac cologne still lingered in the stillness and welcomed her with familiar remembrances. She entered slowly and closed the door behind her. She grew enraged and sad, then at the same time, began to feel so very alone. As she wandered aimlessly around the room, she experienced such a great hurt that she was sure she would never recover. How could her mother just go and drown at a time like this!

Pulling open a drawer, she began to sift idly through the lacy undergarments. Her hand came to rest on a hard object at the bottom of the drawer. She lifted the small black box and carefully opened the lid. The contents puzzled her even more. Inside the velvet-lined box rested an exquisite diamond brooch, obviously an antique by the weathered look of the gold setting. But why was such a rare piece of jewelry here in this box instead of in the safe with the rest of Rebecca's jewelry? At the bottom of the box was a faded and torn photograph. Krystal raised the picture close to her face and studied it. The images of two people could be made out in the center of the tattered photo; a lovely young blonde girl and a reckless looking cowboy stood in front of a large building.

Krystal moved over to the window and strained to make out the name above the door of the building. "Piper's Opera House, Virginia City," were the words printed across the front of the wooden structure. Krystal felt the breath catch in her throat. This was a picture of her parents, probably the only link she would ever have to her lost father. She clutched the picture and the diamond brooch to her breast and allowed the tears to flow freely down her cheeks.

All at once it became apparent to her just what an accomplished actress her mother really had been to be able to convince her of her father's death, while knowing all along that he was still alive. How many other lies had Rebecca Colbert pulled off with her expert acting abilities? Krystal looked around the expensively furnished room, her mind buzzing with questions. Where did all the money come from to support this sort of a lifestyle? Rebecca had been a successful actress, but even her salary could not provide the riches that abounded in this room alone, not to mention the extensive traveling she did. Just how much money did she steal from John Colbert's mine twenty years ago? And what, Krystal wondered, was her mother doing down on the docks, the seediest area of the city, on the night of her death?

Chapter Two

Giant spirals of white and gray clouds bellowed from the tall funnel-shaped smokestack and evaporated into the vast blue sky as the steam powered locomotive began to pull away from the Wyoming station. Drake DeGanahl settled back into the uncomfortable seat and glanced around at the other passengers with a disinterested sweep of his dark green eyes. The car was not crowded, only a few people were scattered throughout the coach and most of them appeared to be elderly people.

It had been such a long journey from New Orleans and his temperament was greatly lacking in sociability, even though he had spent an extra day in Rawlins carousing the various saloons. Still, he hated traveling on a train, and though he was more than a little anxious to reach his destination he was not sure what to expect when he got there. Two years had passed since he had been home, the longest years of his life. The city had bored him, but he really had tried to fulfill the promise he had made to his mother in the dirty brothel two years before. He had even studied law for a brief time, although his mind kept wandering back to the rugged mountains of Wyoming and the wide open prairies with endless clumps of gray and black sagebrush stretching out as far as the eye could see. The West was bred into him and nothing was ever going to change that.

His thoughts returned for a moment to the events that led to his unexpected departure two years ago. A hard knot formed in his stomach as he recalled Franklin DeGanahl's death . . . a bullet in the back from a fifteen-year-old boy, an impulsive youth who blamed Sheriff DeGanahl for the hanging of his outlaw father the day before. The killing had shocked the town of Green River, but it had destroyed Franklin's two sons.

Drake, the eldest son of Angelina and Frank De-Ganahl had abandoned the deputy's badge he had worn with pride and had given up his hopes of someday filling his father's position as the Sheriff of Sweetwater County. Instead, he retreated into the shallow comfort of a whiskey bottle and the luring clutches of the local prostitutes. But the rebellious Devon DeGanahl turned his father's death into a twisted vendetta against all society, using it as a lame excuse for his hellbent ways and violent life of crime.

Drake's gaze wandered across the near-empty coach again, coming to rest on a lithe figure positioned at a window seat directly across from him. Curiosity overcame him as he stared at the petite form. It was almost impossible to determine the woman's age, she was draped in an expensive but overly modest dress of black silk that reached to her chin and covered every inch of her with its heavy dark material. A long matching cape adorned her shoulders and concealed whatever womanly charms she might possess. The large brimmed hat that topped her costume was accented with a black net veil and hid her face from view also.

Drake was intrigued. It was a hot summer day, but the woman had to be wearing at least three layers of clothing. The only portion of the mysterious woman in black that he could see was the luscious pair of pink lips which curved with an enticing slant beneath the veil. Drake found himself mesmerized by that fascinating mouth, although he was not sure why. Perhaps it was the fact that he could only imagine what sort of face would accompany such tempting lips. He could not tear his eyes away from her and began to scrutinize every inch of the woman with his discerning gaze. It was evident that she was a small woman, like his mother. Drake guessed that she would barely clear five feet when she stood up; however she sat tall and straight in the hard seat and her head was tilted up in a proud and almost conceited manner. Tiny gloved hands were clasped tightly around a small black bag that rested in her lap. Beneath the full skirt of her black dress, the sharp pointed toes of her dainty high-topped shoes peeked out in a ladylike fashion. Drake guessed that she was in mourning, since she was dressed in solid black, and he knew he was being very rude to stare at her, but he couldn't seem to tear his eyes away.

The woman, feeling the uneasiness that always comes when one is being stared at, turned from the window and looked in the direction of the inquisitive eyes which watched her in bold observance. The soft lips curved down into an unmistakable frown, and Drake found himself even more interested in this strange lady.

She continued to scowl at him, becoming more and more irritated by the moment. Deciding to beat him at his own game, she began to glare back at him through the heavy dark veil. Though he could not make out her features, it was obvious to Drake that she was staring at him in return. He discovered he was having a delightful time, especially since he could tell by the distinct pout on her mouth that she was growing furious. He was hoping she would soon lift the contraption that covered her face and end the suspense of not knowing what she looked like. A fleeting thought passed through his mind that he might be disappointed when she revealed herself to him, but something told him that would not happen. No indeed, Drake's intuition told him that the face behind the concealing net veil would match those delicious-looking lips and he couldn't wait to see the contents inside that ridiculous covering.

Krystal Dawn Colbert's chin tilted outward in an aggravated scowl. Who was this rude and obtrusive man who stared at her with such a degrading glint in his dark eyes? She could not help but notice how his choice of dress seemed to conflict with his rakish good looks. He was garbed in the tailored clothes of a city slicker; yet, something in his forward gaze almost hinted at a savage nature. Krystal decided that he was no more than a dandy, and without a doubt, a low life who was merely pretending to be someone important. She had seen hundreds like him in Boston, but a more handsome rogue she had never before encountered. Becoming slightly irritated with herself for thinking about him in that manner, she quickly pushed the uninvited thought from her mind and concentrated on her anger instead.

Her journey had also been a long one, filled with sadness and indecision. She did not need this unnecessary distraction. Realizing the lout was not going to back down after an endless amount of time had passed, Krystal decided to confront him. Rising cautiously from her seat, she began to cross the short distance to where he sat.

Drake watched in complete fascination as she almost seemed to float towards him in her flowing black attire. He had not been wrong about her small structure, but she moved with the sureness of a person who appeared to tower over others. When she stopped before him, his eyes strained to make out the rest of the face above the sensuous lips he had been fantasizing over.

She leaned down and in a clipped voice said, "Sir, if you were a gentleman with any manners you would know that it is not polite to stare. But obviously that is not the case, so unless you wish to have yourself removed from this car, I would advise you to avert your obnoxious look to something or someone other than me!"

Drake, expecting an invitation of a different nature, was set back on his heels. Woman did not usually talk to him in that manner. He was amused and even more aroused. If he could just see her face . . .

The sly grin that moved in an instinctive and leisurely manner across his face caused Krystal's anger to flare like an ignited torch. She opened her mouth to hurl another threat at him, but before she could get the words out the train lurched forward, then grinded and screeched to an abrupt halt. The passengers were flung around inside the coach like rag dolls and disorder ruled over the entire train. Krystal found herself in the lap of the handsome stranger and was not too happy at the familiar way he was holding on to her. Her startled mind quickly came to its senses and she jumped up, but not before he was able to tell that the feminine wares she had hidden beneath

26

the heavy garments were more than enough to please a hot-blooded male such as himself.

"I beg your pardon," she huffed in an icy voice, but her outburst of indignation was cut short by the loud intrusion of men that roared into the coach. Krystal turned to the source of the disturbance and felt her breath stop short in her chest. In the middle of the aisle stood two men holding rifles which were pointed at the quaking passengers. Beneath wide-brimmed hats the lower portion of their faces were concealed by red bandanas, leaving only their narrowed eyes exposed. Krystal grew numb with fear. Ever since she had left Boston she had been terrified of having an encounter with outlaws. Her well-meaning friends had tried to discourage her from making this trip by relating stories of brutal holdups and murders that occurred in this part of the country, but Krystal had to come. Finding her father was the only thing that had mattered since her mother's death the week before. Even though she had been warned by the authorities not to leave Boston until after the outcome of the investigation into Rebecca's drowning, Krystal had headed out West anyway. Too much time had already been lost where John Colbert was concerned, twenty years worth   her whole life. Besides, Krystal did not care what the investigation turned up, her mother was dead and nothing could change that fact. Krystal only wanted to remember what a loving and wonderful mother Rebecca had been, and nothing more. Right now, though, she had to deal with the greater problem before her.

Krystal Colbert straightened up and glared at the two men who now stood in the middle of the aisle. The lump of fear in her chest threatened to cause her fluttering heart to stop beating, but Krystal's stubborn nature would not allow them to see how scared she really was. Since most of the other passengers were slumped down in their seats in frightened huddles, the outlaw's attentions were immediately drawn to the small figure that stood in bold defiance before them.

Creed Ward pointed his Winchester .44 Carbine in the direction of the woman in black and grinned behind the red bandana. "Well, well, what have we got here?" He glanced at the masked man next to him and returned his undivided attention to the woman. "What ya hiding underneath all them clothes, little lady?" Both men began to snicker in a crude tone. Krystal sensed the meaning in their lecherous tones immediately. A cold shiver passed through her, but she did not back down.

Pulling her small structure to full height, Krystal held her head up high as she continued to glare at the men through the heavy veil. "What is beneath my choice of dress is hardly any of your business, sir."

Drake groaned inwardly and pulled his little black bowler hat down low on his forehead. Whoever this lady of mystery was, she was about to buy herself a whole load of trouble. And a little voice from somewhere deep inside told him that he was going to end up in that inferno with her. Something about those pouting pink lips had already enslaved his curious senses and he realized with a growing aggravation that he would do just about anything to see the face they belonged to. Damn! He wasn't even wearing a gun. He couldn't believe he'd been so foolish. His uneasiness began to expand into an engulfing feeling of doom as he decided that he had definitely been in the city far too long.

Creed Ward began to move towards her as he chortled behind his mask. Krystal became consumed with terror while she watched him approach. She glanced around with a futile hope, although she realized immediately that there was no escape. When he stood before her, the man reached out and using the barrel of his rifle began to draw up the black net of her head gear. Krystal felt as though her heart had definitely quit beating when she felt the cold metal touch her nose and then pass over her eyes. She closed her lids tightly as the veil slid up past her long lashes. Fear controlled every inch of her as she slowly allowed her eyes to open again. The glint in the outlaw's narrowed eyes was flashing at her with an undeniable look of lust. Krystal grew weak with the terror that was rapidly gaining control of her senses, but still, she remained unmoving.

Krystal Dawn Colbert had spent all of her life being told repeatedly of her rare loveliness, so she was prepared for the outlaws' reaction. The past few years she had learned to live with devouring looks from men, knowing that most of them would soon lose interest once they encountered her outspokeness and prudish attitude. On this trip she had not wanted to be bothered with gawking men and idle flirtations, so she had garbed herself in the heavy black attire in the hopes of warding off any unwanted attention.

A wide grin began to spread across Creed Ward's face in spite of his mask. He decided this was his lucky day and he was not going to miss out on it. With an obvious tone of suggestion he began to speak again. "Well, would you take a gander at this? What I found here is better than any amount of gold." He raised his rifle again and pushed back the brim of her large hat. The bonnet tumbled down her back and landed on the hard floor of the coach, releasing a cascade of strawberry blonde curls that floated past the young woman's shoulders.

Drake DeGanahl strained to see the face in front of that magnificent array of tresses, but her back was still to him and without rising up from his seat he could not see what she looked like. Once again, his thoughts wandered to his luggage where his gun was rolled up neatly in his longjohns. He had wanted to impress his mother so much that he had forgotten what life in Wyoming was really like. Now here he sat, dressed like a damned greenhorn, and without a weapon. He hung his head and cursed silently at his stupidity.

Krystal tossed the reddish-gold mane over her shoulders and glared up at the outlaw. "My name is Krystal Dawn Colbert and when my father hears of this outrage you will rue the day you were born."

Creed Ward began to chuckle hatefully again. "Krystal what?" he glanced at the man beside him. "Ain't that the name of that Saloon gal over in Rawlins that we've been hearin' all about?" The other man snickered and nodded his head.

A horrified gasp escaped Krystal's mouth. "Saloon girl! How dare you? I'll have you know, my father is one of the richest men in Nevada and owns most of Virginia City." The haughty tone of voice she used to belittle the men only served to fuel their already devious minds. Drake DeGanahl shook his head and closed his eyes as he slithered down lower in his seat. Krystal Dawn Colbert — whoever you are — he thought as he let out a sign of annoyance, you've really done it now.

Creed Ward began to exchange thoughtful looks with his partner, a cocky young kid who had assumed the fitting nickname of Sidewinder. Sidewinder's mind was working overtime as he began to back up towards the door. "The boss man is up front takin' care of the conductor, but I think he might like to know about this real interestin' turn of events."

Creed nodded in agreement as he reenforced his stance and continued to hold the passengers at bay with his rifle. None of them made any attempt to anger the outlaws and continued to hunch down in their seats with terror. Train robberies were becoming an increasing occurrence in these parts and the dangerous men who conducted them were a violent breed, born of the cattle depression and rapidly changing culture. In spirit they were reckless and carefree, a side iron was their closest friend and it spoke a deadly retaliation at the smallest provocation. They were men to be reckoned with.

Krystal had no idea what the holdup men were talking about, but the strange quiet that reined over the entire coach caused a feeling of disaster to flow rampant through her veins. She turned her head slowly and lowered her gaze to the stranger she had confronted earlier. The intense expression on his handsome face confirmed her greatest fear. Whatever was happening, she knew it would not be in her best interest.

Beneath the narrow brim of his hat, Drake's eyes raised up and came to rest on the beautiful porcelain face surrounded by the mass of sun-kissed curls. He met the worried gaze of the big golden-brown eyes set within an abundance of feathery dark lashes and a strange sensation passed through him. He knew at that moment that his life would never be his own again.

Sidewinder quickly returned with another masked man from the front of the train. The second man moved down the narrow aisle with a careless saunter.

31

His leather chaps flapped out from the sides of his muscled thighs and the fancy silver spurs attached to the heels of his boots jingled in time with his footsteps. From above a black bandana, his dark eyes moved roughly over the terrified people that were at his men's mercy as he reveled in the power he always felt whenever he controlled a situation such as this. The man continued to follow Sidewinder down the aisle, stopping when they had reached the source of the distraction. His flashing sable eyes did not waver as they took in every inch of the enchanting young lady who stood before him. Sidewinder's description of her beauty had definitely not been an exaggeration.

Krystal had never been so terrified, nor had she ever felt so defenseless. Every horror story she had ever read in dime novels about the brutal western frontier came flooding back to her. Good Lord, she should have listened to her friends. Hadn't they tried to warn her? Now she was in the middle of nowhere, in a desperate situation, and she was all alone. The father she had been bragging about was no more than the faded snapshot she had found in her mother's bureau drawer. Krystal didn't even know if he still existed. She clutched her tiny black handbag tightly beneath the long cape. In it she carried the treasured picture, along with the antique brooch she had found in her mother's room. They were her most treasured possessions, and she was not about to give them up to these vile men, at least not without a fight.

The tall outlaw raked his leering gaze over her again. "I understand you've got a rich daddy. Is that true?"

Krystal nodded slightly, wondering what that had to do with anything. Perhaps desperados feared powerful and wealthy people in these parts and the mention of her father would be the salvation of the passengers on this train. All at once, Krystal began to fear that maybe her mother had been wrong about John Colbert's immense wealth. She forced that thought from her mind, deciding instead that the only thing she cared about right now was getting away from the three men that were standing in front of her with the strangest and most terrifying looks in their eyes.

The men exchanged quick glances before the tall man who appeared to be the leader began to speak again. "Well, sugar, you just did all these nice people a favor. Thanks to you, we're going to leave them alone." Krystal let out the breath she had been holding in with a relieved sigh. But the masked man's next words turned her blood to ice. "If your daddy is so rich, you're probably worth a lot more than we could ever collect on this train." He glanced back over his shoulder and nodded at his men. "Yep, boys, looks like we might have us a gold mine here . . . a rich daddy from Virginia City." The man reached out his hand and ran his fingers over her long tousled curls. "And I bet he's gonna want you back real bad."

A visible tremor of fear shook Krystal's small form as she grasped the exact meaning in the outlaw's lewd tone of voice. Good Lord, she thought wildly, they were going to take her prisoner and hold her for ransom. All of a sudden she realized what a terrible mistake she had made with her careless remarks about her father. Oh why, she thought miserably, couldn't she learn to think before she spoke . . . just once!

Drake did not hesitate to consider his decision as he rose to his feet and drew the girl up against him protectively. "This woman is with me and—" his voice stopped short as his eyes met with the onyx-colored ones that drew into two narrow slits above the black bandana which covered the other man's face. For an instant neither man moved nor spoke, each engrossed in deep shock as recognition sunk into their startled minds. Drake was struck speechless by the irony of encountering his brother on this train and it was evident that Devon DeGanahl was equally as surprised. Neither man made any attempt to verbally acknowledge the other one, though their eyes were flashing silent threats at each other.

Krystal was stunned by the man's sudden announcement and took advantage of the quiet to turn and glare up at him. "I beg your—" his tightening grip around her waist interrupted her indignant retaliation. She sensed that this man, despite his meek appearance, might be her only hope, so she quickly fell silent. His olive-colored eyes were drilling into the outlaw's dark eyes with a deadly look that almost seemed to request some sort of a challenge. Krystal found herself almost relaxing within the strong embrace of the man. Her fear subsided briefly as she became more confident that this man was not as mild mannered as his dress suggested.

The outlaw's cocky exterior dissolved momentarily as he returned the other man's threatening gaze. His voice was slightly hoarse when he spoke again. "Well, I guess you'll be comin' along with us then."

His decision was obviously not one that his men agreed with as they looked to be more than a little displeased. Sidewinder immediately voiced his opinion. "You must be kiddin'? Why would you wanna take him with us? He'd only be in the way." His intimidating gaze slid over Krystal again, then back to the leader. "Let me finish him off right now." The boy pulled a well-used Peacemaker .45 from one of the holsters that hung on either side of his hips. He raised the gun to a poised position and leveled it at Drake's head. His bright blue eyes sparkled with the anticipation of bloodshed. Only eighteen, he was a serious contender for beating out the record number of men killed by Billy the Kid over a decade ago. At twenty-one Billy the Kid was reputed to have killed one man for each year of his life. Sidewinder boasted that he had claimed twelve lives so far in his brief, but brutal career.

Krystal drew in a ragged breath, but the man's gaze remained steady as he continued to watch the leader. He did not even appear to be affected by the deadly gun that was pointed at his head. His arm remained in a tight rein around Krystal's slender waist with a possessive grip. Good Lord, she realized with her knees suddenly growing weak, this stranger was about to get himself killed for her and she didn't even know his name. Krystal's mind was spinning and she had never felt such a tremendous feeling of doom. Oh, why hadn't she stayed in Boston? She thought briefly of Les Macrea. He had pleaded with her to wait until after the investigation so he could accompany her to Virginia City. But as usual, she was too stubborn to listen to him.

Devon DeGanahl's surprise at seeing his older brother was replaced by anger when his authority was questioned by the obnoxious young gunman, especially in the presence of his greatest rival—Drake DeGanahl. He turned and looked at the boy with a chilling narrow-eyed expression. "You don't hear too good? I said, he's goin' with us. Now let's get the hell outta here."

Sidewinder did not lower his pistol for a moment as his uncaring glare drilled into the other outlaw. Then

35

he shrugged and twirled his gun around his forefinger in a showy display of defiance before slinging it back into the leather holster. He hoisted his rifle back up and swung around to face the other passengers. The look of horror on everyone's face was evident. This young man was not one to anger. . . .He emitted a aura of danger with each glance of his cold expressionless eyes, and every calculated movement of his lean wiry body.

Devon motioned for Drake and Krystal to lead the way out of the car while Creed Ward and Sidewinder kept the rest of the passengers at bay with their weapons. No one had made any attempt to dissuade the outlaws from taking the hostages and it was evident that they were all relieved to have the holdup men's attention directed away from them. Krystal was too numb with fear to protest, but as they made their way down the steps, the stranger who claimed to be her companion leaned down and whispered in a strict tone of voice, "Keep your mouth shut and agree with everything I say!"

Krystal came to an abrupt halt and glared up at the man. How dare he tell her to shut up. Nobody tells Krystal Colbert what to do, she thought with fury rushing through her, especially some city slicker that she had never even met properly. Drake did not even break stride when he felt her stop and gave her an indiscreet shove, forcing her to keep up with him. "How dare—"

"Darlin'," he interrupted through clenched teeth, "I'm tryin' to save your rich little hide. Now damn it . . . shut up!"

An instant pout came across the pink lips as she started to protest again, but when she tilted her head up to cast him one of her most hateful looks and tell him exactly what she thought of his interference, she realized that he was dead serious. His handsome features wore a chiseled mask that carried an unspoken warning as his olive-colored eyes flashed down into hers.

"Well, fine!" Krystal huffed in spite of the feeling of dread that his look had provoked in her again. She was not used to letting someone else make any of her decisions, no matter what the circumstances. But, she always made sure she got in the last word.

"Fine!" he repeated as they reached a group of horses that stood beside the locomotive. Krystal did not have time to voice her anger at him because she was being ordered to mount one of the huge beasts that hovered above her.

Devon was growing nervous, they had already wasted more time than they should have. Stopping this train today had been a big mistake in more ways than one. The bank notes that were supposed to be in the train safe hadn't been there. And worse, his older brother, the perfect Drake DeGanahl, had been one of the passengers. Devon's voice was more than a little impatient when he repeated his command to the fiery girl. "I said get up on that horse. You're ridin' with me."

"I will not get up on that smelly animal." Krystal was not about to admit that she had never been on a horse's back in her entire life. The snorting animals had always terrified her and facing the wrath of these heathens seemed less frightening than mounting that hairy four-legged thing.

The group of men all swung around to stare at this little slip of a woman who was defying their fearless leader. Creed Ward returned just in time to hear her remark and exchanged mocking glances with the man who had been tending the horses, an aging gunslinger called Austin. Not too many people questioned Devon DeGanahl's orders. Even Devon himself was taken aback for a second, but he wasn't going to let a woman, especially one no bigger than a mite, tell him what she would or would not do. He glared down into her defiant gaze and cursed under his breath. With one swift motion, he grabbed her featherweight form and tossed her over the saddlehorn. Then equally as fast, he swung into the saddle behind her.

Krystal gasped and clutched the protruding horn with a deathlike grip as she tried to hang on to her small silk purse. Although she had never been a weak person, she wondered now if she might faint from fear. But she didn't have time to worry about it. Another masked man suddenly leaped from the front car and at the same time Sidewinder jumped from the passenger car with both his six-shooters blazing. She heard the man behind her curse again and then order the men to head out.

Drake was issued a command to mount an extra horse that Austin had been holding onto and he did not waste a moment in doing so. Gunfire surrounded them now, and though Drake couldn't tell where it was coming from, he guessed that the few men who were passengers on the train had finally decided to try to come to their aid. But it was a useless effort, because the desperados were quickly out of range, and before long had slowed their horses down to an easy gait.

Krystal finally released the breath that she had been holding since she had been thrown on the horse's back. Devon felt her exhale and eased up his tight grip on her as he allowed his raven-colored eyes to travel slowly down over her back. God, she smelled sweet, kind of like early morning in a fresh green meadow, and the long strawberry-hued curls that were brushing against his face were so soft. He was suddenly reminded that this beautiful woman belonged to his brother, a revelation that made him want her all the more. Bitter reflections of his stormy relationship with his older brother came flooding back to him like a raging torrent. Drake always got the best of everything, ever since they were little children. Drake could never do any wrong. It was always Devon who was the bad one. A deep man's voice from the past flashed through the dark recesses of his mind. "Why can't you be like Drake? He never gets in trouble." Then there was Jennifer . . . Devon would never forgive Drake for what happened to Jennifer.

Devon tried to shake off the fury that the memory had rekindled in him as he drew the lovely young woman closer and pressed his hard body against the gentle curve of her back. Their forms almost seemed to mold together in perfection. Perhaps this time Drake wouldn't be the victor, Devon thought with a new surge of vengeance rippling through him. Maybe it was finally Devon DeGanahl's turn for a change.

Chapter Three

The black dress and long cape Krystal was wearing were much too heavy for this time of year and they attracted the heat of the late afternoon sun like a magnet. Her silky undergarments clung to her damp body without mercy and tiny rivulets of perspiration framed her sunburned face. But she was determined not to remove any of the constrictive clothing, fearing that it would only draw more unwanted attention from the desperados.

Never having ridden on a horse before, Krystal's inner thighs felt like they had been rubbed raw and she was certain her legs would never fit together properly again — that is, if she lived long enough to care. She had a terrible feeling that the horse was going to start bucking at any second and she would undoubtably break her neck when she was thrown from his back.

Krystal had long ago stopped worrying about the way the outlaw was pressing himself up against her in very intimate manner. Since she was shoved up against the saddlehorn and his arms encircled her in a tight embrace as he held onto the reins there was absolutely nothing she could do about it anyway.

Besides, she was too hot and too sore to think about anything other than her discomfort. She had no idea where they were taking her, and she was also too terrified to allow her mind to dwell on what they inevitably had planned for her when they got there. Good Lord, she was alone with six men counting the poor man from the train who was pretending to be her traveling companion, and he was definitely no match for these hardened criminals.

After covering a great deal of desolate territory which was graced only by an occasional clump of colorless sagebrush, they finally stopped at a narrow and nearly dry creek bed to water their horses and quench their own thirsts. The men barely spoke to one another, it was evident they were anxious to put a lot of distance between themselves and the railroad tracks. Krystal got her first good look at her abductors when they paused at the creek. The bandanas they wore to conceal their faces now hung loosely down around their necks, but until they stopped she had been too worried about falling off the horse to notice. She was surprised when she observed the faces that had been concealed behind the masks. In her mind, she had envisioned brutal looking men with scarred faces and diabolical expressions. Much to her amazement, all of the outlaws were a good-looking bunch, with the exception of the leader and the young boy called Sidewinder. These two were exceptionally handsome. In fact, Krystal noticed, the man she was riding with was almost as handsome as the stranger who had come to her aid on the train.

The young gunslinger, Sidewinder, possessed the endearing good looks that were befitting a much gentler personality than the cruel nature he had displayed on the train. With flaxen hair falling long and wavy above sapphire blue eyes, he appeared to be an innocent-faced youth, that is until he became annoyed with something or someone. The look of innocence quickly faded and was replaced by a demonic expression that could cause chills to flare up in the bravest of men. Krystal noted that the other men each wore one holster tied to their thighs. Sidewinder wore two, one on each hip, and the fancy embossed holsters, which were suspended from a wide brown belt that hung below his waist, contained a matching set of engraved pistols that sported smooth ivory handles.

It was Creed Ward who scared Krystal the most. He had not taken his ravenous eyes from her all afternoon, and the sly look on his rugged features was unmistakable each time he allowed his gaze to scrape over her body with a slow taunting movement. He had one thing on his evil mind and Krystal knew exactly what it was. She realized she could never let her guard down around him and hoped fervently that she would never be left alone with him.

But Krystal's eyes kept wandering over to the man from the train. He was risking his life for her and she couldn't forget it. Good Lord, but he was so handsome. Although she had noticed his uncommonly good looks on the train, she hadn't realized just how handsome he really was until she stole a long discriminating glance in his direction and closely observed him.

Nonconforming locks of curly light brown hair intertwined with an occasional strand of gold fell out from beneath the small derby that was perched on top of his head and complimented the deep hue of his green eyes and thick dark lashes. His skin, a natural shade of golden-tan, was unmarred and accented by full lips that had a tendency to curve up on the left corner just slightly, which caused his eye on the same side to narrow in a suggestive manner — a instinctive quirk which proposed that he was thinking indecent thoughts, even if he wasn't. It was a look that women found irresistable and Drake found indispensable.

Krystal kept wondering how they were going to convince all of these men that they were actually traveling together when she didn't even know his name. She couldn't keep her eyes from roving over to him as she began to wonder what it would be like to really be traveling across the country with such a debonair companion.

With a sudden jolt, Krystal realized his gaze was beginning to meet hers each time her look strayed in his direction. A slight smile toyed with one side of his mouth as Krystal quickly averted her eyes. She felt her cheeks grow hot with embarrassment at having been caught; but still, she didn't want to stop. Never had a man appealed to her as much as this one did, and she could tell by the glimmer in his eyes that he was undoubtedly attracted to her in the same manner. But most of all, she found it hard to believe that she could actually be thinking about such ridiculous notions when their lives were in such grave danger.

Drake managed to work his way over to her without arousing anyone's attention as the men watered their horses and drank from the small brook. He reached out and laid his hand gently upon her shoulder. "Are you holding up all right?"

His touch caused an involuntary shiver to travel through Krystal in spite of the summer heat. She looked up at him and gave a weak nod as their gazes locked. A very foreign feeling overcame her and caused her to grow light-headed. It was a sensation

43

that confused her, even scared her a bit, but strangely enough she found it to be a feeling that she didn't want to go away. But reality returned too soon.

"You two aren't plannin' anything over there, are you?" Devon asked with a snide grin. He wondered if now was the time to spring the announcement on his men, but decided to wait awhile. When they found out Drake was his brother, they might be more than a little nervous. Before Drake had given up his badge, he had acquired an infamous reputation as a dedicated lawman, not to mention his reknowned skill with a gun. But Devon had noticed right away that Drake no longer wore a gun, and by the looks of his fancy duds, he had turned into a real city boy. Devon found himself wondering how he could've been so worried about his older brother all this time. In fact, now he thought it kind of humorous that he had ever thought of Drake as his competitor at all.

Krystal jumped at the sound of Devon's voice, but Drake shrugged nonchalantly as he bent down and casually scooped up a handful of water. He held his cupped hands to Krystal's parched lips. "Just getting my lady a drink."

Krystal accepted the water gratefully. The man's bravery surprised her. He didn't seem to be frightened by the outlaws in the least. She wished some of his confidence would rub off on her, because she had never been so frightened in all her life.

Devon glared at them for a second. "Well, be quick about it. We've still got a ways to go before nightfall."

Drake leaned over and whispered, "Don't worry, we'll get out of this. Just keep pretending that we're traveling together, and don't say anything that might get them riled up again."

With a sheepish nod, Krystal began to back away

from him. She knew it had been her rash words that had got them into this awful situation in the first place. But what began to worry her even more was the fact that when he had leaned down to whisper in her ear, their heads had touched for a very short time and Krystal had the strangest feeling flowing through her again. A heated flush seemed to spread throughout her whole body and made her heart pound furiously within her breast. She continued to stare after him as he moved back to the horse he had been riding, wondering why that man had such a profound affect on her and why she was thinking about what it would be like to feel his lips against hers. Good Lord, she thought with disgust, what in the world was wrong with her? She had always been so sensible, but all of a sudden she was thinking lewd thoughts about a man she had just barely set eyes on a couple of hours ago.

Devon watched her and grew confused as his gaze sifted back to his brother. He began to wonder how close these two really were, and if he would have much of a problem convincing Krystal Colbert which of the DeGanhal brothers was the better man? With a sly grin, and a renewed burst of confidence, he decided that he wouldn't have a problem at all.

Krystal spent the remainder of the day in a daze, alternating between the reality of riding within the tight embrace of the outlaw's arms and fantasizing about the man from the train. Regardless of how many times she told herself to stop being so ridiculous, her mind kept swaying to unspeakable things . . . shameful things that a decent woman, especially a school teacher, should never allow to fill her thoughts. Krystal decided the heat was making her temporarily insane. That had to be the reason for her mind's crazy ravings.

The sun was beginning to hang low in the Western sky, casting a brilliant array of dusty rose streaks on the far horizon by the time they began to approach a deserted-looking homestead. Krystal realized that they were obviously planning to stop there for the night and once again her tremendous fear encased her insides with a tightening grip. Her terrified look traveled back to the man from the train for reassurance. He seemed to perceive her fear, and in his warm gaze she found a small portion of the comfort she sought. Yet at the same time, she wondered how they were ever going to get out of this horrible mess.

When they drew their horses to a halt before the rough log structure, Devon swung his long frame down from the horse, then reached up and pulled Krystal down beside him. Her legs felt wobbly and weak when her feet hit the ground and for a moment she was not sure if she could stand on her own. With a compassion she was not prepared for, the outlaw slid his arm around her waist for support. She looked up and met his questing dark eyes. He seemed familiar somehow, but that was not possible. She continued to gaze at him, noting the dark tone of his complexion and the curve of his mouth. With the exception of his ebony eyes, he looked just like—

"Where do ya think you're goin'?" Sidewinder's cold voice sliced through the silence. Already the anxious gunhand of the young killer was holding one of his six-shooters to Drake's throat. Drake glared down at him with a look of annoyance. He had no doubt the kid would kill him without the blink of an eye, but the threat of the icy gun barrel pressing against his skin was dimmed considerably by the vision of his brother holding the woman that Drake had already come to think of as his own. All afternoon, as they had ridden across the barren gray plains, he had done nothing other than to stare at the enrapturing young woman, realizing that if it were possible to fall in love at first sight, then he had managed to do just that.

Devon threw Sidewinder a disconcerned glance. "Leave him be." Devon's eyes traveled back down to Krystal as he added lightly, "His name is Drake DeGanahl. He's my brother."

A strained quiet fell over the group for an instant before Sidewinder threw his head back and began to laugh, sounding more like a schoolboy than a deadly desperado. "Your brother! Now if that don't beat all." He raised his gun and pushed back the wide brim of his hat with the barrel, then with an amazed grin resting upon his lips, he dropped the gun back in the holster with a careless shrug.

Brother! Krystal thought she might burst with the anger that suddenly exploded within her. How could she have missed the resemblance? How did any of them miss it? Unless they had all been in on the deception. The man from the train was a brother to this low-down outlaw and she immediately placed him in the same category. Bolts of gold flashed across the brown pupils of her eyes as they narrowed with a look of betrayal. She twirled around to glare at the man who now had a name . . . Drake DeGanahl! But she quickly renamed him.

"You bastard! How dare you lead me to believe that you were trying to help me. Why," she huffed through gritted teeth, "this whole charade was probably planned by the two of you." Her intimidating gaze raced back and forth between the two men as the rest of the group watched in a disbelieving stupor.

Drake rolled his eyes upward and exhaled an irritated sigh. Although he hardly knew this woman who had fascinated him since the first moment he had set eyes on her, he already knew her well enough to know that if he didn't silence her immediately she would ruin everything. He began to move past Sidewinder with a decisive gait until he stood directly before his brother and the little hellcat named Krystal Colbert.

Drake and Devon DeGanahl's eyes met on the same level with shimmering rivalry. Facing one another, the distinct resemblance was more than evident. Only a year apart in age, from a distance it would be almost impossible to tell the brothers apart. But at close observation the clash of their personalities made them a different as silk and leather. Drake's deep olive-green eyes were set within features which were softer and touched with a gentleness that almost seemed to belie his rugged masculinity. Whereas, Devon's appearance was that of someone who felt life had not dealt him a fair hand and now it owed him something in return. A cold look of hatred was a permanent blemish on his handsome face and his ebony eyes almost seemed to shout out his defiant attitude.

Drake reached out and pulled Krystal away from Devon. She balked, but his massive strength was no match for her as she fell against him. "Krystal is upset," Drake stated firmly, "Give us a few moments alone, so that I can explain things to her."

"Hell, somebody explain it to me," Creed Ward retorted in a snide tone. The rest of the gang nodded in agreement. These five men had been riding together for only a short time, and none of them had ever offered to devulge any personal details to one another. But now, they were all curious to hear about the sudden appearance of their boss's mysterious brother and his beautiful young companion.

Austin turned towards Devon. "Yeah, can we trust him? Didn't I hear somewhere that your brother and your daddy used to be lawmen?" he questioned, making Sidewinder grow extremely fidgety all of a sudden. The young man became nervous without much provocation, a fact that contributed to his impulsive urges to kill without the least bit of regard to human life.

Devon glanced at his men, then turned to face his brother again with a slow and calculated move. "Used to be, but that was a long, long time ago. Now, I reckon we'll just have to ask my big brother whether or not he's trustworthy." Devon's expression and his tone of voice was clear, he was giving Drake one chance to make his stance.

Drake made his decision without hesitation. He was a man without a weapon, up against five men who had chosen a lawless life of chance. They had nothing to lose by killing him and Drake would lose all if his choice was the wrong one. Right now, he realized as the odd feeling he had felt on the train washed over him again, he would do anything to be with Krystal Colbert. Even if it meant she would probably hate him for it.

Drake returned his brother's unwavering look. "We're flesh and blood, Devon. I only returned to Wyoming so we could be a family again. The past was buried with pa." Drake felt Krystal stiffen against him. He hoped fervently that she would hold her tongue this time. Much to his surprise, she did not say anything. But it was evident that all of her trust in him had just dissolved with his last statement.

She was right, she felt all hope drain from her weary body. The man she had thought to be her protector, the only hope she had to ever escape from this madness, had only been traveling to Wyoming to join his brother and this band of cut-throats. Krystal couldn't believe her bad luck, and the fact that she had allowed herself to think she was seriously attracted to him. He was the first man who had ever aroused such overpowering cravings in her, but now she was sickened by the thoughts that had been invading her wanton mind all afternoon.

She looked around at the group of men, feeling totally deserted. The only outlaw who didn't seem to be completely ruthless was a quiet man that she had heard Austin call by the name of Joe. He was the man who had jumped from the front car of the train just before the shooting had broken out. Krystal noticed that he only mumbled a short reply when spoken to and remained silent the rest of the time. A tall thin man, he looked more like a preacher than an outlaw, and Krystal decided that he would be the one she would approach for help the first chance she had. She was positive that the two brothers were in on the holdup of the train together and nothing anyone said could convince her stubborn mind otherwise.

A wry grin curled up Devon's lips as he eyed his brother thoughtfully. "So, you wanna be back in the bosom of your family, huh?" His dark eyes shone with an evil twinkle as they raked over Krystal again. "And I trust you'll be a good brother and share all your good fortune?"

Krystal did not miss his insinuation, and before Drake had a chance to retort to Devon's disgusting remark, she blurted out, "How dare you suggest that anyone will share me! And don't try to tell me that wasn't what you meant by that remark. I'll have you know that nobody—"

"Krystal is much too upset to think about what she's

saying," Drake cut in forcefully as he squeezed her tightly, another indiscreet hint for her to be quiet. "Give me a chance to talk to her and calm her down."

Krystal fell silent, but cast Drake the most debasing look she was capable of producing. Drake did not miss the icy look of hatred upon her face and for a moment he began to wonder if he would ever be able to convince her that he was not really here to join up with his brother.

Devon eyed them with a thoughtful frown knitting his dark brows close together. There was something unusual about their relationship, but he couldn't quite put a finger on what it was. He decided he was going to make it his first priority to find out everything he could about Krystal Dawn Colbert and her association with his big brother. Finally he gave his head a slow nod, his voice carried a definite warning when he spoke. "All right, but don't try anything that you both might regret. It would be a real shame to have to hurt a beautiful lady like Miss Colbert."

Drake shrugged as he returned Devon's cold gaze. "I'm not stupid, Devon. I won't do anything to endanger Krystal's life." He wrapped his arm possessively around her shoulders, although she continued to remain rigid and unresponsive. Drake pulled her to the side of the old house, noting as he did so, the low murmurings of the other men. Devon's admission of Drake's identity had made them all grow nervous and uneasy. It didn't matter that Drake was no longer a lawman. The fact that he had once worn a tin star was enough to cause this group of desperate men to grow extremely leery.

Drake was careful to stop where they would still be in full view, but out of earshot. He would have to prove to these men that they could trust him if he ever hoped to get himself and Krystal safely away. But first he had to convince the headstrong Miss Colbert that he wasn't part of his brother's band of outlaws. Judging by the look of pure antagonism on her face, that was not going to be an easy task. His left eye narrowed slightly as he gazed down into the flashing tawny eyes that were boring a hole clean through him with their sharp accusations. A deep frown creased his handsome features as an irritating thought crossed his mind. Although he towered over her by nearly a foot, he realized he had never felt so small. She had a way about her, a sureness that made him feel completely incompetent. Something told him that Krystal Colbert could take care of herself, no matter what the situation, a realization that made him more determined than ever to claim her unyielding heart as his own.

"You remove your hands from me this second!" she spit out at him in a voice that matched the haughty look in her eyes.

Drake instinctively dropped his hands to his side, then grew even more aggravated with himself as he remembered that he had pulled her to the side of the house to try to talk some sense into her. He leaned down close to her until their faces were only couple of inches apart. "Listen, darlin', there's not much time, so would you try to keep quiet for a minute while I explain?"

"Explain what? It's more than clear what's going on here. And if you think that anything you might possibly say would convince me otherwise, well—"

Her words were suddenly cut off by the feel of his lips crushing against hers with an urgency that consumed her reeling mind and made every inch of her being tingle with an unknown invasion. His strong arms wrapped around her narrow waist and held her in an imprisoned embrace as his unexpected kiss evoked her complete surrender. . . . A kiss that dissolved all semblance of sanity from her deminishing senses and made her whole body grow weak as she began to tremble with a frenzied awakening of her slumbering feminine appetites.

His mouth, bold and fervent, mingling with the arousing taste of her own soft lips was almost more than Krystal's confused mind could handle. She thought — just a brief and fleeing thought — of fighting against his sudden advances. But within the manic emotions of this sweet and almost torturous union of their lips it was washed away like fine grains of sand in a turbulent stream. She had been kissed before, but never in a manner that could even come close in comparison with this impetuous kiss and she began to return the pleasure of this intimate contact with unbound vigor.

What deviltry did Drake DeGanhal possess that could cause such complete abandonment of her control? She never wanted this moment, or this delicious sensation to end. And when his tongue began to trace along the outline of her mouth, she felt like a flame of fire had just burned an insatiable path of scorching desire through her very soul. If this man had been an accomplice in the holdup of the train, it no longer mattered. Nothing was important right now but the way his lips were caressing hers with a tender, yet almost fierce hunger.

Drake was sure he could feel the violent pounding of her heart against his own thundering chest as he drew her closer. Beneath the heavy cape and the constrictive black dress her breasts pressed into his hard, muscled body, rising and falling in rapid succession with her labored breathing. Drake felt like he was being swallowed up by the ache that grew uncontrollably through his loins and devoured him with unmerciful longings. Never before had a woman had such control over him with just a mere kiss. He wanted only to lose himself in this engulfing wave of unrestrained rapture. A minute ago, he had been swept away by her nearness, desperate to experience the feel of those pale pink lips against his own, but nothing could have prepared him for the wild impulses that were surging through him now.

Her arms no longer hung stiff and rigid at her sides, instead they moved on their own accord as they slid up to encircle his head. The small black purse dangled carelessly from her wrist as her slender fingers raked through the tendrils of brown curls that tumbled across the nape of his neck and caused the little black derby to drop precariously to the dry ground below, unnoticed.

It was a kiss that lasted but a few brief moments, yet extended into an eternity. . . . A kiss that bespoke of something bigger than either of them had ever dreamed could exist until this overwhelming moment when time stood still, and it was laced with promises of sweet enchantment that draped their hungry hearts in a web of impassioned tumult.

Chapter Four

Breathing properly was not an easy task, and each of them found that their knees were almost too weak and shaky to support their quaking bodies as Krystal and Drake finally separated. That enflamed kiss had gone beyond mere physical contact, beyond their throbbing lips and was branded deep in their yearning souls.

Krystal's misted gaze raised up to meet the flickering fire encompassed in Drake's dark green eyes. Her arms had gone slack on the top of his broad shoulders, and now she had an irresistible urge to run her fingers through the thick curls at the base of his neck again. Her fingers tingled at the prospect. Confusion was only second to the splendrous turmoil that continued to rage within her. His kiss was like nothing she had ever imagined. Yet, she could not help but wonder what affect it had on him? Did he feel as she did at this breathless moment? Did he feel like someone had just replaced his blood with liquid fire? and was he experiencing the same crushing sensations of complete loss of all natural restraint?

At twenty-nine years old, Drake DeGanahl had kissed more women than he cared to remember. A few of them had been timid virgins, but usually he tended to seek the companionship of the warm and willing ladies who occupied the upstairs rooms of his favorite establishments. With these women of experience there was no need to play games or pretend to have feelings that Drake did not feel he possessed . . . feelings that had never surfaced until he set eyes on Krystal Colbert.

But even with his vast knowledge in the sensual pleasures of life, he had never known the summit of desire that had surged his whole being during that lingering kiss, and he knew that he had to seek all the mysteries that lay beyond such a unique contact. An easy and instinctive grin began to roam across his lips and the look he bestowed upon the bewitching lady before him deceived the true feelings he had just discovered in that exquisite moment of tender ecstasy.

Krystal saw the crooked smile which seemed to strip away the last bit of defense she had left. She grew enraged with him and also with herself for allowing his rash gesture to invade her normally sensible mind. Her arms jerked down to her sides as she took a step backwards. His hands still rested intimately on her hips and she pushed them away as though she was just brushing away a fleck of dirt.

"Well," she said in a voice tinged with indignation. "That was certainly impertinent of you, wasn't it?"

Drake stared down at her in disbelief. He knew without any doubt that she was just as overcome by that kiss as he was, but she was too stubborn to admit it. Never a man to grovel at any woman's feet, Drake wasn't about to start now, even if the woman was as enticing as Krystal Colbert. He bent down and swooped up his black derby from the ground. With angry strokes he began to brush it off, noting when he did so that a small choked cough emitted from Krystal as the dust hit her directly in the face. He pulled the little round hat down upon his head at a careless angle and lightly tipped the brim as he leaned forward in a nonchalant stance.

"Impertinence is my speciality, ma'am. It was nothing at all."

Krystal's fury was every bit as consuming as her desire had been a minute ago. Her jewel-toned eyes narrowed with flashing rage. How dare he think that he could kiss her like he just had, then casually imply that it had been nothing at all! She gathered up her long black skirts and began to twirl away from him, but not until she had the final say.

"It's more than obvious that kissing is not your specialty. And now since we both know that kissing each other is about as enthralling as walking barefoot through a cactus patch, we won't have to bother with such unnecessary distractions again, will we?" She tossed the mass of reddish-blond curls over one shoulder with a defiant flip of her head, content that she had wiped out any emotions that still lingered from that demanding kiss.

Drake reached out and grabbed her by the arm, drawing her closer than he had planned. She was within kissing distance again, and he felt his stomach take a nervous tumble. Damn this woman! She made him more furious than he thought humanly possible. Yet, at the same time, he wanted her with a desperate compulsion. It had been part of his training as a lawman to practice caution, and always to remain calm when dealing with a situation where he couldn't predict the outcome. But with this woman all those years of disciplined instruction were wiped from his memory. She inspired him with impulsiveness with her own haughty attitude.

"Well, I think I would prefer the cactus patch," he

answered in a voice that mocked hers. His dark green eyes grew almost black as he fought against the rapid loss of control that her nearness aroused in him once more. When he spoke again, his voice was strained. "As for everything else, you can believe whatever you want, but I'll tell you this only once. I want nothing more than to get you away from here, unharmed. Either you trust me, or you place your life in the hands of that bunch of outlaws over there. The choice is yours, Miss Colbert."

Krystal's gaze traveled over to the group of dangerous men who were all watching the scene with more than a slight interest. She and Drake's kiss had attracted all eyes in their direction, especially Devon's. The sight of their impassioned embrace had summoned up a dark look of jealous rage upon his handsome features. The heartbreaking memory he had been trying to forget for the past decade flashed before his eyes in painful and distorted images. Briefly, he was swept back in time as he recalled another beautiful young woman, the only woman he had ever loved. But, like everything else he had ever desired, he had to share Jennifer's love with his big brother.

Devon trembled visibly with the angry recollection. It seemed like only yesterday since that awful night when Jennifer had told him the truth about her relationship with Drake. It was an admission which had destroyed Devon's future and had tragically ended Jennifer Holt's young life. This time the outcome would be different, Devon vowed to himself.

Even with the fury she was feeling towards Drake DeGanahl, Krystal knew immediately that coping with his arrogance was better than facing the lustful glares she was receiving from the rest of the men. She relaxed her tense frame and glanced back up at him.

Again their eyes locked. She shivered, once more defeated by the emotional reaction his look caused within her trembling being. Right now, she would have agreed to anything this uncommonly handsome man asked of her. She gave her head a slow nod. He released his tight grip on her arm and stepped back as though he no longer trusted his own actions when he was so close to her.

"Do we have a d-deal, then?" he asked with a vague quiver in his voice.

"A d-deal?" she repeated, while wondering if her waning control could handle a deal with a man who caused her insides to turn to a quivering mass with no more than a glance from his twinkling green gaze.

"You pretend to be my woman and go along with everything I say, and I'll get you safely away from these men. Is it a deal?"

His woman? Why did those words make her heartbeat race even faster? She tried to remind herself of the fact that he was undoubtedly an outlaw and therefore no better than the rest of these men. "Your brother is obviously the leader of this group of heathens and you just admitted to him that you had come here to join up with him. How do you expect me to put my trust in you after all that?"

An acute look of aggravation overcame Drake's features. "I admitted no such thing, but I did have to say something or else I would have had Sidewinder's gun drilling a hole through my brains."

Krystal's face paled at the image his words conjured up in her mind. Even if what he said was true, did she dare place her safety in his hands? He hardly looked like he could take care of himself. How could he take care of her, too? Her skeptical gaze moved over his finely tailored suit and then traveled up to the little bowler hat that suddenly seemed so odd looking upon the tousled mass of brown curls.

"I hardly think that I would benefit from such a bargain." A hint of sarcasm crept into her voice. "Not only are you vastly outnumbered, but you don't even have a gun. Do you really expect me to believe that you are capable of helping me to escape, even if you wanted to?"

"Guess we don't have a deal then," he replied sharply as he turned and began to stalk away from her. Was she always so damned contrary?

Krystal was flooded with terror at the idea of being on her own against the whole band of outlaws, even though she still wasn't sure if she should trust Drake DeGanahl. His reason for wanting the outlaws to believe he was their ally was feasible since Sidewinder was definitely more than a little anxious to use his gun on anybody — for any reason. In spite of her intense aggravation with him, his proposition was still her only hope of getting out of this horrible situation alive. And besides, she really did want to believe him.

"Oh, all right!" she snapped in a voice that did not sound very agreeable.

Drake stopped abruptly and swung back around. He had been holding his breath, hoping she would come to her senses. If she had allowed him to walk away and had placed herself in the hands of his brother and the rest of the men, Drake knew he would have tried to kill the first one who touched her, despite the fact that he didn't have a weapon. Not wearing his gun was something he had been repremanding him- self for ever since they had been on the train, and long before Krystal Colbert had felt the dire need to bring it to his attention. But because she had noticed the absence of his gun, he was more determined than ever to prove himself to this woman. Being caught off guard without his side iron was a mistake he would never make again if he managed to get out of this uncanny twist of fate.

He gave his head a slight nod, but his chest felt like it was about to burst with the relief he was feeling. His tactics had won him the first round, she had agreed to go along with his scheme. He was already fighting one war with himself, he didn't want to constantly have to match wits with her, too. Even amongst the heat of the anger that she aroused in him, and the critical state of their situation with the outlaws, Drake's sanity was waging a hopeless battle with his diminishing senses. He must be crazy, he decided with a defeated sigh, because with barely no more than a kiss, Krystal Colbert had claimed his heart and his soul. And if she commanded it, he would lay his head on the henchman's block, and she could have that also.

Krystal thought she detected a look of victory in Drake's eyes as he slipped his arm through hers and began to lead her back to the curious group of spectators. But she kept silent, and instead found herself wondering why he was so eager to help her to escape? He had never met her before today, so why would he want to place his life in danger for a virtual stranger. Just what did he hope to gain from his offer to assist her? If that reckless kiss was any implication, then she had no doubt of the liberties he would be expecting in exchange for her freedom. Well, Drake DeGanahl, she thought furiously, savor the memory of our first kiss, it was also our last!

As they approached the group of men, Drake was quick to notice the deep scowl on Devon's face. His brother's expression was a familiar look which always signaled the fact that Devon was about to challenge him over something. Drake had no doubt what it was that Devon wanted this time. He had not missed the way his brother had been rubbing up against Krystal all afternoon, or the way his dark eyes devoured every inch of her each time he glanced in her direction. As usual, Drake would not tolerate his brother's behavior. Ever since they were small children Devon always had to have everything Drake had in his possession. And once he had whatever it was, Devon never seemed to care about it anymore. As a result, Drake had learned years ago not to give in to his little brother's whims, and to always be prepared to face a contest with Devon.

"Still sweepin' them off their feet, I see?" Devon said with a crude grin.

Drake gave a careless shrug, escorted by a lopsided grin. "Some things never change, little brother."

Devon's rage was more than evident as he swung around to face his brother, but Drake's look remained undaunted by the other man's anger. Drake was aware that Devon's main goal in life was to make him mad enough to request a showdown. Drake also knew that when that day arrived, there would be no turning back for either of them. They had both been taught to shoot by the best . . . Franklin DeGanahl. In a showdown only one DeGanahl brother would walk away and Drake was not ready to know which one of them it would be.

For a moment Devon thought of tossing a gun to his brother and facing him down once and for all. But, he decided as he took another minute to survey the situation, there would be a better time for a final confrontation . . . a time when Devon would make Drake pay for all the sorrow he felt his brother had caused him. But this wasn't the time. First, Devon wanted Drake to suffer as he had suffered. He wanted Drake to know what it felt like to feel as though his heart had just been ripped from his chest with the pain that accompanies losing the love of a woman that means more than life itself.

Devon glanced over at Krystal and noted the flushed color of her beautiful face, and the pale pink lips which carried the soft fullness that was still reminiscent of that long and ravishing kiss. Drake had always been so good with the ladies, but Devon had picked up a few tricks of his own over the years. Yes, he thought bitterly, there would be a perfect opportunity to show his big brother all the things he had learned, but not until he had shown Krystal Colbert what it felt like to be held by a real man.

"We'll be headin' out at sunrise, so we'll stay here for the night," Devon announced briskly. "You two can keep each other warm, just as long as you don't go to makin' any plans about leaving." He cast a warning look at Drake, then gave the same deadly glare to the rest of the men. It was apparent that their boss was in no mood to put up with any arguments, so without any further discussion they all started to unsaddle their horses.

Krystal stayed close to Drake as he followed the other men's lead and began to remove the saddle from the horse he had been riding all afternoon. It was imperative that she learn the meaning of Devon's remark, but she was not sure how to word her question. She nervously cleared her throat while she gave a discreet tug on Drake's coat sleeve. "Um, I beg your pardon? But did your brother mean to imply that we could—you know—sleep together?"

"Yep," Drake replied curtly as he carried the saddle over to the fence post and tossed it across the rough log rail. An amused smirk sauntered across his lips when he turned back around and glimpsed the supercilious look upon her face. He was unable to suppress the full-fledged smile that replaced his crooked grin when he added, "Wyoming nights can get mighty cold, Miss Colbert."

"Oh, the nerve!" she gasped, then whispered through clenched teeth, "How dare you or that low-down brother of yours think that I would actually sleep with you."

"I reckon you do have several alternatives. But, if you should decide to back out of our agreement, I'd be more than willing to make a bet that you still won't be sleeping alone tonight, darlin'."

A bright shade of red moved into Krystal's pale cheeks as she glared up at him. "Don't call me, darlin'! And let's suppose that I do follow through with this ridiculous idea of yours, just what will you expect in return?" She paused, trying to read the strange expression that had suddenly covered his handsome face. Beginning to feel very intimidated by the complex look he was giving her, Krystal rushed on, "I have a good deal of my own money, and my father in Nevada is extremely wealthy, so you see, I can pay very well if it's money that you desire."

How strange that she had chosen to use the word desire.

"Do you think all I want is your money?" His voice was filled with anger. Was she really so innocent that she couldn't sense how she affected him? The intensity of that kiss alone should have said it all.

"Wh-what do you want from me?" Krystal questioned, growing very nervous beneath his glowering look. Why was her pulse beating uncontrollably in her temples and her heart feeling as though it might stop beating altogether? If he didn't want money, was it possible that he wanted . . . her?

What do I want? Drake asked himself while he stared down at the enchantress before him. Her large tawny eyes misted for an instant with a look of apprehension, but just as quickly the fear disappeared and was replaced by a look of puzzlement. If he were to tell her that the only thing he wanted in return for helping her to escape was to spend every single minute in her presence, to know every little thing there is to know about her, and to touch her where no man has ever touched her before. . . .If he told her of his simple request, would she grant it to him? Drake suddenly realized how foolish all that nonsense would sound to a woman like Krystal Colbert.

How many times, he wondered, had she heard those same words from men who were caught under the spell of her beauty, men who had hoped to win over her stubborn nature with pretty words or extravagant promises? A woman as beautiful as she was, no doubt had been subjected to numerous admissions of undying devotion. She would probably laugh in his face if he were to tell her of his real feelings . . . emotions that he couldn't even explain to himself. Drake tried to shrug off the scorching sensations which were pulsating wildly throughout his body. When she was ready to admit to her true feelings about that kiss and the strange affinity that had first attracted them to one another, then maybe, he would admit to his, too. Until then, she would not add him to her collection of discarded conquests, he decided angrily.

"Well, now that I think of it, money would be nice. Lots of it. And who knows, darlin', maybe if I do a good job, you might be inclined to throw in a bonus?" His eyes glistened with a devilish glint as the suggestive grin curled up one corner of his mouth.

Krystal's hands drew into two clenched fists as she became flooded with rage. "Oh, you'll be rewarded, Mr. DeGanahl!" she spit out between tightly drawn lips. "For a job well done, I can make you a rich man.

As for a bonus? Well, if you were insinuating anything else, I think you have already received more than your fair share, don't you?" Krystal's voice quivered slightly. All at once she had an overwhelming urge to cry. She blinked back the angry and unexpected tears as she pivoted away from him. She could not bear another second of staring into those lucid green eyes now that he had made his real motives clear.

What did it matter if he only wanted her money? Had she really expected anything else from a man who acted as irrational as he did? But to actually hear him admit that money was all he wanted from her was more painful than she could ever have ever thought possible. On the train, and all during the long hot afternoon, it had seemed that there was something so special developing between them. The look of tenderness she thought she saw in his eyes must have been only in her overactive imagination. When, and if he helped her to get away from these outlaws, she would make sure that he received the large reward which he wanted so badly, and then she would never have to see him again.

So why was there such a stabbing pain ripping through the core of her chest? And why had she been hoping so desperately that he was as attracted to her as she was to him? But most of all, what about that kiss? It had only created an endless void in her, and it had left her wanting so very much more. Perhaps he was right though, she decided with a sinking heart . . . maybe it really was nothing at all.

Chapter Five

Krystal did not have time to dwell on the painful subject of Drake's confession because as they all filed into the abandoned house she was being asked a very strange question.

A smirk hovered on Devon's lips as he noted the indignant look on her face. "I don't suppose you know how to cook on one of these old stoves, do you Miss Colbert?"

She drew herself up to her full height as she looked down her nose at the black contraption in the corner of the room. The Monogram stove was the only thing that still remained in the abandoned house, and it stuck out like a sore thumb in the mist of the empty structure.

"Well, not exactly. You see, we have always had servants and—" The burst of laughter that rang throughout the group of men caused Krystal's anger to flare. They were laughing at her and she did not appreciate their humor. "What is so funny about that?" she added, enraged. "Doesn't anyone have cooks or maids out here in Wyoming?"

Through another round of laughter, Devon said, "Well sugar, we lent our maid and cook to the governor for the evening. I reckon we'll just have to figure out how to cook our own supper tonight."

All of the men, even Drake continued to chortle with mirth at her expense, but Krystal refused to let this bunch of criminals make her ashamed of her wealth. She raised her chin in defiance and grabbed the knapsack from Devon's hand.

"I certainly wouldn't want any of you to starve to death on my account. And," she pointed her finger at his chest in a threatening manner, "Don't call me sugar!" Good Lord, she thought furiously as she stomped over to the stove where Austin had just built a small fire; one brother called her darlin', the other one called her sugar! Oh, what madness had possessed her to ever leave Boston?

Austin, still wearing a wide grin on his aging face, quickly stepped out of her way as she tossed the bag of food staples on the narrow counter which was attached to the side of the stove then glared at him with a look that defied even the heartiest of men. Of course, she did not know the first thing about how to prepare a meal on this primitive stove, or anywhere else for that matter. She had always been too involved with books and her teaching career to take the time to learn how to cook. And besides, she had never needed to learn those type of menial chores. She dumped the contents of the bag out on the counter and stared at them; Flour, sugar, dried beef, several cans of beans, assorted spices, a few utensils, along with a bowl and a frying pan . . . She was supposed to prepare a meal from this?

"Could you use some help?" Drake's voice was no longer filled with humor and his expression was understanding. He had known from the first time he set eyes on her that she was from a very wealthy family and her comment about having servants had just proved it. It was normal for a woman of her apparent breeding to be at a loss when confronted with the meager ingredients in a cowboy's grub sack.

She turned away from him. "I'll manage."

"I'll help," he said firmly as he began to dump cornmeal into the bowl. Krystal was too furious to show her gratitude, but she closely observed him while he fixed a meal of corn cakes, beans with some dried beef stirred into them, along with a pot of coffee perking on a back burner. That didn't look so hard. Why, anybody could prepare a simple fare like that, she told herself. Next time she would cook the whole meal without anyone's help. Of course, she hoped that there wouldn't be a next time.

"It just don't make no sense to me," Creed repeated for the second time during the meal. "What are we supposed to use for money until we can get her to Virginia City? We ain't got a dime from the last two jobs we've pulled."

Devon sat his plate of untouched food down on the floor and leaned back against the wall. "I'll think of something."

"I'm with Creed," Sidewinder chimed in. "We can't go back to the Hole without any money. We should've robbed the people on that train if nothing else."

Devon rose to his feet abruptly and looked around the room with his anger flashing in vivid contrast across his dark features. "Since when did anyone start questioning my decisions? If any of you don't like the way I run things, you're free to leave." He motioned towards the door with one hand and instinctively dropped his other hand to his gunhandle, a gesture that did not go unnoticed by anyone in the room.

"None of us want that, Devon," Creed was careful to place his hands in clear view and far away from his gunbelt. Devon had proved himself with his fast draw

69

on more than one occasion and Creed had no desire to match his skill against the other man in a confrontation.

Austin cleared his throat loudly and picked up his bedroll. "Well, I'm turning in," he announced as tension continued to hold the room under a strained composure. The other men began to scout out their sleeping areas in silence.

"I'll put my blanket over here." Krystal said in her clipped Eastern accent as she grabbed the woolen covering from Drake's unsuspecting arms and headed towards a secluded corner of the one room house.

"I had that corner staked out for myself." Creed smiled slyly as he followed her to the far side of the room. "But I'd be only too happy to share it with you."

Krystal stared up at him, her face masked with horror. He was the outlaw who terrified her the most. The last thing she wanted to do was to share sleeping quarters with him. She shook her head in a negative gesture and stumbled backwards before turning to face Drake with a look of despair. An indifferent shrug was all he offered to her while he watched her with an intent gaze, waiting to see how much of a predicament she would manage to get herself into this time.

She was reminded of the deal she had made with Drake earlier. Since she was pretending to be his woman, she supposed that they should appear to be on somewhat familiar terms with one another. "We—well, Drake was going to sleep the-there, too," she managed to say, while at the same time feeling like she was going to faint at the idea of sleeping with a man, actually with six men in this crowded little shack. Good Lord, what had she gotten herself into this time, she wondered? Her eyes widened with a silent plea for Drake to come to her aid. Much to her dismay, however, he only continued to stare at her with a curious expression.

Creed's eyes did not waver as he watched her squirm beneath his unscrupulous look. Krystal Colbert was his discovery and he had determined that if her father was as wealthy as she had boasted of on the train, then he should be rewarded with something extra special. He had decided on what that reward should to be right from the first moment he had got a glimpse of this tawny-eyed beauty beneath her heavy black veil. Like most men who lived on the run, Creed Ward had had a real weakness for the ladies, especially the pretty ones, and this beauty was definitely worth her weight in gold.

"There's room for three in this spot and I don't mind sharing." Beneath the brim of his charcoal grey hat, Creed's dark blonde eyebrows lifted in a wry arch as he idly twisted one of the long drooping tips of the thick handlebar mustache which was of the same hue as his hair and brows. He would gladly give up his share of the ransom money she brought for just a few hours alone with her. He thought of the fancy-dressed man she was traveling with, forgetting that Drake DeGanahl was once a lawman in these parts as he started to imagine how she would respond to a real man's loving. Creed's loins ached with the vision of this sweet thing writhing in esctasy beneath him. It would be nothing but pure pleasure since her city boy had already broken her in for him. Creed's evil grin broadened. Soon . . . real soon, he thought as he ran his hand across his mouth to wipe away the wetness that had suddenly appeared on his anxious lips with those tantalizing fantasies.

"But . . . Drake and I prefer to be alone. I mean— we always—well—" she let out a nervous sigh as she looked back to Drake for some sort of assistance.

"Just what is it that you and Drake always do?" Devon's intimidating voice sliced through the uneasiness which still prevailed throughout the room. "I'm startin' to get mighty curious about that myself?"

"That's a real personal question, little brother," Drake retorted with a forced chuckle that was not conveyed into his flashing green eyes. Creed's lustful look had not gone unnoticed by Drake, and it was obvious that Devon's remark had been meant in a derogatory manner, too. "I think you're forgetting that Krystal Colbert is a lady, and she deserves some respect," his glowering look scanned the crowded house, resting a second longer on Creed Ward as he added with a tone of authority that was not in his power to use, "from every man in this room."

Sidewinder immediately stiffened, his impatient gun-hand dropping down to touch the ivory handle of one of his six-shooters. Creed, noticing Sidewinder's spontanious movement, allowed his hand to poise above his gun in nervous anticipation.

Austin merely continued to roll out his bedroll. The oldest gunman of the outlaw troupe, he had long ago learned to keep his nose out of business that didn't concern him or the need for his fast draw. To him, Krystal Colbert was a lady and should be treated as such. When it came to women, Austin lived by the philosophy that a man should be a gentleman at all times, regardless of his profession.

Unfortunately, Joe Preece lived by a different set of rules. To the mild-looking man who hardly ever uttered a word, this woman was a source of irritation . . . a distraction in the normal flow of his life, and Joe didn't like distractions. He picked up his bedroll and walked to the doorway. As he exited, he paused and turned to study the room and its occupants with his piercing gaze for a final time. His eyes rested for

72

one instant longer on Krystal. Then he continued outdoors without muttering a sound.

Devon ignored Joe's exit, still too engulfed in rage. For a moment, Devon thought of disputing his brother, but just as quickly he remembered his plan. Much to the surprise of everyone he began to shake his head in an agreeable manner. "You're right, Drake." He turned to Krystal with a narrow grin etched across his lips. "I'm real sorry, Miss Colbert. It won't happen again." His expression turned to stone as his ebony eyes flashed across the room, hardening even more when his gaze passed over Creed. "From here on out, we will all remember that Krystal is your woman, Drake."

A shocked silence followed Devon's apology, but the tone of his voice held a threat that no one cared to challenge. Devon's men were not used to seeing him back down from anything, especially since it was so noticeable to all of them that the DeGanahl brothers were like two loaded kegs of dynamite, an explosion seemed inevitable.

Drake was left speechless by Devon's words. The abrupt change in his brother's attitude caused Drake's thoughts to suddenly turn suspicious. It had never been Devon's nature to agree with anything Drake did or said. He knew at once that Devon had something up his sleeve, and whatever his ulterior motive was, it was bound to concern Krystal Colbert in some way.

"Thank you," Krystal mumbled. She allowed her eyes to meet Devon's for only an instant while she wondered if she could believe this outlaw who was almost as handsome as his brother. Was Devon's simple command enough to keep Creed Ward away? She had already made a pact with Drake for her safety, did she dare entrust both of the DeGanahl brothers with her life?

Devon paused in front of her when their gazes made contact. His pitch-dark eyes seemed almost forlorn, and they hinted at a longing for something that he sensed would never be within his grasp. Yet, at the same time, he knew it was something that would take precedence above all else in his quest to possess it. Mirrored in Krystal's tawny pupils he saw another young woman's face with laughing brown eyes and pale pink lips. He did not want to compare her to Jennifer, it would make him too vulnerable. He forced himself to turn away from her as he struggled to discard the alien feelings that had wandered into his calloused mind. Why did she have to be so beautiful? She was so very much like Jennifer — too much like Jennifer.

He had to get away from her, away from his brother, and out from under the curious eyes of the rest of the men. He fled from the house, stopping to lean against the worn column of the front stoop when he realized that his plan would not be so easy to carry out. Feelings he had believed to be dead and gone forever had just floated briefly to the icy surface of his cold heart, and they caused a jagged break in the stone wall he had worked so hard to erect in order to protect himself from such tender emotions.

He took a deep breath of the cool air and stared off into the emptiness of the dark Wyoming night. He fought within himself to recapture the bitter and revengeful feelings he had been experiencing through-out the long day each time he had recalled the hurtful memories of his youth, but he found that they kept eluding him. Instead, he kept having a powerful desire to be close to someone . . . someone like Krystal Colbert, and to remember what it was like to care about another human being in the way he had cared for Jennifer Holt.

"Do you prefer to be next to the wall or on this side?" Drake questioned as he motioned toward the hard wooden floor.

Krystal's eyes followed his gesture. Neither spot appeared to be very welcoming right now. Her mind grasped at the thought that if Drake was against the wall, she might be able to attempt an escape during the night. But logic reclaimed her thoughts as she realized that she would also be in the center of all the other men. If she took the spot against the wall, she would only have to contend with Drake DeGanahl. That would be bad enough, she decided.

She pushed past him and tossed her blanket next to the log wall. "I'll take this side," she said as she started to lower herself down onto the makeshift bed while trying at the same time to ignore the insolent look that Creed Ward was still directing at her.

"I wouldn't get too close to that wall if I were you, darlin'."

"Don't call me darlin'," she hissed at Drake as quietly as possible, then added with a uneasy glance towards the wall, "Why?"

"Cockroaches," Drake retorted nonchalantly as he stretched his long frame out next to her and covered his face with his small derby in an effort to shield his eyes from the wayward moonbeams which were shimmering through the bare window.

Cockroaches? Good Lord! Krystal mouthed silently as she stared in disgust at the roughly-hewn logs she was leaning against. She scooted away from them in a swift movement, but was also careful not to get too close to Drake. She glanced around the darkening room while a feeling of complete hopelessness overcame her.

Devon and Joe had not returned and the rest of the men had apparently decided to heed Devon's orders for the time being and were now busy getting ready for bed. Her gaze ascended again and met Creed Ward's leering face. A terrible vision of impending doom engulfed her when she tore her eyes away from him and forced herself to lay down on the scratchy gray blanket. As she stared up at the uneven columns of log beams which supported the ceiling of the small house, she began to feel the same type of overpowering loneliness which she had felt last week at her mother's funeral. She longed to be back in Boston, in her secure little world on the top of the Hill. Why had she been foolish enough to travel out West alone? If she had waited for another week Les Macrea would have been able to come with her, but he had not been able to leave Boston because of the investigation. Krystal guessed that he was probably furious with her for taking off without telling anyone.

Up to this point, she had purposely avoided thinking about the investigation that the Pinkerton National Detective Agency was conducting at this time into her mother's death. For some reason, she had a such a strange feeling about the investigation that she had been compelled to leave Boston before she even knew of the outcome. In her heart, she believed that her mother could not have been involved in any kind of illegal activities, but there were so many little things that just didn't make sense.

Once again, Krystal clutched the tiny black bag close to her heart and wondered if she had come out West to escape the truth about her mother, or if she had traveled to this uncivilized place in search of the answers. Maybe somewhere beyond this desolate country called Wyoming, somewhere in a distant and equally foreign place named Virginia City, Nevada, her questions would finally be answered. Then maybe, Rebecca Colbert would rest in peace, and

Krystal could resume her life again. The awful realization that she might never go back to the beautiful mansion that overlooked Boston from the top of Beacon Hill, or never again teach in her little brick schoolhouse gripped her heart with regret. But most of all, she began to wonder if she would ever find the father whom she so desperately needed?

Tomorrow, she decided, she would try to talk to the outlaw named Joe. His quiet manner made him appear to be more sympathic than any of the other outlaws. He certainly didn't look or act like a desperado. Krystal was certain she would be able to convince him to help her escape. If she could only think of a way to sneak out to talk to him tonight? Since that was impossible, she had no choice but to rely on Drake DeGanahl, and that was a thought that did little to comfort her.

What was it about that man that made her whole body go limp every time those twinkling green eyes glanced in her direction? Most men were usually no more than a necessary annoyance in her career-oriented life. Since she had blossomed into womanhood, she had definitely had her share of men hanging around trying to snare her attentions—some men because of her rare beauty, others because of her immense wealth, but most of them were after both of her alluring qualities. None of those past suitors had ever interested her even the least bit as much as Drake DeGanahl did, and she had only known him for one day.

Anger began to make its way into her thoughts. How could she permit to herself to be so smitten with a man she barely knew? Usually she was so sensible about the male gender, especially since her mother had always been so exultant around men. Rebecca had thrived on the attention she received from the many men in her life. Without it, Krystal was sure that Rebecca would have just withered and faded away. Although she did not condemn her mother's dependency on men, it had made her more determined than ever to make something of her own life without a man's interference.

Teaching had been that outlet for her, and it was the most important thing to her. Why, it was her whole life. In the past couple of years she had proved herself as a teacher and she had high hopes of furthering her teaching credentials in the future. The last thing she wanted right now, or forever for that matter, was to end up cooking and cleaning for some man. Especially a man as exasperating and arrogant as Drake DeGanahl!

A deep sigh escaped from her mouth as she began to give into the weariness of the long, draining day. Inspite of a determined attempt to stay awake, it was not long before Krystal fell into a exhausted and dreamless slumber. The cool night air penetrated the cracks of the exterior wall of the deteriorating house. Unconsciously Krystal inched towards Drake and pressed her body up against his muscled form as she sought the natural warmth which his body had to offer. Her arm draped across his taut stomach while her hand rested precariously close to his most masculine possession.

Beneath the brim of the little black derby, Drake's eyes flew open as he forced back the breath that threatened to choke him. With very slow movements he tilted back his hat and cautiously looked down at the beautiful young lady who had just curled up against him in such an intimate manner. For just one wondrous second he had thought — well, he had hoped — that she was making a very forward advance towards him. With great disappointement, he realized that she was completely unaware of her hands crucial location, and he was more than a little aggravated that she could be sleeping so contently when she was causing him such an indescribable misery. He carefully reached down and moved her hand up so that it was perched in a safe spot upon his stomach, but instantly it dropped back down and covered the sensitive area that was causing Drake the worst distress he had ever known. He could not imagine a greater torture than the one this little gal was unwittingly subjecting him to at this moment.

Afraid to even breath for fear that she would awaken, and realize what a devastating effect she had on him, Drake spent the better part of the long night suffering beyond his wildest imagination. He decided that he would prefer to be chained to a post and beaten to a lifeless pulp than to be forced to endure this slow and agonizing death. He was certain that his desire for this lady was bound to be his downfall. Never before had a woman even come close to causing such a consuming fire to burn so wildly out of control within his body and he knew that he had to make her his in every way!

As the moon began to fade, making way for the first misty white rays of the dawn, Drake's desire had waxed into an overwhelming frustration. He no longer dreamed of the time when he would make Krystal Colbert his woman in reality, rather than just in fantasy. Instead, he was thinking of ways to cause her as much distress as her wandering hand had caused him all during the seemingly endless night. He was even beginning to think that she was only pretending to be asleep so that she could satisfy her own curiosities.

He rubbed a shaking hand over his sweating forehead as he realized that he was being completely ridiculous. Throughout the course of the night, he had thought several times of going outside to escape her ill-placed palm, but he was more than a little leary about leaving Krystal in the house alone with the other men, especially with Creed Ward. During his years as a lawman, Drake had encountered many men like Creed. It was obvious that Creed considered himself quite a ladies man, and no doubt, he was quick to use his skill with a gun to try to impress his latest conquest. Like the cold-blooded killer, Sidewinder, Creed allowed his weapon to do his thinking for him. Drake planned to make damn sure that Creed Ward never had a chance to lay his filthy hands on Krystal. So, he stayed and forced himself to undergo this unbelievable agony. Without a wink of sleep, his temperament was sorely lacking any restraint and his throbbing loins had reached a point of utter wretchedness.

But with the approach of the morning, he carefully slid out from under her strategically placed arm. It was now joined by a slender leg that had managed to entwine itself around one of Drake's own legs. Stifling a groan, he managed to pull himself up to a standing position. Relieved that no one else was awake to observe his painful exit from the house, Drake let out a loud moan when he reached the front porch. He shook his head and wondered what terrible deed he had done to deserve such an awful punishment as the one he had just been forced to endure during the past few hours.

"Long night, big brother?"

Drake swung around, startled by the sound of Devon's voice. "Yep—real long." He turned away again and stared out across the broad expanse of the lonely prairie that stretched out before them.

Devon rose slowly from the spot on the porch where

he had just spent a sleepless night. He walked over and stood next to his brother, allowing his gaze to wander over the barren land. "Strange, ain't it?"

"What's that?"

Devon shrugged. "When pa was still alive, you and I were constantly at each other's throats, forever trying to prove to pa which of us was the toughest or the smartest. Now that he's gone, we're still here wonderin' who's going to be the best man. Guess it wasn't pa that we were trying to impress all those years. Maybe it has always been just between you and me." He sighed deeply and added with a tinge of regret in his voice, "And I reckon we'll never be satisfied until we finally know which one of us is the best of the DeGanahl boys."

"Doesn't have to be that way, you know?"

A humorless smile twisted across Devon's features as he turned to face his brother. When he spoke his voice was flat and without emotion. "For once you're wrong, big brother. It's gone on too long and that's the way it has to be."

Chapter Six

Krystal's first thought when she opened her eyes was that yesterday had only been a bad dream. But as she began to waken fully she remembered that it was not a dream, it was a living nightmare. However, the face which hovered above her was certainly handsome enough to be in a dream, and the look in his olive-green gaze was the gentlest look she had ever beheld. Still, it was not enough to ward off the fear and frustration of her hopeless situation and the tears that suddenly sprang to her eyes were not deliberate.

Drake forgot about the acute aggravation she had subjected him to during the night as he pulled her into the secure circle of his embrace. He wanted to take away all of her sorrow and bring back the peaceful look that slumber had cloaked her beautiful face in a few moments earlier. It wasn't fair that they had to meet one another under these terrible circumstances. But even though it was not the best of conditions, he knew their meeting was the best thing that had ever happened to him. Soon he hoped to get her away from here so that they could start fresh while he wiped away all the painful memories that encased her innocent heart. He pulled her closer as the sobs continued to rack through her small form.

In his arms she felt safe, she never wanted him to turn her loose. It was the same calming effect that she had felt yesterday when they had first been abducted from the train and he had put his arm around her. She even began to wish that he would kiss her again, just like he had yesterday. Her lips flamed with the recollection and her cheeks grew fevered as she tilted her face upward. But Devon's voice ended her desire when he entered the house.

"Let's get movin'. We've got to make a stop before we reach the Hole-in-the-Wall."

Krystal's gaze returned to Drake as her flood of tears subsided. "I'm sorry. I don't know what came over me. I promise not to break down like this again."

Drake smiled as he tenderly ran his finger along the outline of her face. "The only promise that you ever have to make me, Krystal Colbert, is that you'll trust me."

She continued to look up at him, her tears dissolving as his strength seemed to reinvigorate her. His touch alone was one of the most wonderful things she had ever experienced, second only to his incredible kiss. Everything else connected with the events of the past couple days had been a terrible experience. Meeting Drake DeGanahl was like a long-awaited blessing. He had just asked for her confidence. She didn't trust her own emotions right now, but she would trust him if he asked her to.

"Is she all right?" Devon asked. The scowl on his face was a clue to his disposition — a result of the restless night he had just endured.

"Yep, she's fine now." The silent nod of her tousled curls was proof that she agreed with him. He pulled her to her feet, but noted the grimace on her face when she stood up on her aching legs. Refusing to give into the pain in her limbs and backside, she quickly began to straighten her dress and reorganize her long cape, making sure that every inch of her body was properly covered by the heavy garment. When she looked back up, Drake's crooked smile greeted her.

"I'm ready," she replied in a brisk voice. Only vague traces of the recent tears remained and the stubborn tilt of her head signaled that her moment of weakness had passed.

Devon glanced back and forth between the two, acting as though he was nervous about something. "We—the rest of the men have already taken care of—well—you know, private matters? So I reckon Krystal would like to take care of those things before we start riding again."

"Take care of what?" she questioned, primly.

Drake couldn't help but grin as he wondered if she was expecting them to stop at a powder room on down the road. Of course, he knew better than to say anything to her, so he decided to try to be as tactful as possible. "Devon was wondering if you needed to—" all at once Drake found that he could not find the proper words either. "Well, you know?"

With her hands positioned askew on her hips, Krystal's brows drew together with confusion. Just as quickly though, she became aware of what they were trying to ask her. The color which rushed into her pale cheeks was evidence that she had finally grasped their meaning. Good Lord, how humiliating! What was worst of all, was that there was no way she could attend to those personal things without every one of the men knowing exactly what she was doing. She was too embarrassed to even speak. Why the very idea!

Her predicament caused both brothers to feel every bit as embarrassed as she did. Their respect for women was the one trait they both shared and it was their father's deep love for their mother that had instilled it in each of them. Even now, Devon was struck by a bolt of chivalry.

"We'll take the horses and wait up on the ridge for you two." He leveled his skiddish gaze at Drake. Drake understood his brother's reasoning. Krystal might not be quite so timid if he were the only man hanging around if she had to – well – you know?

Krystal watched in a horrified stupor as Devon and his men mounted their horses and headed off towards the distant horizon. She wanted to crawl into a hole and die. Her cheeks turned crimson with mortification as she swung around to glare at Drake. "Did he leave you to hold my hand or something?" she yelled in a vain attempt to hide her distress.

Drake threw his hands up into the air and let them drop with an aggravated gesture at his sides. Damn this woman! She was always jumping to conclusions, and they were usually the wrong ones. "He thinks we're intimate with one another, remember? He probably thought you would prefer that I stay here rather than one of the other men."

"Oh Lord! How can I ever face any of those men again? This charade is impossible. I just can't go on allowing all those men to believe that you and I have—" She couldn't even bring herself to say it. She turned several more shades of red before she covered her face with her hands.

Drake tried to hide his exasperation with her, but she wasn't making it an easy task. "Listen darlin', the fact that those men think you're my woman, and the fact that I do happen to be their leader's brother are

85

the only two things that have kept Creed Ward away from you. Would you prefer him to me?" It occurred to him that they had gone through a similar discussion before. Was she always so damned stubborn?

As much as Krystal hated to admit it, he was right. She was going to have to face up to this impossible situation. Having those men believe that she was Drake DeGanahl's harlot, even if it wasn't true, was better than being fair game for a man like Creed Ward. She cast Drake a sideways glance as she tossed her head up.

"I'm going out behind the house. If you come anywhere near there, you'll rue the day you were born!"

Drake merely nodded. He had no doubt of her sincerity and he had no desire to test it. She returned almost as rapidly as she had departed. Her cheeks flamed even brighter, and as she limped the distance to where Devon and the rest of the men waited, she did not say a word. Nor did she look up from the ground. She was sure she would never get over this humiliation—ever!

Strangely enough, all of the men seemed to be embarrassed along with her, especially Sidewinder. They all knew why they had been waiting up on the hill, out of sight of the house, and for once no one had anything snide to say about it. Even if Krystal Colbert was traveling with Drake, it was still obvious to all of them that she was a real lady. Her presence had conjured up memories in each of them of a long-forgotten sweetheart, or the mother who loved them, no matter how many terrible deeds they had committed.

No one had time to dwell on these thoughts for long because they had barely started out when Devon announced that they were making an unscheduled stop in Lander. Krystal was still sharing Devon's horse and she wanted to ask him where they were taking her. She had heard him mention the Hole-in-the-Wall this morning. Now Devon was talking about a place named Lander, and from the mutterings of the other men, Krystal guessed that Lander was not somewhere that they wanted to be right now.

Creed drew his horse up next to Devon's mare. "You ain't thinking about pulling a job in Lander, are you?"

Devon turned his icy glare on the other man. "Last night you were all crying about not having any money. Well, Lander has a bank, doesn't it?"

"Yeah, and a real tough Sheriff. Hell, Devon, we ain't even had time to case the place, and we ain't got any relay horses neither. This just don't seem rational to me."

"It's my job to rationalize these things, remember? There's no need to fret, Creed. I know Lander real well, and I'm very familiar with the bank."

"I reckon you are, little brother," Drake retorted with a snide chuckle. "Wasn't that the place where you killed your first man? You must be getting mighty desperate to take the chance of robbing the same place twice."

Devon pulled his horse to an abrupt halt and swung around to look at Drake. The hateful expression on his face did little to hide his feelings of animosity toward his brother. "Right now you're in no position to dispute me, Drake. But, if you have a problem with that, I'd be only too happy to oblige you with a gun."

Krystal felt her fear rise up to her throat. Drake didn't even tote a gun and Devon's whole life was governed by his six-shooter. She noticed Devon tense in the saddle behind her, and her terror increased. Looking back over her shoulder, she focused her pleading gaze on Drake. Afraid to call out a warning to him, she hoped that she could get his attention with her eyes.

He did not return her look. His eyes were watching his brother with steady calculation. One word from Drake was all that it would take and they would finally know which of them was the best of Franklin's sons. Devon had been yearning for that for a long time, but every time it almost came down to the final battle, Drake was reminded of the little Mexican lady who had already had more than her share of sorrow in her life.

"Damn it, Devon. Do you ever stop to think of ma whenever you try to goad me into a gunfight?"

His words hit home. There had been a time when Devon believed that Drake used their mother as an excuse to avoid a gunfight, but time had mellowed his opinion. He realized now that Drake was right about what a showdown between the two of them would do to their mother. Angelina DeGanahl was the only source of conscience Devon still had intact. Their father had never made any bones about his preference . . . Drake was unreproachable, and Devon wasn't worth a hill of beans. But not their ma, no sir, she never favored one son over the other one. It didn't matter how many times Devon let her down, her love remained steady and strong. She had bore two boys and she loved them both fiercely and equally. Angelina was a fearless woman, but Devon and Drake's duel would be the death of her, especially since one of them would have to die.

Devon did not bother to answer Drake. He reached

around Krystal and gave the reins a hard yank. His horse lunged forward and plodded down the incline that led to Lander. There would come a time when not even Angelina DeGanahl could halt what destiny had in store for her two rival sons. Devon reminded himself to be patient.

When the sight of the town loomed off in the distance, the group stopped. Devon had been mulling over his plan since last night, and it was a weak plan at best. But the men were right, they had to have money to survive. They had hit a train belonging to the Denver and Rio Grande down in Colorado last week, but they hadn't gotten more than a couple hundred dollars. The lead they had about a large load of unmarked bills being on the train they had held up yesterday turned out to be a dead end, so they were penniless again. If they didn't do something soon, they would be forced to go back into cattle rustling once more, and this band of elite bandits felt they were above that lowly profession these days. Holding up banks and trains had more class, not to mention the dangerous excitement which was involved.

Devon pulled his horse up next to Austin's. "You're in charge of Krystal while we're gone. The rest of you are comin' with me."

Krystal felt herself being lifted from Devon's horse onto Austin's mount but she was too numb to care. Devon was going to rob a bank and Drake was not objecting. Good Lord, he really was an outlaw. And he wanted her to trust him? The men talked quietly among themselves for a few minutes before they rode off, leaving Krystal with Austin, and her misery. She tried to remind herself that they were riding into that town to rob innocent people of their life savings, but all she could concentrate on was praying that Drake would be all right. Why should she care about what happened to some criminal? she thought to herself. Oh, but she did care, and he just had to come back safely!

"The Sheriff of Lander is an old friend of mine," Drake reminded Devon as they approached the town. "If I ride in there he'll know who you are right off."

Devon shrugged with indifference. He knew Drake was trying to get out of being an accessory to the holdup, even if his words did happen to make sense. Devon had stayed clear of Lander for the better part of two years and the last time he had been here he had not made himself too visible. He was wearing a mask when he had shot that bank teller during the robbery, so there was a good chance that nobody would remember him. He thought over his brother's remark. Drake had always hobnobbed with all the lawmen and important businessmen everywhere he went. Someone just might recognize him as soon as they rode into town. Devon glanced over at Creed. "You and Drake will wait for us at the edge of town."

"The hell you say!" Creed retorted. "I ain't baby-sittin' your brother while the rest of you are getting in on all the excitement."

"Drake's right. Someone might know him. You just be prepared to cover us in case we have a posse on our tail when we hit the edge of Lander." Devon's flat tone of voice did not allow for an argument and the unyielding look he threw in Creed's direction silenced the man's protests.

"Are you gonna give me a gun to protect myself?" Drake questioned.

A sly laugh emitted from Devon. With a gun in his

possession, Drake would be no more than a trail of dust. "How much of an idiot do you take me for?" He glanced back at Creed. "And I trust that you won't shoot my brother while we're gone, since he won't be armed?"

Creed threw his hands up in the air and grinned wickedly. "I ain't too trustworthy if I'm provoked."

Devon moved his horse closer to Creed's mount. His ebony eyes glowed with silent warnings as he talked in a quiet tone of voice. "Well in that case, and just so it's clear, if my brother is dead when we return, you better never show your face in these parts again, cause if you do, I'll shove my gun down your throat so far that you'll be swallowing enough lead to blow your guts clean out of your yellow-bellied hide."

Silence closed in around the group. Drake was struck dumb by his brother's words. It was the last thing he would have expected from Devon. In fact, Drake was shocked to learn that Devon hadn't been leaving him with Creed just so that Creed could do the untidy job of shooting him. Then Devon's hands would still be clean and Drake would finally be out of the way. His remark to Creed made Drake even more leery. Devon definitely had something special planned for Drake, and he was not real anxious to find out what it might be. Devon motioned to Sidewinder and Joe to follow him as he gave Creed one more look of warning.

Drake's gaze moved to Creed where he found that the man was giving him the most deadly glare he could conceive. Creed had more than one reason to despise this ex-deputy now. First, on account of the woman, and now he had been belittled in front of the other men because of him. Drake was familiar with the look on Creed's face, he had seen that same

91

expression on dozens of prisoners when he was a lawman. Vengeance . . . it could eat up a man like a cancer, and the only cure was to inflict the enemy with more pain than they had caused you. Any man who had ever pinned a badge on his chest had a mental register of wrongdoers who would like nothing better than to see him six feet under. Creed Ward was just one more name on Drake's list.

The trio rode the rest of the way into town in complete silence. Devon had not told them of any particular plan, and the look on his brooding face discouraged his partners from pressing the issue. Sidewinder was edgy as usual, but Joe Preece was as calm as ever, nothing seemed to excite the quiet man too much. His confidence in his skill with his weapons was the reason that he was so good at his job.

They did not bother to cover their faces with the bandanas that hung around their necks. The newspapers were always giving them credit for bank jobs that they didn't pull or accusing someone else for robberies that they did partake in, so they only used the masks when the mood struck them. Today, none of them cared if they were recognized as they tethered their horses loosely to the post in front of the brick building which housed the bank. They were good mounts, each having been trained to stand completely still when their riders jumped into their saddles from a dead run. Even the sound of gunfire did not spook them, nor would the loud whistle of a locomotive. The men had spent their idle hours between jobs patiently training their horses for such situations since a dependable horse was extremely crucial in their line of work. A well-trained horse could mean the difference between life and death when making an escape. If a horse shied or began to buck, a man might be dumped right in the midst of his pursuers and that could prove to be deadly.

The interior of the bank was the usual layout and the mid-morning patrons were typical, too. However, three trail-worn men with low slung gunbelts entering a bank at this time of day was bound to arouse some attention. The teller, a short stocky man with a balding hairline immediately took notice, but he was not quick enough to sound the alarm, and he was even more flustered by the fact that he was left alone to face the three outlaws. His boss had just stepped out for a cup of coffee only minutes before.

Sidewinder, being the swiftest on his feet, leaped the counter in one easy stride and held one of his guns to the man's throat while Devon and Joe covered the other four people who occupied the bank.

"Faces to the wall," Devon commanded. In unison, the three men and one woman twirled around to stare at the brick wall of the building. Devon locked the front door and pulled the shades down on the windows while Joe rapidly frisked the men. He found only one gun, a small deringer, which he stuffed into his belt before he gave Devon the signal that he could cover them on his own. Devon nodded back at Joe, then lifted the corner of the shade that covered the window on the door. The activity outside the bank appeared normal. Devon sighed with relief since he was sure they had not drawn any unwanted attention, yet. He joined Sidewinder while he ordered the bank teller to empty the bank drawers into a heavy canvas bag.

A broad smile inched across Sidewinder's young face as he glanced over at Devon. Although it was still early in the day, the teller's drawer already held over eight hundred dollars. Evidently there had been a lot of deposits made this morning or else someone had made a very large deposit. Either way it was a good haul for an impromptu robbery, and since it was so unorganized, Devon made the decision to clear out without wasting time trying to get into the safe.

"Let's go," he hollered when the last bill had been shoved into the bag. Joe and Sidewinder did not argue with his decision. Devon had not steered them wrong so far. In a holdup, his level-headed thinking and intelligence was the main reason none of them had met with a bullet, yet. Sidewinder pushed his gun in the teller's ribs and directed him out to where the other people stood. Joe then ordered them to fall to the floor and immediately they all dropped down with their noses pressed against the hard wood floor. None of them intended to argue or to provoke the outlaws since they were all too frightened to move.

Devon cautiously approached the front door and slid the shade back up to the top of the window. There was still no sign of any trouble. It was almost too easy, the street in front of the bank building was quiet and peaceful. Whenever he exited a building or a train following a holdup, he always felt like every nerve in his body was on fire. A man never knew when he opened the door what would be waiting for him on the other side. With his gun positioned in his hand, Devon flipped the back the bolt on the door and then swung back around to issue a final warning.

"Count to one hundred as soon as you hear the door close. If any of you make a sound or move before you reach that number, I'm gonna come back in here and blow everybody's head off." His threat was backed up by the click of the hammer being pulled back on

Sidewinder's .45. Devon glanced in the boy's direction and shook his head. There was no need for bloodshed today. These people were too frightened to cause them any serious trouble.

Sidewinder shrugged then holstered his gun before he followed Devon and Joe out into the street. The few people that were scattered along the Main Street did not seem to take any note of the holdup men when they exited the bank. In no time at all, they were mounted and headed out of town as though nothing had happened. But the bank teller did not count to one hundred, he barely made it to fifty-five before he dared to look up and noticed that the holdup men were gone. He jumped up and ran to the front door as fast as his stubby legs would carry him, screaming at the top of his lungs, "Help! The bank's just been robbed!"

The quiet and peaceful town from a moment earlier suddenly turned into a wild and chaotic circus. The sheriff had left town a few days ago on some business down in Baggs, Wyoming, and he had left the running of the jail to a glory-grabbing deputy sheriff named Richard Prickett. Prickett wasted no time in questioning the teller and, having come to the conclusion that the bank had been held up by inexperienced bandits since they had not even bothered to break into the safe, he decided to pursue them on his own. He issued an order to one of the townsmen to organize a posse and to head out behind him, but he was certain he could overtake the three men in no time and he would probably have them captured before the posse could even catch up to him.

Deputy Prickett was confident as he galloped out of town, but the only sight he saw as his mount skimmed the top of the ridge was the dust left by the troupe of horses in front of him. There was a hell-sight more than three horses for that much dust to be churning up. Prickett estimated that there was at least eight, maybe ten gunmen up ahead. Though they were seeing more horses than were actually there, his keen eyes were still sharp enough to notice that one of the horses carried two riders, and it sure looked to him like one of them was a woman with hair the color of gold-spun fire.

He quickly made another decision—he was turning back. When he ran into the posse of a half-a-dozen men at the edge of town, he explained to them that they were greatly outnumbered and it would be certain death if they continued to pursue the bandits any further. The choice to give up the chase was quickly agreed upon, along with the dissolution of Deputy Prickett's big chance for glory.

Chapter Seven

The rest of the trip was merciless. The men pushed their horses to the limits, but the animals were used to this rapid pace. Krystal had remained on Austin's chestnut colored horse until they had stopped to water the animals. She wished she could continue to ride with him, he was every inch a gentleman. While they had waited for the rest of the cavalcade to return from Lander, he had chatted idly about the Wyoming countryside and had made Krystal feel completely at ease in his presence even in the midst of her anger towards Drake. Unfortunately, when they remounted, Devon pulled her over to his sorrel mare and placed her up in the saddle.

Drake made several attempts to get her attention, but she deliberately ignored him. His excuses were the last thing she wanted to hear. He had ridden off with the other men and when they had returned they were loaded down with greenbacks from the bank in Lander. What could he possibly say to her that would change the facts?

As they approached their destination, Krystal was once again reminded of her hopeless situation. The stone castles of the Middle Ages with their alligator-

97

infested moats and spiked drawbridges to keep out unwanted visitors were no less impregnable than the outlaw community known as Hole-in-the-Wall. Once a prehistoric lake, this desolate valley was the most northern of all the outlaw stations. Surrounded by rugged mountains and a sheer red-rock wall nearly a 1000 ft. high and over 30 miles long, the Hole-in-the-Wall housed more than one hundred horse thieves, rustlers, desperados, and even a few fallen angels who had left the luxuries of the dance-halls for life in this evil-infested hole.

Nature had carved numerous caverns and crevices throughout the stronghold. If a man was familiar with this area and was in need of a place to hideout, he could elude his pursuers for days on end. But the truth of the matter was that the law enforcement officers had little or no desire to follow anybody into this area, so once a man reached this vicinity, it was a natural assumption that he was safe. When a man left the Hole-in-the-Wall he could ride south on various outlaw trails until he hit the Santa Fe Trail. Through towering mountains, foothills, deserts and vast plains he could follow this trail on down into Mexico making it next to impossible for a posse or anyone in pursuit to catch up to him.

During the summer months there was a pungent odor of hot rock intermingled with the sweet smell of golden tull grass, and in the winter the natural barriers provided the perfect spot to winter stolen cattle that had been herded in by the numerous rustlers. Although there were several trails leading into the Hole, a narrow gorge in a rock wall was the most frequently used entrance to exit from this bandit retreat. As Devon led his outfit through the gap which was carved out of the stone wall, Krystal glanced over at Drake and noted the grim expression he wore on his face. She began to wonder if she would ever be able to escape from here.

Darkness was closing in rapidly by the time they stopped at a small cluster of roughly-built log cabins. The new arrivals caused little excitement. Devon and the rest of his men were not strangers to the Hole, and with the shadows of the night falling upon them, Drake and Krystal were barely noticed either. The people who resided at the Hole-in-the-Wall were all here for some undesirable reason. Socializing was not one of them and everyone kept to themselves for their own safety, if for no other reason.

Since she was beyond feeling any embarrassment over her aching posterior, Krystal gladly accepted Devon's arm as she limped into one of the small buildings. The interior of the log structure housed a shabby cantina. A few men leaned against the bar and an aging woman in a skimpy dance-hall costume eyed Krystal from the lap of a man who sat at one of the two tables in the room. Devon led Krystal to the other table which was empty and pulled out a chair for her to sit in.

Today had been the worse day of her life, she decided as she carefully sat down on the chair. She had not had a chance to get close enough to the man called Joe to ask for his help and she had spent the better part of the day brooding over Drake's apparent deceit. Luckily, the weather was cloudy, so her fair skin did not burn as much today as it had the day before, but her backside and her inner thighs hurt so much from two days of constant riding that nothing else mattered anymore. Just as Krystal was about to come to the conclusion that there was no chance of ever leaving this place, Joe Preece sauntered past her table.

"Um—Joe," she gasped, she did not know his whole name and calling him by his first name sounded so improper. She quickly lowered her voice to just above a whisper as he halted beside her chair. "I must speak to you." She rushed on before anyone noticed that she had stopped him. "If you'll help me to escape from here, I'll make sure you receive a large reward."

His face remained solemn while his deep-set eyes peered down at her with little interest. The whole train job had been botched because of this woman. Joe didn't take kindly to obstructions that hindered his work. Robbing trains was his specialty, as was his precise skill with his weapon. Even now as he looked down at the pleading face of this woman he was thinking about the weapon that he was so proud to own. Just the thought of it made him anxious to be alone so that he could slide the shiny knife out from his boot and polish the long blade to it's blinding brilliance. He snapped his thoughts back to the woman and almost laughed out loud that out of all the men, she had chosen him as her savior. But then he reminded himself that woman were almost always drawn to the strong silent type.

Without uttering a sound, he tipped the brim of his tan hat and gave her a brief nod of his head before he continued on his way to the backroom of the building where a tub of water was kept for community baths. Krystal started to call out after him, but was interrupted before she could do so.

"You sure are a pretty lady.

Startled, Krystal swung around to meet Sidewinder's smiling face. "Wh—what?"

His bright blue eyes began to twinkle as he repeated his statement. He pushed his black hat back on his head, exposing the soft tendrils of his long golden-colored hair. "I said, you sure are a pretty lady."

Krystal tried to swallow down the fear that threatened to choke her as he reached out his hand and gently touched one of the wayward curls that tumbled over her shoulder.

"I had a sister with hair this color. All mixed up with red and gold, just like yours."

"A sister?" Krystal repeated with surprise as she noted the look of tenderness on his young face. All at once Sidewinder no longer seemed so dangerous. He began to remind her of one of her students instead of a cruel outlaw. Although she knew that he was no more than a heartless gunman, Krystal found her heart going out to him. "Where is your sister now?"

"Dead," he replied with a careless shrug. "My ma and pa, too."

Krystal gasped. "Oh, I'm so sorry!" She reached out and touched his arm lightly. "My mother passed away last week." She wasn't sure why she had suddenly felt a need to tell the young outlaw this personal bit of information, but something told her that hidden beneath his cocky exterior he was just a sad young boy in need of a friend.

Sidewinder looked down at the spot where her hand rested on his shirtsleeve. His expression took on a mild look of confusion as his eyes traveled back to her face and as he realized she was sincere when she had said she was sorry. He shook his head slowly and answered in a hoarse voice while he began to back

101

away from her, "I'm real sorry to hear about your ma, too."

"Thank you," Krystal said in a whisper as she watched the boy disappear through the door of the cantina. She looked up and met Drake's intense green gaze.

"I'm sorry, too," he said quietly.

Krystal lowered her head and shut her eyes for a moment. If only she could go back in time—before yesterday, before last week—back to a time when her days were filled with the laughter of children and her nights held the soft sound of her mother's voice. A single tear escaped from one corner of her eye, despite her determination not to allow another show of weakness to overcome her in front of her abductors.

The handkerchief that wiped away the salty tear was held by the gentlest hand Krystal had ever encountered, and when her lids fluttered open again, the look in the dark green eyes that met her gaze touched her with unspoken words of understanding and compassion. She could not speak because of the lump which suddenly appeared in her throat. The feeling that she had been experiencing for the past two days returned with increasing intensity. Her hands began to tremble for no apparent reason and her hammering heart threatened to blow apart within her breast. Why did this man affect her so drastically, and why did she feel so utterly powerless to stop it?

"There's two empty rooms upstairs. Do I dare trust the two of you alone in one of them?" Devon asked with his usual frown. Did they always have to look like they were about to seduce each other at any moment? he wondered with disgust.

Krystal tore her eyes away from Drake while trying

102

unsuccessfully to break the spell that engrossed her spinning mind. "Would be be possible for me to have my own room?" She did not allow herself to look at Drake again as she felt her cheeks flame with humiliation. It was degrading enough for all of these men to think that she and Drake had actually slept together before last night. She felt like she had to at least try to save what was left of her diminishing reputation.

"That's not a good idea," Drake answered firmly. "I think everyone here realizes that you are a respectable woman and that you and I don't normally share a room, but under these circumstances I don't feel it is wise for you to be alone."

Another streak of red soared through Krystal's cheeks. "Well — I've never — I mean — last night was the first —" Oh Lord! Why didn't she stop when she was ahead.

A hateful grunt emitted from Devon as he eyed his brother. "You must be slipping, Drake. You traveled clear across the country with this pretty little gal and last night was the first night you two spent together?" Devon shook his head. A rude chuckle escaped him while he patted Drake on the back. "I'm real proud of you, big brother. You give a new meaning to the word gentleman."

Devon ignored Drake's glowering expression as he walked away, still shaking his head in disbelief. Now he had even more reason to wonder about his big brother's relationship to this lovely lady. And so did Creed Ward.

He had overheard Krystal's admission while he was pretending to be engrossed in his whiskey bottle. It was interesting that Drake DeGanahl hadn't taken his turn with her yet. That bit of information made

Creed's eyes glimmer with malice beneath his dark gray hat. He wasn't particularly fond of virgins, but if he could have Krystal Colbert before Drake De-Ganahl did, he would make the sacrifice. It would be only a small bit of revenge, but it would be a start.

Drake turned his angry glare towards Krystal while he fought to contain his voice in a gruff whisper. "Don't you ever stop to think before you open your mouth? How do you hope to convince any of these men that you're my woman if you continue to say stupid things?"

Krystal tossed her head up as her eyes narrowed with a disdainful glare. "Oh, how dare you talk to me in that manner? I don't even want you to talk to me at all! You lied to me about your association with your brother and his band of outlaws. But that's hardly the issue right now. My reputation is at stake. Good Lord, I am a schoolteacher and my personal life has to be above reproach."

Drake's head tilted back as a loud roar of laughter escaped him. A gesture that infuriated her twice as much. She gritted her teeth and tried to keep her voice low. "I refuse to continue to let everyone think that you and I sleep — just what is it that you find so humorous?" She rose to her feet and placed her hands upon her hips. The pain in her hind side was forgotten in the heat of her fury.

"A schoolteacher?" he said through his mirth as his brows raised into a devilish curve. "You are a schoolteacher?"

"And why, may I ask, do you find that so hard to believe?" she demanded between her clenched teeth.

"Yes, you may ask, darlin'," a smile slanted his lips into a look which leaned towards indecency. "They sure didn't make teachers like you when I was a schoolboy. If they did, I might've studied harder, though I'm not quite sure what I would've learned."

Krystal's face flushed a deep shade of crimson, but it was from anger rather than embarrassment. It was apparent what he was insinuating with that crude remark and the look on his face made Krystal grow even more enraged. "You, sir, are a rude boor!"

Drake nodded in agreement, his crooked smile still intact. "And you, Miss Colbert, always seem to bring out the best in me." He tipped his little round hat with one hand as he held out his other arm. "Shall we?" he asked in a haughty accent. With an mock bow he gestured towards the stairs while he continued to smile at her with a bold twinkle in his olive green eyes.

Krystal remained unmoving, her fury clouding out everything else. How dare he talk to her in that tone? He was an arrogant knave and she was not going to let him get away with treating her like she was some trollop whom he had picked up on the train. Never mind the fact that everyone already thought that about her anyway. That was his fault, too, she reminded herself as she mentally compiled a list of things that she could blame on Drake DeGanahl. It was lucky for him that she was too mad to do any more than stand here in the middle of this gloomy dwelling and grace him with the most hateful look that she was capable of producing.

Drake leaned down and quietly said, "We have everyone's attention, darlin'. It would be real wise for us to go to our room now."

She glanced around the room and noticed that he was right. Everyone in the room was observing their

105

heated conversation. She really had no other choice than to do as he asked. To confess to the other men now that everything about their relationship was a lie might make her situation even worse than it already was. She couldn't help but note the odd expression on Devon's face as he watched them closely, and Creed Ward was giving her the most disgusting smile. With a grunt of submission, she reluctantly placed her hand through Drake's extended arm and allowed him to lead her up the stairs.

'Our room,' he had said. Last night she had slept in a room filled with men. Tonight she was sharing a bedroom with just one man. Good Lord! She would prefer the crowded old farmhouse where they had spent last night, to sharing a room with just Drake DeGanahl, she thought as she cautiously looked at him from the side of her eye. Ever since that overbearing kiss yesterday, her emotions had been running wild, and it was her own reactions to being alone with him that was causing her the most distress right now.

Totally unaffected by her hostile attitude, Drake began to disrobe the moment they entered the room. Tossing his suit jacket on a nearby chair, he quickly pulled his tie from around his neck and threw it on the chair, also. His little black derby rapidly followed and landed on top of the pile. When he turned back to Krystal he was unbuttoning the top buttons of his finely-tailored dress shirt. The slivered daggers of gold which flashed at him from her narrowed eyes did not surprise him. But his next words shocked Krystal.

"I realize how sore your bu—um—" her spine stiffened and he noticed a rush of color paint her cheeks a bright shade of scarlet again when he accidently glanced down towards her hips. It was just his luck, he thought with aggravation, that he should find himself falling in love with a prudish schoolteacher. "I mean — I know that you could use some rest. But that's exactly why Devon won't be expecting us to try to escape tonight. It's now or never."

Krystal immediately forgot about his intimate remark concerning her painful situation and began to mull over his words about escape. Was it really possible that he was sincere about helping her to get away? He moved closer and stood only a few inches away from her now. His tall frame towered above her, making her realize how helpless she would be against him if he should decide to make any sort of advances towards her. If she left with him tonight, she would be completely at his mercy. When she gazed up into those deep green pools she grew weak with the unexplained emotions that wiped away any doubts she was harboring about him, and left her with such a deep longing that all she cared about was being with this man . . . and seeking the fullfilment that his nearness continually aroused within her weakening body.

At first Drake thought he was imagining it, but the softness that flooded her face and lighted her large tawny brown eyes with flickering flames of gold was unmistakable. This woman wanted him as badly as he wanted her. With a determination greater than ever before, he knew he had to get her away from this hellish abode. Leaving her at this moment, he realized, would be one of the most difficult things he had ever done, but if they ever hoped to escape, he had no other alternative.

He cleared his throat, but not his whirling mind as he reminded himself that he had always been a man who could control his own destiny. And at this moment, her destiny also rested in his hands. It didn't matter that they were alone in this room, and it was not important that she was looking at him with a rapturous glow of submission upon her beautiful face. When they were safely away from here, he would take her in his arms and . . .

It didn't matter that precious time was wasting as his mouth descended upon hers in an engulfing wave of unabashed passion. The second union of their lips was no less magical than their first, and Drake felt like he had just crossed the bridge to insanity when he forced himself to pull away from the pliant feel of her soft mouth, and away from the tempting form which leaned against his own awakening body with ardent demand. But he had to break away before it was too late to stop the pulsating urges that were overtaking his rapidly disappearing self-control.

Krystal drew in a ragged breath as she tried to steady her shaking limbs. She had returned his second kiss with the same intensity and profligateness as she had his first kiss. This kiss was much too brief though, and she found herself thinking of tugging on the front of his unbuttoned shirt so she could draw his mouth down upon hers again. An unleashed desire filled her with such wanton yearnings that she grew weak with anticipation. But as she watched him back away from her with a look that seemed to shout forgiveness, she grew outraged with herself. What must he think of a woman who would fall so easily into his arms without a moment's hesitation?

"I'll be back soon," Drake said in raspy voice as he fought to regain his sensibility. "I'll knock three times when I return. Don't open the door for anyone else." He swung around and strode from the room in a stiff stride, realizing as he slammed the door shut behind him, that to be in her presence a second longer would be fatal to their escape.

Krystal remained unmoving as she stared at the closed door. She was numb with mortification over the way she had just behaved. What was it about that man that made her lose every ounce of her restraint? Krystal had no doubt that she would not have stopped him if he had continued to make love to her.

"Good Lord!" she gasped as she cast a quick glance at the narrow bed against the wall. She shook her head trying to clear away the vision which suddenly appeared before her eyes . . . A vision of herself with Drake on that rickety old bed in each other's arms. Covering her eyes with her trembling hands in a vain attempt to block out that inordinate thought, she made a vow to herself: from this moment forward, she would not permit Drake DeGanahl to kiss her again — no matter what!

The sound of footsteps in the hallway outside the bedroom door snapped her back to reality. With her heart rising up to her throat, she rushed to the door and bolted the chain. Relief flooded through her when the steps had faded away. As she glanced around the cramped room with its sparse furnishings she began to wonder about Drake's plan of escape? How could they ever hope to get away from this awful place? There were armed criminals everywhere and Drake didn't even have a weapon. Not to mention that Krystal was sure she could not ride another horse for as long as she lived. Just the idea of straddling one of those horrible beasts again made her whole body throb with a resurgence of pain. She wanted to put her faith in Drake, but he had lied to her about his involvement with the outlaws already, and realistically she couldn't imagine that they would be able to sneak away without being caught.

Waiting for Drake's return brought about such an acute apprehension that Krystal was sure that her nerves would not survive this night. The thought of someone discovering them as they attempted an escape was terrifying, but staying here was even worse. Pacing the floor was beginning to take its toll on Krystal's aching muscles, so she eased herself down into a overstuffed chair which sat beside the bed. She had no idea how much time had passed since Drake's departure because as soon as she allowed herself to relax she fell into an exhausted slumber.

Something—a noise, or just a feeling that she was no longer alone—jolted Krystal awake. "Drake?" In the darkness she made out the form of a man standing before her. Her sleepy gaze fought to focus on the man's face. "Drake is that you?" Wasn't he supposed to knock three times? All at once she sensed that this hovering shadow did not belong to Drake. Jumping up from the chair she quickly regained her awareness and immediately realized the danger she was in. As her eyes began to adjust to the dimly lit room she knew the man was not Drake. "Who are you?"

"Joe Preece."

"Joe? How did you get in here?" She distinctly remembered locking the door.

He held up his pride and joy . . . a bone-handled knife whose eight-inch blade glistened like dozens of tiny silver stars in the darkness. A half-breed army scout had taught him how to throw this miniature saber with deadly precision, and Joe savored each and every time he had an opportunity to use this unique skill. Tonight his trusty little sword had opened the locked door with ease, just one of its many uses.

"Good Lord!" Krystal felt the blood drain from her face. Even in this poor light, the knife shone brightly with an ominous forboding. "Wh — what do you want?"

Joe ran his forefinger along the razor-sharp edge of the knife blade. "How much?"

"How much what?" Krystal questioned with dread filling every pore of her body.

"Money. How much money will you pay me to get you outta here?"

For a moment Krystal could not make her terrified mind grasp what he was talking about. Then she recalled the proposal she had made to him earlier. It was another stupid mistake, she realized with a sick feeling growing in the pit of her stomach. This soft-spoken man no longer seemed so safe. In fact, the man who stood before her now twirling his long knife between the palms of his hands was the most diabolical-looking person she had ever encountered. How could she have ever thought he was so harmless?

"How-how ever much you want."

"Ten thousand," he said with a definite tone, then leaned down so that Krystal could make out his features in the dim light. "That oughta do it."

For a moment Krystal thought she was going to pass out with fear. His whiskey-laden breath and blood-shot eyes only served to fuel her terror. If he was drunk she could never hope to reason with him. "All right. Ten thousand it will be. Do you have a-a plan?"

Where was Drake? Something must have happened to him. She fought back the hysteria she felt rising in

111

her breast. What if Drake had crossed paths with Joe? She was not going to permit her mind to dwell on that right now. Drake had to be safe, she told herself sternly, refusing to give in to the panic flooding throughout her whole body — he just had to be!

"I always have a plan," his thin face hosted an evil smile. "I plan to be ten thousand dollars richer, or else I plan to make that pretty little face of yours look just short of hideous." The sharp tip of the knife touched Krystal's cheek lightly.

She did not move, the icy feel of the blade laying against the side of her face had her rooted to the spot. The awful feeling that Joe had found Drake and had done something terrible to him continued to rule her thoughts. She had no way of knowing where Drake was and there was nothing she could do, she realized in horror, but to go with with this madman. All she could pray for was that someone — anyone — would see them before they got away. She would even welcome Creed Ward's presence. At least with Creed she knew exactly where she stood. Joe Preece's quiet, mild-mannered appearance had fooled her completely and it was obvious to her now that he was the most dangerous of all the outlaws who had abducted her from the train. She had no doubt in her mind that he would carry out his vile threat if she did not cooperate with him.

"You have my word that as soon as we reach Virginia City I'll pay you ten thousand dollars and I'll never tell anyone about your involvement with the train holdup or the bank robbery."

Joe slowly lowered his knife and touched the blade in a loving gesture before he slid it down into the side of his tall brown boots. "Nope," he said with a careless

112

shake of his head. "Ten thousand for getting you outta here. Didn't say that I would take you to Virginia City."

Krystal raised her hands in the air in a defeated gesture. "But I have no money with me. I can't pay you until I reach my father in Nevada." Again, the fleeting thought that she might be putting too much stock in a rich father who might not exist, passed through her mind.

"You'll think of something." His narrow lips twisted into a sly smile when he saw the look of fear consume her beautiful face again. He knew she had grasped his meaning and he was tired of talking. Words were such a waste of time. There were better ways to get his point across. Joe's smile broadened, that had always been his own private joke because it was so fitting. He motioned toward the door and as Krystal moved numbly into the dark empty hallway she realized that up until now everything that had been happening was only child's play. Now the real nightmare was just beginning.

Chapter Eight

Joe was familiar with every inch of this complex and all of the other buildings at Hole-in-the-Wall. This outlaw hideout, along with several other low-life dens along the outlaw trail had been one of his many homes for most of his adult life. Without arousing anyone's attention, he and Krystal slipped down a back stairway and into an open field behind the cabin. He motioned for her to remain silent and to follow.

Krystal had no intention of disputing him. The feel of his cold knife was still too recent. She had not given up her hope that someone would notice them as they attempted to escape, but once they were out of the building, it began to seem unlikely that anyone would see them leave. Through the dim light provided by the moon, she moved clumsily ahead of him for a long distance until they reached a deserted corral where two horses stood, saddled and ready for departure. She felt the last of her hope dissolve when Joe gestured for her to mount one of the horses. She nodded, then turned and stared at the beast in perplexity since she did not have a clue as to how to get into the saddle without someone lifting her up onto the animal's back.

With an irritated grunt, Joe moved to her side. He could tell by the look of confusion on her face that she would never make it up into the saddle on her own. He began to wonder if ten thousand dollars was worth the aggravation of putting up with this highfalutin' woman. Just as he was about to place his hands around her waist, a noise interrupted them. Joe hunkered down as he pulled his knife from his boot with lightening speed.

Krystal held her breath, she had never seen a man move so swiftly or with such deadly intent. Beneath the brim of Joe's light-colored hat, his thin face resembled that of a cunning animal whose predator was about to become his prey. Just enough light illuminated from the moon to make the sharp blade of Joe's skinning knife shimmer with a menacing clarity. Krystal broke out in a cold clammy sweat. This man seemed barely human when he stalked out from behind the horse, and the look which was contained within his steely gaze bespoke of something akin to insanity.

The second man appeared to come out of nowhere. One moment Krystal was frantically peering into the obscured light looking for the source of the noise, the next instant his tall straight frame stood out in bold contrast against the opaque shadows of the night. His features were shaded by a broad hat and the ankle-length duster he wore billowed out at the hem as a faint breeze whistled across the open prairie and through the corral.

Joe did not utter a sound as he raised his hand and, with a flick of his wrist sent the knife flying. His aim was steady and precise. Krystal screamed when she saw the glistening blade slicing through the air. But the breeze suddenly whipped through the stillness again, making Joe's weapon waver just enough to made it's contact a fraction less than deadly.

Everything happened in such rapid succession that Kyrstal was not sure what took place next. The stranger fell and rolled to the side, and in less than a heartbeat, a blinding flash exploded in front of her. Her next scream caught in her throat as the deafening sound of the bullet ricocheted through her bewildered brain. Only sinister silence and the stomach-wrenching odor of expelled gunpowder accompanied the illusory spectors which loomed across the land when Krystal allowed her eyes to open again.

The shapes of two men laying in the settling dust were outlined against the vast emptiness of the dim night. One of them moved, he moaned, then almost immediately sprang to his feet. He came towards Krystal. She backed away, consumed with fright. His big gray hat looked familiar, but she could not make her terrified mind remember which one of the men it belonged to. One of the horses blocked her path when she stumbled against the animal's side. With little effort, the man reached out and grabbed her, then tossed her onto the steed's back. Just as quickly he jumped into the saddle of the other horse.

Krystal barely had time to grab ahold of the saddle-horn before the man was leading her horse out of the corral at a neck-breaking speed. She had never held on to anything as tightly as she did this little lump of leather. Her teeth felt like they were being jarred out of her head and each time the animals hoofs struck against the hard ground she had to fight to regain her balance in the saddle again. The ties of her heavy black cape strained against her neck as the wind whipped the garment out behind her, making her feel as though she was going to strangle from the pressure.

She tried to cry out to the man, to beg him to stop before she fell off the horse's back, but her words were lost to the sound of the wind which howled past them, and to the loud pounding of the animals fleeting departure.

At this neck-breaking speed they covered a great distance in very little time, but daybreak was already upon them. The first pale rays of the sun were beginning to peek timidly through the dark clouds which hovered in mixed disarray across the sky. Even the air seemed to hold a feeling of doom this morning. The wind had picked up, obviously blowing in the storm contained within a gathering of heavy black clouds. Between the jostling up and down on the horse's back, Krystal tried to get a glimpse of her captor. But the only thing she could see of the man who still led her horse across the sagebrush flats were the flaps of his long black duster as they whipped about wildly in the air. The reckless ride through the night had been too terrifying for her to notice anything else, and now she was too exhausted to even care who the man was or where he was taking her.

Krystal closed her eyes tightly in a vain effort to protect her eyes from the cutting wind, but the horse's sudden stop caused her eyes to fly back open. The man's horse stood directly in front of Krystal's mount and she strained forward in an effort to get a look at the man. His wide-brimmed hat still prevented her from seeing his face. Her gaze wandered past him and stopped when she realized what he must be looking at. Several hundred yards ahead of them was the oblong opening in the stone wall which provided the exit from this hell-hole. She glanced back at the man. That hat—it was the gray hat that Creed Ward had been wearing. Oh Lord! Had Creed killed Joe

117

Preece because of his obsession to have her all to himself? He had saved her from one madman, but now she was sure that in a different way, Creed was just as dangerous as Joe Preece had been.

The man reached out to her, but Krystal shied back in her saddle as far as she could without falling off her horse. Expecting him to grab at her, she braced herself for a fight. Joe Preece's chilling personality had paralyzed her with fear, but Creed Ward would not have her without a battle. Much to her surprise, he did not make an attempt to grab her. She looked down at his out-stretched hand, then peered back up into his face. There was not time to acknowledge him as he tossed the leather reins into her hands.

"Just hold on to these, darlin'. We can move faster if you ride by yourself." He gave her horse a hard slap on its hindquarters and the animal reared up in fright before charging off through the rock opening in a frenzied gallop. In her terror and confusion, Krystal dropped the reins and instinctively clutched onto the saddlehorn again to prevent herself from being flipped off the animal's back. Their erratic retreat from the Hole-in-the-Wall was no more than a blurr to Krystal. The only thing she had time to worry about was hanging onto the saddlehorn for dear life. The reins which she knew should be in her hands were flying wildly on either side of the horse and there was absolutely no way she could hope to grab hold of them.

The horse showed no signs of slowing down and Krystal was in such a state of shock she was not aware of the rider who suddenly appeared at her side. It was not until he managed to grab ahold of one of the long reins that she noticed his presence. When he tugged frantically on the rein, the horse swung to the side and came to an abrupt halt. Krystal jerked forward nearing flying over the animals head. Before she had time to clear her spinning senses, the man pulled her down from the animal's back. She fell against him, too dizzy to support herself.

"Krystal? Are you all right?"

She nodded slowly as she raised her eyes up to his face. Drake—it really was Drake! He looked so different, she hadn't even recognized him. For a second back there, she had thought she was imagining that he was the man beneath that big hat. But he was real and she had never been so happy to see anyone in her life. His green eyes peered out from under the wide brim and locked with her golden-brown gaze. Dressed in Creed Ward's tan chalis shirt and denim jeans which were topped by a long dark duster, he looked like another person. Gone was the city-slicker image he had presented to Krystal when she had first met him on the train. This dangerously handsome man who stood before her now looked completely natural in this rugged mode of dress, and Krystal sensed that she was looking at the real Drake DeGanahl for the first time. She slumped against him, too relieved that he had come to her rescue to ask him any questions about his attire or anything else.

"We have to keep moving for awhile," he said in an apologetic tone. He picked her up and placed her back into the saddle. She wanted to protest. If she could just ride with him? But she knew that it would be foolish to subject his horse to the added weight when she could ride her own horse. She took a tight grip on the reins when he handed them to her this time, and with a deep sigh, she straightened up and gave him a brave nod of her head.

He grimaced slightly as he smiled back at her, but

in the misty light of dawn, Krystal did not notice. He swung up into the saddle of his own mount and began to lead the way across the gloomy countryside. Before long the threatening rain began to fall and ran in tiny rivulets across the dry ground. Drake was relieved to see the change in the weather. The rain would wash away all the traces of their trail. With any luck they would elude any pursuers before he was forced to give into the searing pain that was ripping through his left side with increasing intensity.

They had covered a great deal of territory, only stopping for a very short time to water the horses, but Krystal noticed their pace was beginning to move at barely more than a crawl. She assumed Drake felt they were safe now and that was why he was no longer in such a hurry. He seemed extremely relaxed in his saddle as they meandered along through a clump of cedars. Feeling a bit more secure in the saddle, she nudged the animal in the side with her heels slightly so that she could ride abreast with Drake. The sight which greeted her caused her blood to turn to ice.

"Good Lord!" she grasped. "Drake! what's wrong?" He was slumped down and dark purple circles outlined his closed eyes which were set within a deathly white complexion. Her words were wasted on him because he was beyond hearing anything.

"Drake!" she repeated. She reached out and touched his arm. Without warning he tumbled from the horse and landed with a thud in the golden grass which surrounded the cedars. Krystal screamed and jumped from her horse's back before the animal had even stopped moving. She tumbled across the ground, but did not pause even long enough to catch her breath as she crawled over to the spot where Drake had landed. A fear more engulfing than anything she

120

had ever felt before overtook her as she peered down into his stark white face. All at once she remembered the vision of Joe's knife sailing through the air. The knife must have struck Drake somewhere. But why hadn't he said something to her?

She looked around at the broad expanse of barren country that surrounded them. They were completely defenseless out here. If Drake died, she would never forgive herself. He had risked his life more than once for her in the past few days and all she had given him in return was trouble.

There had been an overpowering attraction between them from the first moment they had noticed each other on the train. She would not permit him to die until she understood all the strange sensations which he had aroused in her ever since that meeting. With this determination planted firmly in her mind, she began to search his still form for his injury. Immediately the blood-caked hole in the left-hand corner of his dark coat caught her attention. With shaking hands, she pulled back the lapel of his duster, only to be confronted with a larger and redder stain across the top of his tan shirt. Krystal took a deep breath as she unbuttoned his shirt and pulled the wet sticky material away from his shoulder. She blanched at the gory sight of the jagged wound, but forced herself to fight back the urge to be ill. She tried to remain calm while she studied the terrible hole. It was definitely a knife wound, she decided without hesitation. He had traveled all this way with this life-threatening stab wound just so he could keep his part of the bargain. Krystal wanted to cry over his gallantry, but tending his wound was more important than giving in to her constant urge to cry. Although she did not have the first idea about what she could do for him, she knew

121

she was the only chance he had of surviving. If she didn't do something soon he was sure to bleed to death.

Frantically, she glanced around and noticed the saddlebags hanging from both horses. Rushing to the animals, she grabbed the bags and dumped their contents out on the ground. She sifted through the various articles of assorted dried foods, a bottle of whiskey, matches and other odds and ends, but she found nothing that she could put on his wound. Her eyes traveled back to the pile of useless matter. The whiskey bottle caught her eye. Whiskey was a good disinfectant for an open sore or wound. Hadn't she heard that somewhere? Deciding that it was the only feasible thing she had to use, Krystal clutched the bottle to her breast and tugged on the cork until it finally pulled free from the long neck of the container. Her hands were trembling so hard as she tried to pour the liquor over the gaping hole in Drake's shoulder that the liquid splashed across his whole upper body. Krystal cursed at herself and clenched the bottle in both hands as she carefully doused the wound with the clear alcohol. A small moan escaped from Drake's mouth.

Krystal stared in horror at the hole where the whiskey sizzled and mingled with the fresh blood while she wondered what she should do next. She hiked up the skirt of her dress and yanked on the ruffle of her lacy petticoat. After she had torn off a long strip of the thin material she struggled with Drake's limp form as she fought to pull his coat and shirt off so she could wrap the bandage around the wound. When she finally managed to get that task finished, she placed one of the bedrolls that had been tied on the back of the saddles beneath his head. The other blanket she shook open to use as a cover for him.

When she felt like she had done all that she could for him, she remembered the horses. If the horses got away, she and Drake would be stranded out here in the middle of nowhere. Since she knew virtually nothing about caring for the beasts, the only thing she thought to do was to tie their reins to one of the cedars. She gave a relieved sigh, thankful that she had thought to secure the animals in time. Then she settled down next to Drake to begin a torturous vigil. He looked awful . . . worse with each passing minute. His pale face was drawn and pinched and blood continued to ooze through the bandage. Luckily the rain had stopped, and as the sun began to fall behind the distant mountains, the wind stopped howling. By the time darkness had captured the land, the climate was quite pleasant. The change in the weather helped, but Krystal was still sick with worry. Drake just had to live!

She fretted over whether or not she should start a fire. The smoke might draw attention to their location and she was sure Devon and his group of outlaws were hot on their trail. But for Drake's sake she decided that a fire was a necessity. His survival was more important than anything else and the warmth a fire would provide was bound to be beneficial to his recuperation. As the night progressed, Krystal took advantage of the vague light from the moon to gather an armload of cedar branches. She remembered the matches which were in the knapsacks, but starting a fire was not so simple. The rain that had fallen earlier in the day, had saturated the wood and it was still damp, making it difficult to get a fire going. Krystal tediously lit almost a whole box of the stick matches before she finally had a small flame struggling to stay alive in the middle of the pile of kindling. As the wood began to dry out from the heat the fire emitted, it began to increase in volume and after a time a strong blaze was lighting the small area which was nestled between the cluster of cedars. She reclined back against the gnarled trunk of one of the trees and sighed with weariness. The fire was the first she had ever made in the wilds and she felt a good deal of pride for her accomplishment. If only she could do something more for Drake? But other than change the blood-soaked bandages several times throughout the night, it seemed that she was helpless to aid him any further. If he died—Oh Lord, she was not going to think of those morbid things.

The night seemed endless, and Krystal was a bundle of nerves before it was over. Coyotes howled nearby, the trees rustled and she kept imagining that she saw ominous shapes out in the open prairie beyond the clump of trees where they were camped. Towards morning, Drake began to run a high fever. Through the duration of the fever he ranted and raved in incoherent fragments that made no sense to Krystal. She was frantic as she bathed his sweating body with water from one of the canteens in an effort to bring his fever down.

As he tossed and turned and made a weak attempt to fight off Krystal each time she wiped him down or tried to change his bandages, he continued to talk in disoriented phrases about his mother and father. Several times he mentioned Devon, and he talked about numerous women. Surprisingly, much of what Drake said was spoken in a foreign tongue. Krystal recognized the language as Spanish, although she could not understand anything he said. She could speak some

French, since she had traveled to Paris once with her mother. However, she could not comprehend one word of Spanish. She began to wonder if the deep tan color of his skin was derived from a Latin heritage.

From his ravings in English, Krystal was able to put together bits and pieces of Drake and Devon's life of bitter rivalry. Before his fever broke, it was obvious to Krystal that Drake worshipped his parents, had competed with Devon for all of their lives, and he apparently knew a good many ladies. This last bit of information made her see red, although she could not imagine why, because he had also called out her name several times throughout the long morning.

Still, the idea of all the other women he had known continued to gnaw at her. But each time she glanced in his direction, she could certainly see why women would be attracted to a man like Drake DeGanahl. Her eyes were drawn to his perfect masculine form. She scooted closer to him and ran the damp cloth down through the heavy mass of light brown curls which blanketed his expansive chest. The feel of those thick curls surprised her. They looked wiry, but to her touch, they were so very soft. The cloth remained on his lean stomach as she traced her hand up through the downy hair on his chest, then drew her fingers back down again. Her hand stopped at the waistband of his jeans, but the trail of wispy curls continued past his belly and disappeared beneath the cover his pants. Krystal pulled her hand away, aghast at the lascivious thoughts that were running rampant through her mind. She jumped up to her feet and began to back away from this man who caused her to think the most disgusting things. Why, she had almost been tempted to undo his pants and . . . Oh, Good Lord!

Krystal used the wet rag to wipe the sweat from her

own feverish face as she silently berated herself for her abnormal behavior. She forced herself to concentrate on important things, such as keeping watch in case Devon or his men should catch up to them. This thought caused her to take Drake's pistol out of the holster that hung from his hip and place it in her lap. She did not have the slightest inclination how to use it, but it's presence made her feel somewhat safe.

This day turned hot and by midday Krystal was forced to dispose of some of her heavy black attire. She had placed her little black purse around her neck yesterday morning before they had left the abandoned farmhouse, and it still dangled securely at her side when she removed her long cape. Deciding that she did not want to take any chances with the purse and its contents, Krystal left the bag around her neck. But, the bodice of her black dress was entirely too hot and heavy for this scorching temperature. Dismissing her modesty for the time being, Krystal gave the heavy material a hard tug and ripped the top of the garment from the skirt. It was too hot to wear anything other than her lacy chemise, although once she tore the dress apart, she realized that the thin white covering did not hide much of her full breasts beneath its silky material. She would have to keep her cape close at hand and toss it back on if she needed to cover herself in a hurry.

By evening, Drake's fever had gone down considerably and although he had not regained consciousness, Krystal was hopeful that he would recover. His breathing seemed normal and the wound had finally clotted. As the moon was just barely rising up in the velvety black sky, Krystal had already eaten a simple dinner of hardtack and had even managed to perk a pot of coffee over the hot coals of the fire she had built. She was exhausted, but proud. Her friends back in Boston would not believe their eyes if they could see her now. Even the threatening sounds of the wild animals or the rustling trees did not bother her as much tonight. And besides, she still had Drake's gun clasped tightly in her hands. She sunk down onto the blanket she had spread out beside Drake and fell into a deep slumber.

Drake stirred slightly and forced his swollen eyes to open. His head lolled to the side and for an instant before his drooping lids fell shut again, a fleeting thought passed through his pained mind. He was dead, but much to his amazement, it did not sadden or frighten him. Instead, he felt elated, because an angel with golden-red curls and skin the color of fresh cream had been chosen to lead him to a mystical new land. He fell back into unconsciousness, content that he had just glimpsed heaven.

Chapter Nine

A rare wildflower in a field of drab green sagebrush, the gentlest breeze that floats among the tallest
treetops, or a sweet taste of Utopia in a cruel world
were just a few of the things Drake was reminded of
when he opened his eyes from his close brush with
death. At the edge of the cedars stood the loveliest
creature he had ever glimpsed. She was not aware that
he watched her as she threw her head back and closed
her eyes to the warm rays of the bright sun. The thick
mass of strawberry curls tumbled past her bare shoulders in shimmering shades that resembled reddish-
gold silk. A thin chemise supported the outline of her
high firm breasts with delicate white and blue lace,
and the hem of her heavy black dress was pulled up
on one side and tucked into her waistband, revealing
the jagged edge of her torn petticoat and exposing one
slender leg clear past her knee.

Right now, the last thing she looked like was a
schoolteacher from back East. To Drake she looked
like the angel he had imagined her to be the night
before, and with the bright sunlight shedding its
crowning rays down upon her, she seemed almost
unearthly. Drake moaned, he hadn't gone to Heaven,

this had to be Hell. It was a sin for her to look so sensuous when he was so incapacitated.

His moan immediately drew her attention to him. "Drake!" Her voice showed her enthusiasm as she lifted up the side of her black skirt that still hung down around her ankles and ran in dainty steps to his side. Without thinking she knelt down and gave him an affectionate hug. Her pale complexion, which was now speckled with faint brown freckles across the bridge of her nose from the hot sun, blushed a bright shade of pink as she sat back up. "I'm sorry. I shouldn't have — I mean — I hope I didn't hurt your shoulder?"

Drake felt ridiculous, but he felt a sudden flow of hot blood flood through his cheeks, too. "You didn't," he answered hoarsely. She could have cut his whole arm off and he wouldn't have felt any pain in his shoulder. The pain she caused was much lower and it had appeared when her full breasts pressed up against his chest with no more than a flimsy piece of silk as a barrier between their bare skin. His adoring gaze traveled down over her ripe form in a slow, titilating evaluation. Her beauty was ethereal. . . . He knew he loved her with every fiber of his essence.

Even in his weakened state, the heat of his burning gaze ignited a torch in Krystal that nothing could douse. The look of desire upon his face fanned the flickering flame in her body until it burned out of control. She yearned to be his woman in every sense of the word. She wanted him to show her all the unexplored trails of temptation and beyond. Throwing her previous restrictions to the wind, she leaned closer to him until she could feel the warmth of his breath upon her lips. She was going to kiss him again because it was against her will to do otherwise.

When her lips were no more than an inch or less away from his waiting mouth, she was snapped back to reality. Of course, she wanted to kiss him, but, she also wanted so much more from him. He was bound to lose all his respect for her if she were to give into the primal instincts that his presence continually caused to surface within her, and she sensed something so much greater than mere sexual attraction growing between them. Once again, she reprimanded herself for her loose actions while she forced her mind to concentrate on something other than the impaling feel of his hypnotic gaze.

"You nearly scared the life out of me," she said in breathless syllables while she began to lengthen the distance between them. "Good Lord, I thought you were dead. But I think you're going to be all right now, don't you?"

A deep scowl creased Drake's dark features. Good Lord, indeed! This woman could turn her emotions off and on like a spigot on a pump. He knew he had not misjudged the look of passion on her face again, but there she was rattling on about nothing. "Damn!" he growled.

"Are you in pain?"

He pulled the bedroll up around his chin with his good arm and gave her a glowering look. "Yes, damnit. I am in pain."

A worried frown crossed Krystal's face as she inched up to him again. "Is there anything I can do?"

Inspite of the throbbing pain in his shoulder, Drake managed to smile at her suggestion. "Well," he replied with a sudden quiver of his body. "I am awfully cold."

"Cold?" Her worried expression intensified. The heat was almost unbearable today. He must be getting chills, she assumed with fear racing through her. She

130

had hoped the worst was over now that he had regained consciousness. Kneeling down beside him again, she began to tuck the blanket tightly around his body.

"I don't think that is going to help. Maybe you should — no forget it, you wouldn't."

Her face was covered with sympathy as she leaned dangerously close to him. "Yes, I would. Whatever you need, just ask me."

"Well?" It took every ounce of his willpower to keep the wicked grin from entering into his elaborate expression of pain. "Maybe it would help if you were to lie down beside me. They say that body heat is the best source of warmth." A visible tremor shook his entire body to emphasize his need.

Krystal looked skeptical. Surely he would not make any advances toward her in his condition? "I do seem to recall hearing that before." She bit her lowered lip as she debated. "I suppose —"

Another bout of shivering overcame him. Without any more hesitation, Krystal immediately scrambled beneath the cover and wrapped her arms tightly around his chest, being careful to avoid his sensitive wound. "Is this better?"

Drake sighed, suddenly wondering if the knife wound had affected his brain, too. How could he have thought this would help? The long curls of her silken hair fanned out across his chest, her breasts were crushed up against his bare side and her legs were molded next to his own limbs as though they were ajoined. An unexpected shiver rattled through his body as he broke out in a sea of sweat. He didn't answer her question because he was afraid to move even enough to open his mouth. This was worse than the night they had spent in the old farmhouse.

131

"Drake?" she demanded in a panicked tone. "Can you hear me?"

"Yep," he replied through clenched teeth. This was definitely Hades, he wondered what he had done to deserve such a severe punishment. If his shoulder wasn't causing him so much distress, he would have ravished her this very second, protests or not. But the pain in his left side made it almost impossible for him to do much more than lie there, let alone execute the carefully devised plan he had in mind for Krystal Colbert. He wanted to teach her the meaning of ecstasy and prove to her the depth of his expanding love. However, he would have to wait until his battered body would be more cooperative. "Damn!" he repeated.

Krystal frowned, but she did not say anything. She decided that his fowl temperament was only caused from his pain and the chills he was experiencing. She snuggled up closer, determined that she was going to do everything humanly possible to help him recuperate. After all, he had come to her rescue on the train and had also saved her from that horrible man, Joe. Putting up with his bad mood was the least she could do in the wake of all his suffering.

Drake tried without much success to concentrate on something other than the idea of seducing this lovely vixen. He coughed and cleared his throat. "I'm real impressed with the way you bandaged up my wound. Thank you." Actually he was amazed at the way she had taken care of him and fended for herself out here in the middle of nowhere. He guessed that she had never been out of the city before, and the manner in which she faced adversity made his devotion towards her even stronger.

Krystal shrugged. "It was nothing at all." A chuckle

emitted from Drake, and Krystal found herself laughing along with him. They were both remembering that breathtaking kiss from the other day and the casual remark he had made afterward. Although on that occasion, neither of them had found his declaration very humorous.

Drake flashed her a roguish grin. "Considering what you and I call nothing at all, I can't wait for something important to happen."

Krystal raised herself up on one elbow and leveled a warning glare in his direction. Unaffected by her pouting expression, he only continued to smile at her with a glint in his eye. He was doing it to her again — hypnotizing her with the touch of his eyes, and she could not look away as she found herself studying every detail of his face. Three days of whisker growth gave his features a rugged appearance which only served to make him devastatingly handsome. Even the paleness of his skin did not detract from his good looks. Except for the dark smudges from his illness which were evident beneath his olive green eyes, Krystal thought he was the most perfect specimen of man that she had ever gazed upon.

His smile softened as he looked back at her, and the devilish twinkle in his eyes spread until both his pupils were misted with a lumious glow of tenderness. Krystal's gaze was drawn to his parted lips and she did not stop to think about her actions a second time as she felt an irresistible magnetic force draw her downward again. The heat of his mouth captured her lips before they had even touched him. Her sensibility was once again lost with the consuming contact of their kiss. The longing she had for this man was no less than a volcanic eruption and the passion that flowed within both of their fiery bodies was more searing

133

than sprewing lava.

All at once, Drake became aware of the excruciating pain in his shoulder from the weight of her body crushing against his. Damn! He had been waiting for this woman—and this moment—for all of his life. It just wasn't fair! He summoned every ounce of his strength in an effort to ignore the pain, but her action had been so sudden, so unexpected that he unconsciously flinched and gasped.

Krystal sprang to her feet, her eyes wide with mortification. She had been worried about him making advances towards her? Good Lord! She had just thrown herself at him and he was not even off of death's doorstep yet. She threw her hands over her face, though there was no way to escape the shame that was raging throughout her whole being. How could she ever justify this type of dissolute behavior?

"Drake, I—" She turned away, words eluded her in this moment of self-abashment.

Despite the acute throbbing in his shoulder, Drake pushed himself up on his other elbow. His spinning head prevented him from sitting all the way up. He wanted to tell her that he could survive any amount of pain if she would only come back down here on the ground with him and resume her delicious assault on his lips. But he was still too dizzy and too weak to support his own weight. His arm buckled and slipped out from under him. A defeated groan escaped from him when his pain-racked body thudded against the hard ground.

"Drake!" Krystal screamed as she rushed back to his side. His eyes were closed tightly when she reached him and his body was unmoving. She fell on her knees and shook him with a trembling hand. "Drake?" Silence was her only reply. If he had a relapse it would be all her fault. "Please be all right? I couldn't bear it if something happened to you." His lids remained closed. She placed her hand on his bare chest. Oh Lord, he wasn't breathing!

She slumped down and dropped her head into her hands as a sob of dispair racked through her body. She had killed him with her promiscuous actions. How could she ever live with this terrible guilt? She had never had the chance to tell him of the feelings she had been experiencing since she had met him. Feelings of . . . love? Yes, it was just possible that she was falling in love with him, she realized with increasing sadness. If he died, she would never be able to tell him how she felt about him. Oh, surely life would not be so cruel?

Her eyelids closed over the rush of tears that streamed down her cheeks as she spoke to his silent form. "Please don't die? Don't you know how I feel about you?" Another loud sniffle emitted from her as she lifted her head from the cover of her hands. With dread seeping into every pore of her sorrowful body, she forced her tear-filled eyes to open with slow anticipation. The first sight that greeted her was the most infuriating smirk she had ever seen.

"How do you feel about me, darlin'?" he asked as a crooked grin toyed with the left side of his mouth and caused his left eye to narrow with a suggestive wink.

For a short time, Krystal was too shocked to move. She had thought he was dead. Why . . . he had tricked her! The shock she felt rapidly made way for fury. "The nerve of—Oh, how dare you?" she spit out at him as she rose to the full height of her petite 5-foot frame. Her hands angrily pressed down upon the soft curve of her hips as she tossed her golden-red mane over her shoulder with immense indignation. Flecks of gold shot through the cocoa color of her eyes as they looked down her nose with an expression of disdain that Drake was sure could never be equalled. Damn! he thought again. It was unnatural for a woman to be so beautifully livid!

"I thought you were dead," her voice scathed in a biting tone which more than hinted that she wished he really was. "But, I should have known what a low-down good-for-nothing skunk you really are!" Her voice crescendoed to a tone barely less than a scream. "I'll have you know, Drake DeGanahl, that I have never allowed myself to act with such foolish conduct until I met you, and I am never going to allow it to happen again." She emphasized her last statement with an enraged stomp of her tiny black boot against the hard dry ground. Another defiant flip of her head accompanied one more icy look of abasement in his direction as she swung around and strutted out into the clearing on the other side of the cedars.

Drake was left speechless. Not only was she the most stubborn woman he had ever encountered, not to mention the most beautiful, but she definitely had the worst temper he had ever witnessed. Obviously she did not see the humor in his harmless joke. He stared at the tree she was hiding behind, wondering just what she did feel for him and why she had become so angry? Surely she really hadn't thought that she had killed him when she had kissed him? In spite of the pain it caused in his left side, Drake laughed. The look of pure hostility that peered back at him from around the twisted tree trunk, however, quickly silenced his mirth. He began to feel very guilty. She had really seemed sad when she believed him to be dead. Drake leaned back against the bedroll which served as his pillow and began to ponder over her strange reaction.

The sweltering afternoon sun forced Krystal to seek the refuge in the shade beneath the cedars, but not until she had scooped up her long cape and wrapped it tightly around her half-clad form. Her skirt was no longer tucked up into her waistband in the provocative manner as before, and she had assumed the appearance of a staunch schoolteacher once again. She purposely avoided looking in Drake's direction even though she could feel the touch of his gaze. She would never forgive him, she had decided while she had baked to a crisp under the scorching sun. Making her believe she had killed him with her impulsive kiss was a joke of the cruelest nature and she would not grant him the satisfaction of her forgiveness.

"Those horses should be unsaddled and watered, darlin'," he finally said, although his voice sounded cautious.

She jumped back up to her feet and glared at him. "Just tell me what to do, and don't call me darlin'! Miss Colbert would be more appropriate."

He exhaled sharply. "Well, excuse me, Miss Colbert? But would you mind stepping down from your pedestal long enough to take care of the horses before they drop dead from heat stroke?"

Fury colored her cheeks a vivid tone of red. She opened her mouth to match his insult with one of her own, but decided that he was not worth the extra energy. If he had not mentioned the fact that the horses might die from the heat if they were not cared for properly, she would have jumped into one of the saddles and left Drake DeGanahl to fend for himself. However, common sense took hold and she stomped over to the two animals and waited for his instructions.

Drake was amazed at her ability to take on any challenge which was tossed in her path. Her terror of horses had been evident ever since the first day Devon had tossed her on the back of his horse. And although she was continually forced to confront her fears, she did so with a bravado that Drake admired more all the time.

When the horses were unsaddled and she had allowed them to drink water from her cupped hands, Krystal returned to her spot under the cedars to regain her composure. If she had not been so determined to show Drake that she could do anything that needed to be done, she would have fainted from fear at having to let the tongues of those beasts touch her hands. She still refused to speak to him as she fixed him a light supper of bean soup which she had prepared while he dozed. She sank into the mattress of soft grass and wrapped her blanket around her shoulders to ward of the chill of the night. Was he awake? she wondered just before the sound of his imploring voice reached her questioning ears.

"Darlin'?" There was no answer. "Are you cold, too?"

He really did not expect a reply. He closed his weary eyes, although he did not sleep on this cool Wyoming night. The fact that they had already dallied too long in this spot made him extremely nervous. It surprised him that Devon and Creed had not caught up to them by now. Devon would be after them for all the apparent reasons: Krystal Colbert, the ransom money she might bring, and the fact that Devon believed she was Drake's woman. But Drake had given Creed Ward a whole new set of reasons to pursue them with vengeance. He had stolen Creed's clothes, his holster, and most importantly, his gun.

And if that was not enough, he had then left the man tied and gagged in a manure-filled stall back at the Hole-in-the-Wall. All of those things combined was bound to make Creed Ward mighty anxious to seek revenge.

Drake's gaze wandered over to softly caress the gentle curves of Krystal's sleeping form. They could not remain here another day, regardless of his shoulder. Tomorrow they would head for Green River. She would be safe at his mother's house since Devon would not chance showing his face in a town where he was so well known. Drake's past rivalry with his brother seemed trival when compared with the challenge of their contest for Krystal Colbert. A determined surge of adrenalin made his body tense with a new resolution. He realized that he would do anything for Krystal, especially now that he was certain she felt as strongly for him as he did about her. . . . He would even face that final showdown with his brother.

Chapter Ten

Krystal stretched and pushed back a stray hair from the side of her face before she opened her groggy eyes. The first thing she noticed was that Drake was no longer on his make-shift bed. Panic flooded through her when she bolted up to a sitting position. Her fearful gaze searched the area and spotted him standing outside the confines of the cedar trees. He was slowly lifting a saddle up onto one of the horses. From the pinched look on his face Krystal could tell that he was not ready for this type of exertion. She rose to her feet and rubbed her eyes. She had vowed never to speak to him again, but she knew she had to stop him before he ripped open his wound again.

"Drake?" she said in a voice laced with sweetness as she approached him. He didn't answer as he struggled to tighten the cinch with his good hand. She cleared her throat loudly and received a dark glare as recognition. "Do you think you should be doing that so soon?" she continued, ignoring his unsociable disposition.

He stopped and turned to look down at her. Beads of sweat covered his forehead. "It's time to move on. We've been here too long already."

Krystal glanced around with nervous apprehension. She knew he was right. It was a miracle that Devon and the other men hadn't found them by now. "But do you think you're up to riding?" He gave his head a nod and continued to struggle with the saddle. With a sigh Krystal pushed him aside, "Well, if you're determined to leave, then at least let me do that."

Drake's eyebrows curved into a curious arch as he stepped back and allowed her to take over. A few days ago, she had refused to mount one of these beasts, as she referred to them, now here she was thinking she had enough experience with horses that she could saddle one all by herself. A wry smile crossed his lips when he noted the perplexed expression on her face while she wondered what she was supposed to do now that she had control of the situation. He couldn't help but observe the sensuous way she looked when she first woke up in the morning; Her eyes still looked soft and dreamy and the curls of her long hair were tousled and wild. Restraint was taking its toll on him. His smile disappeared when she swung around and gave him an aggravated glare.

"Well, aren't you going to tell me how to do it?" she stated in an equally irritated voice. Holding back the urge to chuckle, Drake patiently guided her through the steps of saddling the horses. Once again, she proved herself to be quite apt in learning to handle the necessary requirements of this rugged frontier. Drake however, did not want her to become too bigheaded from her achievements, so he just gave his head a slight nod of a approval when she was finished.

"We'd better eat something before we leave because we're not to make any more stops than we absolutely have to today." Drake's mood became even more solemn and Krystal was reminded once again how fortunate they had been thus far to escape recapture from the band of outlaws. She did not refuse his offer of hardtack and coffee before they were on their way since she sensed that they would not be stopping for any cooked meals throughout the day.

Krystal noticed that Drake kept constant watch over his shoulder. His actions made her so apprehensive that she found herself continuously looking over the countryside in search of riders also. They kept a steady pace during the remainder of the day, and by the time they stopped to make camp for the night, they were both exhausted. A secluded overhanging cliff provided a good shelter and Krystal insisted that Drake rest while she struggled to unsaddle the horses. Drake was too weak from the long ride to protest, but it seemed to him that it took her an eternity to get the saddles off of the animals. He was about to finish the job himself when she finally managed to accomplish the task. She scooted under the hanging rock ledge with a proud twinkle in her eyes and the moment they spread out the bedrolls, and ate a meager supper of the leftover hardtack which they had also eaten for breakfast, they were both ready to give into their weariness.

When Krystal woke up the next morning the horses were already saddled, coffee was brewing on the fire, and Drake was watching her intently. She rose to a sitting position and blinked to clear her fuzzy eyesight. Unconsciously she began to rake her fingers through her tangled hair. His close scrutiny of her in this disheveled state caused her to blush a dark shade of red while she quickly readjusted her cape over her thin chamisole. The cape was proving itself to be the biggest nuisance she had ever had to contend with, but in her haste to dispose of the hot garment the other day, she had ripped the bodice of her dress beyond repair. The cape was the only other choice she

142

had besides leaving her bosom exposed for Drake to stare at whenever he pleased. A nervous smile touched her lips. "I see you're ready to go. You should've woke me up so I could help."

He shrugged his slumped shoulders and Krystal noticed how tired he looked. The lower portion of his face had sprouted a dense brown covering of short coarse hair, but his complexion still had an ashen pallor and the dark circles below his eyes made it obvious that he was far from a complete recovery. He poured a cup of the hot black brew and held it out to Krystal. "I figured you could use some extra sleep."

She accepted the cup and sighed, feeling a bit rejected. She thought she had been doing a excellent job of caring for the horses, and of him. She surprised herself at the way she had lost most of her fear for the beasts. But then, out here she really had no choice. It was either ride a horse or walk. She smiled to herself, thinking how happy her mother would be to know that she had finally conquered her phobia of horses. Rebecca had tried to persuade her to take riding lessons constantly throughout Krystal's youth, but being the stubborn girl that she was, Krystal refused adamently. The memory of her mother brought an expression of sadness to her face and she instinctively reached beneath her cape to make sure the little black purse was still secure.

Drake noticed her melancholy mood and the fact that she never parted with the little bag. He wanted to ask her about the contents of the purse, but he wasn't sure if she was ready to confide in him yet. He was just grateful that she was being civil to him once again. She did, however, manage to keep a safe distance at all times, which was probably best for both of them. He was trying to be a patient man, but Krystal Colbert was definitely trying his patience.

When they reached Green River, and he had a chance to rest a day or two, they would pick up where they had left off with their last kiss. This thought made him anxious to reach Green River.

The heat was relentless throughout the day, making it necessary to stop frequently. As a result they did not reach Green River, Wyoming until the scorching sun had already disappeared and a quarter moon hung crookedly in the dark sky. Krystal was beginning to worry about Drake's rapidly disintegrating condition by the time they entered the outskirts of the town. Although he had not said a word, it was obvious he was in a great deal of pain and the left-hand corner of his shirt was soaked through again with fresh blood. As their horses plodded down the darkened street, Krystal begged him to head straight for a doctor, or at least to stay put so that she could go find one. But, he was headed towards a definite destination and he did not plan to stop until they reached it.

They had almost passed through the whole town when Drake turned up a narrow street which headed towards a ridge of towering rock formations. Their jagged shape was barely outlined in the dark sky and it was at the base of these eroded cliffs that he stopped his horse and turned to look at Krystal with an expression of relief upon his pained face. She felt a calming feeling of relief flood through her, too. They were in front of a two story house which sat in the bottom of the incline. Now, maybe, they would get some proper medical treatment for his shoulder. Krystal slid down from her horse and allowed him to take the reins from her, but as soon as she had tied the horses to the hitching post in front of the house, she wrapped her arm around his waist. Drake was surprised by her unexpected gesture, but suddenly he felt too exhausted to walk to the house without her support.

"I take it you do know the people who live in this house?" she questioned as he knocked on the door. Before he had a chance to answer, the door swung open and a pretty dark-haired woman of about the same height as Krystal stood inside with a quizzical expression on her face.

"Mother? Has it been so long that you forgot what your oldest son looks like?"

"Oh, Drake!" she exclaimed as her hands flew to the sides of her face. A rash of Spanish sounding words followed while her dark eyes darted back and forth from her son and the young woman who was attached to his side. She was thinking that both of them looked like they had just been through a rough ordeal when Angelina saw the dark red spot of blood upon Drake's light-colored shirt. "Oh, my God, Drake! You're hurt." Her gaze flitted back to Krystal with a question contained within her fearful look.

"He's been stabbed," Krystal volunteered before Angelina had a chance to ask. "He needs a doctor."

"I just need to rest," Drake replied stubbornly as he continued to lean heavily on Krystal for support. He glanced back at his mother. "Just let me lie down for awhile. That's all I need."

Krystal's worried gaze met the older woman's equally concerned look. Angelina gave a knowing nod, and wrapped her arm around Drake's other side as she quickly led them into the palor. The two woman did not speak as they helped him down onto the sofa. He fell back against the soft pillows, close to unconsciousness once again. Krystal looked back at the other woman. Her panic was showing clearly upon her face. "I'll go for a doctor. Please tell me where I would find one at this time of night?"

For the first time since she had opened the door

and found her son and this young lady on the front stoop, Angelina took time to observe the girl. She did not look like the type of woman that Angelina had become accustomed to seeing in Drake's company before he had left Green River. Unless her eldest son had changed drastically in the past two years, Angelina could only assume that this woman was some harlot whom Drake had hooked up with on his way back from New Orleans. But one thing was apparent, the look of concern on her face was genuine, and Angelina sensed that whoever this young woman was, she cared a great deal for Drake.

Angelina looked back down at Drake, then a strange look came into her dark brown eyes. "How did this happen?" she asked in an even odder tone of voice.

Krystal stared at her, confused by the woman's lack of concern over seeking a doctor for her son. "I think he needs a doctor first —"

Hoping not to sound too rude, Angelina interrupted her. "Did Devon do this?"

All the bitter conflicts that Drake had ranted about when he had been consumed with the fever a few days earlier began to flash through Krystal's mind. Good Lord, this woman thought her sons were capable of killing one another, and with an eery feeling of foreboding, Krystal realized she might be right. Krystal began to shake her head, thankful that she was able to tell the woman differently. "No, it wasn't Devon. He had nothing to do with it."

"You know Devon?" Angelina asked hesitantly.

Krystal grew more puzzled with the woman's unusual behavior. "Yes. I — well, it's a long story and I really think Drake needs a doctor first."

"Was Devon involved in any of this?" Angelina questioned again in a more definite tone of voice.

"He didn't stab Drake, Mrs. DeGanahl," Krystal said with an impatient shrug. "But yes, indirectly Devon was involved with everything that happened to us."

"You should go out and take the horses around to the back of the house," Angelina said rapidly as a worried frown furrowed deeper into her expression. "And hurry—before someone sees them."

Angelina watched Krystal's look become even more confused and fearful as she realized how horrible she must sound to her. How could she make this girl understand that as Drake's mother, she would do anything to ensure his recovery? But as the mother of Devon, she had learned to be extra cautious with anything which had to do with her youngest boy. Without speaking to Krystal again, Angelina leaned over and carefully began to pull Drake's shirt away from the wound. She heard Krystal's reluctant steps leave the room and she knew that the young woman had decided not to dispute her for the time being. She returned her concentration to her son, and with relief, she noticed that his injury did not appear to be badly infected, only very deep. If his shoulder was properly cleaned and wrapped, she was certain he would be all right.

As she straightened back up, she heard Krystal reenter the house. The two women's eyes met as Krystal walked slowly back into the parlor. Angelina was certain this young woman was probably going to think that she was the most terrible mother, but Angelina had two sons and she had spent her whole life trying to protect them both equally.

"I'll clean that wound and put a fresh bandage on it." Angelina said in a low voice. The look of panic that suddenly masked Krystal's tired face tore at Angelina's heart. She was sure now that this woman was not some saloon girl Drake had picked up along his way. She reached out and touched Krystal's arm lightly, "Trust me. I wouldn't take a chance with his life. But, I don't think it would be wise for anyone to know that the two of you are here, at least not yet." She gave Krystal a weak smile and asked, "Did you hide the horses?"

Too tired and much too worried about Drake to argue with his mother about her unreasonable attitude, Krystal gave her head a defeated nod. Angelina let out a relieved sigh and squeezed her arm in an affectionate gesture before she rushed off to get the supplies she needed for Drake's shoulder. Krystal slumped down next to his limp form on the sofa. She stared at his haggard, bearded face. Was it possible to be in love with someone she had only known for a few days? She reached out her hand and picked up one of his large hands. The feelings she had for this man were so overpowering they left her weak. She was hopelessly in love with a man she knew absolutely nothing about, except that it was very probable he was an outlaw just like his brother. Why else would his own mother be so hesitant to call for a doctor?

"Please forgive my bad manners," Angelina said as she rushed back into the room. "My name is Angelina and yours?"

Krystal rose from the sofa and smiled weakly at the other woman. "I am Krystal Colbert," she answered with a straightening of her spine and a tilt of her head.

Angelina continued to watch her with an expectant look upon her face, but Krystal did not offer anymore information. She only stared back at the older woman with her wide eyes and a very uneasy-looking expression on her dirty face. Even though the girl was coated with dust, Angelina couldn't help but notice that the young woman's black cape and the skirt of the black dress which flared out from the long cloak were of an elegant style, and her manner of speech hinted that she was from a well-bred family. But Angelina gave up the hopes of finding out more about the girl as she sat a wash basin of steaming water down on a nearby table and went to work on Drake's wound. He woke up the minute the boiling water touched his sensitive shoulder. A low growl was the only noise he made, but he glared at his mother until she was finished.

"Did you meet Krystal?" he asked weakly as his mother began to gather up the dirty bandages along with his ruined shirt.

"Yes, we met. But we haven't had much time to visit yet." She gave Krystal a friendly grin and the eyes of the two women met for a second. Angelina's twinkling gaze returned to her son while she continued to speak with a lyrical Spanish accent. "We've been too busy tending to you."

All at once Krystal began to feel welcome. At first she was not sure if Angelina DeGanahl wanted anything to do with her. But now, Angelina's dark eyes held a warm look of acceptance. A slight smile rested on Krystal's lips while she watched the woman and thought of her own mother and then started to miss her all over again.

Drake noticed the exchange between the two women and began to feel better. He knew what a kind and gentle person his mother was, but they had arrived here tonight under very strange circumstances and he was worried that she would get the wrong impression about Krystal. Especially since he had never paid any attention to the type of women that his mother would want in her home. But even with her hair hanging down her back in a mass of tangles and her smooth skin all smudged with dust from the trail, Krystal Colbert's dignity showed through and Drake knew his mother had not missed it.

Angelina motioned towards Krystal. "It'll probably take both of us, but I'll bet between the two of us, we could get you up to your old room." Krystal nodded in agreement as she moved to the sofa to help Angelina.

"I would be the last person to dispute either of you," Drake mused while he permitted the women to help him to his feet. He felt lightheaded for just a second, but soon felt steady enough to walk up the stairs with their support. "Krystal is a lot like you, mother."

"How so?" Angelina asked with an obvious tone of amusement in her voice.

He glanced at Krystal and noted the look of warning in her jewel-toned eyes. "She may be small," he continued inspite of the tightening grip of her arm around his wrast. "But what she's lacking in size, she makes up for in stubbornness."

Krystal's glowering look intensified, but Angelina merely smiled with a sudden awareness of Drake's strong feelings for this young woman. Perhaps New Orleans had been good for him after all, Angelina thought as they steered her eldest son into the bedroom he had occupied for most of his life. Tomorrow, when he was feeling better, she planned to find out all about Drake's injury, his relationship with Krystal Colbert, and most of all, Devon's involvement in this situation.

Angelina gathered up a dressing gown and robe, along with a fresh dress and shawl from her own closet for Krystal to wear when she woke up in the morning. She had planned to question Krystal as soon as had she showed her to Devon's old room. She thought better of it, though, when she lit the lamp and saw how tired the young woman looked. Krystal thanked her for the use of her clothes and her generous hospitality, then glanced longingly at the bed. Angelina did not miss her expression and the exhausted sigh which followed. Tomorrow would be soon enough to ask questions, Angelina told herself sternly as she said good night.

Drake's mother had barely left the room before Krystal collapsed upon Devon's bed, deciding at once that this was the most wonderful bed in the world. It had been nearly two weeks since she had left Boston and equally as long since she had slept in a real bed. As she stretched her sore body out upon the soft mattress, she began to think over all the events of the last couple weeks. So much had happened in such a short time span it made her head spin. Her life was even more complicated than it had originally started out to be two weeks ago, because not only did she still have to find her long-lost father, but she also had to deal with her feelings for Drake DeGanahl. She yawned, tomorrow she would worry about all those things, tonight she just wanted to crawl beneath that welcoming quilt which covered this fabulous bed.

Krystal had never slept so late in her entire life and she felt embarrassed when she did finally descend the stairs which led to the lower floor. The whole day was already gone and evening was about to close in around them as she moved through the quiet house and encountered Drake sitting in the parlor.

"Hello, darlin'," he said as his eyes raked over her with distinct approval. His mother's dress fit her perfectly and she looked far better in blue than she did in the black attire that he had become accustomed to seeing on her.

She glanced at the floor. Since he did little to hide

the way his thoughts were leaning as he looked at her, she was growing more self-conscious by the minute. She looked around the room with apprehension, but noticed that Angelina was nowhere in sight. "I'm sorry I slept so late. I must have been extremely tired."

He reached over to the table which stood in front of the sofa and crushed out the cigar he had been smoking. A crooked grin slanted across his mouth as he patted the sofa next to him. "I just got up myself. I think we both needed the rest."

She moved across the room with slow steps and sat down on the edge of the sofa, careful not to get too close to him. Lord, he looked so good to her. He was wearing nothing but a pair of denim jeans and his boots. His mother had bandaged his arm to his side so that he would not be able to move it around. Apparently, he had just taken a bath because his hair was still damp and it hung in loose curls behind his ears and across his forehead. The stubbly beard which had covered his face was gone, and his skin tone was once again a golden tan. Krystal swallowed hard. She did not trust herself around this man.

He gestured towards the sling on his arm. "I don't think this is necessary. I feel much better today."

"Well," she said in a squeaky voice. "I-I suppose your mother knows best." Oh, he smelled so fresh and masculine . . . like soap and tobacco. She slid closer to the edge of the sofa. "So? Where is your mother?"

Drake forced back his urge to chuckle at her performance. She was as skittish as an unbroken colt. Maybe she was wondering about his mother's whereabouts because she was thinking along the same lines as he was right now? "She left us a note saying that she would be back later this evening. She had a previous commitment that she could not get out of without arousing suspicion."

"I see!" Krystal exclaimed as she jumped up and crossed the room in a couple of long strides. She pretended to look out the window while she pulled the delicate lace drapes back and stared through the glass. Her eyesight was a blur and her heart was somewhere in her throat. They were alone in this house and he was half-naked. Good Lord! She blinked and tried to force the breath back into her lungs. When she turned back around, he was standing only a few inches away from her. She inhaled and was lost in his engulfing scent.

His arm reached out and his large hand cupped her chin. She closed her eyes and began to pray that she would be strong-willed enough to fight against his touch. But she realized that it was doubtful since her legs were already shaking and her whole body had acquired an unsatiable ache that she could never hope to control when he was this close. If she allowed him to kiss her again, there would be no turning back. Her eyes flew open as she pulled away from him. The first thing she saw was a massive oak cabinet with a large array of firearms resting inside of its heavy walls.

"Oh, would you just look at all those guns!" she shouted with faked exuberancy. She side-stepped him, ignoring the look of disbelief upon his face. Could he hear the thudding of her heart? When she reached the cabinet, she chanced a quick look in his direction. He had not moved, he was still in a state of shock.

"I was wondering," she began as her mind groped for something — anything — that would divert his attention, and hers, away from the consuming desires of a moment ago. "Would you teach me how to shoot a gun?"

He remained unmoving. This woman was incredible. He knew that the last thing she wanted to do was to learn how to shoot a gun, but it seemed that she would do anything to escape her feelings for him. He stomped over to his father's guncase, reached his good arm up to the top of the cabinet and located the key which was always hidden there. If she wanted to learn to shoot so badly, then damnit! he would show her how.

He grumbled something inaudibly as he motioned for her to follow him through the kitchen and to the secluded area at the back of the house. Krystal had to practically run to keep up with his long strides and she was half-afraid that in his furious state he might turn the gun on her. Once they were outside, she forgot about her fears as she stopped to gaze up in awe at the beauty of the rock cliffs that stood behind the house.

"It's really beautiful here," she said to Drake even though he was making a point of pretending that she didn't exist while he checked the cylinder of his father's old .45 sixshooter.

His glowering look turned in her direction as he thrust the gun into her hand. "It's loaded, but I'm only going to show you the proper way to hold onto it because the shots would attract attention and no one knows that we're here, remember?"

She hadn't thought of that. "Oh — well, it's not really necessary that I —" her words were halted by the feel of his body pressing up against her back as he moved behind her and grabbed hold of the hand where she held the gun. Good Lord, was there nothing that could keep them a safe distance away from one another?

She was void of any muscle control in her body as he lifted her arm and held her hand tightly in his own. She was not aware of the gun in her hand, or of the glorious sunset that was beginning to peak above the gigantic rock cliff referred to as Castle Rock. He said something to her about how she should hold the gun but his words sounded far away. She was trembling too hard to concentrate on anything other than his nearness. Did he notice?

She turned her head slowly and looked up at him. His grip on her hand increased as their eyes met. Could he read submission within her gaze? And did he feel the hand of destiny laying upon theirs as she did at this tender moment? The stillness of the impending nightfall seemed to speak to them with wispy words of promise and Krystal was helpless to disagree. Her love and her devouring cravings for this man made her powerless to hold back the inevitable any longer . . .

"Oh, here's where you two are hiding," Angelina said with a wide smile on her lips. She was dressed with the dignity of her heritage in a dark gold dress. Black embroidery adorned the sleeves and neckline, and a black lace mantilla was draped softly over her dark hair.

Neither Drake nor Krystal replied. They had been so close to approaching the point that their first glance at one another had predestined. And now, it was nearly impossible to return their hungering souls back to normal. Drake stepped away from Krystal and cleared his throat. He wished it was so easy to clear his senses. When he began to speak to his mother, his voice was tense and brisk. Krystal was too dumbfounded to join into the conversation. She had been prepared to give into the passion that Drake De-Ganahl never failed to conjure up in her wanton being, but Angelina's arrival had only served to delay that which could not be avoided. Krystal was not sure if the gripping sensation in her chest was relief or crushing disappointment. She knew that meeting this man, being in his presence, and permitting herself to fall in love with him, had detoured her thoughts away from finding her father, taken her astray of her teaching goals and wiped away all her strict moral codes. To leave him would be more devastating than anything she had ever known, but it was the only sensible thing she could do, she realized with a sadness that brought stinging tears to her eyes and caused her whole body to hurt with the impending loss.

Chapter Eleven

She was doing the right thing, she told herself one more time as the conductor called out the last 'all aboard' before the train pulled out from the Green River station. There would be only one layover in Ogden, Utah—a switch from the Union Pacific Railroad to the Southern Pacific—and by tomorrow night she would be in Virginia City. She was finally on the last leg of the journey in the search for her father. Krystal tried to convince herself that it would be easy to put Drake DeGanahl out of her mind, but sneaking out of the house this morning before anyone was awake was one of the most difficult things she had ever done. It was lucky that the train was about to depart shortly after she had located the station because she had almost went back to him even after she had bought herself a ticket to Virginia City. How could she leave a man whose crooked smile laced her heart with eternal devotion and whose kisses lit the darkest crevices of her soul on fire?

She forced herself to concentrate on finding John

Colbert. The locomotive began to jerk forward with a loud hiss from a steam whistle as it started to roll away from the Wyoming town—and Drake De-Ganahl. Krystal leaned back and closed her eyes, chasing away the vision of his handsome, teasing face that her wandering mind had already conjured up. Instead, she tried to imagine how a man like John Colbert would look. The faded photo offered no assistance because of its aged appearance and also because Krystal knew that in twenty years the man in that picture would no longer look the same. She was sure John Colbert would be a very distinguished man since he was so wealthy, but beyond that she was too nervous at the idea of meeting him to think of anything else. Giving up the idea of creating a mental picture of her father, she opened her eyes and felt her body go numb.

The first thought that ran through Krystal's mind was that Drake had come after her. The rise of her thundering heart nearly caused her to stop breathing while she slowly ascended her gaze past the dusty boots and faded denims and low-riding gunbelt. But before her hope-filled eyes reached the face of this tall man, she knew it was not Drake who sat in the seat opposite her. The pounding in her chest increased, though it was no longer with anticipation. Now fear released a torrent of paralyzing adrenalin through her veins. A pair of ebony eyes met her gaze . . . eyes which held a shimmering look of victory from within their dark depths.

"Ain't it uncanny the way we keep running into one another on the Union Pacific Railroad, Miss Colbert?" Devon asked with a wide grin. His smile broadened while he watched her face pale with the realization that she was on her own this time. Devon had kept close watch on his mother's home all through the night and when he had observed Krystal Colbert leaving the house early this morning, his suspicions were confirmed. Drake and Krystal were staying with his mother, but he couldn't believe his luck when it was only Krystal who boarded the train. Apparently, Drake's appeal to the gentler sex did not have much effect on the strong-willed Miss Colbert. Why else would she sneak off before anyone else was awake and leave town—alone?

Krystal glanced around with the frantic expectation of seeing Creed and Sidewinder, or even worse—Joe Preece. Devon leaned forward and replied casually, "No one else is here but me, sugar." He reclined back in the seat and crossed his arms over his chest. "You should feel real privileged to be sitting here with me. I took a real risk by boarding this train in the same town that I grew up in. I'm a real famous man in these parts. But I figured a sweet thing like you was worth the chance I'd be taking, you and your daddy's gold mine, that is." He pulled the brim of his black hat down lower on his forehead and added, "Oh, and by the way, don't get any ideas about announcing to anyone that I'm on this train. Bad as I may want to get you to Virginia City in one piece, I wouldn't think twice about using you as a shield against any bullets that might happen to fly my way."

"Is . . . J-Joe here, too?" Krystal managed to choke out in her terror. The idea of Devon DeGanahl taking her hostage again, even in the mist of his vile threats, did not worry her as much as being back at the mercy of a man like Joe Preece.

Devon shrugged. "Old Joe's dead and buried. Big brother's aim is as good as it ever was. Joe never knew what hit him. The bullet ripped a hole clean through his hear—"

"Please," Krystal interrupted as she threw her hands

159

over her ears. She did not want to hear a detailed description of the man's decease. It was enough to know that Joe Preece was dead. But she still had to deal with Devon, and that was all she wanted to think of for now. "Drake is somewhere on the train." She lied in the hopes that Devon had not seen her board the train without him.

He gave her a knowing smirk. "I'm not as dumb as I look, sugar. I saw you leave my mother's house alone this morning. Poor Drake. I'd be willing to bet, you're the first woman who's ever rejected my big brother."

Pulling herself up indignantly, Krystal retorted. "I did not reject Drake. Why, I hardly know the man. That day on the train was the first time—" The smile that covered Devon's face suddenly made her realize that she had made another blunder. "Well, I mean—"

"Never mind, sugar. There's no need to explain. I had a funny feeling about your relationship with him." Devon shook his head and chuckled. "That's Drake, always gallant and trying to be a hero for the ladies." His smile faded and was replaced by a distant look of hatred which made a feeling of doom overcome Krystal. She was almost glad that Drake was safe at his mother's home, and as she gave in to the idea of being alone with Devon, she began to wonder what had happened between the two DeGanahl brothers to cause such great animosity between them.

Throughout the long day, Krystal alternated between fitful dozing and staring at nothing through the heavy brown film of dust on the window. But no matter what she did, she felt the constant glare of Devon's piercing brown eyes on her. Several times she was tempted to scream for help, but for some reason, being in the company of Drake's brother did not make her feel any real fear. She found herself glancing at

160

him from beneath the long fringe of her lashes. Except for the color of his eyes, the features of his face were just like his brother's. How could he be so different? In an attempt to understand the bitter relationship between the two men, she decided to ask a few questions to satisfy her own curiosities.

"Why do you hate Drake so much?" Krystal hadn't expected an answer, so Devon's sudden avalanche of honesty shocked her.

"I despise everything that he stands for," he retorted with a shrug of his broad shoulders. "And I resent him even more." Devon grinned slightly as his face became distant once again, but he surprised Krystal when he continued to talk about his past life with his brother. "The only bad part about this whole thing is that Drake probably doesn't even remember what it was that made me hate him so much. To me, it was something that ruined my whole life. But to Drake, it was just one more notch on his headboard."

Krystal was more perplexed than ever. "Headboard?" she repeated in a puzzled tone.

Devon leaned forward in his seat and gave her a smile that reminded her of his close resemblance with Drake once again. "Just one more conquest in bed." Krystal's face flushed scarlet when she grasped his meaning. Devon reclined back in the seat. "Don't look so surprised, sugar. That's just the way Drake is — love 'em and leave 'em. You were real smart to leave before you became just one more notch in his headboard, too." Devon noticed the way his words caused her to bristle with anger, so he decided to add a little more aggravation to her fury. "But then, I'm forgetting that the two of you just spent a few days alone on the trail. I reckon a new notch has already been carved in your honor."

Krystal's face grew livid. "Oh, how dare you! Drake

never laid a hand on me. First of all," she said in a scathing tone. "He was near death, thanks to that horrible man, Joe. And secondly, Drake is a gentleman, in spite of what you think!"

Devon whistled under his breath. "He sure has you fooled. But let me tell you a story that just might help you to see Drake for what he really is. It's a story about two brothers—one who is no less than perfect . . . the perfect son, the perfect scholar, and," a wry grin covered Devon's handsome features, "the perfect lover." His crude words caused Krystal to blush and he couldn't help but note the golden bolts of anger in her big eyes.

"However," he continued, "the other brother had none of these wonderful qualities. He was the kind of son that constantly embarrassed his parents with his wild antics, refused to go to school and never had a woman that his brother didn't have first."

"I don't believe you," Krystal retaliated. "And furthermore, I don't care to hear this story."

Devon pretended to ignore her. "Anyway, one day the brother who was the black sheep of the family had this silly notion that he was in love with a girl who loved him in return. Since he was convinced of the girl's devotion to him, he never doubted that she would accept his proposal when he asked for her hand in marriage. But as usual, my big brother was one step ahead of me." The volume of his voice increased as he became the main character in the tale.

Krystal slumped down in her seat, embarrassed by his brashness, but mostly by the intimacy of his story. She tried to hide her flushed face behind her hand as he continued.

His face distorted into a violent mask of rage. "I had worn my heart on my sleeve for months because of Jennifer Holt; makin' eyes at her like some love-sick fool, spending every dime I had to woo her, and the whole time she was sneakin' around behind my back with my brother!" He wiped away the beads of sweat which had formed above his upper lip. "Of course, he didn't really want her either, not like I did."

Krystal lowered her hands and leaned forward in her seat. "What do you mean?" She was engrossed in his story and had to know the outcome.

"I really did love Jennifer, but not Drake. He was too busy proving to everybody what a big tough lawman he was. Being pa's perfect son was too important for him to be saddled down with any one woman, but it sure didn't stop him from adding notches to his headboard." Devon drew in a deep breath and glanced out through the window. "He must've broken her heart, 'cause a few days later, Jennifer left town. I heard after she had left Green River that she had killed herself. I reckon Drake's rejection was what drove her over the edge. She was always so damned sensitive, but that was one of the things I loved—" His voice trailed off as his eyes misted over with the sorrowful recollections of the past.

Krystal felt an unexpected tear roll down her cheek. It was impossible to believe Drake was capable of such callous actions, but it was difficult to doubt Devon's story, too. "Did Drake admit to his involvement with Jennifer?"

"I never asked him," Devon answered with a snide chuckle. "It just didn't matter anymore. I finally realized that I could never compete with Drake for anything." A spark of fire lit his dark eyes as he sat up tall in his seat. His gaze roamed over Krystal while he added with a chilling grin, "Until now, that is."

Krystal grew rigid. For a very short time, she had glimpsed a part of him she was sure very few people ever saw, the part of him that had once loved and cared. Now, he was back to the cold and aloof exterior he presented to the rest of the world. The twinkle in his dark gaze was obvious. She was just one more token in this long embittered competition between Drake and him. Well, she would not be a trophy for either of them, and most of all, she was determined not to become the newest notch in Drake's headboard. Leaving Drake behind in Green River had definitely been the right thing to do, Krystal decided as she leaned back and returned Devon's intimidating stare with her own narrowed gaze. When they reached Virginia City, she would find her father and be rid of both the DeGanahl brothers!

Since Devon had opened up briefly and told her why he harbored such a deep resentment towards Drake, he had become more distant and hateful than ever. Krystal was relieved when it was finally late enough for her to retire to the sleeping compartment of the train for the night, but she did not leave until Devon had issued her a threatening warning. Krystal only threw her hands up in a defeated gesture. She could hardly escape from him. The only thing she could do was to tell someone on the train that she was being threatened by an outlaw. At first, her feelings for Drake had prevented her from turning his brother over to the authorities on the train, but since Devon had told her the tragic tale about Jennifer Holt, Krystal found herself feeling a tinge of pity for the desperado.

Krystal climbed into the tiny berth and pulled the privacy curtain across the front of the compartment. The sleeping quarters were barely more comfortable than sleeping in the seats, but at least in here, Krystal was away from Devon's never-ending watchfulness. The heat on the train was insufferable, so Krystal unbuttoned the bodice of Angelina's dress in an effort to cool off. She was certain she would not be able to sleep a wink tonight, but the minute she relaxed back against the flat mattress, she fell into a restless slumber.

Drake DeGanahl dominated her dreams with his silly crooked smile and those laughing green eyes. Even now his touch seemed so real that when Krystal first opened her startled eyes she was confused as to what was reality and what was merely a lingering portion of her dream. The hand which was clamped tightly over her mouth, however, was a painful awakening and the face that hovered no more than a few inches above hers was no illusion! It took her whirling brain a minute to regain its complete awareness. Scared as she was, her fear dissolved into fury the moment the man began to speak.

"Hello, darlin'. It looks as though we're sharing sleeping quarters again, doesn't it?" Her eyes narrowed with deadly accusations, and Drake knew right away that she would scream bloody murder if he were to remove his hand from her mouth. Damn! he was getting tired of trying to win her confidence.

"Listen here," he whispered with acute aggravation drawing his teeth into a tight clench. "I'm fed up with these ridiculous games. You've been too busy being a martyr to notice that I've fallen in love with you. God knows why, but I have. Damnit, woman," Drake forced his voice back down to a whisper as it began to grow louder, "Even before I knew what you looked like, I was infatuated with the lady beneath those stupid black veils, and ever since then I've done everything I could think of short of dying for you to prove how I felt. If I release my hand and you scream that just might be the last thing I do for you, 'cause every man on this train will come to your rescue and Devon is not about to give you up again without a fight."

In the faint light of the berth, Krystal searched his face looking for some clue as to the sincerity of his words. More than anything, she wanted to believe that he loved her as much as she loved him. But she kept remembering Devon's words. Did she only represent one more notch in Drake's headboard? Drake's expression grew apprehensive as he waited for her reply. Krystal knew she had to make the most important decision of her life. Devon would no doubt challenge Drake to a gunfight the minute he learned of his presence on the train. Despite the terrible things Devon had told her about Drake, Krystal realized she did love him and the churning in her breast told her she could not bear it if there was a chance that he could be killed. But did she dare admit the depth of her feelings before she knew the truth about what Devon had told her? Her eyes locked with his as she nodded slowly.

Drake gently released her and held his breath. In her gaze, he had sensed something so strong, but what? She sat up while her eyes continued to strain through the dimness into his own puzzled look. She moved her eyes slowly over his face. So much had happened since the first time she had encountered him on the train. She thought of last night, when she had been ready to give all of herself to this man who had imprisoned her heart, and then her thoughts reverted to Devon and a dead girl named Jennifer. There were so many unanswered questions involving these two men whose paths she had been destined to cross in this wild frontier. But Krystal was not sure she wanted to know the answers to any of those questions. Drake's admission of love had taken precedence over everything else, and there was only one thing that mattered anymore. "Do you really love me?" she implored quietly, wanting him to confirm his feelings one more time.

"Yes," he answered in an emotion-filled voice.

"I-I think that I might love you, too." Then as an afterthought she whispered, "Good Lord!"

She might love him? Well, he thought, it was a start — a damn good start. The familiar smile slanted across Drake's face as he leaned over to kiss that inviting pink mouth. The heat in the crowded compartment was minor compared to the combustible explosion that their admissions of love had ignited when they touched again. Drake's impatient mouth devoured her soft lips with a thirst which was unquenchable.

Krystal's resistance began to wane within the towering peaks of his enslaving embrace. She knew that she would have to stop him again, but she wanted this sweet torture to last just a little longer. His mouth began to trace a searing path down the side of her neck and across the soft flesh exposed by her unbuttoned dress. She felt too weak to protest as he slowly slid her down upon the hard berth mattress and covered her shivering body with his own trembling form. His lips had descended in the transition and were now traipsing gently along the lacy outline of her chamisole. Each spot where his hot lips touched remained inflamed and as his hands began to push her dress away from her shoulders, Krystal realized that the entire length of his lean body completely imprisoned her and his legs were wedged between her own separated limbs in the most intimate manner possible. There was no denying Drake's intention or the extent of his passion as Krystal felt his bulging virility press against the curve of her hip. Her body became drenched with perspiration and her senses seemed to disappear within the fiery rage which soared wildly through her being.

She vaguely noticed that his hand had worked its way downward and was now moving under the skirt of her dress as his fingers slid up along her leg. She gasped as his hand began to delve into the warm glen between her thighs, yet she could not seem to put an end to this ecstatic madness. His fingers began to caress that secret area, gliding over the silky material of her undergarments until she was sure she was about to lose the last of her sanity. She had to stop him . . . but not just yet!

Krystal felt like she was in a hazy trance and she was fighting a losing battle in her efforts to return to reality. How could anything so wonderful be so wrong? Every inch of her burning flesh tingled with the feeling of sensual discovery and she was certain that she was quivering so hard that the whole berth was shaking violently, too. She would tell him to stop if she could only speak, but her breath was hung up somewhere in her throat and it would not permit her voice to pass. His mouth was relentless and his fingers were without mercy as they continued to ravish her flushed body and make her mind senseless with rapture.

In spite of her resolution to end this forbidden desire, she continued to return each of his kisses with an insatiable devotion. Her body acted of its own accord and responded to every one of his inquisitive embraces by arching against his muscular form with eager anticipation. His kisses were deepening and his expertly positioned form, ripe with unspoken innuendo, was molded tightly against the curves of her wanton body. Krystal felt him undo the brass buttons of his jeans and she was aware of the searing touch of his passion-laden member as it rested against her thigh. He moved from between her legs and stretched out beside her as he began to work diligently at tugging her garterbelt down over her hips. She felt incomplete without the blanket of his tall frame and she yearned to pull him back into the refuge of her aching limbs. Oh Lord! within seconds her indecision would be past the point of pondering.

She had run away from him to avoid this happening, but once again, it had taken no more than his nearness to chase away all of her moral sensibility. He said he loved her, but to what extent? The idea of making love to any man out of wedlock defied her whole existence and she could not abandon her beliefs. But to halt this excessive delight now was going to take every bit of strength she possessed and she could only hope that he would understand.

"Drake?" she whispered feebly. His lips covered her parted mouth in response while one of his hands masterfully brought one enslaved tip of her breast to its taut and swollen splendor. His mouth pulled away from hers as his head began to proceed downward. The touch of his tongue trailing softly over her chin and neck left a blazing rivulet of ecstasy which was nearly Krystal's undoing. "Drake?" she pleaded in a louder tone, though she was beginning to wonder if it was already too late for protests.

Drake stopped his sensual descent and took a deep breath before he answered her. "Yes?" he finally asked in a very choked tone of voice.

Krystal swallowed hard, wondering if she really wanted him to stop. She had never known such rapture as she did a second ago, but she had never felt so confused either. "It's just—well, it's so wrong to do this, don't you agree?"

The sound of Drake's loud exhaled breath was the only reply she received.

"I mean, it's not as though we were married or

169

anything," she added quickly. Oh, Lord! That made it sound as though she was expecting a proposal just because he had told her that he loved her.

Drake bolted up to a sitting position and stared at her. "Married?" he repeated with shock.

Krystal raised up on her elbows and stared back at him. "Good Lord, Drake," she began indignantly. "I was not raised to be promiscuous."

"Good Lord!" he mocked. "May I be struck dead by a bolt of lightning if I ever thought any differently."

Krystal began to scoot out from beneath him. The passionate mood from a moment ago had rapidly disintegrated with his snide remark. "Lucky for you it's not a stormy night, but I wouldn't stand out in any open fields if I were you!"

Drake fell back against the far wall of the narrow berth and dropped his hands down angrily on his thighs. His first thought was to toss a snide retort back in her face, but he realized that it would only be wasted breath. Krystal Colbert, he was sure, could top anything that he could think of with one of her own biting remarks. Marriage! he thought with invigorated anger and the sudden anticipation of a new goal for him to pursue in the near future.

Chapter Twelve

"How is your shoulder?" Krystal questioned from her corner of the berth.

"It hurts, damn it!"

She folded her hands in her lap and sighed. So far, nothing had gone as she had planned. Her original objective had been to get away from both of the DeGanahl brothers, and now here she was with Drake in her sleeping compartment and Devon waiting for her out in the coach car. Was there no way to escape these two men? She glanced back at Drake's brooding face.

"How did you get here?"

"What difference does it make?" He didn't care to tell her that he had not been able to sleep because of the state he was in after their encounter behind the house last night. Nor did he want to explain how he had heard her sneaking out of the front door early this morning, or that he had been about to take out after her when he had seen his brother sneaking out from the side of the house. In order to avoid any trouble at his mother's home, or in the town of Green River, he had decided to follow them both onto the train and not make his presence known until it was necessary.

Krystal could tell that he was in no mood for polite conversation by the tone of his voice so she tried to think about something else, but it was not easy. Sitting across from Devon's glowering face had been less torture than being two feet away from Drake. It was impossible to be so close to this infuriating man and not want to be in his arms. But she just kept reminding herself how close she had come to being another notch in his headboard. That only reminded her of his kisses and the feel of his firm body laying between . . . Good Lord! All she seemed to think about since she had met Drake DeGanahl were things associated with immoral desires. She ran her tongue along her throbbing lips and tried to force herself to think about more pressing problems.

"Well, not that it matters, but what do you plan to do now that you are here?" she asked with a snide edge in her voice.

Since he was growing used to her haughtiness, he retorted casually. "This train should pull into Odgen about daybreak. Do you suppose you could coax Devon out to some secluded area where the two of you could be alone?"

"Alone?" Krystal huffed, aghast at the idea. "Not hardly!"

Drake drew in a defeated sigh and dropped his head into his hands. "I would be waiting there," he added with exasperation.

"Oh, well, that makes me feel so much better!"

Drake closed his eyes and forced himself to hold his tongue. Never had he known a woman who could make him so furious. He could spend his whole life trying to match wits with her and still he would never get in the last word. His eyes opened and darted across the close quarters into her narrowed gaze. "Just do as I tell you to, just once, and maybe you might get out of this mess you've gotten yourself into."

She leaned forward until she was only inches from his face. "Well, you are correct about one thing. I did get myself into this situation and I can get myself out of it. I don't recall asking for anything from you."

"Well, you're right about that, too. I must've been crazy to think that you would appreciate my help." He pulled back the curtain and peered into the empty corridor. As he slid out of the compartment he whispered in a low growl, "Next time you get yourself kidnapped because you don't know when to keep your mouth shut, don't expect me to come to your aid." He tipped the brim of the brown hat he was wearing, and backed out into the narrow passageway. "Good luck, darlin'. You're going to need it."

The curtain flapped back in her face, but not before she whispered through the opening with clenched teeth, "Good bye and good riddance to you, too, Drake DeGanahl!"

Damn! Drake thought with rage. It would serve that hard-headed woman right if he did desert her. He exited from the car without caution, too angry to care whether he came face to face with Devon or not. But Devon's hat was placed over his face and he appeared to be dozing when Drake stomped past him and found a safe place to wait out the remainder of the ride.

Alone in the small compartment, Krystal was forced to face up to the enormous mistake she had

173

just made. Why did she allow Drake DeGanahl to antagonize her so much? She knew that she loved him, and he had seemed so sincere when he had told her that he was in love with her, so why couldn't they say a civil word to one another?

The conductor's loud voice announcing the train's imminent arrival in Ogden jolted her thoughts back to Devon. She quickly ran her fingers through her tousled hair, wishing that she had some hairpins to hold the long tendrils into the tight bun she always wore when she taught school. She took a deep breath before pulling back the heavy curtain which separated the berth from the corridor. There was no telling what she would encounter when she left the security of this compartment. Where was Drake? she wondered.

A lazy smile sauntered across Devon's deeply tanned face as he watched her emerge from the berth. She glared back at him as she began to smooth down the wrinkled skirt of his mother's blue calico dress. She glanced around at the other passengers who were emerging from the sleeping berths, nervously scanning every face while she walked towards Devon with a clumsy gait. She knew Drake was somewhere on the train and the last thing she wanted was for the two brothers to confront one another. In an unconscious gesture she clutched her little black bag tightly against her side.

The train jerked to a halt as Devon's gaze traveled down to the bag. A curious expression filtered in his eyes. He remembered that bag being in her hand ever since the first day he had met her on the train. "What is it that you guard so carefully in that little bag there?" He motioned down toward her hip where the purse was hanging. Krystal's body grew rigid.

174

She clasped the bag up to her chest with both hands and gave him a defiant look which told him the importance of its contents. He started to say something, but suddenly his expression changed from an inquisitive look to one of fear. He grabbed her arm and pulled the brim of his hat down to shade his face. As he pushed Krystal towards the back of the train, he warned her to remain silent.

Krystal managed a quick look back over her shoulder, half expecting to see Drake somewhere behind them. Much to her relief, she only caught a glimpse of a man with a shiny star pinned to his chest emerge through the doorway of the front train car. She did not have time to see if Drake was anywhere among the passengers who were unloading from the train because Devon was pushing her through the back exit and down the narrow iron steps. The last step was a great distance from the ground so Devon slid past her and jumped down ahead of her. His strong arms encircled her waist as he quickly lifted her down beside him. She had no other alternative but to follow him when he clasped onto her wrist and began to walk swiftly away from the locomotive.

Her frantic gaze searched the crowd for Drake again, but he was nowhere in sight. Devon was headed toward the opposite end of the station where the Southern Pacific tracks met with the tracks of the Union Pacific Railroad. Krystal felt helpless as Devon pulled her across the yard to the other train track. Suddenly she remembered Drake's suggestion that she try to coax Devon off someplace where they would be alone. She knew how upset Drake was with her, but she was sure that he would not leave her alone. She was counting on him when she skidded to a halt.

175

"Wait!"

Devon paused and glanced around. "What is it?" he asked with annoyance.

Krystal's spinning mind tried to think of something. "Why — why don't we just go somewhere for a few minutes and give ourselves a chance to calm down before we board the other train." His skeptical look did not deter her as she rushed on. "If we board the train in this state, someone is bound to notice the fugitive looks on both our faces." She glanced around in a frantic gesture.

"Over there," she shouted much louder than necessary, as she pointed to a deserted-looking building. "We can slip behind that shed for a second and compose ourselves. Please? I just need a minute or two?"

Devon noticed the bright red flush across her face and the wild look in her golden-brown eyes. If they got on the train right now, her appearance would draw unwanted attention to them. He raised his hands in the air in defeat, then motioned for her to lead the way. She tried not to appear suspicious, but she felt like every pair of eyes in the station were watching them. All she could hope for now was that Drake was nearby and that he was witnessing her attempt to lure Devon to a secluded location.

Behind the ramshackle building there was nothing except an open field of range grass that was already beginning to turn light brown from the heat of the summer. The early morning sun had not reached this area, so it was still partially shaded by the building. The couple slipped behind the old shed and leaned against the rough wall. Krystal felt like her pounding heart was about to crash through her chest as she pressed her bag against her heart in a vain effort to slow down the loud thundering from within.

Devon glanced down at her and his attention was immediately drawn to the purse again. His curiosity was beginning to get the best of him. She certainly kept that little bag well guarded. "Now, that we're alone, how about telling me what's in your little satchel there?"

In an instinctive gesture, she drew her arms behind her back. Devon was even more intrigued with the contents of that mysterious bag. In a swift motion he grabbed her arms and pulled them out from behind her. Krystal was so startled by his sudden act of brute strength that she dropped the bag at his feet. They both stared down at the little bag for a second before Devon bent over and swooped it up. She grabbed for the purse, but he held it high over his head and gave her a wicked smile.

"You have no right to take that from me. The contents are of no worth to anyone other than myself." Her anger had brought tears to her large eyes, but her tears did not affect him. He lowered the bag slowly, and for a moment Krystal thought he was going to give it back to her, but all at once he pulled open the gathered top and dumped the contents into his hand, then casually tossed the purse down into the dirt.

A weak sob escaped Krystal when she grabbed for the yellowed photograph as it floated towards the ground. When she straightened up she saw a greedy glint flicker through Devon's dark pupils. In his outstretched hand rested the exquisite diamond brooch. The sun, which had just began to shed a single ray of light over the top of the old building, caught the reflection of the brilliant ring of jewels and set off a series of blinding flashes. Devon's hand quickly closed over the circle of light as his questioning gaze met Krystal's startled look.

"Would you kindly give that back to me?" she asked through tightly-drawn lips.

A low whistle emitted from Devon when he carefully reopened his hand and held the brooch up to his face so that it would not catch the sunlight again. "Did you steal it?" he inquired with awe.

"How dare you insinuate that I stole it? It belonged to my mother and I demand that you give it back."

Her uppity attitude caused Devon to burst out laughing. He found this woman unbelievable. The top of her head barely reached to his chin, and she was completely defenseless against anything that he might choose to do to her; yet, she continued to issue orders to him as though she were in total command. The DeGanahl boys always had liked fiesty women and this one was beautiful, as well. It was no wonder Drake was so anxious to claim this lady for his own. But since it was obvious that she wanted nothing to do with his brother, perhaps it was time for Devon to make his move. He could not imagine a better revenge than to win over this woman, especially since it appeared that his brother wanted her so badly that he had even chanced his life in order to protect her against a band of train robbers.

Krystal stumbled back against the building as he stepped closer. The look in his ebony eyes was undeniable. Where was Drake? She thought about screaming for help, but Devon was so close now that he would be able to silence her the minute she opened her mouth. His muscular frame was brushing against Krystal's trembling body as she raised her pleading eyes to his

178

passion-misted gaze. She was caught off guard by his sudden switch from crudeness to tenderness and for a moment she felt powerless to do anything. All she could think about was how much he resembled his brother, and that thought only served as a reminder of how much she loved Drake.

Devon mistook the soft glow that consumed her delicate features for surrender. He thought briefly of Jennifer Holt, and the feelings he had buried with her when he had heard of her death. It had been a long time since he had made love to a woman with any emotion other than a basic need. He wondered if he was capable of holding a woman like Krystal Colbert with the tenderness that she deserved. A vision of this woman in the arms of his brother on that first day he had witnessed that long intense kiss suddenly flashed before his eyes, reminding him of his long-time vendetta. He thought of Jennifer again, only this time it wasn't his love for her that he was remembering. It was the memories of her shameless deceit.

The gentleness rapidly disappeared from his face and he saw a look of terror spark Krystal's brown eyes with flecks of gold. He no longer felt confused, the alien feelings were gone and he was in control of his emotions once again. Revenge, his constant companion for the past decade, had returned and forced his mind back to its heartless mode of detachment and emptiness. He knew now that it would be easy to make love to Krystal Colbert. He would just keep remembering how much Drake wanted this woman. He was thinking about kissing that trembling mouth as he lifted her chin with his hand and began to lower his head to meet hers. His desire to possess this woman whom he knew his brother was also hankering

179

for, made Devon deaf to his surroundings, and he was unaware of the man who suddenly appeared from the side of the shed.

Drake's blow was so swift that not even Krystal was sure what had happened until it was over. Only a second ago, Devon's hot breath was about to snatch hers away as his mouth began to brush against her lips, and the next moment he was a crumpled heap on the ground. Krystal suppressed the scream she felt rise up in her throat as she fell back against the building. Good Lord, if Drake hadn't shown up right then, Devon would have proceeded to kiss her. She had begun to doubt that Drake would come to her aid, but he always seemed to be there when she needed him the most. Her gaze met his, but she quickly looked away when she felt her face grow hot and flushed as it always did whenever she glanced at him.

"Is he . . . dead?" She motioned down at Devon's still form.

"No, just out cold." Drake tossed away the piece of wood which he had used to club Devon over the head with and began to lift his brother's limp body up from the ground. Krystal remembered the brooch. Frantically she searched the ground and saw the shimmering diamond circle laying in the dirt several feet away. She rushed to the spot and grabbed the pin, then quickly returned to where Devon had dropped her bag. When she had replaced the photograph and the brooch back into the little black purse, she turned her attention back to Drake and noticed him grimace as he struggled to support the weight of his unconscious brother. She was reminded that he still had an unhealed stab wound in his shoulder as she rushed to

180

Drake's side to help him drag Devon around to the front of the shack.

"That door is unlocked," Drake stated breathlessly. He had already checked out the shed and had decided that it would be the ideal location to leave Devon until he woke up from his unfortunate accident. Drake was proud of Krystal for being able to divert his brother's attention so that he could get the drop on him. He was not, however, pleased with the method she had chosen. But since there was not time to discuss the use of her enticing wares, Drake decided to dismiss his aggravation for the time being.

Krystal turned loose of Devon and opened the door as Drake quickly pulled him into the empty room. She glanced around outside before she slammed the door shut, but much to her surprise, no one seemed to be paying any attention to them. Most of the people had already boarded the other train or were busy mulling around the ticket window across the train yard. When she turned around, Drake was busy tying up Devon's feet and hands with a long rope.

"Will he be all right?"

Drake stood up and nodded. "He's gonna have one hell of a headache, but that's about all."

Krystal glanced around the interior of the dirty building. She felt a twinge of guilt about leaving him in this shabby place. 'How long will it be until he wakes up?'

"Not long, but it's going to take him awhile to undo the ropes and he's not about to call for help." Krystal gave him a questioning look. Drake shrugged and explained. "He took a big risk by boarding that train in Green River, and he was real lucky that he was able to pull it off without getting caught. He's not

181

going to take another chance that someone would recognize him now." Drake shook his head, surprised at his brother's carelessness.

"That man that Devon was so worried about on the train was Cameron Reed. He's the Marshal of Sweetwater County and he's an old friend of our father's, but he would like nothing better than to hang Devon's neck in a noose. He had been on the train all the way from Green River, but he was riding in a private car with some Pinkerton detective. I had to do some mighty fast talking to divert his attention away from you and Devon while you two got off of the train."

"Oh," Krystal replied quietly. His mention of the Pinkerton man made her feel uneasy, though she could not understand why. All at once she realized that her fears about Drake had been unfounded. It was obvious to her now that he was not one of Devon's cohort's in crime or else he would not have been able to acknowledge the law officer on the train.

"I thought you'd never get here," she said bluntly, unaware of the way her voice sounded.

Taking a defensive stance, Drake retorted, "I didn't know I was expected. I seem to recall that you told me you could handle Devon by yourself and it appeared that you were doing a damn good job of it, too."

She started to defend her actions, but she was forced to admit to herself that she had been foolish to think that she was capable of handling a man like Devon all on her own. "I'm just relieved that you showed up in time. And I'm sorry I was so rude to you in the train berth."

Drake tried to hide his shock. The last thing he had expected was an apology from her. "It's just as much my fault as it is yours. I don't know why I'm so hot-tempered whenever I'm around you. But then," he stepped closer to her, "I've never felt like this before."

"Neither have I," she replied, feeling her pulse quicken. She gazed up at him and fell in love all over again. Like a bee drawn to honey, she pressed her body against his taut form as her moist lips parted slightly with the expectation of another sweet attack of his mouth. It was an invitation he couldn't deny as he swept her petite form into his arms and brought his mouth down to claim hers. The lonely sound of a train whistle snapped them back to reality.

He pulled away. "That's your train to Virginia City, darlin'. I know you wouldn't want to miss it."

Krystal grew terrified and confused. "Aren't you coming?"

He glanced down at his brother than returned his dark green eyes to her tense face. "You're safe now. There's no reason for me to come, is there?"

Her eyes misted with unshed tears. "Isn't the fact that I love you reason enough?"

Drake studied her face closely. The threatening tears surprised him and they weakened his guarded position. He wanted to know for certain that she wanted him to accompany her to Virginia City. She had already run away from him once, what would happen when they reached Nevada? When she was back in the safety of her father's domain would she no longer have any use for him? He was not sure if his battered heart could take another attack of Krystal Colbert's sharp rejections. His love for her was growing too strong, and at the same time, it was so new that it was still very fragile. If she did not want him as badly as he wanted her, he was sure he could not

183

stand to be in her presence any longer. To love her this much and to not have her completely was causing him too much distress.

Another shrill whistle caught their attention again. "Last call, darlin'."

Krystal couldn't believe that he was actually going to let her go on without him. They had been through so much the past week that she could not imagine tomorrow without him. She didn't want another tomorrow unless he was there to greet it with her. "If you're not going, then neither am I," she stated simply.

Drake remained unmoving, her declaration had left him speechless. He had thought that nothing was as important to her as reaching Virginia City. Yet, she was willing to miss that train if he didn't go with her. He felt like something had just exploded inside him, and he realized that it was only his love for her increasing with boundless limitations. He would not allow her to miss her train. He would go to Virginia City with her, or to the ends of the earth if he was by her side.

He grabbed her hand, "Come on, darlin', we've got a train to catch."

Chapter Thirteen

Krystal traveled the remainder of the trip in a veritible daze. There was nothing that could compare to this wondrous new feeling of being in love with a man like Drake DeGanahl and knowing that he loved her in return. Neither of them had said a snide or even remotely derogatory remark to the other one since this morning. The whole journey was pure bliss. Krystal blushed profusely every time Drake cast her one of his suggestive grins and she kept having the urge to pinch herself to see if this was just a dream. She had come out West with the determined hope of finding her father and already she had found more than she had ever imagined. Each time Drake leaned across the seat to point out something of interest to her through the train window, she felt her heart miss a beat, and when he casually rested his arm around her shoulders, Krystal felt such a consumption of love rush through her tingling being that she knew that in his arms was where she wanted to spend the rest of her life.

Whenever she stole a glance in his direction she found it hard to believe this was the same man who she had mistakenly thought to be a silver-tongued dandy the first time they had met. His light brown curls framed his face from beneath a chocolate brown cowboy hat. It was adorned with a wide band which was made from a rattlesnake hide, and he was dressed in a white pearl-snapped shirt that was topped by a body-defining vest in the same shade as his hat. His looks, Krystal discovered throughout the long day, were not his only assets.

Since they had never really had a chance to converse in a calm manner before now, they spent the whole day excitedly learning about one another. As she listened to him speak of his parents and about the dedication he had felt as a lawman, Krystal glimpsed the private man behind that crooked smile and those devilish green eyes, and she discovered that Drake DeGanahl was one of the most compassionate and sensitive men she had ever met. The fact that he conspicuously avoided talking about his relationship with his brother made Krystal all the more anxious to ask him about Jennifer Holt. But she decided they were getting along too good right now to bring up Devon or anything remotely associated with him, so she remained silent. But someday, she told herself, she had to hear Drake's side of the sad story that Devon had related to her about the dead girl and her involvement with both of the DeGanahl brothers.

Krystal confided in him about her mother's death and the letter which had revealed the surprising secret about John Colbert. However, she did not devulge any information about the money her mother had taken from her father's mine, nor did she mention the diamond brooch. Ever since this morning, when Devon had asked her if the pin was stolen, Krystal found herself wondering once again what such an expensive piece of jewelry had been doing in her mother's bureau? Since it had been with the photograph of her parents, she rationalized that perhaps John Colbert had given the brooch to her mother and she had kept it in the drawer for sentimental reasons.

But still . . . Krystal had a strange feeling about that piece of jewelry and felt it best to keep quiet about it, especially to Drake. When he had talked about his life as a lawman, his fierce pride and strict obligations had been visible in his face and in his strong tone of voice. Krystal wondered how he would feel if she were to tell him what she suspected about the brooch? But that would almost be the same as accusing her mother of being a jewel thief. That was a suspicion she would never voice. So she remained silent about the pin and about the Pinkerton Detective Agency's investigation back in Boston.

By the time the train had deposited them at the station in Virginia City, Krystal had come to the conclusion that she had been destined to travel out West just to meet Drake DeGanahl. Of course, when she mentioned it to him, Drake told her that he had known that from the first moment her lips had beckoned to him from below her heavy black veil, and she was reminded again of how irritating Drake De-Ganahl could be at times.

"It shouldn't take too long to locate my father," Krystal quickly changed the subject. "My mother's letter said he was probably the wealthiest man in Virginia City."

"Your mother hadn't seen him for twenty years," he reminded her. "Besides it's two o'clock in the morning.

187

I suggest we get a room and start hunting for him in the morning."

Krystal opened her mouth to argue with him, but realized that dropping in on a man in the middle of the night and claiming to be his long-lost daughter might be rather rude. So, she tossed her head indignantly and in an attempt to hide the fact that Drake was partially right, she retorted, "Did you say — a room? I hardly think so. Two rooms would be more like it." She began to walk briskly away from the station as though she knew exactly where she was headed.

Drake rolled his eyes upward and nodded in agreement as he followed her from the depot. Today had been too perfect to ruin it with this ridiculous argument again. Two rooms it would be, for now anyway. Once they were standing on the wooden planks of the sidewalk she turned to him with an aggravated glare.

"Have you ever been to Virginia City before?" she asked. He nodded and graced her with a slanted smile. "Well," her voice raised with irritation, "Which direction is the hotel?"

Drake tried to suppress the chuckle he felt well up in his throat with a slight cough as he took her arm and began to lead her away from E Street and towards C Street and the International Hotel. Despite the early morning hour, Krystal was amazed at the amount of activity in the town. There were more saloons on this one narrow street than she had ever noticed in all of Boston. During the great boom of the past thirty years, Virginia City could boast of having over 100 saloons, and though many of them had died out with the gradual decline of the ore discoveries,

188

there still were enough saloons to keep the town lively.

Drake noticed her curious expression and realized how different this rough mining town was from the city life she was accustomed to living. Off in the distance a shrill whistle blew, signaling the shift change for the miners who still worked around the clock in the dark caverns. With the approach of the new century, the city which had been built on silver was now merely a shadow of the fabulous mining camp it had been during the twenty years following the discovery of the big bonazana of silver and gold in '59. But even now, its rich earth still continued to yield around $500,000 in ore a year.

Clinging to the side of rugged Mount Davidson, Virginia City had literally grown up on the Comstock Lode, and until the last of the big mines ceased operation nearly a decade before, the town had always seemed to tremble with a constant vibration as the giant Cornish pumps sucked boiling hot water away from the area where the men pounded and dug through the hard rock. But with new and refined methods of mining the once noisy town seemed eerily quiet to the oldtimers who still hung onto the vanishing hope of discovering another bonanza somewhere within the time-worn ground of the Washoe Valley. Many of the men who had spent their lives in the company of the thundering noises of the old stamp mills were so used to yelling above the constant roar of the machinery that shouting became the normal way for them to speak for the rest of their lives. It was a common sight to see two old miners screaming in one another's ears on the street corner or a table in a restaurant simply out of habit.

189

As they continued along the crooked boardwalk, Drake couldn't help but notice the startling contrast of Krystal Colbert's refined dignity against the harsh background of this fading boomtown. With a sinking feeling, he wondered if she would be willing to give up her fancy house on Beacon Hill and her life among the high society of Boston in return for the meager life he could offer to her out here in the West? All at once, Drake was forced to take a good long look at his life. What did he have to offer a woman like Krystal Colbert? He didn't even have a job, and his pride would never permit him to live off of her wealth. The only money he had was the trust fund his Spanish grandfather had set up for him almost thirty years ago. Drake had vowed ever since he had first heard about the money never to spend a dime from that account, no matter how desperate he was for money. The memories of his mother's heartbreak passed through his mind and he felt a new surge of anger towards his grandfather, Migel Ramirez. He would never take a penny from a man who would deny his own daughter because she had followed her heart and married a man who was not from her same ethnic origin.

Drake glanced down at the beautiful woman who walked beside him again, and surprised himself with the sense of responsibility she aroused in him. He knew he had to make some decisions about his own life before he could ask Krystal to share her future with him. By the time he had steered her into the lobby of the luxurious International Hotel he had become furious with himself for the direction he had allowed his life to take. He was almost thirty years old, and he had nothing to show for it except a trail of bitter memories and a tarnished badge that he hadn't felt worthy of wearing for the past two years.

"Do you know John Colbert?" Krystal asked the drowsy-eyed man behind the desk. Her question jolted Drake out of his self-pitying trance.

The man pointed at the hotel log as he handed Krystal a pen so that she could sign the register. "Nope, can't say as I do, ma'am. Room 203, second floor, take a right after you leave the elevator," he glanced at her signature and added as he turned his attention towards Drake, "I'll call a bellboy for your luggage, Mr. Colbert."

Flustered, Krystal shoved the pen back at him and snapped, "We don't have any luggage and he is not Mr. Colbert. And further more we need two rooms! Now, you must have heard of John Colbert?"

Drake shrugged and took the pen from the confused desk clerk. "Krystal," Drake began in a patronizing tone, "It's late, you're tired and you are not being very cordial right now. Tomorrow, when you are rested, and in better spirits—I hope—we will find your father."

Krystal's eyes flared with rage as she turned her wrath on Drake. "I am in fine spirits, thank you. I certainly do not need anyone, especially you, to tell me how I am feeling. Did you forget that the reason I came to Virginia City was to find my father? How do you expect me to think about sleeping when I am this close to finding him?"

Drake took the two room keys from the man behind the desk. The desk clerk carried an amused expression on his face now that this woman's fury was no longer directed at him. Drake wrapped his arm around her shoulders as he pushed her toward the hydraulic elevator. "Damnit!" he scowled, his own problems making him more irritable than usual. "I said we would find him tomorrow and I meant it."

Krystal skidded to an abrupt halt at the entrance of the elevator. "How dare you speak to me in that manner?" She placed her hands on her hips and tossed back her head as her defiant look drilled into his dark eyes. When he retaliated by crossing his arms and glaring back at her, Krystal began to sense a vague feeling of defeat. As she gathered up the long skirts of his mother's dress and stomped into the iron cage with him hot on her heels, she realized that he was the first person who could command her surrender with no more than a glance from his unyielding green eyes. By the time they had reached the first landing, she had decided that being in love with a man who was more stubborn than herself was complete insanity. But right now she was too furious with the dolt at the desk for not knowing who her father was, and at her self for loving Drake DeGanahl so much, but mostly she was mad at Drake because, well, just because!

She turned sharply to the right the second he opened the hinged elevator door, and resumed her huffy stride until she reached the door marked 203. She grabbed a key from him, and shoved it into the key-hole. He did not utter a word as he watched her struggle to unlock the door. When he finally realized that she was not going to give in, he tapped her lightly on the shoulder and held up the other key. Krystal threw him a challenging look over her shoulder, then looked at the key he was holding in front of her face. She turned a livid shade of red as she realized she had the wrong key. She grabbed the other key, and immediately opened the door. As she started into the room, Drake tapped her shoulder once more.

"What now?" she said as she spun around. He gave her a crooked smile and held out his hand. With another flush of scarlet turning her cheeks a darker shade of red, she realized she still had the other key. She shoved the key to his room into his outstretched hand, then slammed the door in his face.

"Damn!" he muttered as he continued down the hallway to his own room. At times she could be impossible!

The International Hotel was one of the finest hotels in all of Nevada, but as Krystal threw herself down on the bed in a self-imposed rage, she did not even take notice of the lush surroundings. In her travels with her mother she had stayed in so many elegant hotels that they all looked the same to her, and right now her thoughts were too engrossed with Drake DeGanahl. That man made her furious, with his cocky attitude and that silly grin which was almost always present on his wickedly handsome face. It was pure torture to be separated from him, and what was worse, her love for him continued to grow each time they were apart.

He had been correct about one thing, however, she was tired and tomorrow would be soon enough to find the father she had not known existed until two weeks ago. In spite of her exhausted state, Krystal could not sleep. Every time she forced her eyes to close, she experienced the strangest hot flashes throughout her whole body until she was drenched in perspiration.

She tried to concentrate on tomorrow and finding her father, but all her deceiving mind wanted to think about was the feel of Drake's large hands caressing her the way he had in the train berth, a thought that created a new outbreak of sweat and a fierce trembling in the pit of her stomach that threatened to make her insides explode with lustful yearnings. She felt as though she were teetering on the edge of a bottomless pit and at any moment she might tumble in to this dark, beckoning hole.

No doubt, Drake DeGanhal was the devil who was waiting at the bottom to catch her when she fell.

Until she had met this man, it had been beyond her wildest imagination to ever consider making love before she was properly married. But Drake had acted shocked when she had mentioned the word marriage on the train. Being the scoundrel that he was, Krystal was sure he hoped to coax her into his bed without the proper formalities. And the most shocking development in this whole mess was that she wanted him so badly that she was actually considering the idea. It would be so easy to sneak down the hall to his room. Who would ever know—Good Lord! How could she even be thinking such torrid things? How could love make her so miserable? How could she bear another night alone?

The restless slumber Krystal had finally forced herself into was rudely interrupted much too early. Krystal felt like she had been hit over the head with a sledge hammer when she sat up in bed. A dreaded glimpse in the mirror above the dresser told her that she did not look any better than she felt. She stumbled to the door and swayed up against it. "Who is it?"

194

she asked in a hoarse voice as she tried unsuccussfuly to make her glued eyelids remain open.

"Drake."

She gasped as her heavy lids flew open. She rushed to the dresser and began to smooth her tangled hair down with her hands. He couldn't see her looking like this. She pinched her pale cheeks, but it didn't help. The long night had been pure hell, and it showed all over her haggard face.

"Krystal, are you all right in there?"

"Of course. I'll be right there." This is ridiculous she told herself while she straightened the bodice of the dress she had not bothered to remove for the night. This was hardly the first time he had seen her in the morning. This was, however, the most disheveled she had ever been . . . something she could thank Drake DeGanahl for since it was his fault she had spent such a horrid night.

When she opened the door, she expected him to remark about her obvious lack of sleep and she was already planning a retaliation. But, much to her surprise, he did not seem to notice. He was too proud of retriving her trunks from the station where they had been waiting for her to catch up to them.

"My luggage! Oh, how can I ever thank you enough?"

He leaned against the frame of the door in an easy stance. "I'll think of something, darlin'." He smiled and added, "I couldn't sleep so I decided I might as well do something. They were still sitting in the baggage room."

Krystal swallowed hard and turned away to hide the sudden rush of hot blood she felt color her cheeks

195

again. She hadn't blushed as much in her whole life as she had in the past week. But his admission that he hadn't been able to sleep reminded her of the thoughts that had robbed her of a decent night's sleep. Well good! she said to herself. It would serve him right if he were as miserable as he was making her. When she turned back around, he was dragging the trucks into the room and ignoring her.

"I'll be down in the restaurant. Come on down when you're ready." He slammed the door shut as he exited quickly. In the hallway he stopped to catch his breath. He could not stand to be in that room with her, and he refused to subject himself to that painful torture again. She had no idea how sensuous she looked in the mornings with her eyes slanted seductively from drowsiness and the mass of reddish-gold curls hanging softly around her shoulders. He grunted and started towards the elevator, but when he reached it he continued past it and stomped down the stairs instead. Damn, if this kept up, she would be the death of him yet.

Krystal stared at the door and wondered about his odd behavior. He acted as though his mind was a million miles away and she needed him more than ever today when she went in search of her father. With a sigh, she began to unpack her trucks. While she spread her clothes across the brocaded bed covering and filled the porcelain tub in the small adjoining bath with water, she contemplated her first meeting with John Colbert. How would he react to meeting her after all these years? Did she resemble him, she wondered? Her nerves were getting the best of her by the time she finished smoothing the last of her perfectly coiffed hair into place and stood back to view the results in the mirror above the marble-topped dresser. This would have to do, she decided as she wrinkled up her nose at her reflection. Taking a deep breath, she opened the door and headed down to meet Drake at the restaurant.

When she entered the restaurant, she immediately spotted Drake sitting in the corner. He was absently stirring a cup of coffee as he stared off into space with a distant expression. Krystal stopped and watched him for a moment. He seemed so sad, so unreachable, and she began to wonder if he regretted coming here with her? He sensed her presence and his eyes snapped up and met her questioning gaze. They could not tear their eyes away from one another when they locked with an invisible hold. Drake slowly rose from his seat as he drank in every exquisite inch of this sweet vision. Even the elegance of this fabulous hotel seemed shabby compared to Krystal Colbert. She was dressed in the latest Paris vogue in a high waisted gown of creamy-colored silk and delicate crocheted lace. A plumed hat of the same hue and fabric topped her carefully French-braided hairdo and in the palm of one of her white kid gloves was a matching parasol.

A smile lit her cocoa eyes with flecks of gold and Drake was sure the room suddenly became brighter. As she began to move towards him, he felt an overwhelming feeling of love consume him and it was all he could do to keep from grabbing her and kissing those soft pink lips right there in public. He wanted to shout out his love for her to all of the world.

He pulled out a chair for her and as soon as she

was seated he sat down across from her and resumed his obvious appraisal. He thought she was the most beautiful sight his eyes had ever beheld. Krystal lowered her head in a bashful manner, suddenly embarrassed by his open observation. His gaze boldly traveled the full length of her for a second time then came to rest on her face as a twisted smile curved his lips.

"Drake," she whispered, "People are staring at us. Must you be so brazen?" He chuckled and narrowed one eye with a wicked insinuation as the color in her cheeks deepened. "I mean it, Drake. We did just get into town and since we arrived together, I feel that we must be extra careful in order to protect our reputations."

Drake could not contain the loud roar of laughter which abruptly escaped from him, despite the icy glare that darted from her narrowed gaze. "Darlin', my reputation is far past the point of protecting," he laughed again when he noted her horrified expression. "But, I'll sure do my best to help you protect yours."

"You're arrogant and insufferable, but I am too concerned about finding my father to go into that again."

The smirk faded from his face as he became serious. "Speaking of your father, I've been asking all around town about him. But, no one seems to know of any one named John Colbert."

The color drained from Krystal's face and her eyes widened with a sheet of threatening tears. "That's impossible. He has to be here."

Drake wished he could magically produce the father

she wanted so desperately, but the fact remained that no one he had spoken with had ever heard of anyone of that name. "I talked to the Sheriff while I was waiting for you to come down this morning. He said there are still a few of the wealthy miners who struck it rich living in the area, but no one named John Colbert." He saw the look of hopelessness cover her face when he added, "I'm sorry, Krystal."

She blinked back the urge to cry and squared her shoulders as she pulled her tiny frame up tall in the chair. "Well, I think the sheriff must be mistaken. I know my father is here, I just know it!"

Drake sighed heavily with regret edging into his voice as he made a suggestion. "We might check the cemetery. It's possible that he's there." Her eyes grew fearful and he quickly continued, "But there is also a good chance that he moved on to another mining town when his vein ran dry here, or even more likely is the possibility that he moved to San Francisco like many of the other wealthy men from this area." He reached out and picked up one of her small gloved hands. "Wherever he is, we'll find him—together."

The sincerity of his words and on his face convinced Krystal that he meant what he said. She was tired of trying to be strong and independent all the time. She felt a deep need to have someone to lean on and someone to protect her . . . someone like Drake DeGanahl. "Can we start looking for him right now?" she asked quietly.

Chapter Fourteen

The trip through the cemetery had only depressed Krystal in spite of the fact that they had not found any grave markers with her father's name on them. There were, however, many graves which were distinguished only by two sticks tied with old ropes in the shape of crosses or with a large rock, and it was those nameless graves that made her spirits sink even lower. It was possible that her father's remains rested beneath one of those crude markers and she would never know it. They exited through the tall wood columns of the cemetery entrance and Drake closed the gate behind them.

"Where to now?" Krystal sighed. Virginia City was not that big, and there were only so many places to search. So far they had not turned up any clues to John Colbert's whereabouts.

They had already made a visit to D Street, despite Krystal's vehement protests. She had been humiliated just to be seen in that area, especially since nearly every establishment was a house of ill-repute and provided homes for a good many soiled doves. Drake, it seemed, had lulled down there longer than necessary and on more than one occasion, Krystal had caught him snickering whenever he glanced in her direction. It was hard for her to hide her feelings of disdain and she was offended with everything she saw on D Street. When the red light district turned up no clues, Krystal graced Drake with an I-told-you-so look and insisted that they check at the bank to see if there was a bank account listed in John Colbert's name. But that only proved to be another dead end, and now, luckily, so had the Virginia City Cemetery.

"The assayer's office," he stated with a definite nod of his head.

Krystal brightened up. "Of course. Why didn't I think of that?"

Drake shrugged in a nonchalant manner. "I can't believe I didn't think of it sooner." Krystal gave him a wry smile as she allowed him to wrap his arm possessively around her waist and lead her back to C Street, and quite possibly to their last hope in finding her missing father.

"John Colbert?" the man rubbed his chin thoughtfully. "John Colbert? Sounds familiar, yes it does."

Krystal felt her hopes soar as she pulled the faded photograph from her purse. "This is a picture of him with my mother. It was probably taken sometime between 1874 and 1876." Drake strained to get a glimpse of the couple. Was that old photo what she had been guarding so vehemently throughout the trip?

The man took the photo from her and produced a magnifying glass from beneath the counter. "Well," he said as he studied the man's image through the glass, "I've been here since '71, so if he mined any in this area, I've probably seen him on more than one

201

occasion. But," he handed the picture back to Krystal, "I can't tell anything by this." He leaned back and shouted over his shoulder, "Hey, Malcom, come out here a minute."

Krystal held her breath as she waited for the man called Malcom to appear from the next room. A whiskered man of about sixty years old scurried into the main room of the assayer's office and looked at Drake and Krystal curiously, then turned to the man who had requested his presence.

"Malcom, you ever hear of a man called John Colbert, a miner who was in this area 'bout twenty years ago, maybe longer?"

Malcom leaned against the counter and drew his heavy brows together in thought. "Colbert," he repeated then grew silent with concentration. Krystal was still afraid to breathe while she inwardly prayed that this man would remember something which would aid them in their search. All of a sudden, Malcolm snapped his fingers and gave them a broad smile. "Colbert!" he turned to the other man behind the counter, "Ain't that the crazy red-headed Frenchman who has that useless old claim up on the other side of Sugar Loaf? Been up there fer years, he has."

Krystal gasped. "I hardly think that man would be my father." She turned to Drake, "I don't think we are going to find out anything here."

Malcom shook his head. "I'm real sure that's the man yore lookin' fer. His mine is called, um, somethin' like—"

Krystal shook her head defiantly. "I'm sure you are mista—"

"Sunrise!" Malcom yelled as he smacked the

counter top. "No, that's not it. But it's on that order."

Krystal drew in a deep breath, not sure if her anticipation was dread or excitement. Sunrise? It was just too coincidental. "Krystal Dawn?" she asked tentatively, but almost wishing that she had remained quiet.

The man brought his hand down upon the counter again, and Krystal nearly jumped out of her skin. "By Golly, that's it. Krystal Dawn is the name of that old goat's mine." Malcom shook his head and chuckled as he retreated back to the room he had just come from. "Crazy as a loon, that one," he said before he disappeared through the doorway."

Drake's arm encircling her shoulders snapped Krystal out of her shocked state. John Colbert, a crazy old goat? "He must be mistaken," she muttered as her wide eyes looked to him for reassurance.

Drake only shrugged as he wished that he could give her some sort of reassurance. "I reckon we better take a trip up to Sugar Loaf and see for ourselves."

The journey up the mountain referred to as Sugar Loaf was no more than a blurry haze to Krystal. The vivid image of her father had been shattered by Malcom's description of the crazy red-headed Frenchman who lived up on the side of the mountain. She knew without a doubt that the man would turn out to be someone else, but she could not leave Virginia City until she proved it to herself and to Drake. The image of her beautiful mother passed through her mind. It was unthinkable to try to imagine Rebecca Colbert married to someone who was considered to be crazy as a loon!

Drake had rented a carriage in town, but the road

disappeared to no more than a weather-beaten trail before they had reached the location that the man at the assayer's office had given them of the mine. They were forced to go the remainder of the distance on foot. Krystal's dainty white leather shoes were hardly designed for mountain trekking and by the time they had spotted a cabin perched on the side of the mountain, she was about to admit to defeat.

"I just know this is a waste of time," she repeated determinedly as they climbed the last steep knoll to reach the cabin. But the end of Krystal's reserve faded when she came face to face with a weathered old sign perched at the summit which held the inscription, 'Krystal Dawn Mine, Proprietor: John Colbert.'

She was at a loss for words because her breath seemed to stop short in her chest. But she wasn't sure if the feeling of suffocation she was experiencing was because she was glad to find her father's mine, or if it was because she was wondering if coming to Virginia City had been a terrible mistake. For twenty years she had built the man and the legend bigger than life itself, and now the reality was almost too much for her confused mind to except as it all came crashing down around her. Her eyes traveled around the expanse of desolate countryside of sage and rocks, not even a tree cared to grow up here. It was a barren land, with the shabby crumbling cabin only creating a jutting eyesore on the side of the bleak mountain. . . . This was her legacy.

Drake felt her disappointment as greatly as if it were his own. She had been boasting of her father's wealth since the first day he had met her and he knew that she had believed in her perceptions with all her heart. There was no way she could have been prepared for this terrible letdown. Her gaze met Drake's worried look and she couldn't stop the solitary tear that escaped from one corner of her eye and rolled down her face. He reached out and gently wiped the teardrop away with his fingertip.

"Oh Drake, I've been such a fool. All that talk about my father's wealth — Good Lord, you risked your life for me and this — " she threw her arms up and gestured around at the bleak land, "This is hardly the reward I promised you, is it?"

His look changed as he watched her face. Did she really think he still wanted a reward for bringing her here? If she did, she was a crazy as her father was accused of being. "You're right, you are a fool if you still believe that I want any money from you. Your love is the only reward I ever hope to collect. Why can't you understand that?" He grabbed her by the shoulders and drew her up to him. "Just your love," he repeated hoarsely.

She felt her knees begin to tremble, the feeling working its way through her limps and into her stomach and chest until her whole body was quaking. Another tear followed the trail of its predecessor and dropped precariously upon the delicate lace of her crocheted collar. He was right, she was foolish to keep trying to deny her feelings. Her gloved hand reached up and softly touched his tanned cheek. "If my love is the reward you seek, then you shall be rewarded through all eternity."

A simple 'I love you' would have sufficed, but her fancy choice of words caused his whole body to break out in a rash of goose bumps. A trace of that crooked smile appeared on Drake's face for a fleeting second before he scooped her small form into the tight circle of his embrace and lifted her from the ground while his lips put a lasting brand upon those maverick lips that beckoned to him with such tantalizing promises. When he set her feet back on the ground and they separated, the look that covered her lovely features was full of softness and emotion.

"It's bigger than both of us, darlin'," he whispered. Her eyes, ablaze with golden flames peered up at him from underneath the wide brim of her bonnet. She realized that their thoughts were exactly the same and for a moment, they were both unaware of their surroundings, unaware of anything other than the overpowering love that swathed the future with wild expectations.

When at last, they were forced back to the present, and reminded of the latest obstacle they had to overcome, Krystal's look of despair returned. She drew in a deep breath, "Well, I guess I've come this far, and I can hardly leave here until I meet him, can I?"

Noticing how weary she looked, and sensing how much she dreaded the impending meeting, Drake made a decision. "I'll look around and see if he's anywhere in the vicinity and you stay here and rest."

She opened her mouth to dispute him, but realized that he was right again. Her feet could not handle much more hiking in the shoes she was wearing, and quite frankly, the longer she could delay the meeting, the better. She nodded and permitted Drake to lead her to a chair that stood on the front stoop of the old shack. She pulled a dainty white lace handkerehief from her silk purse and spread it on the seat before she sat down, while Drake managed to suppress a chuckle. He wondered how she would feel if she knew that her face was covered with a layering of dust from their walk up the mountain, and the tears her eyes had deposited a few minutes ago, had left dirty tracks down the side of her face. But, he sighed, a little bit of dirt hardly dimmed her beauty.

He thought of kissing her good-bye, but decided against it. First he would find her father, then he would take care of the unfinished business which had begun with their first breathtaking kiss and had been building to an unavoidable climax ever since. With that thought making him extremely anxious, he rushed off in the direction of the little stream that trickled down the embankment, since he figured that area would be the most logical place to look for the old man. It was on the opposite side of the mountain from the trail they had just came up on, so they wouldn't have seen him if he was somewhere along the creekbed.

Drake had only gone about a quarter of a mile downstream when he got his first glimpse of John Colbert. Walking towards him was a colorful little figure of a man, dressed in suspendered overalls, red long johns and a floppy hat of distinct character. Below the distorted old hat was the brightest mass of red hair Drake had ever seen, and it hung from his chin in the form of a long pointed beard and down to his shoulders from the back of his head. Oblivious to anyone's presence, he was leading an old speckled mule and singing incoherently at the top of his lungs. When the old man spotted the tall cowboy at the top of the ravine, he knew it could only mean one thing—claim jumpers!

Before Drake could utter a word in his own defense the old man had a sawed-off shot gun aimed at his head and was issuing a deadly threat. "That there is about far enough, young fella. One more step and I'll blow your head clean off."

Drake was caught off guard. The man's appearance definitely fit the description that Malcom had given to them and Drake was wondering if the old man was crazy enough to shoot him before he had a chance to explain everything to him. He threw his hands up into the air, far away from his gunbelt and tried to sound calm. "Whoa there, I think you've got the wrong idea."

John Colbert lowered the gun a couple inches and squinted into the glare of the afternoon sun, then drew the shotgun back up to a level position. "I know a claim jumper when I see one, and you look like one of them lowdown varmits to me!"

Drake smiled inspite of his precarious predicament. This old man had no idea how much he sounded like the daughter he had not seen for two decades. Drake raised his hands higher. He had no desire to rile this man if he was as hot-headed as his daughter, and maybe just as crazy, too. However, he knew that he had better do some mighty fast talking. "You're John Colbert, I presume?"

The gun did not waver. "You presume right," the older man's voice carried just a trace of a foreign accent.

"My name is Drake DeGanahl. I've just accompanied your daughter, Krystal Colbert, to Virginia City."

The man's mouth falling open between the droopy mustache, and even shaggier beard was the only indication that he had unerstood Drake's words. The old shotgun remained steadily perched on the man's shoulder, and the silence was heavy as Drake waited for a reply.

"Hells-a-fire! My daughter?" was the only thing that emitted from the old minder as he finally began to lower his weapon. Drake drew in a relieved breath as the other man began to relax slightly.

A crooked grin consumed Drake's face. "Hells-a-fire," Drake repeated in spite of himself, "is a mild way to describe your daughter, Mr. Colbert."

John Colbert began to smile. His baby girl—here! "You've really brought my little girl back to me?"

Drake began to edge down the incline, careful not to make John suspicious of him again. "I've traveled with her from Wyoming, but she came all the way from Boston to see you."

"Boston! So that's were they took off to?" His face suddenly took on a pained expression as his mind made a brief visit with the past. "Is her mother with her?" He did not bother to wait for Drake to answer. "Of course she's not. She hated it out here too much to come back again."

Drake stood only a few yards away from him now, close enough to see the sadness in his brown eyes. It was Krystal's place to tell him about her mother's death, so Drake was relieved that the man seemed satisfied with his own answer. John Colbert raised his gaze and began to observe the other man with a close scrutiny. It was possible that this man was lying to him, but how else would he know about Krystal

209

Dawn? "You brought my daughter here from Wyoming, you say?" Drake nodded. "Well, are you her husband then?"

Drake's composure crumbled slightly. "Husband? Well, no."

"Hells-a-fire! Just who in tarnation are you?"

Drake's first thought was of the descriptive language that the Colberts used . . . Hells-a-fire? Good Lord? There was no question in his mind that John Colbert would get along just fine with his daughter. "I'm—I am her—it's a long story, Mr. Colbert," he finally managed to choke out. How was he supposed to explain what he was to Krystal, when he wasn't even sure himself? She had admitted to their love, but with a woman like Krystal Colbert a man still could not be sure where he stood.

His answer did not satisfy John. "Young fella, I ain't too sure I like the sound of you traveling around unescorted with my daughter? But I'm real anxious to meet my little girl again, so I'm gonna let you off the hook for now. But I want an answer to my question 'fore too long, and it better be the proper one."

Drake nodded again, wondering what the old man might consider proper? All at once, Drake realized that he had nothing to fear. Once John Colbert met his little girl it would be more than obvious to him that Drake's relationship with her could hardly be anything but proper. Drake's tall frame straightened again, he felt very secure that he would not have to face John Colbert's wrath because of Krystal's chastity. "She's waiting up at your cabin."

John continued to give him a skeptical look. He decided to test the other man's knowledge a bit further. "What's she like?"

Drake shrugged. "Why don't you go up see for yourself."

This cowboy had a stubborn streak, John liked that. "I will. But while we're a gettin' there, why don't you tell me something about her. 'Bout how old is she now?"

They began to walk slowly up the mountain. "Twenty, last April." Thank goodness Krystal had told him her age and what month her birthday was in when they had talked on the train yesterday. He understood what old man Colbert was up to now. This third degree was designed to find out if he really was who he claimed to be.

John gave a satisfied nod. He didn't really feel the need to ask anything else. If this young fella knew his daughter's age and birthdate, then he must be authentic. But he still was getting more irritated with each step he took, wondering just why this man had accompanied his daughter to Virginia City when he wasn't her husband. Now he was concerned. Just how had Rebecca raised their girl? "What's she do back there in Boston?"

"She's a schoolteacher, Mr. Colbert." He wanted to add that she was every inch a prim and prudish schoolteacher also. But that would hardly be the appropriate thing to say to her father, so he stopped himself.

Again, John smiled. A real respectable profession — schoolteaching. So what in tarnation was she doing with this gun-toting cowboy? He tugged on Abigale's rope, the old white-and-gray mule always lagged behind on the last steep embankment up to the cabin.

John was still mulling over the fact that she was in the company of a man who could not even explain who he was, only that he had traveled with her from Wyoming. He had not seen his little girl for twenty years, and already he was wondering if he was going to have to protect her honor.

His thoughts sifted back in time again as he said, "Bet she's real pretty if she looks anything like her mother."

Drake reached the top of the ridge a few steps ahead of the old man. He began to grin wistfully as his eyes ascended and caught sight of her on the front stoop of the cabin. She was still sitting on the old chair in a very prim pose . . . her tiny feet were crossed at the ankles, and the lace parasol was perched daintily over her shoulder as it shielded her delicate complexion from the harsh sun. She was breathtaking, by far the most beautiful sight Drake had ever looked upon. Against the drabness of the falling-down cabin and the barren mountain, her beauty was even more outstanding. Pretty, John Colbert had asked? Damn! That didn't even begin to describe the way she looked. "Why don't you decide for yourself, Mr. Colbert?"

John drew in a deep breath as he topped the last of the slope. His eyes immediately followed Drake's gaze, stopping to rest upon the vision of loveliness sitting in front of his home. *"Magnifique!"* he muttered in his native tongue.

Chapter Fifteen

The sound of the men approaching the cabin caused Krystal's head to jerk around with a start. She had been lost deep in thought, thinking about her parents and Drake, but mostly the latter. She rose slowly from the chair, her eyes glued to the short wiry man who stood beside Drake at the edge of the slope. Good Lord, it was worse than she had expected. Surely this hairy old character was not John Colbert? In a frantic moment she looked at Drake. Her expression almost begged him to tell her that this was not her father. But Drake only smiled that crooked smile that she was becoming so accustomed to seeing and gestured towards the other man with his hand. "Krystal, this is your father."

All her fantasies of this man were shattered with Drake's confirmation of his identity. Oh, how could her mother do this to her? Her shock was too great for her to do anything other than stand rooted to the spot with her eyes wide and her mouth hanging open. John was too startled to move, also. He had always believed there would never be another woman who could equal Rebecca's rare beauty. But the young woman who stood before him now proved to him that he had been wrong. A wide grin separated the long scraggily hairs surrounding his mouth as he slowly approached the girl. There was no doubt in his mind who she was. . . . She had every one of Rebecca's exquisite features, along with the unique golden-red combination of his and Rebecca's hair colors. Even the hue of her eyes was a mixture of his cocoa brown irises and Rebecca's jewel-colored topaz ones.

John was in awe of her, especially since he had long ago given up any hopes of ever seeing her again. He wanted to hug her, or at least touch her, just to prove to himself that she was real. But he could tell by the disbelieving look on her face that she was not sure what to think of him. He didn't blame her if she was disgusted with him, either. After Rebecca had taken Krystal and the money, he had given up on himself, and on life in general. It was no wonder that his daughter was appalled at the sight of the man she was forced to claim as her father.

During their careful observation of one another, they had inched forward and now were only a few feet apart. Krystal opened her mouth as though she wanted to say something, but words eluded her. She kept trying to imagine this man with her mother, but she couldn't draw anything but a blank. She thought of the picture she had found of the two of them together. Twenty years had passed and people changed a lot in that length of time. He must have been a man that Rebecca had found attractive all those years ago.

Krystal began to grow furious with herself for the shallow thoughts which were passing through her mind. She was judging him by his looks and forgetting that there was a person with feelings hidden beneath that mass of red hair. This man was her father . . . the man she had believed to be dead for all these years. Her father! Nothing else mattered in that moment of realization as she threw herself up against him and wrapped her arms around his neck. "Hello father," was all she managed to whisper as she continued to hold on to him as tight as possible.

For a minute John was too surprised to move. Her sudden gesture was the last thing he had expected. His shocked gaze flew to Drake, then traveled back down to the Krystal as his stiff arms finally began to rise so that he could return her hug. It was too good to be true, Krystal Dawn had finally returned home!

When they pulled apart, not a dry eye remained. Even Drake found the reunion between the father and daughter to be quite an emotional scene to witness. He had been worried that she might still deny that this man was her father when she actually met him. But Drake reminded himself that beneath that prim and haughty exterior was a very sensitive woman, and that side of her had just shown through vividly. He sighed with relief and with a touch of pensive reflection as he thought of his own father. Franklin De-Ganahl had been the most prominent figure in his life when he was a child, and Krystal had been deprived of her father's influence while she was growing up. He began to wonder what terrible deed John Colbert must have done to make Krystal's mother lie about his supposed death? His questions would soon be answered, because both Krystal and John began to talk rapidly as soon as they backed away from each other.

"I thought you were dead all this time. Mother told me you had been killed in a mining accident when I was an infant."

215

John smiled wistfully while his teary eyes continued to study her closely. "Well, in a way, I reckon you could say that I did die back then, 'cause when your mama left me and took you with her, my whole life ended."

Krystal raised her hands to touch the sides of his whiskered, weather-beaten old face. Had this pitiful little man been here all this time, pining over his wife and daughter? Krystal thought of the extravagant and carefree life her mother had led and the comparison was almost too much for her to bear. John Colbert was definitely not the prominent business man she had expected, but that no longer mattered. Krystal's heart went out to this man along with the love that she had savored for so long.

"I only found out a couple of weeks ago that you were still alive or I would have come a long time ago."

John was too choked up to speak for a moment. He couldn't make his mind accept the fact that she was really here. The only thing that could make this meeting more perfect was if Rebecca had come back here with her. His eyes scanned the area behind her, although he knew it was a wasted gesture. Still he had to ask the question. "Your mother? Did she come too, cherí?"

Krystal's face paled. It was so obvious that he still loved Rebecca, in spite of everything that had happened between them. She looked away while her mind searched in desperation for the right words. "My mother—"

John didn't bother to let her finish. "Oh, I know what you're goin' say and I ain't sure if I can bear to hear it." He began to tremble visibly and almost looked like he might pass out. Krystal reached out to him, but Drake was already at his side and the two of them supported the older man as they walked him over to the chair that Krystal had just vacated. Krystal had never observed such a heartwrenching moment. How could her mother have treated him in such a cold and cruel manner?

"My mother is dead," Krystal said angrily as she knelt down beside him. "But she stole money from your mine and she took me away from you. Doesn't that make you resent her?"

"Oh no! I could never hate Rebecca." He shook his head and gave her a sad smile. "I loved Rebecca with all my heart, nothing will ever change that. I was so lucky to have her for the short time that I did and I understand why she left. She only wanted a better life for you. How could I resent that?"

Oh this dear, sweet, old man. Krystal suddenly felt like a wicked, unforgiving shrew. But she couldn't help the rage that was pulsating through her veins right now. It was just so unfair that she had grown up without the benefit of knowing what a wonderful man her father was.

"I'm sorry, but I just can't stand the thought of what she did to you." Her eyes suddenly filled with angry tears at the idea of him wasting away up here on this godforsaken mountain, while her mother had been living a life of luxury all this time.

He patted her shoulder softly. "She wasn't to blame, chéri. What woman would want to live in a place like this?" He waved his gnarled hand out towards the desolate countryside. "Especially a woman like Rebecca."

Drake moved closer, more curious than ever to learn about Rebecca Colbert and everything else that concerned Krystal. Her face was a mask of hurt and confusion. Drake wished he could do something to

217

protect her from anymore pain. Just from the bits and pieces of her life that he had already learned of, it seemed like she had more than her share lately. But he was only an outsider here, there was nothing he could say or do to help her, so he remained quietly in the background.

"She wrote in her letter that you were probably the wealthiest man in Virginia City, and that the money she stole from you was nothing compared to the amount of gold in your mine. But—" Krystal's misted gaze traveled past her father, taking in the old cabin and crumbling outbuildings. All at once, she understood. "Good Lord—she stole the only money you ever made from this mine, didn't she?"

John tilted his head to the side, and the long red strands of hair tumbled over his shoulder. "Letter? What letter?"

Krystal realized that she had not explained anything to him yet. So far it was all too confusing and the extent of her mother's deceit was more than a little unsettling for her to comprehend. She could only imagine how confused her father must be.

There was no doubt in her mind that her mother had stolen every cent John had ever made from this mine even if he didn't want to admit to it. Why else would he be living like a pauper up here in the middle of nowhere? She took a deep breath and rested her eyes on his face. Beneath the wild abundance of red growth was such a quiet gentleness. Krystal looked beyond the unruly hair and floppy hat and no longer noticed the soiled old rags that covered his thin form. There was so much expression in those pale brown eyes that she suddenly began to understand how he had won her mother's heart even if he had not been able to retain it.

218

"Mother was killed in a tragic accident a couple weeks ago. But she had written a letter to me sometime before her death and enclosed it with her will. It was in the contents of that letter that I learned that you were still alive, and also how she had stolen money from your mine so she could run off to Boston after my birth."

"Accident?" John repeated in barely a whisper. His expression was drawn and sad as his eyes looked down at the ground in an effort to hide the tears which were teetering in their corners.

Krystal wondered if he had heard anything else she had said to him. It was apparent that he did not care about the money Rebecca had stolen from him, or the way she had run off with his infant daughter. It seemed that he had justified everything she had ever done to him in order to keep her memory untarnished in his mind. Krystal felt terrible for him and for herself.

Despite the fact that her mother was dead, and wasn't even able to defend herself, Krystal felt a growing contempt for the woman, and that made her feel even more horrible. Rebecca had destroyed her father's whole life and it just wasn't fair. An even worse thought began to plague her. . . . What if her mother had only married him because of his mine and the gold she might have suspected was in it? Was she capable of something so conniving? That was something she intended to find out. There were a lot of questions Krystal had to ask her father, but it didn't have to be right now, she decided. First, she would try to understand the depth of the love her father obviously had harbored for her mother through the past two decades, then maybe she would not despise her so much, either.

"No one knows exactly how she died. It looked as though she might have tripped and fell into the river. Maybe she was knocked unconscious, because she was a very good swimmer." Krystal began to wonder about the Pinkerton investigation, and what else they might have come up with by now? Perhaps she could have waited to see what the detectives learned about her mother's death, because as she repeated the explanation it suddenly sounded so unlikely—especially in the sudden light of all of Rebecca's other discrepancies. Krystal remembered the brooch again. She just had to know if it had been in the box with the photograph for a reason.

"Did you ever give mother any expensive jewelry?"

John remained unmoving, still staring down at the ground. He couldn't imagine that Rebecca was gone forever. It had always been his greatest wish that someday he would see her again. His sorrowful gaze returned to the girl before him. She was the only tangible proof that a woman like Rebecca had really loved him, even if only for such a brief time. He sighed deeply and shook his head in response to her question. "The only jewelry I ever had a chance to buy for Rebecca was a cheap wedding ring. I always thought that I would buy her a real diamond someday, but . . ." his voice trailed off as he was consumed in memories once more.

He studied his daughter's sorrowful face for a few minutes. Over the years, there had been many times when he wondered if his brief time with Rebecca had just been a dream or only a figment of his vivid imagination. It didn't seem possible that a woman as talented and as beautiful as Rebecca could have been his wife, but Krystal Dawn's return was enough to remind him that he was not as crazy as everyone said he was.

He began to smile through the heavy growth of whiskers. "Hells-a-fire! I can't believe you're really here. I want to know everything about you. I already know you're a schoolteacher back there in Boston," John's eyes shifted over to Drake, taking on a distrustful glint once more as he pointed an accusing finger at him. "And I know that he ain't your husband. So just who in tarnation is he?"

Krystal's mouth gaped open as she also turned to stare at Drake. She immediately forgot about the brooch and the fact that it was hidden in her mother's drawer for some reason other than as something sentimental. The last thing she had expected from her father was to be reprimanded because of Drake De-Ganahl. "Him?" she said in a shocked tone of voice which sounded as though she was surprised that Drake was still present.

Drake retaliated with a placid smile, wondering how she intended to explain their relationship to her father since he certainly had not done a very good job of it when John Colbert had asked the very same question of him earlier. Krystal looked away from him, growing annoyed with Drake's patronizing attitude.

"Oh, him," she laughed, forcing her voice into a casual tone. "He's well . . . he is . . . it's a long story."

Drake covered his urge to chuckle with a loud clearing of his throat. John's eyes narrowed with an instant parental disapproval as he glared up at Drake. "That there is the exact same words he used. Well, I got plenty of time and I ain't goin' nowhere 'til I hear this long story." He leaned back in the chair and crossed his arms over his chest in a defiant gesture as his eyes flashed back and forth between his daughter

221

and this cowboy, whoever he was!

Krystal drew in a deep breath. All she could do was to start at the beginning. She made the mistake of glancing in Drake's direction again. The evil smile which was curved across his face made her all the more flustered. "Well, you see, in the beginning, when I first left Boston, I was alone," she said breathlessly.

Drake tried desperately to suppress a chuckle. Her story sounded like something from biblical times . . . In the beginning? She ignored the rude noises Drake emitted, refusing to look at him again. "Then we—I mean—the train stopped in Rawlins, Wyoming, and he, Drake, boarded the train. But," she said with a snooty tilt of her chin, "I didn't really notice him until much later."

Drake coughed and Krystal's voice quivered slightly as she began to talk faster. "In fact, we probably would have never even met if his brother had not held up the train." Her voice crescendoed slightly, but John remained unmoving. He was not going to make any judgments until he heard the entire story. "And Drake saved me when I was taken captive by the band of outlaws."

John's scowl deepened. "Why in tarnation didn't you just thank him for saving you and leave it at that? Did you have to bring him to Nevada with you? Hells-a-fire! That ain't even proper!"

Krystal gasped. "Oh, but we've never—" she glanced up at Drake with a look of distress, but the smirk that covered his face was no help at all. He only made her stumble over her words all the more. "I mean—he just—well, he only accompanied me here because he knew his brother had followed me to the train station that morning after we had spent the

222

night at his house in Green River." Oh why did that sound so horrible? "What I mean is—"

John rose partially from the chair. "You spent the night with him and his brother at a house in Green River?"

Krystal sprang to her feet. "No, not Devon, just Drake." Oh Lord, she was only digging a deeper hole for herself. She quickly added, "And Drake's mother was also there, of course." John's quizzical look deepened while Krystal gently pushed him back down into the chair. She dropped her hands to her side in exasperation. "I told you it was a long story and I'm afraid I'm not doing a very good job of explaining it all to you." She swung around and glared at Drake. "You might help me to explain it to him, you know?"

"I'd be happy to, darlin'," he replied with a narrowing of one eye as he sauntered up closer to her in an intimate manner. The dark flush in her face made him smile twice as wickedly while he pressed even closer to her. "Should I start in the beginning, too? Right from the part where you sat in my lap on the train, or would you prefer that I tell him about the wonderful job you did of taking care of me all those days and nights out on the lonely prairie. Or maybe I should tell him about the other night when—"

"Oh, how dare you!" she screamed, and emphasized her fury with a forceful shove against his chest. "You are the most despicable man I have ever met! Now, you can tell him the truth, right this minute!"

Drake laughed and staggered back when she pushed him, but his humor began to sober rapidly when John's sawed-off shotgun was eyeballing him once again. Drake threw his hands up in the air and tried to sound serious. "I'm sorry, Mr. Colbert, but you must realize by now that your daughter is most

223

respectable, and I," he patted his chest in a patronizing manner, "respect her completely. Our relationship has been extremely proper." As he said the last two words with intensity, he glanced at Krystal. The deadly threats issuing forth from her golden-brown eyes made him thankful that she was not the one holding the shotgun.

"We're all gonna sit right down here," John stated forcibly, still waving the gun in the air. "And I want to know exactly what has been going on between you two. My little girl just came home after being gone for twenty years, and if she's been accosted in any form while she was tryin' to come back to me, there's gonna be hell to pay!"

Drake didn't doubt John's threat for one second as he realized how foolish he was being to test this old man. Even though Krystal had never met this man before today, she had obviously inherited every one of her father's ideas on honor and esteem. Who was Drake to dispute the two of them, or especially John's unfriendly-looking weapon?

"I apologize again, Mr. Colbert. I've been making light of this whole situation, and you're right . . . we should all sit down and talk rationally." He looked at Krystal and grinned sheepishly. "And I apologize to you, too."

Krystal continued to glare at him for a few seconds longer. She was so mad at him that she wanted to shove him off the side of this mountain. But when he smiled at her like he was at this moment, how could she stay mad at him? "Do you swear to tell him the whole truth?" she asked while she continued to eye him with a distrustful look.

He nodded and held up his left hand as he placed his right hand over his heart. "And nothing but the

224

whole truth." His smile made his deep green eyes twinkle even brighter as he began to sense her weakening composure.

She shook her finger in front of his face and said, "If you say anything out of line again, I will have my father fill your pants with lead! Is that understood?" She looked back at John and gave her head a satisfied nod as their eyes met.

John returned her smile, he was confident that his daughter would not lie to him. Drake DeGanahl on the other hand had better watch his step from now on or else John planned to fulfill his little girl's threat and this cowboy's britches would be smokin' lead all the way down Sugar Loaf!

Chapter Sixteen

John puffed vigorously on the skinny brown cigar that Drake had offered him while he poured another round of tequila for the two of them. He leaned back against the rail of the front stoop and contemplated everything they had just told him about the events of the past week. It was not the most feasible story he had ever heard, but John decided that it was very probable that a man like Drake DeGanahl would come to the aid of a woman he had never met, especially if the woman was as lovely as Krystal. Being relatively new at fatherhood though, John felt a dire need to be reassured that his little girl had not been involved in any compromising situations along the way. But after listening to Krystal and Drake talk about all their adventures, John had come to two conclusions: there was absolutely no way that a man with any conscience could take advantage of his daughter unless she wanted him to, and it was obvious that in the short time she and Drake had been together, they had fallen in love with each other.

The first observation made him proud of the way his little girl had turned out, the discovery that she was in love with this cowboy though, worried him. He had just met Krystal again, and because of Drake, it looked as though he would never have a chance to have her all to himself, even for a little while. Although it had been a very long time since John had dealt with a woman, he was wise enough to know that if he ever attempted to keep them apart, he would lose Krystal for good. She was undoubtedly a Colbert—stubborn and hot-headed. Besides, John was beginning to like Drake DeGanahl, and if he had to turn his little girl over to another man, this young fella might do.

"Please come back to town with us tonight, father? We'll get you a room at the hotel where we're staying."

John frowned while he gave his head a negative shake. He only went to town twice a year and that was often enough for him. "I don't take to crowds and they ain't real fond of me either."

Krystal decided to give up. He had asked them to spend the night up here on the mountain with him, but after glancing at the primitive cabin and not even caring to look at the interior, Krystal had decided that she preferred the comforts of the hotel. They would just have to be content with visiting him during the daylight hours. Anyway, she needed some time to herself. There were a lot of things to think about now that she hadn't planned on. If her meeting with her father had gone as she had originally hoped it would, she had planned to ask him to return to Boston with her. But now that she had met him and knew how dedicated he was to this mountain and his hopes of finding another vein of gold, she knew that she would never be able to convince him to go back East. He was an old man who had lived his whole life on the few bittersweet memories that his young wife had left him with twenty years ago, and with the elusive dream that someday he would see Rebecca and Krystal again.

By the time they had said farewell to John, Krystal had managed to make herself sick trying to come up with some sort of solution to her dilemma. Every time she glanced at her father, her heart broke and she told herself that she would never leave him alone again, even if it meant giving up the life she had back in Boston. They were bound to need schoolteachers in Nevada. But could she survive this kind of life? The very idea of actually staying here made her a little more sympathic towards her mother's plight. But that still did not justify Rebecca's actions and the more Krystal pondered it, the more she felt a need to make the past up to her father. Just when she had herself convinced that she was going to remain in Virginia City, she would look at Drake. And he would glance back at her with his twinkling gaze which was always accompanied by that crooked smile, and she would grow weak with those strange sensations once more.

Drake would not want to stay in Nevada, and Krystal knew it would not be fair to ask him to stay. He had once been a dedicated lawman, and she was sure that one day he would want to return to Wyoming and to his chosen profession. Virginia City was a dying frontier, practically a ghost town, and it had nothing to offer a man like Drake DeGanahl. Krystal had never been so confused. There just had to be a way to work everything out, because she did not want to live without Drake or her father now that they had both entered into her life.

The sun fell behind the mountains early in this part

of the country, so Krystal and Drake were forced to leave after a couple of hours of visiting with John. But even in that short time, they had learned a great deal about one another. He was a gifted storyteller and he told them one story after another about his adventures as a miner. Krystal felt like she had known this little man all of her life, and she was grateful that she had been given this chance to get acquainted with him.

"Everything went well, didn't it?" Drake asked as they started down the trail. He had not been too sure in the beginning since they had managed to start off on the wrong foot, but when John had broke out his treasured bottle of gold labeled tequila, Drake knew he was going to get along fine with the Frenchman.

"I suppose." She had come to a decision and it was shattering. His arm encircled her waist as he helped her walk down the rocky trail, but all she could concentrate on was the fire which was raging in the pit of her stomach. How would she ever make him understand that she was not going to see him again after tonight, and yet how could she stand to let him go? But if she didn't make a clean break away from him immediately, she knew she would never be able to part with him. With every passing second and with every breath she took, she fell deeper in love with him. It was almost too late already.

When they reached the spot where they had abandoned the team of horses and buggy, Drake hitched up the horses while Krystal stared at the magenta hues of the setting sun on the distant horizon, and fought back the irresistable urge to break into tears. She had always been so strong in the past and she had to be extra strong when she told Drake about her decision. If she didn't sound definite, he might try to coax her into leaving here with him, and she could not allow him to do that.

Drake eyed her quizzically while he lifted her into the carriage. She had hardly said a word all the way down the mountain, and that was certainly not normal for her. He had thought things went extremely well with her father this afternoon, but now he wasn't so sure. She seemed depressed and foreboding all of a sudden, and he began to wonder if she was truly disappointed that her father was not the important and wealthy man whom she had hoped he would be.

"You're unusually quiet this evening, darlin'," he commented casually as the buggy jerked forward.

"I can't see you anymore," she blurted out while closing her eyes tightly to hold back the sudden rush of tears. She did not want to see the look on his face, but she could not help herself. Expecting to see an angry or hurt expression, she was aggravated to notice that he was ignoring her.

Drake flicked the reins again as the horses precariously dodged the treacherous rocks in the narrow trail. "It sure gets dark early in these parts. Maybe we should have left sooner."

"Drake? Did you hear what just I said? After tonight, I don't want to see you again. I have not been thinking clearly the past few days with all the crazy things that have been going on, but now I realize how impulsive I've been about—about my feelings for you." She swallowed hard, but the lump in her throat did not go away, and neither did the searing pain in her heart. Why didn't he say something? She began to get angry. That was good, she decided. If she was mad enough, it might take saying goodbye a little bit easier.

"I only pretended to care about you so that you would help me to find my father." Oh, that made her

230

sound awful. He would surely hate her for saying something so horrible, but it was the only way. Good Lord, if he would just answer her!

Drake's jaw muscles drew rigid, but he knew better than to say anything to her right now. It was obvious that she had decided her loyalty to her father could not be combined with her love for him. Did she really believe that he would ask her to choose? He had known right from the beginning how important her father was to her, he wouldn't ask her to leave him when she had just been reunited with him.

Drake was too furious with her to even give her the courtesy of an answer. Damn this woman! He should have made love to her days ago. As long as she was hung up with all her chaste virtues, she was the most impossible female he had ever met. But there was one way to cure her, and if he could just manage to remain calm until they reached town, he was confident he would be able to show her that the only place she belonged was in his arms. And it wouldn't mean she would have to give up her father, but Drake was not going to give her up either.

Nothing made Krystal more furious than to have someone purposely ignore her and that was exactly what he was doing. "Doesn't it bother you that I lied to you about my love for you? Or that I was only using you for my own selfish purposes? Good Lord, Drake! Aren't you going to say anything?"

"Nope, damn it!"

Aha, so she was getting to him. Well, she wanted him out of her life, but not that easily. "I thought you loved me, but I guess you were lying about that—"

The buggy jerked to a halt and his lips crushed against her mouth so abruptly that for a moment Krystal was not sure what was happening. This kiss was not meant to be a tender gesture, only a crude way to silence her, and she realized it immediately. If he thought he could shut her up with a mere kiss every time he chose to do so, well, he had another thing coming. Krystal threw her hands up to his head and grabbed hold of both his ears and twisted with every ounce of her strength. It was a sure-fire method that always worked when one of her students got out of line, and as far as Krystal was concerned, Drake was acting just like some juvenile who deserved to be reprimanded for his vile behavior.

It was Drake's turn to be caught off guard. What in the devil was she trying to do? He pulled away from her and glared down into her flashing eyes as she continued to crank on his ears. Something in his dark gaze told Krystal that she was treading on dangerous ground. She quickly turned loose of him and scooted as far away from him as possible. "Well, I never!" she huffed in her most indignant tone of voice.

He tipped his hat by the wide brim and narrowed one eye, then grabbed up the reins again and gave them a sharp flick with his wrists. "That, darlin', is quite obvious. Maybe if you had indulged in some of the sweeter pleasures of life, you wouldn't be such a snobbish prude. But don't worry, I intend to take care of that problem as soon as we reach the hotel."

"Oh, don't you wish?" She drew in a short breath and rushed on in a degrading tone. "If you're insinuating what I think you are, well, you would be doing it against my will and that is called rape, Drake DeGanahl. If I don't kill you myself, I'll see that you hang from the highest tree." She glanced around at the barren land and added with disdain, "If there was a stupid tree to hang you from, that is!"

Drake began to wonder if he would be able to keep

his temper under control until they made it back to town. Why was he putting himself through this kind of aggravation? Was love supposed to be sheer hell? Hells-a-fire! he repeated in his mind as he thought about John Colbert. Maybe the old man had come up with that expression while he had been married to Krystal's mother. Drake could certainly understand how that saying would be appropriate if Rebecca Colbert had been anything like her stubborn daughter. Drake gave the reins another hard flick. He was not going to give in to Miss Colbert that easily. He loved this hellcat for some mysterious reason, and he knew she loved him, too. And it was high time that she started learning what it meant to be Drake De-Ganahl's woman!

The remainder of the trip was tense and silent, but not for the reasons it should have been. Krystal felt like her pulse was going to explode and she had broke out in a cold sweat just from the thought of Drake forcing himself on her. She kept telling herself that she would kill him if he even came near her, but the visions that were consuming her wanton mind at this moment did not match that threat at all, though they were just as deadly . . . to her honor and pride anyway. Good Lord, she was almost wishing that he would force himself on her, then she wouldn't have to blame herself for the loss of her respectability.

She shook her head and closed her eyes in a vain attempt to clear her sordid mind. She was disgusted with herself as her brain continued to draw the vivid pictures of the two of them locked in an enraptured embrace. She could not believe the path that her mind — and her body — had taken since she had met this infuriating man. Well, he had another surprise coming if he thought he was going to make her another notch in his headboard, she told herself one more time.

The carriage slammed to a halt in front of the International Hotel, making Krystal's heart leap up to her throat. She blinked and looked around. She hadn't even realized they were back in town. She had been too wrapped up with the prospects of his tantilizing threats. It was difficult to even breathe in a normal manner. Was her face as flushed as it felt?

"I'll let you out here, then I'll take this rig back to the livery." Drake did not look at her while he spoke, and since he was not feeling very much like a gentleman right now, he did not offer to help her down from the coach.

"Well fine!" Krystal said as swung herself down from the seat and landed promptly on her rear end in the dirt. A horrified gasp escaped from her mouth as she quickly glanced around to see if anyone had noticed. Oh, the humiliation!

"Are you hurt?" Drake questioned as he leaned over to the side and looked down at her from the seat of the buggy. His expression, which was a mixture of mirth and concern, rapidly turned into a crooked smirk when she turned her reddened face up to glare at him and he realized that the only thing she had injured was her over-expanded ego.

"Hurt! Oh, how dare you even bother to ask? If you were any sort of a gentleman, you would not have allowed this to happen in the first place." She rose up from the ground and tossed her head back as though she had planned her clumsy retreat from the buggy with exact precision. "This is just one more thing that I can add to the list of things I already owe you, Mr. DeGanahl." She narrowed her eyes and added, "And I always repay my debts." She readjusted her hat, then swung around and stomped into the hotel, her rage making her blind to the curious stares of the gathering crowd who had been observing her performance with great interest.

Drake laughed inspite of himself. The sight of her entering the hotel with a large smudge of dirt across the back of her expensive Paris dress outlining every line of her ripe form was extremely humorous when combined with her haughty attitude. His humor began to fade though, when he contemplated her last remark. Being paid back for all the wrongs she thought he had done to her could prove to be drastic measures coming from a woman like Krystal Colbert. Maybe, when he returned to the hotel, he should try to make amends.

Krystal flung her hat across her room with a violent toss. And the minute she stepped out of her soiled gown, she threw it on the floor, too, then stomped on it in an irrational moment of rage. Oh, that infuriating man! Somehow she would pay him back for all his interference in her life before it continued to get worse than it already was. She could not think of anything without his aggravating face pushing its way into her mind, and his image was always accompanied by the remembrance of his burning touch. By then it was useless to try to concentrate on anything else, because the lustful yearnings would consume her without mercy.

Krystal pulled out a blue satin robe from the closet and wrapped it around herself, then flopped down cross-legged on the bed. She had to face the facts . . . she was obsessed with Drake DeGanahl and nothing was going to change that. If he did leave her because of the stupid things she had said to him this evening, she would probably go in search of him. But they could not continue the way they were going much longer, or else they would both go insane. The only consolation, insignificant as it might be, was that Krystal was certain he was suffering just as much as she was.

A knock on her door was nearly Krystal's undoing. She sprang from the bed and made a quick lap around the room before she realized how utterly ridiculous she was acting. Of course, it was Drake, and he probably had come to apologize for his obnoxious behavior once again.

"Who is it?" she asked innocently as she leaned against the door in a fevered panic.

"Who were you expecting, darlin'?"

Oh, why did he always have to be so snide? "What do you want?"

"For starters, how about letting me in?"

"Ha!" she huffed with an unmistakable tone of contempt. "After you threatened to abuse my body? I hardly think so."

Drake slumped against the door in an irritated gesture. Damn, she had no idea how close she was to pushing him over the edge. "Krystal!" he said though clenched teeth, "I'm going to count to three. If you have not opened this door, I'm going to break it down."

Oh Lord, he was just crazy enough to do it. It would serve him right if she didn't open the door. The hotel officials would not waste any time in hauling him out of here if he attempted to break into her room. But that was the last thing she wanted.

"One — two — thr —" the door flying open stopped his words short. The grin of victory that curved up his lips and made his eyes flash with shimmering bolts of green lights was too much for Krystal. She gave the door a vicious shove, slamming it back in his face. But he effortlessly pushed it back open before she could bolt the lock. With one angry stride, he stepped into the room and shut the door behind him. His smile from a second ago was now replaced by a dark scowl. Krystal did not back down as she stood her ground and stared up at his towering form with her own defiant look of fury.

He had come here to ask her to forgive him for all his rude actions. In the back of his mind was even the vague idea of asking her to become engaged to him. He knew she would like the idea of a proper arrangement between them. But damn it! Here she stood with her luscious curves covered only by a flimsy robe, and it was a satin one no less. And to make matters worse, it was gaping open in front to an indecent plunge between her perfectly rounded breasts. . . .Breasts with taut peaks pressing against the thin material as they rose and fell in rapid succession with her enraged breathing. Drake reminded himself of the self-control he had always prided himself on possessing. But it had just disintegrated into thin air with the tempting picture she presented to him, even though she had no idea how inviting she looked right now. Drake knew that what he was about to do would probably turn whatever feelings she had for him into raging hate, but he was only a mortal man, and she was too beautiful to resist.

Krystal's breathing grew heavier, but it was no longer from her acute anger. He was only standing there, yet he was doing it to her again. He was too close, too dangerous, and this feeling was too powerful

237

to fight against any longer. She had never wanted anything or anyone as much as she wanted this man . . . at this moment. Forgotten were all the hard-driven lessons of respectability and honor that she had chosen to live her life with before she had met this man. She was in too deep now, and she was not strong enough to be immuned to his touch, his kiss, or to anything else that involved Drake DeGanahl.

They had talked about destiny having a hand in their meeting once before, and now Krystal was aware of the depth of that settlement. It had been fate which had put them both on that train. It was destined for her to be kidnapped by those desperados, and it had always been in the stars for them to be led to this glorious moment of unrestrained longings. Tomorrow might bring yet another turn of fate, maybe it would even lead them on separate paths, but for tonight nothing could interfere with this predetermined course of events that neither of them could change.

Drake drew her into his arms, and the intense heat of their bodies penetrated through the barrier of their clothing. In this moment nothing existed beyond the aura of their essence when they touched one another without physical or mental resistance.

"Make love to me, Drake," Krystal whispered softly. Her arms wrapped around his neck as he gently gathered her small form up into his strong arms and carried her to the soft bed which held the sweet dreams of awakening passion.

Chapter Seventeen

Krystal had not bothered to light any of the lamps in the room when she had entered earlier. She had only lit the fat candle that had been on the table beside the bed, and as Drake placed her upon the dark red brocaded bedcovering, the reflection from the candle flickered across the bed, making her blue satin robe shimmer in shades of lavender. Even her pale skin took on a light sheen of purple and her soft golden-red curls fanned out across the bed in an emblazoned array of pink hues. Her eyes were closed and those tempting lips were parted just a fraction

To Drake, she looked like a goddess. He was almost afraid to touch her, if this was a dream, he did not want to wake up. If it was real, he was sure she would soon regain her senses and scream for help. He wondered if this was the revenge she had threatened him with, but he decided he would take his chances.

Krystal opened her eyes and looked up at him. His expression was tender, yet apprehensive. She understood why he was hesitant. She had allowed him to caress her before, but she had always cut him off abruptly. Couldn't he see that it was no longer in her power to stop him? Her body ached with such an

239

incredible yearning that it was impossible to deny it, or him. For a minute neither of them moved, they just drank in the sight of one another in the flickering shadows of the candle light. Her arms raised up towards him, an invitation for him to come to her.

Drake placed his hands in hers and pulled her up to a sitting position. The satin robe hung loosely around her silken shoulders and he pushed it back until it slid down her arms into a soft heap around her waist. She gasped, and closed her eyes again as her arms instinctively drew up to cover her exposed form. Drake's hand cupped her chin and raised her face upward.

"Don't ever be ashamed to let me see your body, darlin'. It's a vision of beauty that can never be equalled," he said quietly.

Krystal's eyes opened again as he continued to hold her face in his large hand. Through the dancing flames their enchanted gazes locked. His tender words caused a new surge of warmth to spread throughout her body. She realized that she wanted his eyes to caress her like they were doing at this moment. She yearned for his arms to hold her, and for him to teach her everything about love that she knew he was capable of showing her. Her tawny eyes glistened with the strange excitement which stirred within her. Her arms dropped down to her sides as she turned her head and lightly kissed the inside of his palm. A tingling sensation bolted down Drake's spine. Her kiss had been such a simple gesture, but it had completely captivated him.

His limbs suddenly grew too shaky to support his weight, so he released his grip from her chin, and slid down to his knees beside the bed. As his lips scorched a trail across her throat and down through the soft crevice between her breasts, the wide brim of his dark brown cowboy hat tapped lightly against her bare shoulder and was knocked from the back of his head. It landed, noiselessly upon the carpeted floor in much the same manner that his little derby had tumbled onto the dirt the first time they had kissed.

His mouth grew eager as it encircled the hard nucleus of one rising mound while his tongue flicked across the protruding kernel, making it enlarge to its full potential. Krystal's fingers knitted into the tousled curls of his thick brown hair, as a small moan escaped from her mouth. She had never known such a supreme pleasure, and this was only the beginning.

His tongue flitted to the other swollen knoll and taunted it into its full blooming glory, also. Krystal's whole being felt as though it was consumed in a raging fire. She had to have more, she had to learn all that there was to know about this exquisite ritual, and about this man whom she loved more with every frantic beat of her heart.

Drake pulled away from her and drew in a ragged breath. She was the most beautiful creature he had ever seen, and he found it hard to believe that she was going to belong to him in every way possible. He wanted to savor every second and he wished he could make this night last forever. As he rose to his feet once again, he pulled her back up with him. The bothersome robe became only a memory as it slid the rest of the way from her trembling body and surrounded her feet with soft folds of blue satin. Standing here before him, without the security of her clothes, she had never felt so vunerable. Deep down, somewhere in the darkest recesses of her mind, her conscience was wrestling with her heart, shouting out to her how wrong this was. But it was a useless battle, because her body was possessed by this man, and right now, she would do anything he desired of her.

Her tender skin rubbed against the rough fabric of

his shirt and pants, while the cold brass buckle of his gunbelt pressed between her ribcage. In his boots, he easily measured six feet in height. Without shoes, Krystal barely cleared five feet, and next to her tiny build, he was a giant of a man. For a second, she became fearful that he would hurt her, and not even realize it. But her fears quickly dissolved when he reached around her small waist and lifted her up so that he could kiss her lips with the most tender touch she had ever known. When he placed her back on the floor, she wanted to beg him to take her the rest of the way.

Drake knew she wanted him as urgently as he wanted her; he couldn't miss the smoldering flames in her passionate gaze. She no longer tried to hide her modesty when he stepped back and appraised her perfectly formed body in the dim light of the candle. Only in his dreams had he imagined how lovely she would be and he was not disappointed. With haste, he began to unbuckle his gunbelt. He placed it upon the table next to the bed, and quickly shrugged off his suede vest, but his eyes never left Krystal, not even for an instant. He could see her tremble every so often, though he was not sure if it was from fear or anticipation. The idea that no other man had ever gazed upon her luscious form in the intimate manner which he was looking at her now only increased his appetite for her. Drake reminded himself how innocent she was and to be gentle with her as he showed her all of love's sumptuous addictions. He wanted this to be his most superior accomplishment, because after tonight, she would be his for all eternity.

Krystal was not sure what was expected of her. But with his penetrating gaze scanning every inch of her unclad body, she was too helpless to move. He began to undo his pants, and as his fingers started unfastening the heavy brass button, her heart missed a beat. She thought briefly of the time she had doctored his stab wound while he was unconscious and of how she had slid her hand down through that very trail of soft brown curls that led past his waistband. The memory evoked such a vivid recollection that it caused a violent tremor to shoot through her body. Good Lord — she had been wanting this to happen even back then.

His hands moved up to the pearl snaps of his shirt, and all at once, she had a wild urge to rip the garment off of his body. Her arms reached out, almost as though they were moving on their own accord, and she impatiently began to tug on the snaps. He moved his hands out of her way while he permitted her to undo the front of his shirt. When the last snap was undone, she pushed back the material to reveal his broad furry chest. How would it feel, she wondered, to have that soft expanse of curly hair rubbing against her bare skin? The same sensual thought was passing through Drake's mind, but he did not want any barriers to come between the first complete union of their flesh.

"I gotta get these damn boots off, but darlin', please don't lose that mood." He bent over and tugged on the heel of one boot in a frantic gesture. The tight boot finally pulled free and he began to do the same to the other one. He did not wait for her to help him with the remainder of his clothes, time was suddenly too precious to waste with such trivial nonsense.

Krystal exhaled a deep breath and tried to think clearly, but she was too far past that point now. She ran a shaky finger across her sweating brow, and when she looked back up, Drake stood before her like a sleek golden statue. Never having seen a man completely in the buff before, her eyes immediately

243

fell to the area of a young girl's most intense curiosities. Her startled gaze flew up to his face as she felt a hot flood of perspirations cloak her whole body.

"Good Lord," she gasped, more to herself than to him, but her meaning was not lost on him. Women of vast experience had told him on more than one occasion that he was every woman's secret fantasy. But Krystal was too innocent to realize that Drake had been specially gifted, and soon, she would be, too.

"I'll be gentle. Please don't be frightened?" He took a step towards her.

How could he say that? she wondered as she grew more frightened with each passing second. She had heard how painful it always was the first time, and she was sure that most men were not as well-endowed as Drake obviously was. She began to back up, but the bed was directly behind her. She plopped down upon the mattress, and before she could move, he was kneeling beside her on the bed.

"I think maybe we should reconsider this rash action?" she cried out in alarm.

His illusive grin was the only answer he took the time to give to her as his muscular form pushed her back onto the brocaded bedspread. It was too late for second thoughts, he could never stop now, and the minute their bodies brushed against one another, the last of her protests were gone, too. The heat of his body seared Krystal with its touch, and once again, she was lost to the natural phenomena that his mere presence aroused within her. Her fears from a moment ago were absorbed in the mania of uncontrollable feelings that only this man could cause, and those cravings which could only be curbed by his love.

It was as though every one of her senses had suddenly sprung to life for the first time as his large body completely blanketed her small quaking being.

His fresh masculine odor made her grow heady and the taste of his lips against her own hungry mouth was like a rare delicacy. She suddenly became aware of his knees pushing between her thighs as he sought out the hidden feminine mystique which was contained in that secret area. She closed her eyes tightly and tried to brace herself against the imminent pain, but instead she felt the gentle touch of his strong fingers prodding into her moist aperture. An incoherent sound escaped from somewhere deep in her throat while his skillful fingers continued to move within her until he had brought her to the brink of delirium.

Drake sensed that she was eager to accept all of him and he could not hold off any longer. Krystal felt him readjust the position of his hips between her legs as the tip of his monumental organ pressed up against her damp orifice. Instinctively, she prepared to cry out with pain, but his mouth covered hers as he plunged deep within her and drew away her gasp with his kiss. The initial pain was everything that Krystal had feared it would be, but it subsided so quickly that her spinning mind was left in a state of confusion. For a moment he remained unmoving and then he began to pull away. Was that all there was to it? Oh how she hoped not, because the uncontrollable fire in her had not even began to subside, and she still wanted so much more of him.

As though he could read her mind, Drake suddenly began to move within her again, and now there was only a vague stabbing sensation that soon evaporated until it was replaced by a feeling that was so engulfing that Krystal never wanted it to go away. His movements intensified in a rhythmic motion that gave Krystal the overwhelming urge to move her hips in time with his. Her body arched up to meet his and she felt his hands grasp ahold of her buttocks as he

245

helped her hips to rise and recede with each of his thrusts. Good Lord—this was sheer ecstasy!

As a rule, everything must eventually come to an end, although Drake had prolonged this wonderful ceremony longer than he had ever thought humanly possible. Even with her inexperience, Drake decided this woman was amazing. She had transported him to heaven and back, and he had never even left her embrace. Their bodies clung to one another as he made a final, dynamic plunge and filled her with his life-giving nectar.

Krystal cried out and dug her nails deep into his back, though she was not aware of either action. Her whole being had journeyed to the same celestial place where she had taken him, and together they slowly descended back to reality. Beneath her hands, Krystal could feel the tense muscles in Drake's back begin to relax. At first, she had hoped he would never stop, now she was too weak to care.

For a time, neither of them attempted to move, they were each memorizing every detail of this fabulous night. Eventually, Drake pushed himself up from her limp form and sighed with contentment. However, he still did not speak as he reached over and scooped up her exhausted body from the bed. She thought of asking him where he was taking her, but since she trusted him completely now, she just snuggled up against his warm, furry chest.

Just when she was certain nothing could even come close to comparing with the pleasure of the intimate contact they had just found in one another arms, Drake surprised her by carrying her into the adjoining washroom. He tenderly stood her on the floor and began to sponge off her perspiring body with a cool damp washcloth. His strokes were so gentle that Krystal experienced a whole new feeling of joyous discovery. He was teaching her that being in love and making love was limitless. It meant so much more than just a mere sexual act, and Drake was only beginning to show her the infinity of this spectacular ceremony. She felt only a moment of embarrassment when he wiped away the faint streaks of red from between her silky thighs, the last evidence of her lost virginity, but his actions were so caring and natural that it seemed as if they had been touching one another like this forever.

She had never imagined that a man could be so loving, and if she could return only a small portion of the delight he gave to her, then she wanted to do so. She took another cloth from the wash basin and began to rub it over his body in slow and senuous motions, being careful to avoid the stab wound which was still evident upon his shoulder. The look of rapture that masked his features told Krystal that her actions were pleasing him as much as his tender thoughtfulness had done for her. There was not one inch of one another's body that they did not know after this night of total abandonment. This had to be a sin, it was too extraordinary to be anything else.

All at once, Drake grabbed her hand and took the washcloth away from her. "If you continue to do this, I'm gonna have to ravish your body one more time and I'm not sure if I have the strength to do that again this soon." The suggestive grin rested upon his lips and Krystal had the distinct impression that he would not have any trouble complying with his innuendo if he so desired.

She fluttered her long lashes in a precarious manner and smiled sweetly. "Perhaps at your age, one does have to be careful about overdoing such strenuous activities." She laughed and dodged him as he reached out to grab her. She retreated back into

247

bedroom and took refuge beneath the covers on the bed.

Drake jumped onto the bed and dove under the blankets after her. Since she was not hard to find, he quickly had her in his arms once more. As their laughter filled the room, they clung to each other, too deep in love with one another to care about anything outside of the boundaries of the four walls.

When their mirth subsided, Drake cleared his throat and suddenly began to speak in a serious manner. "Well, I reckon I'm going to have to make an honorable woman of you, darlin', so what would you say if I asked you to marry me?"

"What? Marry you?" Good Lord, she was not ready to plan her whole future just because of one night of passion, no matter how much she loved him. She pushed the blanket away from herself and sat up. "I suppose it would be the proper thing to do under these circumstances, but I don't think it's anything we should rush into. Marriage is hardly something to take lightly, you know?"

Drake threw the covers off himself and raised up on one elbow. In a matter of seconds, she went from being a carefree woman of unrestrained passion, and had reverted back to her staunch and snooty schoolteacher attitude. He had hoped that once she learned what it felt like to be a complete woman, she would begin to shed her pruddish eastern approach to life, but it appeared that she had not changed at all. How could she actually think that he could take marriage to her lightly?

"Well, you're probably right," he said in a nonchalant voice. "There's no reason to worry about marriage, yet. We'll just wait until you get pregnant, that way we'll have a good reason to rush into something more serious."

"Good Lord," she said, aghast at the idea. "Do you—I mean—would it be possible that—tonight—I could have—" Oh, the humiliation! How would she ever explain that to her father? Her brows drew together in deep thought. Maybe it would be wise for them to get married right away. After all, they were in love, and that was the natural thing to do when two people felt so strongly about one another. It's just that marriage sounded so—well, so enslaving!

Drake hoped he would never forget the way she looked right at this moment. The tendrils of her long strawberry-blonde hair were curled around the frame of her face and they tumbled in soft abundance past her creamy shoulders. She still carried the rosy glow of their exuberant love-making upon her pale complexion and her expression was priceless. The turmoil in her mind was evident upon her beautiful face, and Drake could almost guess exactly what was going through that stubborn mind of hers. He knew that she loved him, she would not have allowed him to make love to her if she didn't have very strong feelings for him. But he also knew how damn autonomous she was. Right now, she was probably wondering how she was going to protect her lost honor, and at the same time, retain her complete independence.

She chewed nervously on her lower lip as she contemplated the rest of her life in a span of a couple minutes. "If we were to get married, would you still allow me to teach school?"

"Maybe."

That certainly would not do for an answer. "Then forget it. I'll have to take the chance that I didn't get—you know—"

"Pregnant?" he mocked.

"Yes, that's what I meant to say. And we just won't ever do this again."

"Damn!" he growled as he fell back against the pillow in a defeated gesture. They were right back where they started. "Well, if you did get pregnant tonight, it damn well better be a boy!"

"Oh really?" she retorted icily. "And why is that, may I dare ask?"

"Because one female like you is all a man should ever have to cope with in one lifetime, that's why?"

She huffed with indignance. "How dare you say something so rude after we just —"

"After we just did this?" he replied as he swiftly swung around and pulled her into the circle of his arms again. A startled cry escaped from her mouth, but almost immediately she fell silent. Just being this close to him was enough to evoke her total surrender and the incandescent glow in her tawny gaze was all the invitation Drake needed to arouse his desire once more.

"Drake?" her voice was feeble, too filled with emotion to be articulate, but he heard.

"Yes, darlin'?" he questioned, hoping that her thoughts were running along the same lines as his were at this moment.

She raised her face up as she ran her tiny tongue along the outline of her lips, leaving them moist and full of kissable temptation. Drake was rapidly losing what little restraint he had left.

"Make love to me just one more time," she said in a breathless sigh.

He closed his eyes and smiled to himself. How could he refuse this woman anything?

Chapter Eighteen

Krystal opened her drowsy eyes and sighed with contentment. It was hard for her to believe that this incredible man had walked into her life such a short time ago, and already she had given all of herself to him. But Drake DeGanahl needed to do little more than glance in her direction, and she grew weak with desire for him. It was no wonder that he had been able to break down her defenses so easily. What was even worse was the fact that he had spent the whole night here in her room and that she was the one who had asked him to make love to her — not once, but two times. He would probably never let her live that down.

She tilted her head back and watched him as he slept. He looked so peaceful and innocent, almost like a little boy. But he certainly did not behave like a little boy last night. Just the thought of it was enough to make Krystal want to wake him up and ask him to make love to her again. Did she have no shame at all? she wondered as she broke out in a fevered flush.

Her head was resting on his chest and she burrowed her cheek deeper into the the thick mat of curls which ran across his muscular body while her eyes traveled down the length of his flat abdomen. The lower part of his lean form was graphically outlined by the thin white sheet which was tossed carelessly across the bed. She could not resist running her fingers down through that beckoning trail of fur, a trail that led below the sheet and ended at paradise. Good Lord, it was bad enough that she was now a fallen woman, but did she have to be an insatiable one, too! With great effort, she pulled her hand away and tried to force her mind away from her lascivious cravings.

"Don't stop now, darlin'," Drake's eyes were still closed, but a devilish smile had consumed his handsome face.

Krystal jumped at the sound of his voice. "Oh, you're awake?" She hoped her voice didn't sound as anxious as her body felt once she realized that he probably knew exactly what she was doing.

He opened one eye lazily and looked down at her. It hadn't been a wild figment of his imagination. He was really here. And last night was definitely not a dream. His arms tightened around her small form, and just as he was about to suggest that they take up where they had left off last night, there was a loud banging on the door.

Krystal's heart felt like it just bolted up to her throat. "Oh Lord! Who could that be?"

Drake shrugged with indifference. "It's probably just the maid checking to see if you need something."

Her nerves were getting the best of her, he was probably right. "Um—who is it?" she cried out in an unsteady voice.

"It's your father," was the booming reply.

252

Krystal sprang from the bed in one leap. Her eyes grew wide with fright as she spun around, trying to figure out what they were going to do now. She spotted her blue robe on the floor and scooped it up as she swung around to Drake. He had not moved, he was too intent on watching her erratic performance. "Don't just lay there," she hissed. "Do something!"

"Krystal? Are you gonna let me in?" John asked from the other side of the closed door.

"I'll be right there." She glared at Drake for a second longer. How could he just lay there? With an impatient grunt, she grabbed hold of the blanket and pulled it away from the bed, and off of Drake. "You'll have to hide." She looked around the room in a heated panic. "Under the bed, quick!"

Drake shook his head and frowned. He had no intention of crawling under the bed. "Sorry, darlin', but I'm not going to hide under the bed and I'm not going to hide the way I feel about you."

She clenched her fists at her sides, growing more frantic by the second. "I'm not asking you to hide your feelings, just your body!" He was insufferable at times. She would rather die than to allow her father to find out about last night.

Drake climbed out of the bed and grunted with aggravation. "I'm going to tell your father how much I love you and that I plan to marry you. I'm sure he will understand that."

"Oh really?" she said in a huffy voice. "But you're forgetting one thing, aren't you? I have to accept your proposal first, and I don't recall saying that I would marry you." How dare he think that he could decide her whole future just because of one passionate night. She would marry him when she was ready and not a moment sooner.

"Krystal? What's going on in there? Are you talking to someone?"

She froze to the spot as she turned to Drake with a look of terror and desperation. He knew he must be crazy to give into her foolish demands, but damn, she looked so horrified at the prospect of her father finding out that she was less than perfect. He pointed a threatening finger at her as he grabbed his pants up from the floor. "All right, you win—this time. But as soon as he leaves we're going to settle this once and for all." He quickly gathered up the rest of his clothes and retreated into the bathroom with an angry stride.

Krystal sighed with relief and started towards the door, but before she could reach it, John pushed it open and stomped into the room. "Hells-a-fire, chéri! Don't you know better than to leave your door un-locked. Lucky for you it was only me."

She remembered that when Drake had bullied his way into her room last night, she had never bothered to lock the door again. Good Lord, anybody could have walked in on them. "I—I—" she suddenly realized that her father looked completely different than he did when she had first met him yesterday. His long hair was trimmed to his shoulders and the shaggy beard was neatly shaped around his face. "You look very nice, Father," she said as her gaze traveled down over his clean shirt and pants.

A proud smile claimed his mouth, he was hoping she would notice how he had fancied himself up for her, but his smile quickly faded. "Well, you look terrible. Are you ill? And what in tarnation took you so long to answer the door?"

Instinctively she smoothed back her unruly hair and then gathered the front of her robe together tightly at the neckline. "Uh—well, I'm just . . . tired.

I didn't sleep too well last night, and I just feel so listless today." Now Drake DeGanahl had turned her into a liar, too. Could her father see the guilt written all over her face?

John eyed her cautiously as he placed his shotgun against the wall for safe-keeping. His eyes moved past her and paused at the sight of the messed up bed. Krystal held her breath. Surely he didn't suspect anything?

"Hells-a-fire!"

"What?" she screamed, nearly fainting with fright. She was too afraid to turn around, so she remained frozen to the spot. What had he noticed?

"What is tarnation is that gun and vest doin' on your table?"

"Oh, that?" Her mind searched for a logical explanation. "I . . . was nervous about being alone last night, so Drake let me keep his gun in my room. And the vest? Well, I was cold." Now she had produced two more lies because of Drake DeGanahl—oh, that incorrigible man.

John began to look doubtful. "Nervous and cold?" Well, she was sure acting nervous, right now. Since he was nervous about coming into town himself, he decided not to ponder over her strange behavior any longer.

"Seein' how I came into town today just so that I could spend more time with you, why don't you go get yourself dressed up real pretty so you can go to breakfast with your daddy?"

Krystal nodded quickly. Thank goodness he had changed the subject. "Oh, that would be wonderful. You can go on down to the hotel restaurant and I'll join you as soon as I make myself presentable."

John smiled broadly, picked up his shotgun, which

255

was never far away from him, and headed towards the door. "What room is Drake's? I'll stop by and invite him, too."

"No! I — I would rather spend some time alone with you, if you don't mind? Drake can join us later."

"That's fine with me, chéri," he said with a pleased grin. "I like the idea of havin' you all to myself for awhile." He exited from the room as Krystal exhaled the breath she had come close to suffocating on. Before she had a chance to call out to Drake, the bathroom door swung open and he stalked out. He had not wanted to make any noise, so his pants still remained only partially buttoned and his shirt and boots dangled from one hand. With his other hand, he shoved his hat on top of his head, then glared down at Krystal.

Why on earth was he so upset? It was, after all, her reputation that was on the line. "You'll have to leave now," she stated blatantly. "I'm having breakfast with my father."

"Well that's just fine. And what am I supposed to do . . . starve?" He dropped his bundle of clothes on the floor with a thud and placed his hands on his hips. What was it going to take to make her realize that she could not continue to turn her emotions from hot to cold whenever she so desired?

"I'm not hungry anyway. Being in love has made me lose my appetite for some reason. But later, when we're alone, we are going to have a long talk. That is, if it's all right with you?"

"Just fine!" His snide tone only fueled Krystal's irritation with him, but she knew he had a point. They did have to work out their differences, because they were in love. Last night had proved that, and she was really getting tired of this constant bickering.

Perhaps, over breakfast this morning, she would tell her father that she and Drake were in love with one another. "Drake?" she said quietly.

"What?" he snapped as he bent over to pick up his discarded clothes again.

"I do love you, you know?"

Damn contrary woman! Well, he loved her, too. Instantly he straighted back up and reached out to her. In less than a second, she was in his arms once more. Their lips joined in a sweltering kiss that ignited a wild flame in the center of their existence.

"Krystal, I just wanted to remind you to lock the do—what in tarnation?" John's words sliced through the air like a knife as the door swung back open. Shock and the unexpected sight of his daughter in this rascal's arms made him see red for an instant. But he regained his senses in a matter of seconds. The sawed off shotgun leveled at Drake without a moment's hesitation. "I just knew you were dallyin' with my little girl's affections."

Drake's arms instantly dropped away from Krystal as he stepped back. The look upon their faces did not need explaining. Their guilt at being caught was an unspoken admission which was written all over their expressions. But Drake felt the need to say something. "John—I mean—Mr. Colbert, I realize what a surprise this must be, but—"

"Surprise? Hells-a-fire! Dang near caused me to have a heart attack. She's barely more than a baby, and you took advantage of her innocence, now you're gonna pay for that." His gun raised higher in the air.

Krystal screamed in horror as she stepped in front of Drake. "Don't shoot him, Father. I'm the one who asked him to make love to me." Good Lord! had she really told her father that? She squeezed her eyes shut but the look of disgust upon her father's face was still vivid in her mind. What a disappointment she must be to him now.

"Don't you be tryin' to protect that varmint, Krystal Dawn. I know his kind. He's only after one thing." His frown deepened, "And it appears that he already got it. But don't you fret none, chéri, 'cause I'll take care of everything."

Krystal wanted to die, this was the most humiliating thing she had ever been involved in. The fact that her father was trying to justify her actions and place all the blame on Drake made this situation even more degrading. But she couldn't allow Drake to take all the responsibility.

"No, father, you're wrong. I'm as much at fault as Drake, and I will not let you harm the man I love." Drake's eyes widened as he stared down at her. He was proud of her for standing her ground with her father, but especially for admitting that she loved him.

John's thick red brows drew together in thought as he contemplated this situation. He had figured out that they were in love with one another since yesterday, but he didn't think his little girl had let her feelings interfere with her common sense. Drake De-Ganahl had violated her, and now it was his job as her father to set things right. He narrowed his eyes at Drake and spoke to him over the barrel of the gun. "You're comin' with me, young fella." With a glance in Krystal's direction, he added, "You get some clothes on, we'll be back shortly."

Drake did not waste any time in fastening his breeches and following John Colbert from the room, while continuing to dress. As they departed, he gave Krystal a confused look which was accompanied by a helpless shrug. He had no idea what her father was up to, but since he had learned long ago never to argue with a man whose weapon was aimed at his head, Drake complacently complied with the older man's orders.

Krystal remained unmoving. She was too numb to do anything else. This was horrible, nothing could ever compare with this shame. And it was as much her fault as it was Drake's, so she knew she could not allow her father to harm him in anyway.

She grabbed a pearl gray suit from her wardrobe. Back East it was the most elegant daytime fashion a woman could wear. The skirt was of a slim fit through the hips, flaring out at the hem, and was teamed with a frilly blouse that boasted an abundance of white ruffles down the front. It was topped by a closely tailored jacket which was nipped at the waist line and had leg-o'-mutton sleeves trimmed with delicate ribbons of pale pink satin. She quickly pulled her hair up into a loose swirl of curls and placed a large gray hat with a pink plume on her head to hold the thick mass in place. She did not bother to appraise her apparel in the mirror before she fled from the room, she was too worried about Drake to care how she looked.

She had not even reached the end of the hallway when she met Drake and her father, along with a strange man whom she had never seen before. Drake gave her an odd grin that almost appeared to be more of a grimace. What were they up to now? and why had her father involved someone else in this? It was bad enough that he knew what had happened last night. Too embarrassed to even glance in the direction of the stranger, she turned to Drake with a questioning expression.

He leaned down and whispered, "You're not going to like this one, darlin'."

259

"Just what is going on?" Krystal demanded. Drake's brows raised slightly as he motioned towards her father with a toss of his head. Krystal swung around to John. "Father," she said in a hushed tone of voice. "I would rather that we keep this just between you, Drake and me."

John prodded them all back towards Krystal's room with a wave of his shotgun. Krystal huffed with indignance. She was starting to despise that stupid gun. When they were in front of her room again, John reached for the doorknob, but Krystal had locked it when she had left a few minutes ago.

"Now you lock it?" John grunted. "When there's nothing goin' on in there, it's locked. And awhile ago, when you and him was—"

"Father!" Krystal cut in angrily. "I hardly think this is the proper place or time to discuss such private matters." Her eyes shifted to the unknown man and back to her father again. "Who is he?"

The man, tall and extremely thin, pushed his wire rimmed glasses up from the bottom of his nose with his forefinger. They immediately slid back down, looking as though they might slip off of the narrow tip at any second. Much to everyone's amazement, the little round spectacles stopped and teetered in a delicate balance at the very end of his pointed nose. Dressed in a worn black suit and white shirt, the man's garments contrasted sharply with the deep shade of red which his face had turned during Krystal and John's brief exchange of conversation. In response to Krystal's question, he cleared his throat with a nervous cough and held out his hand. "I'm Father Lester."

Krystal immediately noticed that he did not look at her directly, instead, he stared at the ground while he

260

offered her his hand and when his gaze wandered upward, his eyes peered over the top of the wire glasses in a quick and uneasy glance. "Father Lester?" she repeated while she gave his hand a lame shake, growing more confused by the second.

"Unlock that door, chéri. We're goin' to your weddin'," John stated with a firm nod of his bright red head.

"Wedding?" she repeated. Surely he wasn't serious? She placed her hands on the soft curve of her hips and angrily faced her father. Beneath a wave of golden-red hair which hung casually across her forehead, she blinked with arrogance and spoke in an even more supercilious manner. "I beg your pardon? Are you suggesting that Drake and I get married right now just because of one night of—" She glanced in the direction of the preacher. The look of embarrassment upon his face suddenly made her feel like the worst kind of trollop, and to make matters even worse, they were standing here in the middle of the hotel hallway announcing it to everyone who passed by.

Krystal pushed past her father and hastily shoved the key into the keyhole. "I think we should discuss this in private." The trio of men followed her into the room, each of them wearing distinctly different expressions across their faces; John's was stern and determined, poor Father Lester looked as though he feared that he might be swallowed up by the bowels of Hell at any moment, and Drake, well, he appeared to be enjoying every minute of this ridiculous charade. Krystal graced him with the most abasing look she could project upon her face, but he returned her gesture with that infuriating smile which always seemed to border on thoughts of indecency, and if his thoughts were on last night, no doubt they were running along those very lines.

Oh, if she were only a man, she would knock that smirk right off of those lips—those lips whose kiss was so very extraordinary. Now why, she thought furiously, did she always have to remind herself of those things? Without any sort of warning, the memory of last night flashed before her eyes and unconsciously she glanced towards the unmade bed. Her cheeks flamed with the recollection as she tore her eyes away and met with Drake's look of mocking amusement. How dare he make a joke out of something this serious? A shotgun wedding—Good Lord! She intended to see to it that Drake DeGanahl regretted this day for the rest of his life!

"Where do you want the bride and groom to stand?" John asked Father Lester, oblivious to Krystal's fiery rage. The preacher jumped at the sound of John's voice and threw his hands up in despair. This was the first wedding he had ever performed at gunpoint and he was not sure if one followed the normal procedure, or if it even mattered in a case such as this.

"This is outrageous. Drake and I have no intention of marrying one another under these circumstances." She swung around and dared Drake to defy her as she added, "Do we?"

Drake wiped the smile from his face the moment her flashing gaze was directed his way. "I never argue with a loaded shotgun, darlin'." Actually, he rather liked the idea of a simple ceremony, no fuss or bother, and then they could get right to the honeymoon without any further interference. However, he knew better than to tell her his real feelings on this subject.

Krystal could tell that it was useless to try to reason with him when he was in this patronizing frame of mind, so she turned back to her father. "Well, I refuse. I'm old enough to make my own decisions and I will not marry anyone until I choose to do so, and I'm sure Father Lester would not marry a woman against her will." She glanced at Drake, back to her father, then leveled her angry gaze on Father Lester.

Father Lester swallowed hard, his large adams apple bobbed like a buoy in the ocean above the collar of his white shirt. "I—I—" he looked to John Colbert and began to ring his thin hands together with nervousness.

John waved the gun into the air again, "Hells-a-fire, no offense intended Father, but there's been enough talk. Now, let's just get on with it." He aimed the gun at Father Lester.

"Dearly Beloved," Father Lester gasped out in terror.

"Skip all that fancy stuff," John grunted. "Just say the necessary words, and they ain't got no rings, so don't worry about that part either."

Krystal and Drake were both in a state of shock as they stood mutely facing each other. Krystal opened her mouth, but nothing escaped, this was just too unbelievable for words. Her mind only half grasped what Father Lester was saying.

"Do you—um?" the preacher glanced at John with a question on his face.

"His name is Drake—Drake DeGanahl. And my daughter's name is Krystal Colbert."

Father Lester nodded. "Do you, Krystal Colbert, take Drake DeGanahl as your lawfully wedded husband?"

"She does," John answered with a wave of his gun.

"I don't believe it will be legal if the young lady does not answer for herself," Father Lester replied as

263

he shoved his glasses up on his nose again.

Krystal blinked and stared at the preacher with a numb feeling working its way through her weak limbs. Did she want Drake for her lawfully wedded husband? Did she have any choice? Her gaze traveled over and met Drake's intense look. She began to tremble, two words and she could spend the rest of her life in his arms like she had last night. After he had showed her the true meaning of love, she knew she never wanted to live without it again, or without him. Perhaps she had sensed that this was where her life was headed ever since the first moment her gaze had been drawn to him on the train.

"Oh yes . . . I do," she said in a whisper.

Drake's look softened, his green eyes sparkled with love when she answered Father Lester's question. She was the woman who stalked the secret passages of his dreams and now she would belong to him forever. "Do you, Drake DeGanahl, take Krystal Colbert to be your lawfully wedded wife?" Drake reached out both hands and Krystal instinctively moved forward. As their hands clasped together, he replied quietly, "I do."

Father Lester sighed with relief, this was the shortest ceremony he had ever performed and he was never so glad to get anything over with as much as he was this wedding today. "I now pronounce you man and wife." He nodded at Drake, "You may kiss the bride."

Drake pulled Krystal closer, until they were only inches apart. He was sure he could feel the pounding of her heart, or maybe it was his own? She raised her face upward and her eyes shut as her golden-tipped lashes fanned down across her cheekbones in anticipation of his kiss . . . the kiss which would seal this unorthodox union for all time. Drake's spinning mind suddenly recalled the language which his mother had patiently taught to him when he was a youngster. It was his Spanish heritage, Angelina had told him proudly. Someday, his mother always prophesied, he would live in Mexico in the beautiful hacienda which he would inherit from his grandfather, Migel Ramirez. Back then, his mother's native tongue had seemed so foreign, but now, for some strange reason, the words came naturally to Drake.

Before he leaned down and claimed her as his bride with a gentle conjunction of their lips, he said softly, "*Mi mujer, mi esposa, mi destino . . . hoy yo donar de mi nombre, mi corazon de ya poseer.*"

Krystal's eyes opened, his words had touched her to the very core of her existence. Although she did not know the meaning of anything he had just said to her, she knew it was the most beautiful thing her ears had ever heard. Her mouth opened to ask him what he had said, but his lips cut away her breath and also wiped away her question with their burning touch. When he pulled away, they stared at one another for several seconds, each of them was trying to grasp the meaning of what had just taken place. It had lasted but a few brief minutes, but it would encompass an eternity. Married . . . they were really married.

"Damn," Krystal stated in quiet awe.

Drake sighed and added, "Good Lord!"

Chapter Nineteen

"This is not necessary, you know?"

"I don't care," Krystal replied as she tossed the last of her wardrobe into the trunk and slammed the lid down. She swung around to give Drake a look of exasperation. Her tawny eyes flashed with annoyance while she quickly glanced around the room to see if she had forgotten anything. She unconsciously pushed back a wayward curl from her forehead, the rest of her naturally wavy hair had come loose during her packing and had tumbled down from the top of her head. It now hung in an unruly reddish-gold mass over one shoulder. The heat of the summer had made the thick tendrils more curly than usual and they framed her lightly tanned complexion in a wild abundance.

Drake couldn't believe that she was really his wife. The fact that their wedding had been held at gunpoint did not matter in the least to him. John Colbert had unwittingly solved half of Drake's problems, now Drake just had to figure out how he was going to support his new wife.

"I refuse to stay in this hotel one second longer than necessary. I have never been so humiliated in my whole life. Can you just imagine the talk that must be circulating throughout this whole establishment because of what my father did today? Why, our marriage is probably the biggest scandal in the history of Virginia City." She threw her hands over her face again, a gesture of shame that she had repeated several times during the hasty packing of her belongings.

"I hardly think so, darlin'," he retorted with a slanted grin. "Virginia City has had more than its share of scandals throughout the years, a shotgun wedding was probably the least monumental of them." But he was not surprised that his prim wife would think that their wedding was the most disgraceful of them all. Drake pulled his hat off of his head and ran his fingers through the thick brown curls which covered his head. The heat was close to being unbearable this afternoon so he decided not to replace the heavy felt hat. As it sailed across the room and landed in the middle of the bed, it occured to him that it was very probable that their children would have naturally curly hair, too. It was a comfortable thought which brought another easy smile to his face. Marriage and children, they had a nice sound to them. They were things that had always been in the back of his mind, but since he had never met a woman who interested him enough to consider as a lifelong mate, they had always remained only a distant illusion. Even though he had not known this lady for very long, there was one thing Drake was certain of — life would never be dull with a woman like Krystal Colbert — Krystal DeGanahl, he reminded himself as he leaned back in

267

the large winged-back chair and observed the tempting way his bride's tight fitting skirt emphasized her luscious curves.

Dressed in her elegant gray suit, and with an indignant look upon her pouting face, she looked as proper and formal as the high-bred Eastern lady which she was raised to represent. But last night Drake had learned what a seductive siren was contained within that staunch and haughty exterior that she displayed to the rest of the world. She had been reborn with the discovery of unboundless passion and incessant love, and she had taken him to a new height of sensual pleasure that he had never known with any other woman before her. Now that they were properly married and she no longer had to worry about moralizing her conduct, Drake knew their love would have no limits.

"So, are we leaving Virginia City, then?" Drake asked in a casual tone, his thoughts were concentrating on a problem of a different nature. Would she object to a brief interlude of romance before they left the luxuries of the International Hotel, he wondered?

Krystal's gaze came back and focused on her husband's face. "I can never show my face in this town again." Why was he staring at her with such an obvious look of suggestion on his face? The twinkling glint in his dark eyes was unmistakable and when his gaze shifted to the bed, Krystal knew immediately what was on her groom's mind.

Like an aphrodisiac, his look was all it took to consume her whole body in a fiery flame of wanton desire, but she fought a frantic battle to draw her thoughts away from the lustful feelings that this man continually aroused in her. How could he be thinking such thoughts now? It was those concupiscent

268

thoughts which had placed them in this situation in the first place. Krystal's voice cracked slightly when she spoke, her mind continued to journey into that newly discovered territory of ardent yearnings which she had encountered in Drake's arms last night. But she could not permit that to happen—not here in this room—not after her father had made it public knowledge that she had shared this bed with a man who was not yet her husband.

Krystal forced herself to turn away from Drake as she moved a safe distance away from the beckoning bed. "I refuse to remain in this hotel a moment longer. Maybe we could stay with my father for awhile."

"In his cabin?" he asked in an incredulous voice while his thoughts were briefly diverted away from the delectable idea of ravishing his lovely bride once again. Drake had only glimpsed the interior of John Colbert's cabin yesterday when they were up on the mountain and there was absolutely no way the three of them could stay in the falling-down shack were her father resided. It was impossible for him to imagine Krystal staying in a place as primitive as her father's cabin up on Sugar Loaf. Drake almost laughed out loud at the picture his mind painted of her wiping off the layers of filth in that dirty, crumbling abode with her dainty white-lace handkerchief.

"Of course," she retorted in defense. "It wasn't all that bad. Anyway, what other choice do we have?" A thoughtful expression furrowed across the delicate features of her face. There was always her home in Boston, but she was no longer sure if she wanted to return to the East now, if ever. The life she had lived only a short time ago was like a fragment from a distant dream; the lavish house on Beacon Hill, elaborate dinner parties with visiting royalty from far-away lands, the grand opening nights at the theater — it just didn't seem real anymore. . . . Only Drake's embrace was reality now.

She felt as though her life had only begun last night, or was it the first time her eyes had wandered across the train coach and met with Drake Da-Ganahl's intense gaze? Nothing could even begin to compare with the marvelous discovery of emotional and physical love which she had found in Drake. Their location was not what was important, she realized, as long as they were together nothing else mattered.

Drake was equally as thoughtful as he contemplated their uncertain future. He had been thinking about that problem ever since he had first realized that he was in love with Krystal, and now that she was his wife — his responsibility — he knew he could no longer avoid the issue. He felt completely incompetent to provide her with the sort of life that he wanted to give her. It was beyond reason to think that he could even begin to compete with the fancy lifestyle she had lived in Boston. Being a lawman was the only thing he had ever known and a man sure didn't choose that profession because he hoped to become rich.

Drake thought of his own mother and the parallel path that Krystal's life was following. His mother had given up a life of extreme wealth in order to follow her heart. But did Krystal love him as much as Angelina Rameriz had loved Franklin DeGanahl? Would Krystal have ever consented to marry him if it hadn't been for John Colbert's unyielding demands? Drake unconsciously touched the spot over his heart where the shiny tin star had once adorned his shirt with pride. There had been a time when he could not imagine doing anything else with his life besides being a lawman. But since his father's brutal slaying, wearing a badge no longer held the glory and intrigue that it once had. He wondered if he could still be reinstated, and if he was, would he still be able to abide by the rigid standards that he had set for himself as a defender of law and order?

He thought of the large trust fund which belonged to him, a gift of extraordinary generosity from his grandfather and he grew enraged with himself for allowing that thought to enter into his mind. Drake's grandfather, a Spanish aristocrat, had bestowed the large sum of money to his first born grandchild, along with the title to his vast estate in Mexico in a vain attempt to lure his cherished daughter away from the young Texas Ranger whom she had met and impulsively married during a visit to a distant relative in El Paso, Texas.

Migel Rameriz, beside himself with shame and rejection, was positive he could convince his daughter to return to Mexico, even after he learned that she was already carrying the ranger's child. But Angelina loved Franklin DeGanahl more than life itself, and her father's wealth did not impress her, not even when he bequeathed it all to her unborn child. Unaffected by her father's lavish gift, she left Texas with her husband to live in an even more distant place called Wyoming. During a rash moment of distorted rage, Migel sent a message to Angelina to inform her that until she left the scoundrel who had stolen her away from her family, she would not be welcome to come home again. Although Angelina was heartbroken over her father's denial to accept her marriage to Franklin DeGanahl, she knew the choice she had to make would be ruled by her love for her husband, so she

271

had not returned to her homeland for over three decades. From friends of the family, Angelina had heard that, at seventy-two years of age, her father's health was failing and many times he had said that he regretted the ultimatum he had given his daughter. He was too stubborn to tell her that he had been wrong though, and like her father, Angelina was still filled with pride and lingering resentment, too. She would not return to Mexico until he personally asked her to come home.

Even though she had further defied him by fleeing to Wyoming, Migel had left nearly all of his wealth in his first grandson's name, and had even set up a smaller, though still an extensive trust fund in Devon's name after he had learned of the birth of a second grandson. A man who had always allowed his family's overbearing wealth to do his talking for him, his money was the only way Migel knew to show his daughter that he had not deserted her completely. Since Angelina was Migel's only child, her boys were the last of a proud family.

When each of Angelina's sons reached the age of twenty-one, the money became their sole property. Devon immediately began to siphon out his funds on the day of his twenty-first birthday. Even Drake's dramatic lectures on the heartbreak their mother had suffered because of Migel Ramirez and his unfeeling methods of controlling people with his money could not deter Devon's wild spending sprees. Devon was obsessed with the money he had inherited — it gave him power over the people and the situations he could not normally monopolize. He had not had to work to earn this money, so he had no qualms about spending it. He threw it away on wild women, gambling, and every form of low-life activity he could engage himself in. Within a couple of years, every last penny of his money was spent, and a rift of irreparable damage had been created between Devon and Franklin De-Ganahl.

Drake, on the other hand, vowed never to touch a dime of his grandfather's money unless the old man relented and apologized to Angelina for all the heartbreak he had caused her through the years. Since Migel Ramirez had not retracted his insenible conditions, Drake had put the money out of his mind and pretended that it did not exist. He grew more furious with himself for thinking of it now.

"I'm going to take your luggage down to the train station," he said in an angry tone as he stomped over to the bed, grabbed his hat and pulled it down upon his head. Thinking about the money and his own shortcomings only made him more furious with himself, but it did not help to solve his problems.

Krystal jumped at the sound of his foul tone. "I can't just leave my father. I'm going to try to talk him into going with us." She frowned and added, "But I still don't know where we're going?"

A deeper scowl consumed his face. How could he tell her something that he did not know himself? When he had left New Orleans a couple of weeks ago, his plan was to return to Green River and to try to pick up the broken pieces of his life. That had been a difficult task even when he had only himself to think of, now that he had acquired a wife, it was overwhelming.

"I'll tell you when I return," he retorted, sourly. He grabbed her trunks by the handles on the sides and hurried through the door as she opened it for him. His eyes darted away to avoid her questioning look. He didn't like his life to be at loose ends, and it had been like this since his father had been killed over two years ago.

By the time he had checked Krystal's trunk in at the train station for storage until they decided to leave, he was frantic to find a direction for his life . . . their life. In spite of his indecision about his future, he realized that today was still the second luckiest day of his life, his first had been the day he had spotted the tiny black-clad figure sitting by the window during that fateful train ride. His stride began to pick up as a plan began to formulate in his mind. They would return to Wyoming, he would ask the Marshal of Green River for his old job back, and Krystal could teach school. Everything would be perfect.

Back in the hotel lobby he picked up a copy of the *Territorial Enterprise*, the local newspaper and began to whistle as he skimmed over the articles which did not hold much interest to him, especially since he was thinking about the blissful life he would live with his new bride in Wyoming. His elated step suddenly jerked to an abrupt halt as he drew the paper closer to his face. He reread the excerpt which had been reprinted from the Lander, Wyoming newspaper — *The Fremont Clipper*. His stomach felt like it had just overturned as his eyes focused on the article once more. This was not possible!

Without bothering to wait for the hydraulic elevator that the International Hotel was the proud owner of, he bolted up the stairway in several long strides. Krystal's door was not locked, so Drake shoved it open harder than he had intended. She gasped as the door hit the wall and bounced back. His large hand stopped it before it reclosed. The look on his face immediately told her that something was horribly wrong.

"Drake! Good Lord, what is it?" The first thing which occurred to her was that something awful had happened to her father. "Is—is it my father?" she said tentatively, while she prayed fervently that it wasn't.

He entered the room slowly and kicked the door shut with his sharp-toed boot. His eyes did not leave her terrified face as he began to recount everything he knew about his new bride. He realized that he knew virtually nothing about her former activities back East, was it possible that there could be some truth in this outrageous story? Without speaking, he stuck out his arm and pushed the paper towards her. Krystal shied away from it. She did not want to know what it was that would make him so hostile.

Drake rattled the paper in her face. "Tell me they've made a terrible mistake, darlin'." His voice was cold, controlled.

She began to break out in cold chills. Why was he acting so strange? The ominous paper rustled before her face as she reached out with dread filling every pore of her being. When her trembling hand clasped onto it, she gazed back up at her husband, hoping to find some sort of reassurance, but his look did not offer any. Slowly, she raised the paper up and allowed her eyes to descend. "What?" she questioned with confusion. There did not seem to be anything among the printed lines that she could see which would bring on such an adverse reaction in Drake. He pointed angrily to one of the articles, a seemingly insignificant piece in the lower righthand corner.

Fremont Clipper—Lander, Wyoming—Dateline: July 25, 1896: BANK ROBBERY—A daring holdup was conducted at the bank in Lander on Tuesday morning. Three armed men entered the establishment at approximately 10:00 a.m. and relieved the bank teller, William Kelsy, of almost nine hundred dollars. Although none of the bank's patrons were injured during the holdup, it was a terrifying experience for the unfortunate people who happened to be in the vicinity at the time.

A posse was formed by Deputy Richard Pickett, but was disbanded a couple miles north of town where the brave men realized that they were vastly outnumbered. The three bandits who had robbed the bank were met by no less than a dozen or more men at the outskirts of the city. Only Deputy Pickett was close enough to make out any of the desperados, though they were still too far away to provide a clear description. However, Pickett was able to distinguish one of the riders as a woman. It is assumed that the men were part of the Wild Bunch, a group of bandits who have been conducting raids throughout Wyoming, Colorado and Utah for the past couple of years. The outlaws were undoubtedly headed for the secluded country known as Hole-in-the-Wall in the Lost Cabin area.

The mysterious woman who accompanied the men is believed to be Krystal Colbert. The woman was supposedly abducted several days ago when a train belonging to the Union Pacific Railroad was held up up a band of outlaws approximately twelve miles west of Rawlins. The kidnapping is suspicious, however, because of a news bulletin which was received at the Sheriff's office on the same morning as the bank robbery. The bulletin, issued by a branch of the Pinker-

276

ton National Detective Agency based out of Boston, Massachusetts contained a wanted poster and vital statistics of the young woman known as Krystal Colbert. Miss Colbert is being sought by the agency for questioning in an investigation which was being conducted in Boston at this time concerning the murder of a woman who has been linked to a lucrative jewel-smuggling ring that has been operating out of Boston for more than a decade.

Krystal was too stunned to speak in her own defense. This was not possible, how could they be allowed to print such ridiculous lies without any sort of proof? Through eyes which were beginning to blur and hands that trembled so hard that the rustling of the newspaper sounded deafening, she tried to read it again, hoping that she had interpreted it wrong the first time. But Drake grew impatient and snatched the paper from her unsuspecting hands.

"Damn it, Krystal! I want some answers. What murder? What investigation? And most of all, are you running from the law?" Drake's voice grew louder, despite his inner attempt to remain calm. He kept telling himself not to jump to conclusions, but the lawman in him was rapidly gaining control, and his mind was filled with growing suspicions.

His thoughts flashed back to the day he had met her on the train. . . . Why had she been garbed in a heavy black veil on such a hot summer day? Was she lying about her mother's death, or was her mother's death the murder the newspaper spoke of? Drake's mind began to spin with the possibilities and he hated the conclusions he started to perceive. Surely Krystal would not have lied to him about her mother's death?

But now that he began to recount the story she had told him, he realized that she had been very elusive about her mother and the life they had lived in Boston. The idea of Krystal being involved with jewel thieves was not only the most far-fetched thing he had ever heard, but he did not want to believe that his wife could be a liar.

The fact that they had found John Colbert was proof that her journey out West was legitimate. Maybe it was possible, Drake suddenly realized, that Krystal was only trying to protect her mother — the mysterious and deceased Rebecca Colbert? From the bit of information he had picked up from Krystal and John's conversation about Rebecca, Drake knew she sounded like the type of woman who would do anything to get what she wanted. His dark green eyes searched Krystal's face for any sign that might signal that she was lying to him, but her look was so confused, so terrified, he instantly became convinced that she was innocent of any wrongdoing. His anger was redirected to whomever was responsible for the pack of lies printed in this newspaper.

"We're going to the authorities and straighten this mess out, right now!" Drake reached out and started to grab a hold of Krystal's arm, but she pulled away from him in fear.

"Drake, I swear, I know nothing of a jewel-smuggling ring. Good Lord, they — the Pinkerton men — must think my mother's death was a murder! But why would they want to question me?" Tears began to fill the rim's of her large eyes with the fear that was running rampant throughout her quaking body. A wanted poster had been sent out on her! The very idea petrified her. Why would they go to such drastic measures to seek information from her?

Drake's anger began to subside at the onset of her tears. He was sure that she was telling him the truth and he intended to prove it. "Krystal, I'm sorry," he said in a softer tone of voice. "I'm not upset with you, not now anyway. I let my imagination get carried away and I wasn't thinking clearly. I know you could never be involved with anything unlawful." He reached out and drew her up to him.

Krystal allowed him to cradle her in his powerful embrace, it was the only place she felt safe, and she wished he would never have to turn loose of her. He was right, of course. She knew that they should go to the authorities and find out what the Pinkerton's investigation had revealed about her mother. Yet, she was not sure if she wanted to know the whole truth. She been curious about her mother's vast wealth and extravagant lifestyle ever since her mother's funeral. And what about the brooch? Krystal's blood ran cold as she thought of the diamond brooch she had found in her mother's bureau drawer. The strange feeling she had felt about that elaborate piece of jewelry intensified even more now. Was it stolen, just as Devon had suggested? If it should turn out that it had been stolen, then it would prove that her mother had been involved in something illegal, and Krystal knew she could not slander her mother's memory with a scandal such as that would cause, even with the anger she had felt towards her mother because of the terrible way she had treated John Colbert.

"Drake, I can't go to the Sheriff, or anyone else about this."

He pulled away in an abrupt manner. "What are you saying? Don't you realize that you will be considered an accomplice to whatever crime has been committed if you don't comply with the law?" His brows

279

drew together as his face settled into a deep frown. "There is no reason you should be afraid to go to the Sheriff, unless—" he couldn't finish the thought which had just entered his mind again. Only moments earlier, he had been planning their whole future, together . . . a future which promised a lifetime of happiness. If it turned out that she was wanted back East for criminal activities, their life together would be over.

Krystal knew exactly what he was thinking, she could read the accusations written all over his face. Had his mind already sentenced her without a trial? She wouldn't beg him to believe her. If he did not love her enough to put his faith in her, then there was nothing left to say on the subject.

"I'm going to my father's cabin," Krystal stated in a quiet voice. She avoided his eyes as she pushed past him and exited through the door. In the beginning, she had not trusted him, but her feelings for him had remained strong, even through her doubts. Was it possible that his love for her was not strong enough to see him through something this devastating? Or was it that his love had just been shattered into a million shards . . . just like her heart?

Chapter Twenty

For a second, Drake was too numb to move. The slamming of the door echoed through his tortured mind and ricocheted across the silent room. Krystal had not admitted to anything, but she had not really denied anything either. A part of him was clinging to the rigid lawman creed which continued to rule his life. Yet, his heart was shouting at him to go after her. He wanted to forget what the newspaper said, forget whatever dark secrets she might have in her past. But could he, Drake DeGanahl, the uprightous man of frontier justice, forget that his wife was wanted by the Pinkerton National Detective Agency?

In barely more than one panicked beat, his heart made the decision for him. He yanked the door open, nearly pulling it off of the hinges with the force and bolted from the room. She stood at the end of the hallway, her eyes large with fright, and filled with a desperate hope. A force greater than both of them pulled them towards one another until they were only inches apart. The tender look contained within his misted green eyes told Krystal that he had made a choice. The affinity which had first drawn them to one another had developed into a passion of their flesh and of their hearts, and it had made them not only lovers, but also man and wife.

She closed the narrow gap between them until they were so close that their bodies touched and their breathing rose and fell in unison. She lifted her face up as his head tilted down to meet hers, but they did not kiss. They just stood in the middle of the hallway, their lips almost touching, and their bodies merged together as though they were one. Each of them sensed that their relationship had just added another dimension to the affection they had already had for one another. In this instant of complete acceptance, intermingled with overpowering devotion, words were not necessary.

The trip back up to Sugar Loaf was made in silence, too. Drake had rented horses and purchased a corduroy riding suit for Krystal to wear before they had left town. But she remained aloof whenever he tried to talk about anything other than her increasing riding abilities, especially now that she had the proper riding attire. Drake keep reminding himself not to pressure her into telling him why she was afraid to go to the authorities, but it was hard for him to remain quiet about the subject since it was eating away at him without mercy. But when she had walked out of that hotel room, he had made a decision that he was going to stand beside his wife—no matter what the consequences turned out to be.

Krystal was struggling with her own feelings of confusion and despair. She wanted to tell Drake about the diamond brooch and the fear she had about her mother's activities in Boston, but would he understand why she did not want her mother's memory destroyed if her suspicions should turn out to be true? Or would he insist that she go to the Pinkerton men and tell them what she suspected about her mother? Krystal could not forget that Drake was once a lawman, although she couldn't help but wonder how dedicated he still was to his former profession. The only thing they did agree upon, however, was that Krystal would have to stay out of sight until they could find out more about the wanted poster issued on her by the Pinkerton Agency. She wondered if Les Macrea had told the detectives about the letter contained in her mother's will. If he had, it would probably be just a matter of time before they would be looking for her in Virginia City, too.

When she related this latest worry to Drake, he instantly decided that they should leave Nevada at once. This was foreign territory to him since he did not know anyone here. Whereas, if they returned to Green River, he could use his past connections with the Wyoming law enforcers to learn about the investigation which the Pinkerton detectives were conducting of Krystal and her deceased mother. He still had many friends who were lawmen, friends who had tried to persuade him to return to his job after his father's death. It had been mentioned on several occasions that Drake should take over his father's position as Sheriff of Sweetwater county, but Drake had been too disillusioned at the time to even consider it. It seemed strange to him now, because only a couple of hours earlier he had actually been thinking about applying for that job when they reached Wyoming. But now, just as it had been for the past two and a half years, his life was once again in a turmoil and a simple solution was not within sight.

Krystal knew it wasn't safe to be in Virginia City if Les Macrea had told the detective agency about John Colbert. But leaving here would also mean leaving her father, and even though she was furious at him for his rash decision to force her into marrying Drake, she still hated to be separated from him again. "I'm going to try to convince him to leave here with us," she stated firmly as they rode their rented horses over the last knoll which led to the Krystal Dawn Mine.

"He won't go," Drake replied. John Colbert had been on this mountain too long. Drake knew the only way to get the old man off of here would be to blast him off of Sugar Loaf.

Krystal cast a smug look in his direction. He didn't know everything, and she could be very persuasive at times. Tonight she planned to use every ounce of her feminine wiles on her father in an attempt to convince him that he should go to Wyoming with them.

John was reclining in the old chair which stood on the front stoop when they arrived. Since it was late in the day, he knew that they were obviously not going to go back to town tonight. "Hells-a-fire! What in tarnation are you two doing here on your weddin' night?"

Krystal blushed profusely. Good Lord, it was their wedding night. Suddenly she wished they had not left the International Hotel with such haste, one more night might not have made any difference. A devilish smile curved Drake's lips when he noted the strange look on her reddened face. He wondered if her thoughts were equalling the same sweet expectations that his mind was envisioning of their wedding night.

284

Krystal quickly turned away from Drake when she caught sight of the crooked grin on his mocking face. Was he always thinking lewd thoughts, she wondered? But then, since she met him, her thoughts were constantly engrossed with lustful yearnings, too.

"We — well, we wanted to talk to you," she managed to stutter while trying to focus on something besides the memories of last night and the anticipation of the next time.

John approached them with a cautious look upon his weathered face. " 'Bout what?" He helped her dismount, then handed the reins to Drake, who led the horses over to a nearby clump of sagebrush which served as a hitching post.

"About going to Wyoming with us," Krystal gushed enthusiastically. "Drake and I are leaving right away and we want you to go with us."

John shook his head in a disbelieving manner. "Wyoming? Now why in tarnation would I want to go to Wyoming? I got my mine to work here."

Krystal's hands dropped to her side with aggravation. "This mine? Surely you're not serious? There's nothing here anymore, and mother stole everything there ever was in this godforsaken mountain." Krystal stopped herself, she had already said more than she should have. The Krystal Dawn Mine was all he had and it had been his whole life for more than twenty years. What right did she have to belittle it? "I'm sorry, Father. I shouldn't have said that, but please come to Wyoming with us? I couldn't bear to leave you again."

John's expression of hurt began to fade with her last words. He didn't need anybody to tell him how worthless this old mine was. But to leave here after all this time? John glanced around at the crumbing shack, the bleak countryside and the crooked sign which he had erected on the day of Krystal's birth. A lifetime of shattered dreams and forgotten plans were sunk into the dry soil of this mountain.

"I can't go with you, chéri. This is my home." He smiled through the red whiskers as he glanced towards the cabin. "I still got a roof over my head, I ain't never been hungry, not for too long anyhow, and there's always that faint chance that someday —" he paused as his eyes took on a gleaming, faraway look. "Someday, I just might hit a new vein, or discover one more of them big gold nuggets like the one I found up here on the day you were born."

Krystal wanted to dispute him, to tell him how foolish he was to cling to such an impossible desire, but how could she steal his dreams away from him? Her protests stopped short when she looked at his enthusiastic expression. She nodded her head and gave him a wistful smile. Who knows, she thought hopefully, maybe someday he will discover another bonanza up here on this lonesome mountaintop. "We'll be leaving for Wyoming in the morning then. So could Drake and I spend the night here with you?".

John was taken aback with surprise, he was not accustomed to having house guests, and he rather liked the idea. "Why, of course. I just shot a rabbit for my dinner and it'll be plenty for all of us. And I got a bottle of scotch, too. I've been savin' it for a special occasion. Ain't nothing more special than my little girl's weddin' night."

Krystal laughed and glanced at Drake. He had been watching the touching scene in silence, but now he moved to Krystal's side and laughed along with her. He could think of better places he would like to spend their wedding night, but so far, nothing which involved Krystal followed the normal course of things.

John reached down into a canvas bag and pulled out a skinned rabbit while a wide grin crossed his face. "I'll start supper right now."

"I'll cook dinner," Krystal blurted out, ignoring the chuckle which emitted from Drake's direction. "You and Drake can enjoy that bottle of scotch while I prepare that — that thing." She wrinkled up her nose as she cautiously reached for the dead animal. "Did you say this was a rabbit?" The poor thing was dark red and terribly skinny with gray veins running through the meaty parts of its hindquarters. It certainly didn't look like any of the little furry bunnies she had seen in Boston. Krystal swallowed hard, but refused to give into the unexpected urge to vomit. Drake's smirking face was all it took to make her more determined than ever to show him that she was capable of cooking, or anything else that was expected of her now that she was his wife . . . and especially since there were no servants out here to do it for her.

She tossed her head back defiantly. "Are all the cooking utensils in the house?" She tried to sound knowledgeable in spite of the loud noises Drake was making as he chuckled and faked several short coughs.

"Yep," John answered, wondering what Drake found so humorous. "Right by the stove. Are you sure you don't need any help, chéri?"

"Of course not," she replied through gritted teeth. She was thinking of smacking Drake in the face with this hideous excuse for a rabbit if he didn't quiet down

287

as she swung around and gave him a look of amazement which did little to silence him.

"Maybe you would like some help, darlin'?" he choked out with his mirth. "I seem to recall that you don't cook too often."

"Oh, really? Well, why don't you just go drink your scotch while I prepare a fabulous feast out of this—this poor animal." Holding the rabbit at arm's length, she hurried into the dimly lit cabin. Oh Lord, it was worse than she thought it would be. Yesterday when Drake had left her here while he had went in search of her father, she had been too nervous about their meeting to even notice the inside of the old shack. And when Drake had returned with him, they had stayed outside while they conversed. Krystal was not impressed with the interior of her father's home. In fact, she could not even imagine a human living in such filth.

Against one wall was a narrow cot with a tattered quilt rumped up at one end. Beside the bed leaned a chair which was held together by several bands of baling wire, and a small, rectangular table with a nauseating array of half-eaten food staples stood in the center of the room. The only other thing in the one room abode was the iron stove which adorned the far wall. It was a Monogram stove just like the stove which had been in the old farmhouse where Krystal had spent the first night with Drake and the band of outlaws. She had watched Drake closely that night while he had prepared a meal, and she was sure that she could cook on this stove without any problems.

Finding a clean spot to lay the rabbit down on while she attempted to light a fire in the stove was a different matter, however. She finally resorted to taking out the white lace handkerchief from her little black handbag and laying the animal down upon it. Carefully she lifted one of the round lids from the front burner by the coiled handle. She was in luck, it was already filled with kindling, and a box of matches sat on the shelf above the stove. In a matter of seconds, she had a fire burning in the stove and was feeling quite confident that she was going to show Drake DeGanahl a thing or two about cooking. She couldn't wait to see his reaction when she presented a delectable feast before his smirking face. She about jumped through the roof when his voice bellowed through the door of the one room cabin.

"Are you needing any help yet, darlin'?" His eyes instantly took note of the skinned rabbit resting in the middle of her elegant lace handkerchief. It was apparent to Krystal that he was finding this to be extremely humorous since he could barely contain his urge to laugh.

She bristled with indignity. "No, thank you. I'm doing just fine all by myself." She waved proudly at the fire which she had just started in the burner.

It was obvious to him that she was in one of her more stubborn moods, so he decided to let her have a go at cooking the whole meal on her own. "If but if you should need anything—"

"I can assure you that I won't," she cut in with a forceful tone. Did he think she was completely helpless when it came to menial chores? Well, she thought angrily, soon she was going to prove him wrong and then he would be choking on his laughter.

Drake smiled and tipped his hat by the brim before backing out of the door, but not before he took one more intimidating look at the rabbit and its formal

289

mattress of linen and lace. Krystal's hands clenched tightly into fists as she twirled back around to the stove. She glanced over at the slaughtered rabbit with dread. Somehow, she was going to turn that lump of pitiful red meat into a feast fit for a king! Perhaps, she would even allow Drake DeGanahl one small morsel, but unless his attitude improved a great deal, it was doubtful. More furious than cautious, she shoved a large handful of wood kindling into the burner, then dropped the iron lid back down on it with a loud thud.

Her father had been right about the cooking utensils being next to the stove. He had forget to mention however, that they had not been washed for at least a decade. The pans, along with all of the spatulas and assorted cooking implements were covered with thick layers of blackened grease and soot. Krystal picked up one of the cast iron skillets by the very tip of its slimy handle, being extra careful not to touch her light-colored riding suit with the dirty mess.

"I do believe there is a skillet hidden somewhere beneath all this filth," she announced as she exited onto the front porch. "Is there a—a sink or something where I could wash it?"

Drake and John both jumped up in unison at the sound of her voice. "A sink?" John's voice echoed. "Up here?"

Drake sat back down on the step where he had been sipping from the bottle of scotch. A look of immense humor twisted his face into a taunting smile, and it was all he could do to keep from laughing out loud again. "You know, John?" he chortled. "A sink is one of those things which requires indoor plumbing and running water. You're bound to have at least two . . .

290

one in the kitchen, and another one in the wash closet."

John immediately grasped the meaning of Drake's mocking remarks. "Oh yes, of course. And just for emergencies, I keep an extra one in the living room, next to the Davenport."

Krystal grew livid and directed every bit of her fury at her husband. He was not content to make her look foolish on his own. Now he was luring her own father into making snide jests at her, too. Storming over to where he was sitting, she purposely dropped the skillet into Drake's unsuspecting lap. The greasy black substance rapidly covered his pants with distorted streaks of oily grime.

"Well that's fine, Mr. DeGanahl," she added in a haughtier tone than normal. "And since you apparently know where the sink is, then you can wash the pan." Her perfectly shaped brows arched upward as she graced him with a triumphant smirk.

A look of disgust joined the frown that was already present on his face as he looked down at the dirty pan sitting in his lap. Why was it, he wondered, that he was the one who always ended up taking the blunt end of his innocent jokes? "Guess I'll go down to the creek and try to scrape some of the grease out of this skillet."

"I reckon I could help ya," John added sheepishly, because he knew he was every bit as guilty as his new son-in-law.

Krystal watched as the two of them sauntered off in the direction of the tiny rivulet of water which they called a creek. Good Lord, a woman won't have a chance against those two. Krystal smiled to herself and drew in a deep breath of the cool evening air before she started back into the cabin. Even before she turned around, she sensed something was not right. The air she inhaled had a strange heaviness in it and it seemed to stop short in her chest. The reason for the odd feeling became apparent the minute she glanced back into the cabin, and her terrified scream broke the quiet atmosphere of the impending nightfall with a chilling foreboding.

Drake froze in his tracks, but for only a second. Krystal was in danger, and he moved faster than he had ever moved before, with John hot on his heels. Krystal was backing out of the cabin door as spirals of black smoke were trailing up from the roof and rapidly covered the last of the golden sunset with hazy streaks of gray.

"What the . . . hells-a-fire! Get away from there, cheri!" John yelled as he began to hasten his step. Drake was already on the stoop beside Krystal. But when John reached the front of the cabin his voice screamed out another deadly warning. "Run! There's a box of ammunition and an old keg of dynamite in there, the whole top of this dang mountain could blow."

Drake grasped his meaning at once. Fear made him move like a man possessed as he swooped Krystal into his arms and charged off of the porch past John in a frantic retreat back down the mountain. John stopped long enough the untie the horses and his old mule. The animals wasted no time in galloping down the side of the mountain as soon as John let out a war-whoop and slapped them on their hindquarters.

Everything was happening so fast, Krystal had no idea what her father was yelling about. She couldn't understand why they weren't trying to put the fire

292

out, instead of running wildly away from it, but there was no time for questions. All at once there was a round of small explosions that sounded like rapid gunfire.

"Hit the dirt," came the next panicked command from John Colbert. "That was the ammo, the dynamite will be next!"

Krystal felt the wind rush from her lungs as she crashed to the ground with the full weight of Drake landing directly on top of her. Her pain was quickly forgotten though, because in the next instant there was a deafening noise and the whole earth seemed to shudder with violence. The deadly eruption spewed rocks and dirt upward from the trembling mountain and then showered Drake, Krystal and John with a downpour of crushing debris. Then there was a calm almost as unnerving as the explosion had been seconds earlier, as the mountain slowly became still once again. All that could be heard was the steady roar of the fire which raged beyond control in the spot where the log cabin had stood just moments ago.

Still too frightened to be coherent, Krystal was vaguely aware of Drake's body rolling off of her. Then she became aware of the pain in her lungs from the force of the fall. As she turned over slowly, she gasped and inhaled the foul air which was thick with smoke and dust. Strong arms were suddenly cradling her within their embrace. She let her quaking form go limp against him, secure now that she knew Drake was taking care of her.

"Are you hurt?" he implored. Krystal gave a negative shake of her head. Her voice eluded her as the air forced its way back into her pained lungs. She became aware of her father's hand resting on her arm while his concerned eyes studied her closely.

"I — I'm sorry, Father," she cried. Good Lord! she had just blown his house up.

John shrugged, "Ain't your fault, chéri. That old stove's been in there since your mama lived here, and I don't hardly ever use it so I reckon it was just all clogged up with grease and such. I should've cleaned it, or better yet, I should've cooked supper myself. You're my guests, if anyone's to blame, it's me." He patted her arm and a gave her a weak smile.

Krystal felt horrible. He was trying to place the blame on himself and she knew without a doubt that she had caused the fire when she had shoved extra wood in the burner and then covered it with the lid so that it could not get any air. When she had turned around and first spotted the fire, it had been shooting up the stove pipe, but before she could even open her mouth to scream, the roof had erupted into an inferno of flames.

"Oh no, Father. It's my fault, I know it is and I'm not going to allow you to take the blame." Her voice bordered on hysteria, but John remained firm as he continued to shake his head vigorously.

"That's not important, all that matters is that no one is hurt," Drake said as he held Krystal tighter. When her blood-curdling scream had first reached his ears, he had been filled with a fear like he had never known before. In the brief span between the sound of her scream and the time it had taken him to reach her, he realized how important she was to him, and how his life would mean nothing without her.

Krystal glanced up when she felt his tightening grip. The night was alive with dancing lights from the huge fire and it cloaked them with a hazy, coral-colored glow which enhanced the love in both of their gazes as they sensed how lucky they were to be in one another's arms. "I guess I should have accepted that offer for help," she said.

Drake gave his head a knowing nod before his look was drawn upward, toward the funnel of twisting black smoke that was intertwining with long fiery arms of orange flames, each fighting to control the other against the black velvet of the night sky. Krystal stared up at the sight with fascination and horror. In Boston, she had witnessed many fires, but never one with such fierce intensity, and never one which she had caused because of her stubborness. Her father's whole life had just been blown from this mountain. She would never forgive herself.

The fire burned itself out within a couple of hours, leaving only dying orange embers and the twisted remains of John's few belongings amongst the gray ash. As though to serve as a reminder of the terrible deed, what was left of the old stove jutted out from among the smoking ruins like a messenger of doom. There was nothing left to salvage, so after a sleepless night, the trio started down the mountain on foot. Halfway down Sugar Loaf they encountered John's old mule and near the bottom they came across both of the rented horses, so they were able to ride the rest of the way back to Virginia City. John remarked several times how lucky they were that there wasn't a lot of vegetation around his cabin or else the whole mountain would have gone up in flames. Virginia City and most of the surrounding areas had always had a severe problem with fires and most of the journey back to town was spent listening to John relate stories of all the fires he had been a witness to, or had heard other miners talk about.

Krystal didn't hear a word he said, but she nodded or smiled whenever he seemed to be speaking in her direction. She was too engrossed with her self-pity over starting the fire. She had forced her father to leave the mountaintop that he had been so devoted to all of these years and she would never be able to make it up to him.

All at once she was reminded of something her father had mentioned when they had first arrived at his cabin yesterday. Last night had been her wedding night and she had missed it! Oh, how could she even be thinking about something as unimportant as that with all the awful things that had happened? She fought with herself to concentrate on more important things, such as the wanted poster the Pinkerton Agency had issued on her, and the fact that in one careless moment, she had destroyed her father's whole life, and, Drake's scorching kisses trailing down through the heaving valley between her breasts. Oh, Good Lord!

Chapter Twenty-one

Staring out the window of the noisy locomotive, Krystal was stunned by the drastic way her life had changed since she had boarded that first train a few weeks ago in Boston. She smoothed down the folds of her black dress with shaking hands and glanced around the train coach with apprehension. She felt like a real criminal and wearing these clothes as a disguise made her feel even more guilty. Drake had been worried that the sheriff might be looking for her after the article appeared in the paper yesterday, so he insisted that she dress herself in the concealing outfit as soon as they reached town. The outfit had not been difficult to obtain from her trunk since she had another black dress and veil almost identical to the one she had been wearing on the day she had met Drake. She simply slipped into the ladies room at the train station and waited until Drake had fetched it from her trunk. In no time at all, she transformed herself into the same lady of mystery who had first inticed her future husband with her tempting pink lips.

Drake reclined in the seat next to her and as his gaze wandered over towards her direction, a slow smile began to curve the corners of his mouth. Beneath the heavy black veil which covered most of her face, Krystal smiled back. She found it hard to believe that this handsome cowboy was her husband. Even after all the bad things that had been happening in her life lately, her shotgun marriage to Drake — degrading as it was — was the one good thing that had come from it all. If her father hadn't taken matters into his own hands, she and Drake probably would have bickered about marriage for a very long time since that seemed to be the usual course of their relationship.

She looked across the aisle and noticed that her father was sound asleep in his seat. Finding him was another blessing she was grateful for. Even though she would never forgive herself for blowing his house to bits, she was secretly happy that she did not have to leave him behind in Virginia City. Although it had not be easy to tear him away from the town where he had spent the last thirty years, Krystal was beginning to think that deep down, John was glad to be going with them, too. While they were waiting for the train to leave Virginia City, she explained to him about the Pinkerton's quest to find her. Telling him about the wanted poster had been a difficult task after everything else that had happened, but by the time they had boarded the train, John was as determined as Drake to prove that Krystal was not involved in anything unlawful.

Just as she had related the story to Drake, she also

told her father everything, except the part about the diamond brooch. Even though she knew nothing of where the brooch had come from, she had a feeling that it was somehow the fatal link between her mother and the jewel thieves the newspaper had written about. The condemning piece of jewelry was once again tucked away in the little black bag which was clutched tightly in her hands and she had no intention of letting it out of her sight until this whole mess with the Pinkerton Agency was cleared up.

Sitting quietly on the train gave Krystal plenty of time to rehash everything about her mother's life that she could recall. But for the past few years they had each been involved with such separate lives that Krystal discovered she really had no idea how her mother spent her time when she was not performing on the stage. Becoming weary with all the dead ends she kept coming up with, Krystal switched her thoughts to what waited for them back in Wyoming. Devon would undoubtably cross their paths again and now he would resent her as much as he did his older brother since she had helped Drake to ambush him behind that deserted shack. She could not help but think about the girl, Jennifer Holt, and the sad way she had contributed to the brothers' bitter fued so many years ago. All at once, she had a compelling need to hear Drake's side of the story.

She twisted around in her seat and eyed Drake thoughtfully. He was reclining back against the back of his seat, but he was not asleep. When he felt his wife's intent gaze focusing on him, he turned and narrowed one eye beneath his wide-brimmed hat. "A penny for your thoughts, darlin'?"

"I want to know about Jennifer Holt," she blurted

out.

"Who?"

"Jennifer Holt — the girl you stole away from Devon, and the reason for the battle that has been going on between you two for so long."

Drake pulled himself up abruptly. "What in the devil are you talking about?"

Devon had been correct, Krystal assumed, Drake did not even remember the girl. But she intended to refresh his memory. "How could you be so heartless to forget a girl that your brother loved with all his heart and whom you destroyed with your cruel rejection?"

Drake slumped forward, his face a mask of confusion. "Whoa, darlin'. I don't know what nonsense my brother told you, but it sounds like he filled your head with a pack of lies." Drake's jaw squared as anger colored his olive eyes with a dark fury. "He's not going to get away with this, damnit!"

"Are you saying there never was a girl named Jennifer Holt?" Krystal was confused now. Did Devon make up that tragic story just in the hopes of turning her against Drake? Devon had seemed so sincere when he told her the tale of his lost love. His heart-break had been every bit as convincing as Drake's rage was now. The last thing she wanted to do was to cause more conflict between the two brothers, and if it turned out that she was repeating a lie that Devon had conceived just for that purpose, then she would feel as angry towards Devon as Drake did right now. "Think hard, because I have to know if Devon was lying to me."

Drake's brows drew together as he searched his memory. Jennifer Holt? "No, I don't — " he slapped his knee and then pointed at Krystal as a look of recognition lit up his face. "Wait a minute! I do remember a girl named Jennifer. But . . . that was years ago."

Krystal felt her blood turn to ice. There was such a girl, and perhaps there was also a reason for Devon's feelings of animosity towards Drake? "Do you remember anything else? Such as the night Devon proposed marriage to her, but she turned him down because you were the one that she loved. And do you also remember why she was so despondent after confessing her love to you that she would kill herself?" Krystal tried to keep her voice at a controlled level, but it was difficult to do with the anger that was rapidly taking over her sensibility.

Drake's mouth gaped open in shock. "Is that what Devon told you?" He didn't need an answer, it was written all over her face . . . she believed that Jennifer Holt had committed suicide because of some terrible injustice he was supposed to have done to her. He fell back against the seat and stared at his wife in disbelief as a slow boil began to work its way through him. Devon would never be satisfied until he lured Drake into a final confrontation, and if his conniving lies caused a rift between him and Krystal, then it was possible Devon would finally succeed.

Krystal pulled the heavy black veil up and flipped it back over the top of her black hat. She wanted nothing to obstruct his face from her probing gaze. She had closely watched Devon's expression when he had told her about Jennifer Holt, and the pain in his ebony eyes had convinced her that he believed what he was saying was the truth. If she could see the same sincerity in the depths of Drake's deep green gaze, then maybe she might be able to piece the two stories together and begin to make some sense out of this strange tale.

She reached out and touched her husband's arm lightly. "I'm sorry. I have no right to jump to conclusions, especially when it is not any of my business. But I implore you to tell me your side of the story. I have only Devon's account of what happened to cause this terrible resentment between the two of you, and I feel I can't let it rest until I have tried to sort it all out."

Drake's eyes moved down to the spot where her slender hand rested on his sleeve. He stared at her delicate fingers as he tried to will his mind to travel back in time. He realized that he had not had a chance to buy her a wedding ring yet. That was one of the first things he intended to do when they reached Green River. He pushed that thought from his mind and returned his wandering mind to Jennifer Holt. He could not even recall her face because Krystal's beautiful angelic face was the only image his spinning brain could conjure up. She had filled his life with dreams of a future that would be graced by her precious beauty and the timeless love they had discovered in each other arms. No woman he had ever known, or would ever meet again, could even begin to complete with the overpowering feelings he had for her. How could she ask him to remember a girl he had vaguely known ten years ago?

His gaze ascended and he was lost in those pools of golden-brown that watched him with dread and hope. He could see the questions that begged to be answered floating in their jeweled depths and he knew she was wrong about one important thing. His life was her business now, and all that concerned her was his business, too. He would tell her all he knew of

Jennifer Holt, and then, he would ask her to tell him about Rebecca Colbert.

"It was so long ago, and at the time it seemed so trivial," he began.

"A young girl's death seemed trivial?" Krystal asked, wondering if her husband was not the compassionate man she had first thought him to be.

Drake shook his head. "That's not what I mean. I was talking about what happened between me and Jennifer Holt." Krystal grew rigid in her seat. She had been praying that he would tell her that nothing had ever happened between them, but it appeared her prayers had not been answered.

"I didn't learn of her death for several months after it supposedly happened, and no one told me she had taken her own life. I heard she was dead, nothing more. I had no idea she used me as the reason she couldn't marry Devon. He never mentioned anything to me. What I know about her is mostly what I remember hearing from other people."

She clasped her shaking hands together tightly and placed them in her lap. "What happened the last night you saw her?"

He leaned his head back against the hard train seat and took himself back through the misty passages of time, back to the days when his life was still filled with the challenges that accompany youth, back to that fateful spring night. His mind envisioned a young girl with big brown eyes and hair the color of harvest wheat. He could not tell Krystal about that last night without talking about the type of girl that Jennifer Holt been, too.

"Reverend Holt's daughter, as I recall, was as wild as her father was gentle and kind. I reckon that's why folks around Green River always looked the other way when she was up to one of her high jinks. Now that I think back on it, she and Devon were like two peas in a pod when it came to being hellbent and rebellious." Drake sighed as his mind continued to trek into the deep trenches of his memory. He had not thought about those long ago times for many years and so much had happened since then, it all seemed to be lost in a distant haze.

"I had heard from the grapevine that Devon had been seen in her company several times, but then, nearly every young fella in the county had been involved with Jennifer Holt at one time or another."

"Even you?"

Drake squirmed uneasily in his seat as he rubbed his sweaty palms down the length of his thighs. "I had more than one opportunity. Miss Holt was always sending me come-hither signals with those big brown eyes of hers. I might've been young, but I was nobody's fool." Drake shook his head while an amazed look covered his face. "I guess the same couldn't be said for my little brother though. He must have asked her to marry him the night of the annual spring church social, because that was the night she came to me and declared her undying devotion to me. She was real persuasive, if I remember correctly. And I won't lie to you, she was a pretty little gal, no doubt about that. But she was used goods in Sweetwater County."

Krystal felt her face grow flushed at the insinuation of Drake's words. If it was true that Jennifer Holt had been such a trollop, why had Devon become so involved with her? "But . . . Devon must have loved her immensely."

Drake sighed as he leaned back in the hard seat, his

mind groping even deeper into the faded past. "She cornered me out behind the old barn where we always held the social gatherings during the warm months, and she told me," a bitter chuckle emitted from him, "how she had loved me for a long time and that all her other beaus had not meant anything to her. I thought she was bluffing when she told me that someone had proposed to her that night and how she had turned him down because I was the one she loved." He swung around and gazed at Krystal with a pleading look. "I really believed she was just making it all up so that I would make some sort of a commitment to her. I never knew Devon's feelings for her were so strong."

"What did you say to her after she told you of her love for you?" Krystal felt like she was asking questions that she really did not have a right to ask, but she wanted to understand what had really happened.

"I laughed. I told her there wasn't a man in all of Sweetwater who was stupid enough to marry her after she had rolled in the haystack with half the men in the county."

Krystal gasped. "You didn't!"

"I did. How as I to know my own brother was that big of a fool? I had better things to occupy my time with besides keeping track of Devon's social life."

"Oh, is that so?" Krystal asked coldly. "Well, if you had never paid any attention to — this — Jennifer Holt, why would she tell Devon that you loved her, too? You said it yourself, she had been intimate with half the men in the county. Were you included in that tally?"

Drake's expression grew taut. The more he thought about the past, that night in particular, the more furious he became. It no longer mattered that he had

305

planned to answer anything Krystal might ask of him. Why should he have to defend himself to his own wife because of Devon, or anyone else!

"Whether or not I was one of Jennifer Holt's lovers is hardly important, darlin'. Maybe you should concern yourself with the problems at hand instead of something that happened ten years ago." Immediately Drake cursed himself for losing his temper. A look of defiance flashed into Krystal's eyes while she drew herself as far away from him as she could in the narrow seat. "I didn't mean anything by that re—"

"Oh, I think you did!" she cut in sharply. "And you're right, of course. I have enough problems of my own. I hardly need to be worrying about your and Devon's past love affairs."

Damn! She was drawing her own impulsive conclusions again. Drake watched as she pulled down her black veil across her face in an enraged gesture, making him all the more defensive. The events of a decade ago were unimportant when compared to the enormous problems they were facing now. But they had to learn to trust one another if they ever hoped to overcome them. He imitated her gesture by yanking on the brim of his hat and pulling it down low on his forehead before he sunk back against the seat. He knew he should apologize to her, but he had an unyielding streak that equalled Krystal's when it came to being stubborn. His crossed his arms over his chest and began to contemplate his next meeting with his little brother.

By the time they reached Odgen, Utah, Krystal had come to the conclusion that she hated trains. She was sick of riding in the hard coach seats and she was tired of traveling from one place to another. She

306

wanted to live a normal life again, but that seemed impossible now. As they descended the train coach of the Southern Pacific Railroad, Krystal's thoughts returned to the last time they had been in this train yard. She had helped Drake trick Devon and had left him in an abandoned building — tied and gagged. She shuddered at the memory. Devon would be more revengeful than ever, and part of his anger would be directed at her.

"Drake! Am I glad to see you again. Are you headed back to Green River?" A rugged looking man sauntered up with a wide grin etched upon his weathered face. His friendly greeting went unnoticed by Krystal. She was too consumed with fright as her gaze locked on the glistening badge which adorned the front of his shirt. Instinctively, she began to tug on the corners of her net veil.

"Cameron!" Drake answered with more enthusiasm than he planned. He couldn't believe that the Wyoming marshal was still in Odgen and for a moment he was at a loss for words.

Cameron Reed shook his head as his smile began to fade. "It's a stroke of luck that I ran into you here."

Drake chuckled, hoping his face didn't give away any of the nervousness he was suddenly feeling. "Oh, why is that?" He glanced over his shoulder and noticed that Krystal and John were nowhere in sight. His uneasy feeling from a moment ago began to turn into an engulfing feeling of panic.

"I'm taking Devon back to Green River on the train today. He's been in the Odgen jail since his arrest."

"What did you say?" Drake demanded loudly when his mind snapped back to Cameron's statement. "Devon was arrested?"

307

Cameron Reed blinked, Drake's tone of voice momentarily setting him back on his heels. "You haven't heard about it? It's been on the front page of the local newspaper for the last three days."

"I'm just returning from Neveda." His voice was still louder than necessary although he was trying to act normal. "I don't know anything about Devon being arrested."

Cameron shrugged. He had known the DeGanahl's for a long time. At one time he had worked beside Franklin and Drake as a fellow lawman, and for the past couple years he had hunted Devon DeGanahl with a relentless obsession. But he had always been one step behind the cunning outlaw — that is, until a few days ago. Devon had been careless, and Cameron was finally there at the right time. But it was Drake's behavior that aroused him now. Drake DeGanahl had always been so calm mannered. Cameron was curious as to what would make Drake so edgy.

"I helped the Odgen sheriff arrest Devon several days ago. He was on a drunken rampage and more than likely would've went unnoticed by the local authorities if I hadn't been in town." Cameron shrugged as he eyed Drake closely. "But I'm taking him back to my jail in Green River."

"Damn!" Drake said without thinking. If Devon was to be incarcerated in Green River, then it was safe to assume that his whole gang would be somewhere in that area. That meant Drake not only had to worry about protecting his wife from the authorities, but also from the likes of Creed Ward. He glanced at Cameron Reed and noted the strange expression on the marshal's face. Immediately Drake sensed the other's man suspicions.

"I'm sorry, Cameron. It's been a long day and your announcement caught me off guard." Drake attempted a weak smile, hoping to lighten the mood. "Why are you extraditing Devon back to Wyoming?"

Cameron spit on the ground and narrowed his eyes. "Because I wanted him real bad. It's over for men like Devon and I'm intending to use him for an example."

Drake wasn't surprised by Cameron's cold attitude. Cattle rustlers, holdup men and killers were having a heyday in Utah, Wyoming, Colorado, and their surrounding states. There wasn't a lawman in the territory who didn't have his hands full trying to crack down on the outlaws' increasing activities.

"I wish I could return to Green River with you today, but I have some pressing business here in Odgen." Drake lied. "I'll be tied up for a couple days. Will you permit me to see him when I do get back to Wyoming, though? I don't know if it would matter to Devon, but it might make my mother feel better." Drake glanced around again. There was no way he could take Krystal on the same train that Cameron and Devon would be traveling on today. He was getting more nervous by the minute, but he forced himself to at least try to act normal for the time he was in the marshal's presence.

Cameron's tense stance relaxed. He began to feel slightly guilty for the suspicions he had been forming about Drake. Lately he had so much on his mind that he caught himself suspecting everyone he came in contact with. Franklin DeGanahl's oldest son didn't deserve the consequences of his little brother's life of mayhem. "You'd be allowed to see him, but you're right, it probably won't have much effect on him. He's a bitter man, worse than I expected him to be. If his attitude doesn't change before he goes to trial, he doesn't have much hope of escaping a noose around his neck."

Drake nodded in agreement. Devon had obviously been arrested right after he and Krystal had left him tied up in the train station. He could only imagine the extent of Devon's hate towards him now.

"If it's not one thing, it's another," Cameron continued in an aggravated tone. "Worryin' about Devon's cohorts trying to break him out is more than enough, but I've been up here Odgen for the last few days with some Pinkerton man and some lawyer from back East. This was the last thing I needed right now."

Drake's heart took a violent jump in his chest. He clenched his hands tightly at his sides in an effort to hide their visible shaking. A dozen questions were whirling through his mind, but he didn't dare trust himself to speak. When he had met Cameron the other day, he had mentioned the Pinkerton man then. Drake had no doubt that the detective was here because of Krystal. Drake knew he had to find her and get her out of Odgen before they encountered the detective who was obviously hot on her trail.

"I'll see you in a few days," he managed to choke out as he made a hasty retreat from Cameron Reed. Drake could feel the marshal's curious stare following after him, but he did not break stride as he hurried into the station. Once he was inside the building, he paused to catch his breath. The seriousness of Krystal's situation hit him like the blast from a cannon. The Pinkerton National Detective Agency had sent an investigator clear across the country to look for his wife. The article in the newspaper had said she was wanted for questioning, but what did they hope to learn from her? What was the extent of her involvement with the jewel thieves and the murder mentioned in the paper?

Drake's mind was whirling with questions of his own — and accusations — when his brooding gaze ascended and met with Krystal's worried look across the room. She had sought refuge in the ticket office when Drake had stopped to talk to Cameron Reed. If she had nothing to hide, why was she so frightened of talking to the authorities? Drake felt betrayed, he did not want someone else to tell him whatever it was that she was trying to hide. He wanted Krystal to love him and trust him enough to tell him on her own. But was it possible they had not known each other long enough to develop the clossness that a strong relationship could be built upon? Drake ran a trembling hand across his upper lip to wipe away the beads of sweat which had suddenly appeared there. Had they even known one another long enough, he wondered, to be man and wife? Or was their marriage some crazy charade that they would both come to regret?

Chapter Twenty-two

The only thing Krystal could attribute to Drake's sour attitude was his encounter with the marshal in Ogden. What could the man have told him to affect him so drastically? Since they had left Ogden under the shadow of nightfall several hours earlier, he had been cordial to John, but he had not even made an effort to be civil to her. At first, Krystal had been hurt by his cold indifference, but as the long night wore on, anger began to replace her hurt. Why was he so mad at her? He was the one who refused to answer her question about his relationship with Jennifer Holt. The more she dwelled on their conversation about that subject, the angrier she became. He had not admitted to an affair with the girl, but he had certainly not denied it, either. Krystal knew she was being foolish to worry about something which had happened ten years before she had even met Drake, but she had a nagging feeling that whatever had taken place back then, would somehow affect their lives now.

"Did he say anything to you?" Krystal asked her

father in a whisper as she brought the mare which Drake had rented for her to ride up next to her father's horse.

John eyed the back of his new son-in-law thoughtfully and shrugged. "He only said it was too dangerous to travel on the train anymore and from now on we would be travelin' by horseback."

Krystal's fear increased. Why was it suddenly too dangerous to travel by train? She nudged her horse in the side and the animal moved forward with a jerk. When Drake had demanded that she and John hide in the same abandoned shack where they had tied up Devon she had not wanted to argue with him, and when he had returned with three horses his mood had been so hostile that she was afraid to ask him any questions.

She was getting used to the idea of riding across country on a horse again, but she was aghast at the getup that Drake had insisted on her wearing for the trip. She had never worn britches in her entire life and she felt ridiculous wearing a man's shirt and a pair of boy's jeans with her dainty black hightop boots and black bonnet. And underneath the scandelous outfit were the lacy undergarments she had been wearing with her black dress. He didn't even have the decency to provide her with a complete outfit, but she was afraid of increasing his foul mood so she did not mention the fact that her ruffled garterbelt was not the most comfortable choice of underwear to accompany the tight pants he had purchased for her.

Since they had sneaked out of Odgen, he still had not offered her any explanations as to his strange behavior. Instead, he had grown more distant and sullen with each passing mile, and Krystal was not sure how much more of this she could take. Drake's eyes remained fixed on the old stagecoach road they

313

were following when she rode up beside him. He tried to concentrate on the dim outline of the road, which by now was lit only by the star-studded sky, but it was nearly impossible. Even when she had been riding behind him it was difficult to deal with his acute sense of her deception along with his strong feelings of love for her. Now that she had moved her horse abreast with his mount, the wild thrashing of his heart threatened to explode within his chest. It was useless for him to attempt to decifer his emotions. His thoughts were still too jumbled and confused. When they reached Green River he would take her to his mother's house until he had a chance to talk to Devon. Drake could not perceive what his next step would be past that point because he loved her too much not to have her complete confidence.

"Drake? Her voice trembled when she spoke his name. He did not answer, but the ache in her heart deepened. "Are—are we still going to Green River?"

The stony expression he wore did not disappear as his words sliced sharply through the cool night air. "Yep, Devon was arrested in Odgen. He was shipped back to Green River today and I need to talk to him."

"Good Lord!" Krystal's mind immediately flashed back to the day they had left him in the deserted shack. "It's our fault! If we hadn't—"

"Damnit Krystal!" Drake cut in as he turned in his saddle to look at her. His dark eyes narrowed, their coldness matched by the icy tone of his voice. "Devon is a wanted man. Not only is he wanted for robbery, but he's also a cold-blooded killer. I refuse to take any of the blame for anything that has to do with him. He made his choice a long time ago . . . the wrong choice. Maybe you should take a lesson from his mistakes."

Stunned by the cruel sound of his words, Krystal

314

grew limp in the saddle. Her horse, a gentle gray mare, sensed her riders loss of control and seized the opportunity to stop and nibble on a clump of range grass. Krystal stared at the sight of Drake's back moving away from her, but she could think of nothing to say in her own defense. She wanted to cry out to him, to ask him why he was acting so hateful toward her and to demand that he tell her why he would insinuate that she was the same as Devon, but she couldn't make a sound.

"I'm going to ride on ahead," John said quietly when his horse was beside Krystal's mare. "I think you two young folks need some time to be alone."

She did not answer as John continued to move ahead. When he caught up with Drake, the two men had a brief exchange of words before John rode on up the road. The darkness soon swallowed up the last of him, leaving only Drake and the shape of the black horse he sat upon outlined by the silvery moonbeams. He swung his horse around so that he was facing Krystal. She could not make out his features beneath his dark brown hat but she sensed his look even from a distance. He did not want to stop to talk to her, in fact, she wondered if he was not wishing that he had never even met her. She was too frightened to move. If he had suddenly decided that he did not love her after all, she was not sure if she could go on without him.

Realizing she was not going to ride up to meet him, Drake finally nudged his horse in the sides and headed back in her direction. Even his horse seemed to walk with dread-filled steps as they slowly approached the spot where Krystal still sat unmoving on her mount. Drake tried to tell John that it was not necessary for them to talk, but John insisted. Now they were alone . . . and Drake had nothing to say to

315

her.

Krystal peered through the shadows of the night, seeking some hope that his mood had changed. But there was enough light illuminating from the moon to lend proof that his attitude towards her was still the same. His expression had not changed, it was still filled with the same extreme aversion as before.

"What have I done?" she asked in a feeble voice that teetered on the verge of tears.

Drake leaned forward in his saddle as he inhaled the sweet flowery scent of the night-blooming sand puffs. If she would only tell him what it was that she had done to warrant a Boston detective to chase her all this way, then maybe it would make his decision just a little bit easier. His pleading eyes searched her face for an answer. She was just so damn beautiful in the purplish glow of the desert moon against the deep red clay of the earth. His insides twisted into a knot. The mere sight of her was too tempting for him to be this close. He saw her lower lip tremble as her large eyes filled with the threatening teardrops. Forcing his eyes to shift a different direction was almost impossible, but he had to look away before he lost what was left of his diminishing senses.

A tremor of pain filled Krystal's chest when he turned away from her. For a moment she thought she had seen a glimmer of the love he had felt for her before they had stopped in Ogden. But it disappeared as fast as it had appeared and the detached look that overcame his expression was more painful than she could bear. If he regretted their marriage, nothing else mattered. She had to get away from him, and away from those dark eyes which only held contempt where they had once contained the soft glow of his love.

"I won't beg you to tell me what's wrong, so I can

316

only draw my own conclusions." Her voice quivered as she added, "And I don't want to be somewhere where I don't feel I am wanted."

"What is that supposed to mean?" he asked with aggravation.

Krystal drew her hand roughly across her cheek to wipe away an unwanted teardrop. "It means that I am not going to Green River with you. My father and I will part company with you here."

"Don't be rid—"

"I'm not!" she interrupted in a restrained voice. "You have to think of Devon and your mother now. You don't need to be burdened with my problems, too." Drake opened his mouth to speak, but Krystal shook her head with vigor. "No, let me finish. I know how hard it is for you to deal with your own conflicting feelings concerning my situation with the Pinkerton Detective Agency, but I have to handle it my way. I had hoped you would understand, but I realize now how selfish I've been."

Drake exhaled deeply. He had been praying that she was finally ready to confide in him. Instead, she was willing to leave him in order to keep her dark secrets from him. "Aren't you forgetting something?" he asked in a sarcastic tone.

"Such as?" she retorted with a faint hope that he would reconfirm his love for her.

A crooked, forced smile moved across his face. "Such as the fact that you're my wife now and you'll go where I go."

"Oh, really!" How dare he think that a few words said in front of a preacher who had a gun pointed at his head would give him the right to dictate the rest of her life. "Well, there is a simple solution to that problem. I do seem to recall that our marriage has not been consummated, so an anullment should not

317

be too difficult to obtain." Without warning, she kicked her horse in the sides and jerked forward in an erratic plunge.

Drake did not take time to mull over her rash words as he spurred his horse and took off behind her. His powerful black stallion immediately overtook her little mare and even though she attempted to outrun him, Drake easily reached out one arm and pulled her from her saddle in one swift movement. With his other hand, he yanked hard on the reins as his steed slid to an abrupt halt. Krystal kicked and hit at him with her fists in a vain attempt to escape from his tight embrace as he struggled to remain balanced in his saddle. But between her violent thrashing and the horse's sudden stop he was unable to support himself. They both tumbled from the horse and landed with a thud among the range grass and low brush which covered the ground in dense profusion. The impact of the fall caused Drake's hat to be knocked from his head and it fell beside Krystal's wide-brimmed black hat in a wild rosebush which grew from the ground several feet away. The thick, heavy curls of her long hair cascaded across his face and blocked her from his view for a minute.

"Damn you, Drake DeGanahl!" Krystal cried out in breathless gasps. He had managed to hit the ground first, absorbing most of the fall for both of them, but as soon as she could double up her fists again, she began to pound on his chest. "Turn loose of me this instant, or I'll — I'll —" her words were severed by the feel of his inflating manhood pressing against the thigh of the snug fitting jeans she was wearing.

The wind had been knocked from Drake's lungs when they fell but he was finally able to talk as he asked in a choked tone, "You'll do what, darlin'?"

Shocked that even in the mist of their intense anger,

their desire for one another could overpower everything else, she could do no more than stare at him through the pale moon light. She wanted him to make love to her as badly as she wanted to get away from him. It was terrifying to know that this man could have such a power over her mind and body. "Turn loose of . . . me," she repeated weakly.

"If that's what you really want?" Drake's shoulders heaved nonchalantly as he raised his hands up into the air, freeing her from the imprisonment of his embrace. Wanting her this strongly and giving in to her demand was sheer torture. But he would not take her against her will, not unless she gave him no other choice.

Krystal swallowed the heavy lump in her throat as she pushed herself up. The lower part of her body still rested against him and it was undeniable what he was feeling. But she had to know there was more than just a sexual attraction between them, and he still had not explained the reason for his hostile treatment of her. If she allowed this consistent weakness to overcome her now, he would win . . . their marriage would not only be consummated, but he would also expect her to bow down to his every command. Well, Krystal thought with venom, no man would ever put her in that situation—not even Drake DeGanahl! She raised up to her knees, her legs straddling his muscular limbs in her attempt to get up from the ground. Another wave of desire, which she silently swore not to give into, consumed her searing body with a yearning like she had never imagined.

Drake waited until he could not stand her indecision a second longer. She was too stubborn to submit to the emotions that he could see flashing across her face, even in the dim moonlight. But he was ready to take the responsibility for himself, and for her too. As she slowly began to rise up from him, Drake grabbed both of her wrists and pulled her back down. She gasped as their bodies made contact once more. He felt her tense and prepared himself for another assault of her fists when he turned loose of her. But she did not move, not even a breath escaped from her lips as she waited for him to make the next move.

She had been afraid that he would allow her to leave, but thank God, his insight went beyond her stubborn exterior. The breath she was holding began to escape from her mouth in a quivering exhale as she sensed that no one would ever understand her complex nature like this man did. He had known how much she wanted him, even when she was trying to deny her passion. Opposite as it seemed they were at times, there were the fleeting moments like this when their emotions merged together and all the diversity in their troubled lives was forgotten like the insignificant grains of red dirt which blew softly across the vast desert floor.

Their bodies were molded together so tightly that they were almost inseparable and their lips on the verge of touching. Outside of this moment, somewhere beyond this garnet desert ground, pungent with the herbage odor of the low brush that covered the dry soil, were the deep conflicts which threatened the love they had discovered in each other's arms. But now they were whisked away to another place and time . . . a fantastical land of enchantment were nothing else was important, except the cherished remembrance of holding one another so close that even the night air could not wedge in between them, and a time where the erratic beating of their impassioned hearts did not care to distinguish between sweet esctasy and harsh reality.

Krystal could not douse her desire, it was raging

out of control as she crushed her parted lips down against his waiting mouth. His tongue darted into the warm cavern of her mouth, intertwining with bold intrusion with her less aggressive one. Their fury from a moment ago evolved into a torrid passion which neither of them could ever hope to corral. The first kiss led to another, and then still another, each devouring union of their starving lips more forceful and demanding than the one before it.

Knowing his kisses only served to increase this ravenous hunger, Krystal pulled away from him long enough to tug on the black scarf which was knotted loosely around his neck. Too impatient to wait until she had disposed of the troublesome obstacle, Drake pushed her hands away and laid them upon the snaps that ran down the front of his shirt. At once she grasped his meaning and began to pull them apart with her trembling fingers. Beneath this obtrusive garment was the soft carpet of light brown hair that her small hands yearned to caress and explore.

Drake, anxious to feel her pliant skin against his own hardened flesh, occupied his hands with the row of buttons which ran down the front of the plaid cotton shirt he had bought for her today. Her legs were still straddling his awakening body as he raised her to a sitting position and dismissed the shirt from her shoulders. Now the only barrier between his wandering hands and the creamy mounds of her rising and falling bosom was her lacy white camisole. A narrow row of tiny hooks caused him little concern as his nimble fingers quickly undid them and pushed the thin straps back, allowing the flimsy material to disappear from sight as it floated down her back.

His eyes, which were dark with excitement, ascended, drinking in the heavenly vision she presented above him. A visible tremor caused his whole being to quake with anticipation. She looked like a beautiful angel outlined by the ethereal slivers of the shimmering beams of moonlight. Her wavy tresses, a halo of fiery golden strands, flaired out around the soft hollows of her cheekbones and fell lightly past her silky shoulders to the middle of her back. The dusky glow enlightened the jeweled tones of her tawny eyes which were enhanced by the glimmer of passion that hung heavy upon her half-closed lids.

His attention was diverted by the rapid heaving of her full breasts as they seemed to beckon to him with their taut pinkish-brown summits. As if some unseen force had taken control of his actions, his head automatically moved forward until his moistened lips locked onto one alert knob. Krystal cried out, not in pain, but with the indescribable pleasure that his mouth was causing to surge throughout her shaking being. Her slender arms encircled his head, pulling him closer in the hopes that he would never stop this erotic agony.

But the relentless throbbing which caused her insides to pound with such an intensity that she could no longer ignore it soon made her ache for much more than just his lips could offer. She remembered the night he had first make love to her in the hotel room in Virginia City and she immediately knew what was needed to extinguish the raging ardor within her.

Once again, Drake almost seemed to read her thoughts. His mouth released his possessive grip from her swollen breast as his hands grasped around her small waist. With little effort, his strong arms levitated her tiny form while his tall frame followed her to a standing position. He began to unbutton the front of the jeans which she despised so much, and she retaliated by undoing the buttons of his matching jeans. His hands began to roam slowly downward as he pushed the pants over the gentle curves of her hip bones. He permitted her to slide the pants past his hips, but then grew too eager to wait for her to finish. Taking command of the situation, he bent over and tugged off his tall boots, then kicked the pants from his body. With a quick movement, he shrugged his shirt from his shoulders, leaving nothing except the black scarf around his neck to cover his masculine form from her imploring view.

Krystal also wished to hasten the disposal of their bothersome clothing, so she reached down and attempted to loosen the laces of her high-topped boots. But her hands were trembling so violently that all she managed to accomplish was to tie them both into a succession of tight knots. She grew angry with herself and pried them from her feet, not bothering to take note of the pain her rash action caused to flare up in her ankles as she pulled the jeans over her feet and flung them across the desert ground.

Her breathing grew heavy with expectation as he gently lowered her back down onto the ground. His straight white teeth glistened in the darkness as a slow smile spread across his handsome face. All that remained to remove from her curvaceous form was her ruffled garter belt and the black silk stockings which were attached to them. He had not realized that she was still wearing the feminine undergarments beneath the jeans and he grew even more excited with the prospect of removing them for her. Seldom did he have the pleasure of relieving a woman of her hosiery since most of the ladies he associated with were in the habit of wearing nothing more than a flimsy robe in their line of work. Even Krystal had only been clad in a satin robe the first time they had made love. His movements were slow and deliberate as he unhooked each of the tabs which were connected to the garter-belt and then spread his fingers around her legs as he rolled the delicate stockings down to her ankles and past her tiny feet.

In spite of the warm night air, he shivered. He wanted this woman so much he ached with desire for her. This petite seductress held his whole life within her grasp. He had tempted destiny and she had overpowered it. Moving down between the warmth of her satin thighs, his masterful scepter spiraled downward into the moist portal of her womanly domain. A shudder worked its way throughout his body. Nothing had ever compared to the rapture he felt when their bodies came together in this ardent union.

A soft moan escaped from Krystal as his weight closed down upon her, crushing her against the hard ground. But she did not notice the tiny rocks that cut into her back or the prickly feel of the sharp range grass biting into her tender skin. She did not care because all that mattered was the extreme pleasure her virile husband bestowed upon her with each precise movement of his strong and skillful body. She felt as though she might burst with the love she felt for him. How could she have ever thought she could walk out of his life? He was like the air she breathed, without him she would die.

He suddenly grasped hold of her hips and rolled over, taking her limp form with him until she was impaled on top of him. For a second Krystal grew confused. This was all so new; but, she was an eager student. His hands guided her to an upright position as his hips continued to thrust forward, deeper and more powerful than ever before. A strange sensation passed through Krystal as she flung her head back and rode the engulfing waves of his passionate tide. He was almost more man than her small frame could accommodate and it was oddly painful because it was a hurt that made her crave the affliction more with each arch of his ascending body.

If it were possible to remain suspended in time, Krystal wished they could abide forever beneath the velvet expanse of the starry desert sky. She had handed him her heart the first time he had made love to her. But now, she was committed to him in mind and spirit, too. She would never allow herself to be separated from him, she decided in one brief second of coherency before their bodies reached the vertex of this exquisite ostentation.

Afterward they clung to one another, reluctant to let this magical feeling escape from them. It was more than physical, more than an elaborate act of emotion . . . It was the eternal blending of two wanton souls.

Chapter Twenty-three

Drake had practically grown up in this jail. These crumbling old stucco walls was his second home when his father had been sheriff of Sweetwater County and during the years that Drake had been a lawman. His pensive eyes moved hesitantly around the small room. He hadn't been here for over two years, but nothing had changed in appearance and he could still feel his father's presence heavy in the atmosphere. All at once he realized that virtually everything *was* different. His father was gone, this was Cameron Reed's domain, and Drake was now an outsider in this room. He began to feel ill at ease and nervous as he was consumed by an overpowering urge to turn and run back through the door. He grew angry at himself. Why should he feel like an outlaw? It was his brother who was in the cell block in the next room.

Krystal drifted through his mind. He thought about the kiss she had given him before he had left her awhile ago. It had been a lingering kiss, the kind that made his lips throb with stimulating memories for a long time afterward. He was already beginning to miss her.

"Hello Drake." Cameron said in greeting as he entered through the doorway which led into the area where the prisoners were held. He gave Drake a curious going over with his eyes. "I mentioned to Devon that you were coming to see him when you got back to town and it seems that he's real anxious to see you."

Drake shrugged with a gesture of unimportance, but his heartbeat quickened without warning. He hoped Cameron did not see past the facade he was trying to present to him. For years it had been a well-known fact around Green River that the DeGanahl brothers were on less than friendly terms. No doubt, Cameron Reed was wondering why Devon would even care if his brother showed up at all.

"I'll bet he is," Drake retorted coldly. "And he's probably hoping that I can help him avoid the end of a rope. But he made his own bed and now he can lie in it!" Drake did not regret the fact that Devon's life of crime had finally been halted. He only regretted the sorrow that his incarceration was undoubtedly causing their mother. His wife's brief involvement with Devon also worried Drake. If Devon had mentioned Krystal's name to Cameron Reed then there was no way she could continue to elude the detective who was looking for her. Drake had to force himself not to ask Cameron what he knew about the investigation which was being conducted by the Pinkerton Agency, but he had given his word to Krystal that he would not interfere with the way she had chosen to handle that situation. It was extremely difficult for him to remain on the sidelines, though.

For a second Cameron continued to study Drake

327

with an unreadable expression. He trusted Franklin's eldest boy, but as a lawman, he also had a very cautious nature. Something didn't sit right with him. Devon was anticipating Drake's visit with too much enthusiasm. There had to be more to their impending meeting than just wanting to make Angelina feel good that her oldest son had taken the time to visit his brother in jail?

Cameron recalled that Drake had mentioned he had been in Nevada. What part of Nevada? Cameron found himself wondering? That Pinkerton man had been headed to Nevada when Cameron had left him in Odgen a few days back. It was even stranger still that a man had supposedly been abducted from the same train that the elusive Krystal Colbert had been taken from several weeks back. Drake DeGanahl could easily fit the description of that man, with one exception . . . the passengers had all said the man was a real city slicker.

Cameron moved his eyes slowly over the other man's rugged mode of dress and sighed. Drake's denim jeans and shirt which were topped by a suede vest and a dark scarf knotted loosely around his neck was the code of dress that Cameron had always seen this man wearing. No doubt, the man traveling with Miss Colbert was some shady character from back East, probably her cohort in the jewel-smuggling operation the detective had told him about. Cameron decided he must be letting his job get the best of him as he shook his head to clear his thoughts.

"Leave your guns on my desk before you go in to see Devon."

With a nervous feeling in the pit of his stomach, Drake began to unbuckle his gunbelt. Evidently Cameron did not know anything about his and

Devon's association with Krystal or else he would not trust him to see Devon. Drake avoided the other man's intent stare while he continued into the next room. As the door slammed shut behind him, Drake's eyes fought to adjust to the dimness of the small area which contained two separate cells. No noise emitted from either cubicle when Drake began to walk down the short corridor. The sound of his heeled boots echoed loudly on the hard planks of the wooden floor which only served to increase his dread at seeing his brother again. But he had a score to settle with him. Devon could push him a long way, now he had involved Krystal in their feud and Drake could not forget that so easily. Drake walked past the first cell which was empty with the exception of a narrow cot, then took one more long stride and stopped before the rigid black bars of the last cell.

Devon's tall frame reclined casually back on the bunk as his ebony eyes peered up with a evil glint. His brooding features showed no surprise in them when his gaze met with his brother's unfriendly glare.

"Well, well, look who we have here?" Devon did not try to disguise his feelings of animosity when he spoke. He had been contemplating this reunion for days and he had anxiously awaited his brother's return from Virginia City so that he could spring his surprise on him. "I knew you couldn't stay away. You've been waiting too long to see me behind bars and now . . . here I am." He rose precariously from the narrow bed and swaggered to the bars. "So, tell me, big brother? Since you are the reason that I'm here you must be planning to stay around for the hanging, or has city living weakened your stomach for that type of excitement?"

Drake did not answer. Devon disgusted him with

329

his cocky attitude. Even in the wake of his imprisonment and possible death he still refused to admit that his wicked ways had finally led to his own destruction. Drake began to wonder if coming here was a good idea. It certainly wasn't going to help improve his relationship with his brother, nor would he be able to relate the truth about his visit with him to their mother. It would kill her to know how much bitterness and hatred festered inside her youngest son.

His thoughts drifted to Krystal once more. Maybe he should have brought her into Green River with him? He had left her and John waiting for him outside of town until nightfall when he planned to take them to his mother's home. But now he was overcome with a feeling of foreboding. Perhaps they should not have returned to Wyoming at all. Somewhere there had to be a place where the past and its lingering ghosts would be buried for good. His dark green gaze focused on his brother. He wanted his marriage to Krystal to begin with a clean slate and it would not be possible to do that until he had set the record straight about the past.

"I'm not leaving here today until we've settled a few things. Such as why you have blamed me all these years for what happened between you and Jennifer Holt."

For a second, Devon's mask of disdain faded. He had not expected Krystal to tell Drake all the personal things he had related to her about Jennifer. But then, he had not expected Drake to come after Krystal when she had run away from him, either. Was it possible that Drake really cared about this woman?

A snide chuckle emitted from Devon. "Jennifer Holt is nothing more than history. Why don't we discuss something more tantilizing. Like Krystal Colbert, for instance?"

Drake's jaw squared with unspoken anger. He refused to let Devon goad him into another battle of snide barbs. But if Devon made one more derogatory remark about his wife, Drake knew he would not be able to contain his fury any longer. "Krystal has nothing to do with what's been going on between the two of us for all these years."

"So, she's still around then?" He could tell Drake was fighting to hold his temper in control and he found that to be quite interesting. His big brother had always been the one to remain calm and in charge of his reactions at all times. And it was unusual for Devon to be able to put Drake on the defensive, the situation was usually reversed. However, it appeared that Krystal Colbert had changed all that.

Drake moved closer to the bars of the cell. "I'd advise you to choose your words carefully when you talk about Krystal."

His brother's protective attitude towards Krystal Colbert made Devon even more anxious for revenge. "Miss Colbert must be quite a woman to keep your interest for this long."

Drake's eyes became livid with rage. His brother was extremely close to pushing him too far with his disrespectful references to his wife. Through all the years of resentment between the two of them, nothing had ever come this close to making Drake feel the need to face a deadly contest with his brother. But he would not allow Devon to say anything which was unwarranted against his wife. He was almost too angry to speak so he remained conspicuously silent.

An evil grin curled Devon's lips. He had never seen Drake so furious and he had not even told him the best part about Krystal Colbert yet. "I don't suppose you took the time to check over the wanted posters out on the wall when you came in?" Devon rested casually against the bars while he enjoyed the pained look which moved into his older brother's face. For a second he was afraid that Drake might already know about Krystal's unlawful activities back East. Then he reminded himself that this man was his brother . . . the unreproachable Drake DeGanahl. Drake would never allow himself to be in the company of a woman who was even remotely implicated in anything illegal.

Drake's hand's rested on his narrow hips which felt strangely barren without his gunbelt. The tightening in his chest was a reminder that his brother's indiscreet suggestion was almost more than his taut nerves could handle. Had Devon said something to Cameron or was it just coincidence that he had mentioned the wanted posters which adorned the jailhouse wall? "I had other things on my mind. Besides, I've seen your face on wanted posters before. They don't impress me."

"Is that so? Well, would you be impressed to see a poster with the face of that sweet little thing, Krystal Colbert on it?" Devon gloried in the look of fury which overcame Drake's face. It was more than obvious that his low-hitting question had struck a nerve.

Without warning, Drake reached through the bars and grabbed Devon by the collar of his shirt, yanking him roughly up against the bars. "You're treading on dangerous ground. You'll welcome a noose around your neck if you're not careful what you say about Krystal."

An unnerving smile curled Devon's lips as he pushed Drake's hands away from his shirt collar. Drake's violent reaction was more than he had even hoped for. "What's this? Is it possible that the noble

332

Drake DeGanahl has been taken in by a jewel thief?"

"You don't what you're talking about," Drake answered through clenched teeth. His face became a mask of disciplined hatred as he clutched hold of the bars tightly with his hands. If he could break into that cell, Devon would finally have the fight he had been goading him into all through the years. "Those wanted posters are a mistake. And I intend to prove it!"

Devon was thrown off guard by Drake's admission. He found it hard to believe that Drake would know about Krystal's outlawry and still want to be in her presence. His brother's granite beliefs on law and order could not have changed so drastically in the past two years, so there had to be something more to it. Devon tilted his head to the side and shrugged. "If I didn't know better, I'd think you were in love with that woman. But we both know that you could never love someone who was less than perfect . . . such as yourself." He stepped back out of Drake's reach. But Drake remained unmoving while his knuckles whitened with the tight grip he still had on the bars. His eyes continued to drill through the barrier, though his intense rage was blinding him.

He released his tight hold on the bars and took a step backward. "I only came here so that I could tell mother that I saw you. But I don't have to put up with any of your bull. And since this might be the last time we see each other I would like to clear up something from the past." Drake leaned closer to the bars of the cell again. "I never touched Jennifer Holt. I was not one to follow suit with every other man in the county. If I wanted a woman with Jennifer Holt's experience, I always went to the other side of town. You know where I mean, don't you, little brother?"

Devon's black eyes glowed with deepening hatred. He had not been totally blind to Jennifer's permissive behavior when they were young. But after all these years he had justified the girl's bad habits in his tortured mind. He did not want to be reminded of the painful memories that he had tried to bury in the deepest caverns of his subconscious.

"She may not have been perfect, but compared to Krystal Colbert, she was practically a saint."

"I've listened to all that I intend to from you." Drake backed away from the cell, his expression draped with fury. "I only wish now that I was still wearing my badge, and that I was the one who had put you behind these bars." Drake moved farther back, his flashing eyes never leaving Devon's dark glare. As he turned and began to stalk down the short gloomy corridor, Devon's voice filled the narrow space, almost seeming to echo from every direction.

"Why don't you ask Krystal what she's carrying around in that little black purse that she guards so closely?"

Drake's footsteps slowed, coming to a halt at the end of the hallway. He turned and met his brother's gaze once more. A tension so great filled the cramped area so that it threatened to suffocate the two men. The rivalry which had always been between the brothers seemed to surface and then to explode within the confines of this one challenging look. Devon's words rang through his head as Krystal's vision blurred before his eyes. Had she confided in Devon when she could not even trust her lurid secrets to her own husband?

Devon knew that at last he had found the weapon of subversion to use against Drake. A tight smile came to his lips as his raven eyes glistened with malice. "She's the one thing you hate most in all the world, Drake. Your precious Krystal Colbert is just a good-for-nothing outlaw. . . .Why she's just like me." Devon's wicked laugh filled the air as Drake took a threatening step toward his cell.

"She's nothing like you. There's not an inch of your worthless hide that even comes close to comparing with Krystal." Drake pushed open the door with a forcful shove, but paused as he started to exit. He turned back to Devon with a look that distorted his face with rage. "If you're ever fortunate enough to get out of that cell, I'll be waiting!"

Devon's sinister grin broadened. A desperate urge consumed him as he feverishly wished that he was not behind these imprisoning bars and that he was wearing his gun on his hip at this moment. He had no doubt that his brother was furious enough at him to make a move if the situation had been different. With the exception of Jennifer Holt, Devon had never wanted anything as much as he wanted this final showdown with Drake. He would never have Jennifer, but someday, despite these bars, or regardless of their mother, he knew that he would finally meet his brother for one last conflict.

Chapter Twenty-four

Drake was like a man who was obsessed as he rode away from the town of Green River. He had not even bothered to answer Cameron Reed when the marshal had spoken to him as he exited from the jail. He could not concentrate on anything other than what Devon had just told him. What type of incriminating evidence was Krystal carrying around in that little bag she always seemed to have within her grasp? He was continually trying to conform to her idea of justice and it went completely against his grain. There was nothing he wanted more than to trust her, but until she confided in him about everything, he was left to draw his own conclusions. Right now, he did not like what the evidence was leading him to believe.

He had left Krystal and John a couple miles out of town. A rock overhanging which was carpeted with a dense growth of grass provided shelter from the hot August sun. By the time Drake reached them, he was nearly out of his head with rage. Forgotten were the tender and loving thoughts that had surrounded them for the past couple days. They were replaced by the clouded feeling of deceit . . . the one thing Drake knew he could not live with when it came to anyone, especially his wife.

Krystal had only to glance at the expression on his face to sense that his trip to town had been less than successful. But she had no idea that his fury was directed all at her until he had dismounted from his horse and swung around to face her with the look of a violent storm brewing within the dark green depths of his icy gaze. The bright smile quickly faded from her face and was replaced by a puzzled frown which drew her brows into a rigid arch.

"Is it Devon?" she asked, almost fearful of his answer.

"You know damn well it isn't," he retorted in a crude tone. His tall frame seemed even larger in comparison to her small structure when he was this angry. Her pensive eyes searched his face with frantic hope that his vile mood was not because of his discontent with her again. The past couple of days had been so perfect, she was not sure if she could face another round with his suspicious nature.

Drake felt like someone had just stuck a knife through her heart. How could she stand there and act so innocent while at the same time clutching that little black bag tightly up against her chest. His eyes fell to her hands and to the mysterious purse.

Instinctively, Krystal's own eyes followed his gaze. Her hands tightened around the bag whose narrow strap still hung around her neck. She did not know what part the diamond brooch played in this tangled web, but if it was a link to her mother's innocence or guilt, she was not going to allow anyone to take it from her until she knew the answer for herself.

Drake saw the glint of defiance in her eyes, and he knew she was not prepared to confide in him, even now. Words had proved to be only a wasted effort with this woman. He was at his wits end, and he was too furious to care what he said or did at this moment. If only she would say something to give him some sort of encouragement that she was not guilty of any crime. But she just stared up at him, her jewel-toned eyes shimmering with tears of determination and resolve.

He glanced over the top of her head and caught a glimpse of John. The old man carried a worried frown on his whiskered face, and when his eyes met Drake's, his look turned to one of pleading. Drake blinked and glanced back down at Krystal. She had not moved, nor had her expression changed. The only thing different he noticed was that the tears which had been only a threat an instant ago were now flooding down her smooth cheeks. Drake tried to tear his eyes away. He did not want to feel the emotions that were surging through him. It was too easy for him to love this woman, even though he knew he would have to leave her. His head jerked to the side as his eyes closed tightly. For his own sanity, he had to forget the way she looked at this moment.

Krystal did not even fight against the tears that blurred him from her vision. She was losing him, yet she felt powerless to stop it. He cared nothing about her feelings of devotion to her mother's memory. All that seemed important to him was his unyielding opinions of righteousness. She felt like she was on a never-ending seesaw of emotions. One minute he was the most compassionate man she could ever hope to know; the next second, he was a tower of aloofness, content only if she conformed to his domineering attitude. Krystal tossed her head back as she clutched

338

the little bag closer to her body. No one had ever made her do something that she did not want to do without a fight. . . .Drake DeGanahl was no exception! Her golden-edged lashes fanned down for an instant over her tear-ridden eyes, and when they opened again, her look matched Drake's with a stubbornness that could not be broken.

The desert air suddenly felt lethal as they both realized that they had hit a stalemate. Yet, each of them was too proud to back down. Drake turned slowly and placed his hand upon his saddlehorn. For a second he did not move, he was silently praying that she would say something . . . just one word muttered from those soft lips and he would never leave her.

Krystal had the urge to reach out and touch the muscles in his back that curved beneath the cloth of his shirt. She wanted to feel the heat of his hard flesh against her own soft skin . . . just one more time. Her hand trembled on the verge of fulfilling her desire. But she allowed too much time to pass. As she started to move forward, he suddenly swung up into his saddle. His frustrated face glared down at her as she pulled her hand back and clasped on to the little bag again. He pretended to ignore her gesture, but it only caused the pain in his heart to take another dramatic plunge.

"If you decide to put an end to this game of cat and mouse your playing with the Pinkerton Detective Agency, I'll be in town waiting for you. But if you insist on hiding the truth from me and living your life on the run, then don't bother to come looking for me. It seems to me that the choice is simple, but the final decision is yours to make." He paused while his eyes searched for a clue to her thoughts, but she remained silent. He pulled the wide brim of his hat down low on his forehead, his sinewy body leaned forward in his saddle as he added with a definite tone of voice, "If I don't hear from you by tomorrow, then I'll know that you made your decision."

The hand that yearned to reach out to him, raised slightly. But she quickly pulled it back against her body. He did not understand and she would not beg him. Her head barely moved with the nod she gave to him in response, but he saw her gesture. He tipped his hat again and turned the big black stallion around. As Krystal watched him ride away, a hurt so great filled her whole essence and she was sure she would not survive another minute without him. He became only a dark speck on the distant horizon, but still, she did not move. Tears streamed down her face as her father placed a comforting arm around her shoulders, but neither of them spoke.

"He'll be back, chéri," John stated in a hushed tone of voice when he could not longer stand the deafening silence.

Krystal shook her head. "No, he won't be back." She choked down the rest of the sobs that welled up in her throat and squared her narrow shoulders. "But someday—" she turned and focused her intent gaze on her father, "Someday when I have cleared mother's name, then I will go to him." She drew a shaking hand across the side of her face to wipe away a lingering teardrop and looked back in the direction where Drake had just disappeared from view. Someday, she thought, we will be together again . . . in a place where the past no longer matters and the reality of our love for one another will overpower everything else.

Without removing her eyes from the distant horizon, she said, "We'll rest here tonight. Tomorrow we'll head back to Ogden and catch the train."

"Train?" John asked in confusion.

"We're going to Boston," Krystal answered as she twirled around and began to roll out her bedroll upon the mattress of green vegatation which covered the ground.

John watched his daughter in mute astonishment. Boston? He had no desire to go to Boston, but he dared not argue with her about it. She would undoubtedly take off by herself, and John did not want her traveling alone again. So he remained silent and began to help her set up a temporary campsite for the night. Maybe by the time they reached Ogden he could convince her not to return to the East. There had to be a way to clear Rebecca's name without going back to Boston. At least that's what John was hoping as the shadows of the impending night settled in around the rock ledge and cast distorted shapes across the area of grass where they sat beside the small campfire that he had built to ward off the chill that accompanied the rising of the moon.

"You should try to get some sleep." John received no answer. He was beginning to get worried about her. She had been staring into the center of the fire with a distant look upon her beautiful young face for hours without saying a word. John's heart went out to her, but he felt helpless to do anything for her. She was too hardheaded to go after Drake, and John knew Drake was equally as stubborn.

But John was determined, too. He was not going to let her leave for Boston until they had tried all the options available to them out here in this part of the country first. He was hoping that she would come to her senses before tomorrow and realize how sorry she would be if she were to leave Drake DeGanahl and return to the East. But if she still refused to be sensible, John was planning to head for the nearest jail, where they would face this Pinkerton business head on . . . with or without Krystal's cooperation. Tarnation, he thought with an aggravated grunt as he glanced longingly towards his bedroll, young folks act so foolish at times!

John's eyes refused to stay open a second longer, especially since he had already settled the problem in his mind. "Let's get some sleep, or neither of us will be able to travel tomorrow," he pleaded once more.

Krystal shrugged. "You go ahead. I'll come to bed soon." She tucked her legs up tightly against her body and rested her chin on her knees as she continued to watch the hypnotizing flames flickering against the blackness of the night.

John mumbled under his breath while he crawled beneath the cover of his bedroll. She could be as stubborn as she wanted to be tonight. In the morning he was taking control of the whole situation. With this thought firmly planted in his mind, John was sound asleep in no time at all.

Krystal remained beside the campfire, moving only long enough to stoke the fire when the orange and gold flames threatened to diminish or die out. Her life was in too much turmoil to think about sleeping and she was becoming more confused with every breath she took. She had thought that returning to Boston to clear her mother's name from the great injustice bestowed upon her memory was the only logical plan. And now, she was not so sure. She knew she had to fight against the charges made by the Pinkerton Detective Agency, but she wondered if she could bear the idea of leaving Drake behind, even though it would not be for long. They had known one another such a brief time, and their love was only beginning to blossom with boundless potential. Did she dare take the chance that his love for her might not survive if she left him? Drake said he would wait until tomorrow for her decision. Well, it was the woman's prerogative to change her mind, and Krystal was going to take advantage of that feminine privilege.

She would prove her mother's innocence, but with her husband by her side. She had never dreamed that she would find a man whom she could love as much as she did Drake DeGanahl. She knew that she was not going to be able to leave him tomorrow, or ever. Her love for him was an insatiable hunger and she would surely starve to death if she were deprived of it. She began to feel the ache that was becoming such a common occurrence since she had met Drake, but she was defenseless to restrain the sweet agony. Her yearning body would never be able to survive the long night that was stretching out before her. Good Lord! Krystal, she told herself for the umpteenth time, just don't think about him!

A noise, like the sound of a twig breaking beneath the footstep, rang out from the other side of the rock ledge and jolted Krystal from the fantasy she was composing in her mind. For an instant, her blood ran cold as her eyes searched the surrounding darkness for the source of the disturbance. She glanced at her father. Only the very top of his head was protruding from his blanket, but it was apparent that he was snoozing peacefully. Deciding the noise must have been in her imagination, Krystal reached over and grabbed her bedroll. As she wrapped herself in the warmth of the blanket, her mind wandered back to her husband once again. An anxious sigh escaped from her lips. She couldn't wait for daylight to break

343

so they could head into Green River, and so she could be back where she belonged . . . in Drake's arms.

Another noise, louder and more distinct than the one before it, echoed out in the quiet. Krystal gasped, but the moment her eyes caught sight of the man who had just stepped within the radius of the campfire glow, any further vocal sound was lost to her fear. She wanted to cry out to her father, but terror ruled her whole being. She could neither move nor speak as her eyes widened in horror.

Creed Ward smiled with this new sense of power. It was a feeling he had been experiencing a lot since Devon had been in jail. The rest of the men looked to him for guidance now, and he was thoroughly enjoying his position of authority. His long handlebar mustache moved up and down while he worked a large wad of chew to the front of his mouth, then casually spit the brown waste to the ground. As he wiped the excess from his chin, his evil smirk broadened into an even more chilling smile. His hunch had been right. When he noticed Drake DeGanahl entering town earlier today, he had wondered if Krystal Colbert was also in the area. But when DeGanahl rode out again, and then returned back to town alone, Creed was beginning to doubt that Miss Colbert was in the vicinity.

To satisfy his nagging curiosity though, he decided to scout out the likely spots for a campsite. She was not hard to find. Creed just took out in the same direction that Drake had been coming and going in all day. And low-and-behold! Here she was, looking even more enticing than he remembered, and twice as lovely in the soft glow of the campfire. His loins flared with lustful anxiety, but there was no time for pleasure now. Creed had no idea if Drake was planning to come back here tonight, and he had just become aware of the man who was sleeping nearby.

When Krystal noticed his crazed look turning toward the still form of her unsuspecting father, her lost voice suddenly returned. "Please don't hurt him," she cried out. Her outburst startled John from his peaceful slumber. Instinctively, he grabbed for his sawed-off shotgun. Creed saw the glimmer of the short gunbarrel, and in one effortless motion, he slid his side iron from the leather holster which was tied to his thigh.

Krystal's scream pierced the night air, but it was lost in the thundering aftermath of the exploding bullet. Her father slumped forward in the grass without uttering a sound. She did not see where he had been hit, and Creed did not allow her the time to go to him. He yanked her to her feet and dragged her behind him as he quickly headed back to his horse. Krystal pulled against him and begged him to let her go to her father, but Creed was deaf to her pleading. He barely even noticed her resistance as she struggled to free herself from his tight grip. His thoughts were filled with the excitement of knowing that he had Krystal Colbert in his possession, and there was no one around who could stop him this time. His only regret was that he had shot the old man, and if he was dead, Creed would not have the satisfaction of Drake DeGanahl knowing who had his woman. Creed chuckled to himself as he tossed her twisting form across the saddle. DeGanahl would know eventually what had happened to Miss Colbert, but only after Creed had finished with her.

Krystal did not see what direction they were headed in, she was in too much pain from the calloused way Creed was making her ride on the horse. He had thrown her over the saddle as though she was a sack of flour and even when he had swung himself into the saddle, he did not allow her to sit up. She could not even cry out to him because she was completely immobile. As his horse charged across the dusty landscape, her throat felt as though it had closed up from the dust which was hitting her directly in the face. Her mind continued to fight against this unbelievable turn of events, but the little fight she had left in her aching body soon dissolved.

Creed felt her go limp and suspected that she had fainted. He began to grow concerned because his intention was not to harm her. He only wanted what he felt was rightfully his. It was his curiosity that had uncovered this beauty on the train in the first place. But Devon had pulled rank on him, and claimed her for himself, in spite of the fact that she was supposed to be Drake's woman.

It was the older DeGanahl brother, though, who Creed wanted to avenge with a raging obsession. He would not rest until he had paid Drake DeGanahl back for humiliating him at the Hole-in-the-Wall. The rest of the men still laughed whenever they thought his back was turned. Creed would never forgive Drake DeGanahl for stealing his clothes and tying him up in the stable. But the most degrading part of all was that DeGanahl had also stolen his gun. Creed figured a woman like Krystal Colbert was the only compensation for payment of his cherished six-shooter.

The distance between the spot where Krystal was camped and Creed's campsite was easily covered before dawn. Krystal had hardly stirred the whole trip, and by the time Sidewinder helped lift her down from Creed's horse, Creed's concern had begun to turn into fear.

"Is she hurt?" Sidewinder questioned as he placed

346

her upon his bedroll. He gently pushed back a stray hair from her dirty forehead as he leaned closer to her limp form.

Creed knelt down on the ground beside her. "I don't think so." A worried frown burrowed across his face. "I think she just passed out." He patted the side of her face in an attempt to rouse her.

She coughed as her heavy lids slowly began to flutter. Another cough cleared her throat, but her mind still refused to grasp reality. She forced her eyes open against their will. The young face of Sidewinder was the first thing she focused her blurry vision upon. Growing confused, she thought for an instant that she was back in Boston and that Sidewinder was one of her students. She shook her head as she attempted to clear her jumbled thoughts and met Creed Ward's face on the opposite side of her. The horrible recollection of the previous night came back to her in a blinding flash and her terrified scream shattered the early morning stillness as she flung herself against Sidewinder's chest in a futile attempt to flee from the other man. Sidewinder's arms immediately encircled her trembling body with a comforting embrace as his blue eyes drilled into Creed's faked look of innocence.

"What did you do to her?" he demanded angrily.

Creed shook his head and raised his hands into the air. "I—I—"

"He shot my father!" Krystal gasped, as she pressed closer to Sidewinder. He tightened his hold on her when he felt a violent tremor shake her whole body which was accompanied by the memory of the vicious attack of her father.

Austin approached the group and eyed Creed with unspoken accusations burning across his aging face. "Is that true?"

347

Again, Creed only shrugged in an ignorant manner. His guilty eyes raced back and forth between the other two men. "I didn't know he was her father. Anyway what difference does it make? He drew a gun on me first."

"You didn't have to shoot him." Krystal cried. She wanted to say so much more to this unhuman beast, but her words were lost to the rush of tears that she could no longer control. The father she had only known for a few short days, but had loved for a lifetime, could be dead or dying and there was no way she could help him. It was almost more than her mind could comprehend.

Sidewinder continued to hold her until she had cried herself into a state of exhaustion, his unnerving glare never leaving Creed's sheepish face. Sidewinder had killed numerous men and had not thought twice about it. But this little flame-haired lady reminded him so much of his dead sister that he was consumed with a protective attitude toward her right from the first moment he had set his clear blue gaze upon her beautiful face.

Creed rose to his feet and glared at the other men. "It wasn't my fault," he said in his own defense. "And I don't give a hoot what the rest of you think. That woman is payment for a debt that was owed to me. Ain't nobody gonna interfere with that." In spite of his brave announcement, Creed retreated to the other side of the camp and crouched down in front of the dying fire.

Austin's gaze met with Sidewinder's and a silent vow was made between the old gunslinger and the young killer. Austin gave his head a satisfied nod as he walked over to the circle of rocks that enclosed the fire. He poured himself a cup of strong coffee from

348

the pot that was perched on one of the rocks and sat down to sip on it while he observed Creed Ward.

Creed avoided Austin's look and did not glance in Sidewinder's direction either. He knew the two men were feeling defensive over the woman right now, but he didn't see that as any big threat. Creed planned to head into Brown's Hole today. Krystal Colbert was going with him, regardless of Austin's or Sidewinder's objections. No one would dare follow them into Brown's Hole. Creed fingered his new Colt .45 which hung on his hip. He was not as partial to this gun as he had been to the one Drake DeGanahl had stolen from him, but it served its purpose.

Krystal's spinning mind finally began to clear, but she continued to tremble every time she tried to take a breath. Sidewinder never left her side. She raised her reddened eyes up to his face. When he felt her movement, his blue eyes lowered to meet her teary-eyed gaze. He smiled, it was a gesture laced with warmth as he remembered the way she had touched his arm and told him that she was sorry when he had told her about his family. It had been a long time since someone had treated him kindly and Sidewinder would not forget it.

Through the last of her tears, Krystal managed to smile back at him. It did not seem possible that this angelic-faced youth was a cold-blooded killer. His kindness began to have a calming affect on her as she thought about her father and the chance that he could still be alive. All of a sudden, twinkling eyes of deep olive green suddenly danced before her face. Drake . . . Oh Lord! He would have no way of knowing what had become of her. He might not return to the spot where her father had been shot, so he would believe that she had chosen to run away from Green

349

River instead of proving her love to him by returning. The vicious circle that her life continually spun around in settled down upon her like a heavy spector of doom. She did not know where she was, or what Creed Ward had in store for her. If her father was dead and if Drake believed that she truly was a desperado, she wondered if there was anything left to fight for?

She glanced through the heavy veil of smoke which signalled that the fire was nearing its finish and spotted Creed's hovering form. As his gaze met hers, a powerful emotion overcame her with a unmeasurable degree of fierceness. It was a new feeling which she had never experienced before this moment, and the intensity of it was all directed at Creed Ward. Her tawny eyes narrowed in the bright glare of the morning sun. Creed could see the hate she felt for him, it was so apparent on her face that it startled him. Her delicate features took on a harder appearance as her eyes remained unwavering. This was not the end of the battle, she realized, it was only the beginning.

Chapter Twenty-five

The light of the day brought little peace. He had not seen her since last night, and that was much too long. Drake leaned his full weight against the rail of the balcony which was suspended from the wall outside his bedroom. Down below him, life went on as usual. But in the house which stood above the town of Green River, and at the base of the towering stone cliffs of Castle Rock, Drake was filled with such a great feeling of indecision that it threatened to tear him apart.

He ran a hand through the thick curls of his light brown hair while his weary eyes wandered down towards the street where the jailhouse stood. Damn his brother! Damn that woman! Drake hit the wooden rail with his doubled-up fist. Would he ever live a normal life like the serene-looking people who walked down the streets of the quiet little town? If he only knew what he wanted to do with his life, but that was something that constantly eluded him. It was foolish dreaming to think that he would ever be able to undo the resentment which had built up through the years with his brother, especially now that Devon would soon face the end of a rope, or a lifetime of imprisonment. But did he dare to hope that there was still a chance for him to share his future with Krystal?

He sighed and went back into his room. Now that the day had begun, he knew there was no use to worry about getting any sleep. He shouldn't have come home last night. He could have paced the floor of the local saloon just as easily as he had walked back and forth in the narrow confines of his old bedroom. He tucked the tails of his beige shirt down neatly into his jeans, then tightened the brass buckle on his low-riding gunbelt before donning his suede vest. His hat received the worst end of his turmoil as he nervously rolled the brim into a tight cylinder with his fingers.

"Can we talk, *hijo*?"

Drake swung around abruptly at the sound of his mother's soft voice. She had not called him *hijo* for a long time. He lowered his eyes to the floor briefly before he answered her in a hoarse voice. "I reckon so."

Angelina entered the room apprehensively. She had not wanted to pressure him into talking last night when he had arrived because he had been so upset, but now she felt a compelling need to help him if he would permit her to do so. "Krystal did not return to Green River with you?" she asked. There was no reason to wait for him to tell her who was behind his melancholy mood.

Drake sighed. His mother had always had an uncanny perception. "Yes, but I left her last night."

"And now you're sorry?"

Was she always correct with her assumptions? He shook his head slightly as his mother approached him and touched his arm lightly. "Then you must go back to her before it's too late."

Drake shook his head. "She knows where I am." He swallowed hard and turned away from her dark probing gaze.

Angelina drew in a ragged breath. All of the men in her life had always been too stubborn to relent to anything that might make them appear to be less than impeccable. It broke her heart to see that both of her sons had allowed that affliction to destroy their chances at happiness. She was determined to see to it that Drake did not allow his obstinateness to get in the way of his love for Krystal.

"In everyone's life there comes a time when they have to follow what is in their heart." Angelina said from experience as Drake turned to look down at her. "And sometimes that is not an easy thing to do, *hijo*. But true love is so precious that one can not allow it to slip away, even if it means rejecting all the rules that you have previously lived by up until that time."

Drake did not speak as he allowed his mother's words to mingle with his confusion. She was talking about herself, yet the outcome of her story applied directly to her oldest son. Submission was not easy for him, but then love had not been an emotion he had known before he had met Krystal Colbert, either. He knew it didn't matter that she had not come back to him last night or this morning. She probably would not come on her own accord because she was just as inflexible as he was. But it no longer mattered. She was his wife, and he loved her more than he had ever thought it was possible to love a woman. Krystal was his future, he was not going to let her escape their destiny.

Angelina blinked back her tears as her son — her

hijo — grabbed her by the shoulders and kissed her cheek before he pulled his hat down over the heavy mass of hair on his head and rushed from the room. He would thank his mother for her wisdom later, but now he was too mad at Krystal for allowing him to leave her last night, and he was furious at himself for actually going. That woman was too damned independent for her own good, Drake thought with an aggravated grunt. He was going to give Krystal her first lesson on how to be a good wife just as soon as he arrived at their campsite.

From a distance, everything appeared to be fine. The two horses he had rented in Ogden still grazed in the same spot where they had been hobbled last night, and it looked as though John and Krystal were still asleep. But as Drake ventured closer, it was obvious that nothing was as it should have been at this time in the morning. There were no flames in the circle of rocks which had been strategically placed to enclose a fire, and one bedroll was laying in a discarded heap next to the cold fire. The form of a man was straddled across the other bedroll and it was apparent that he was not merely asleep.

Drake unsnapped the strap across the top of his holster as he approached the camp slowly. His cautious gaze did not miss one minor detail of the foreboding scene. Panic washed over him when he realized that Krystal was nowhere to be seen, and that it was John's unmoving body that was slumped over on the ground. He slid down from his horse and rolled the man over carefully. A sickening knot formed in his stomach when he saw the gunshot wound in John's ribcage which was caked with a thick layer of dried blood.

A weak moan barely made it past John's cracked lips, but it was enough to raise Drake's hopes. If the old man was still alive, then maybe he would be able to tell Drake what had happened here, and where he would find Krystal. Drake knew the only chance John had was to have a doctor remove the bullet which was probably still lodged somewhere in his side. Working against time and with an obsessive determination, Drake quickly constructed a travois out of Juniper branches and John's bedroll to haul the injured man back to town.

Drake tried to put Krystal out of his mind while he concentrated on transporting John into Green River, but it was impossible. He would always blame himself for whatever had taken place at their campsite during the night. If he had not been so selfish and unyielding again, they would have spent the night in the safety of his mother's home. But old habits were not so easy to break and even now he had a selfish reason for wanting John Colbert to pull through . . . John was the only person who knew what had happened to Krystal.

John Colbert was also a stubborn man, and before the doctor took him into surgery to remove the bullet which was lodged in his ribcage, he had given Drake the clue he had been praying to receive. Drake left the doctor's office with his destination clearly mapped out in his mind. John had been too weak from his loss of blood to speak audibly, but he had managed to put a shaking hand up to his mouth and trace the outline of a drooping mustache above his lips before the anesthesia the doctor had given him took hold. It did not take long for Drake to figure out that the old man's feeble hand gesture was meant to represent Creed

Ward's long handlebar mustache.

Cameron Reed looked up from his desk with surprise when Drake pushed through the front door of the jailhouse. The marshal's first reaction was to go for his gun, but he sighed with relief when he recognized the man who had caused the distraction. His tense stance relaxed as he slid his gun back down into its holster. "Drake? Something the matter?"

"Damn right, something's the matter!" Drake's rage was spewing from him as he ignored the fact that the other man had just drawn a gun on him. His eyes scanned the room, stopping to rest on the poster with his wife's beautiful face plastered across the center of it.

"I want to be reinstated," he said as he turned to face the shocked marshal.

Cameron gave an uncertain chuckle. "Well, now, it's not that easy, you know?"

"You have the authority to deputize me. And I want to be a lawman again." He closed the short distance between them and stood inches away from the older man. His determination glistened in his unwavering gaze. "I was a damn good lawman and you know it!"

Cameron shrugged. "It's not that, Drake. It's just — well —" Cameron searched for sound reason to discourage the younger man, but he could not think of anything. Drake was exactly the kind of man Cameron would like to have as his deputy. He was sure the rest of Devon's gang was still in the area and he had no one who was qualified enough to send in search of them. If Drake was fired up over something to do with the outlaw bunch, there was no doubt in Cameron's mind that he would also be the man who could bring them to their end. Cameron drew in a

356

heavy breath as his gaze met Drake's steely look. He was struck by the similarity that Drake had with Devon at this moment and an apprehensive sensation passed through him. Whomever or whatever Drake DeGanahl's rage was directed at, Cameron hoped that he would use it to bring justice rather than to just destroy anyone who crossed his revengeful path.

"All right, Drake. You've got your old job back."

Drake's gaze filtered up to the wanted poster on the wall again as Cameron's eyes were drawn in the same direction. He tore his attention away from the poster and stared at the marshal. "Can I have my badge now?"

Cameron blinked and nodded slowly as he walked to the other side of his desk and pulled open one of the drawers. He lifted a shiny tin star from the interior of the drawer and held it out to Drake. Drake felt his insides twist into a ball of knots. When he pinned that badge above his thundering heart, he would be committed to uphold the law. He wondered if he could face the challenge of his decision once again. He wanted Creed Ward at all costs, but what about Krystal? The urge to look at her image on the poster once more became so strong that Drake had to turn in the opposite direction in an attempt to fight against it. His tortured mind could only handle so much pain.

The light shedding from the glistening star hit him squarely in the eye and snapped his mind back to reality. With a hand that shook so badly that he was unsure if he would be able to control his actions, Drake reached out and took hold of the star by one pointed tip. His whole body trembled visibly as he positioned the shimmering emblem on his chest and latched the back of the pin. He smoothed his brown suede vest back down over his shirt and took a deep breath. His father's strong influence was reborn in him, but not with the pride that he felt when he had previously been a lawman. The memory of his father was accompanied by the engulfing fear that he was not deserving enough to wear this badge again. He thought of the young boy who had killed his father in cold blood, of men like Joe Preece and Creed Ward and he knew there was not time to waste wondering about his own qualifications.

"I need to speak to my brother."

Cameron gave his head a slight nod. He had been right; Drake was going after the rest of Devon's gang. His hand reached around to his back pocket as he removed the keys to Devon's cell, then handed them to his new deputy. Talking to Devon would not be nearly as effective if Drake had to speak through the bars.

A knowing expression crossed Drake's face. His thoughts were identical to Cameron's, physical contact might be the only conversation Devon would submit to in his hateful frame of mind. Drake pushed through the door which led to the cell block. He paused and took a deep breath before he continued down the hallway. From the corner of his eye, he caught the shimmering of the silver badge as it moved beneath his vest with the shifting of his walk. The pin was almost weightless, yet he could feel it hanging on his shirt as though it weighed at least a hundred pounds. He paused before Devon's cell and unconsciously placed his hand on his hips. It was a gesture that drew his vest back and revealed the badge he was wearing upon his chest.

Devon glanced up from his bunk when he heard footsteps approaching his cell. Unconcerned, he glanced back down at the week-old newspaper Cameron had allowed him to read. But something caught his eye. His gaze flew back up to the stature of his glowering brother and came to rest on the glistening silver star. His ebony eyes traveled up to Drake's stony face. He did not try to hide his surprise as Drake inserted the long skeleton key in the keyhole and entered the cell. He pushed the door open and let it bang against the bars of the ajoining cell with a loud crash, but he did not bother to close it again.

The younger DeGanahl folded the newspaper he had been reading and placed it on the end of the bunk before he leaned back against the wall. His brother's attitude was more than apparent. Only once before he had seen Drake in this state . . . right after they had learned about the murder of their father. Back then Drake had taken off his badge, knowing that revenge could not take the place of justice. Now, Devon realized with a growing feeling of uneasiness, Drake had replaced the badge for the same reason he had once felt unworthy to wear it.

A nervous chuckle broke the thick silence. "Well, well, it looks like there's a new deputy in town. Should I feel honored to have my lowly cell graced with his. presence?"

"Where's Creed?" Drake was not going to play word games with his brother again.

Devon gave his shoulders an indifferent shrug. "How would I know? It's kinda hard to keep track of anybody from these surroundings." He gestured around at the dingy cell with a wide sweep of his arm.

Drake reached out and grabbed him by the front of his shirt as he pulled him to his feet. Devon did not resist, nor did his victorious smirk fade from his face. "Ain't this a little unfair, big brother? I'm a defenseless

359

man." His evil smile broadened. "Why, not only are you wearin' a badge, but you're also wearin' a gun. But then . . ." Devon's dark eyes narrowed as they met Drake's gaze on the same level. "We both know that you don't want to finish me off now. That's not the plan, is it?"

"You'll never be a free man again, so what does it matter?" Drake released his tight grip on his shirt and stepped back as though Devon carried a deadly disease. "All I want from you is to know where Creed Ward is holed up."

Again, Devon shrugged nonchalantly. "He could be any place by now. Why such an interest in him anyway? Or is it just that you're just hell-bent to wipe out every bad man in the West now that you're a big important lawman again?"

Time was too important to waste listening to his brother's cynical remarks again. It had already been hours since he had found John in the desert. Creed could have taken Krystal to any number of hideouts by now. The two most likely places being Robber's Roost in southern Utah, or Brown's Hole which was primarily in Northwestern Colorado. Either location was legally out of Drake's jurisdiction, but that was a minor distraction.

"Creed was in this area last night and the only thing I want from you is to know where he was headed?" Drake took a step forward until he was close enough to hear his brother's steady breathing. Devon was undaunted by his closeness.

"Why is it so important to find Creed? He's small potatoes. Why don't you go after somebody like Butch Cassidy if you're trying to regain your prestigious reputation again?"

Drake shook his head and backed up to the door of

the cell. His eyes burned a path in Devon's direction one last time. "Creed Ward is not worth the dirt beneath my feet. But last night he kidnapped Krystal and shot her father. For both of those actions, he will pay in spades." Drake's voice was too controlled for any dispute as he swung around and moved out of the small enclosure. Almost as though it was an afterthought, he pushed the cell door shut and strode to the end of the hall.

For a moment Devon stared at the steel plate on the door where the latch had just snapped into place while Drake's words penetrated his mind. "Wait!" he called out just as Drake started to leave the cell block.

Drake felt his heart skip a beat. Was it possible that Devon would give him some clue as to Creed's whereabouts? His hand froze on the doorknob, but he did not turn around.

"I think Creed was planning to head into Brown's Hole," Devon said, wondering why he had suddenly felt the need to help his brother find Krystal Colbert. He heard the door at the end of the hallway open, then Drake's footsteps click against the hard floor as he exited from the cellblock.

Drake paused to gather his thoughts. He had not other choice but to trust his brother, but he would not thank him for the information until it proved to be accurate. He glanced up and noticed Cameron watching him intently. "I'm going after Creed Ward."

"Did Devon tell you where he was hiding?"

"He told me where he thought he was headed. But I'll find him." Drake moved to the front door, and barely paused before he exited with a final statement. "I'll be back in a couple of days."

Cameron opened his mouth to protest, but Drake was gone before he had a chance to utter a sound. It occurred to the marshal that he was the one who should be issuing the orders to the younger man since he was in charge of this jail. But if there was a chance that Drake could bring in the rest of Devon's band of outlaws, then Cameron was not about to stop him. He scratched his chin thoughtfully and relaxed back into his chair. There was still something else that kept bothering him. His eyes darted to the opposite wall which was covered with the various wanted posters of wrongdoers. He opened a desk drawer and rummaged through a stack of documents and notes. He pulled out one of the small slips of paper and studied it. This was the name of the fellow he had met up in Odgen, the lawyer who had been traveling with that Pinkerton man. Cameron recalled that the man had told him that he was planning to remain in Ogden, in case Krystal Colbert happened to turn up in that area. Maybe he should send a telegram to this Les Macrea, and ask him a few more questions about that pretty little gal whose poster seemed to interest his new deputy so much?

Chapter Twenty-six

Creed Ward regretted his hasty decision to take Krystal Colbert to Brown's Hole within seconds after they had begun their journey. She was unequaled when it came to stubbornness. She refused to mount the horse when he had ordered her to, refused to hang on to the saddle horn when they had started out, and undoubtedly would have allowed herself to topple onto the ground if he had not held on tightly to her waist the whole time they rode. It did not matter what Creed instructed her to do, she would not comply.

The fact that Austin and Sidewinder chortled under their breath each time she defied him was not improving Creed's disposition. Her presence threatened his authority more than having Devon DeGanahl around to issue the orders. By nightfall when they had reached the outskirts of the area Krystal had heard the men refer to as Brown's Hole, she was more than pleased with herself. It was obvious that she had already managed to intimidate Creed Ward and in the process had made allies out of the other two men.

Creed was rapidly learning that she was not some placid female whom he could order around like some lowly servant. Servant? Good Lord, it was hard to imagine that just a short time ago she had been issuing orders to her own servants. For a moment, her thoughts traveled back to Boston and to the mansion on Beacon Hill, then she remembered her father, and her thoughts were snapped back to the present as she reminded herself of her contempt for his possible killer.

"Here's a bedroll for you," Sidewinder said. He hesitated when he noticed the strange look on her face. She snatched the blanket from his hand, then reminded herself that she should not take out her anger on this boy. She forced a smile as she muttered a thank you to him. His look brightened, and Krystal's fury toward Creed intensified. It was men like Creed Ward who influenced young boys like Sidewinder. Beneath those ornamental weapons which he wore constantly on his hips, Sidewinder was probably just a troubled child who could easily be put on the right path if he wasn't in the presence of murderers such as Creed Ward. That was one more thing she could add to her ever-growing list of reasons as to why she planned to see that Creed Ward received his just reward.

She flung her bedroll out on the hard ground and thought of how nice it would be to sleep in a real bed again. Her own bed—not a train berth or a bed in a hotel room. It seemed so long ago that she had actually slept in her own bed, that now she could not even remember how it felt to snuggle into a soft mattress of feathers and heavy quilts which had the faint smell of lilac cologne. Krystal realized she was remembering the times she had crawled into her mother's big brass bed when she was a little girl. It was a sense of security that had never been matched, not until she had found a similar feeling of contentment in Drake DeGanahl's arms. If only she had some way of knowing where he was or if he was thinking about her at this same moment as she was thinking about him . . . and if he was missing her, and discovering that he loved her more every minute, too?

She stretched her weary body out upon the blanket and fought against the urge to cry. Her mother was dead, and now because of her, her father was probably gone, too. If she had lost Drake, she would have no one. She had felt lost and alone after her mother's funeral, but not even that could compare to the terror she felt tonight. Would she continue to lose everyone she loved and cared about? She thought of Les Macrea. He had not entered into her thoughts much lately, but she knew he would always be her friend. He was in Boston though, and that was in another lifetime.

The feeling that she was being watched caused her to sit back up. Creed was staring at her and the tears which had been so close to the surface of her tawny eyes rapidly disappeared. Creed Ward would not have the pleasure of watching her cry. She laid back down and focused her eyes overhead. Only the outline of the half moon had appeared, but not one star was out in the darkening sky yet. She could still feel Creed's intent gaze, and she was determined not to let him get the best of her. It took all her willpower to keep from looking in his direction, but finally she heard him relax back against his bedroll. Her eyelids began to feel heavy as she wondered how she could feel tired when her life was in such constant despair. Tomorrow she would formulate a plan, but tonight she gave into the weariness of her body. She would need to rest tonight, she told herself, so that she would be prepared for whatever tomorrow might bring.

Night passed too quickly in the sense that Krystal did not feel refreshed when she opened her drowsy lids, and it did not pass fast enough to elude the phantoms of her shadowy nightmares. Each time one of the demonic spectors had filtered through the hazy passages of her sleeping mind, she would awake with a start. But she could never remember what her dreams had been about. She was relieved when morning had finally arrived and she would no longer be tormented by those terrifying illusions.

She blinked and glanced around. Was this Brown's Hole? She had expected a barren 'hole' in muted shades of putrid brown. What she saw in reality was the ethereal beauty of a timeless creation. Surrounded by the brooding presence of Diamond Mountain to the south, Cold Spring Mountain to the north, and nestled between O-Wi-Yu-Kuts Plateau and the Uintah Mountain range, Browns Hole was literally what the name suggested. The floor of the hole, 35 miles long and six miles wide, was carpeted with sage in hues of silver and cedars of a rich deep green. Juniper trees and pinyon pines jutted from the gentle slopes of the low ridges, their craggy shapes defined by the spectacular maroon buttes and sandstone promontories. The beauty of this area was enhanced by the permeating quiet of the desert aura, and Krystal found herself in awe of this place called Brown's Hole.

"Are you hungry?"

She jumped at the sound of Sidewinders voice booming out in the silence. She almost had the urge to whisper when she answered him. Instead she just gave her head a negative shake. She wished now that she had paid more attention when they had ridden into this area last night. From this location, it appeared that there was no exit from this secluded valley. How would she ever find her way out of here?

"Well, let's get movin'," Creed said in a voice that was less than sociable. He stalked to where the horses were teetered and began to saddle his own horse with little regard to the rest of the group.

Krystal dragged herself up from the ground as she wondered if she would ever become accustomed to riding on those beasts. Her backside was screaming that she was not built to ride in a saddle and that she would never grow used to it. She inched her way towards Sidewinder. He was busy saddling his horse and smiled down at her when he noticed she had approached him.

"Where are we going now? I thought this was Brown's Hole."

"You're right, this is Brown's Hole. But we're going to be in this area for a spell, so we're going on over to the river. There's a cabin where we usually stay." His childish grin broadened. "When we get there, I'll show you Lodore Canyon. You ain't never seen a sight to compare with the Canyon."

Krystal shrugged. She was amazed by this part of the hole. Lodore Canyon must be spectacular, she decided as she spun around to take in one more glimpse of the breathtaking countryside.

"Are you ready?" Creed asked in a hesitant voice. He was preparing himself for another episode like the one they had the day before when she had refused to mount his horse, and she had made him resort to physical force in order for him to get her atop of the animal. But today she tossed her golden-red curls in defiance and stomped straight over to his gelding. Creed was even more intimidated by her behavior than he had been before. She turned her narrowed gaze in his direction as she waited for him to help her into the saddle. At that moment, he began to wonder if it would have been more revengeful to let Drake DeGanahl have this woman. A frown crossed Creed's mustached face as he swung into the saddle behind her. Perhaps DeGanahl was thanking him for taking this female off his hands and had no intention of coming after her. Creed grunted as his heels dug into the sides of his horse. That would be just about his luck, he thought with aggravation.

In a very short span of time, the group reached their destination. If possible, Krystal thought this section of the hole was even more beautiful than the spot where she had awakened this morning. The Green River lived up to its name just as Brown's Hole did. Entering abruptly through the dramatic rock walls of the Red Canyon from the northwestern corner, the river meanders along the eastern edge of the hole and then drops into the jaws of the vermillion walls of Lodore Canyon. Krystal gasped as her eyes met Sidewinder's shining blue eyes.

"Beautiful, ain't it?" He smiled proudly as though this land was his personal discovery. "After we get settled, I'll take you up to the top." He pointed toward the splendorous maw of the canyon where the midday sun cast glorious rays of light upon the brilliant orange-red walls of rock.

Krystal shook her head with enthusiasm. She glanced toward the cabin. Good Lord, not another one room cabin. Well, at least her odds were getting better. This time she would only be sharing a room with three outlaws instead of five, not counting Drake, of course. The thought of Drake caused her excitement of seeing the canyon to disappear. Had he bothered to go out to their camp yesterday morning? Or did he just ride in the opposite direction without so much as a backward glance? The sound of men's

368

voices engaged in a heated discussion snapped her back to the reality of her devastating situation.

"I ain't goin'," Sidewinder said flatly. He knew why Creed wanted to send him and Austin off to Lay for supplies. With the two of them headed into the small town of Lay, Colorado, Creed could be alone with Krystal Colbert. His blue eyes took on a shimmer of chilling magnitude as he faced Creed with bold defiance. A shiver bolted down Krystal's spine. She remembered that look on the young outlaws face the first day she had saw him on the train. His kindness the past couple of days had temporarily blocked his evil nature from her mind. Her terrified gaze moved to Austin, whose elderly eyes watched the scene in quiet reserve. He ignored Krystal's imploring look, too involved with the men to divert his attention. She riveted her eyes back to Creed and Sidewinder as fear inched it's way throughout her body. She was paralyzed with the indescribable horror of remembering how casually Creed Ward had shot her father. These men drew their guns as easily as they enhaled a breath of fresh air. It did not matter if they were right or wrong, their side irons were the ruling factor in every situation. Krystal closed her eyes, but they would not remain shut. She hated the thoughts which were racing through her mind. . . . Please God, let Sidewinder's hand be faster. Good Lord, was she really asking HIm to aid one man in killing another?

Creed smiled . . . a smile as cold as the look in Sidewinder's translucent pupils. He was getting real tired of this youngster's attitude, maybe it was time to teach him a lesson. Creed stepped back, his right arm rigid at his side. He had always wondered how fast the kid really was, today was as good as any other day to find out.

A look of surprise filtered across Sidewinder's face

while he watched the other man's actions. Seldom did a man make a voluntary choice to draw against him in a gunfight. The boy's reputation with his guns was well deserved. Creed Ward was letting his obsession for the woman cloud his thinking. Sidewinder thought of Krystal. He would not allow his eyes to waver from Creed, but if he was to look in her direction, he knew what he would see on her face. Her jewel-toned eyes would be wide with fear, her soft pink mouth would open with a silent plea, though she would probably be too scared to make a sound. His young mind had a permanent picture of that face implanted forever in his memory. He had seen that expression before . . . on his sister's face, right before a bullet that had been meant for him went astray and struck her instead.

Sidewinder saw the light flicker in Creed's eye, the signal he always watched for in his opponent. It never failed, a man's eyes always lit up for just an instant or less, but it was always just a flash before he went for his gun. Sidewinder had first noticed that fleeting glimmer in the eyes of the man who had killed his sister. He saw it now, in Creed's eyes. Sidewinder's hand fell to his hip in a movement so swift, it was blurred. Although he wore a gun on each hip, today he would only need to draw one. His sister's face flashed before his eyes, or was it Krystal Colbert's? Sidewinder's thumb cocked the hammer as his nimble forefinger pulled the trigger. The bullet made a whizzing sound that sliced through the air as it zeroed in on the target.

Creed's .45 tumbled to the ground. He had only began to pull it out of the holster. His shocked look drilled into the kid's sky-blue eyes. "Why?" he asked in a hoarse voice.

Sidewinder twirled his gun around his forefinger, then dropped it neatly down into his fancy holster.

His hand, the same hand he had just drawn his gun with, raised up and pushed his wide-brimmed hat to the back of his wavy blonde head. An innocent smile curved the corners of his mouth as he lowered his hand once again and pointed his finger at Creed. "Bang, bang, you're dead."

Krystal's blood froze as Sidewinder turned to look at her. Her terror-stricken body shook in spite of his warm smile. She glanced at Creed Ward as he sunk to his knees in the silvery sagebrush. His wide-eyed gaze looked up at her as he shrugged. "Why?" he asked again.

She turned to Sidewinder in confusion. What was going on? He had just shot Creed, hadn't he? Sidewinder's chilling smile remained intact. He almost seemed too proud of himself to speak.

Austin began to move toward Creed, who still hunkered down in the dense vegetation on his knees. A dark red stain had began to soak a small spot on his shirt above his gunbelt. Austin helped him to his feet and glanced at Sidewinder. "Why did you gut-shoot him? You could've just killed him, outright. No man deserves to suffer the long death of a gut wound."

Sidewinder threw his hands up into the air in a casual gesture. "If you get him outta here soon enough, Miss Colbert won't have to watch him die. She shouldn't have to see that, should she?" His head tilted to the side as though he was asking the most simple question in the world.

Austin shook his head and started toward the horses. He agreed with Sidewinder on one thing only. Nobody should watch a man suffer the agony of a gut shot, especially a woman. He had never known anybody to shoot a man in the gut on purpose. Usually a man was hit in the stomach by someone who was not skilled enough to hit his heart or lungs, areas which would result in a quick death. Austin was angry at the boy. After he disposed of Creed Ward, he was going to come back and teach the youth some manners. An outlaw should have a code of honor to live by just like any other man, and Austin decided it was high time Sidewinder learned how to conduct himself with a gun.

Krystal watched in horror as Austin flung Creed over the saddle of his horse. Creed's eyes were open, but he appeared to be in shock. A related feeling of fear began to seep into Krystal's being. She was going to be alone with Sidewinder and she had understood enough of what Austin had said to know that Sidewinder's strategically aimed shot was a cruelty of unspeakable proportion. Her insides quivered so violently she was not sure if she could control her actions. She wanted to cry out to Austin not to leave her here with this crazy man, but she didn't want to anger Sidewinder. So she kept silent, though she was sure they could hear the deafening thud of her heart and the thundering of her shaking body.

Sidewinder held out his hand. "Want to walk to the top of the canyon now?"

He was almost like two separate people. Moments ago, he had carried a message of death in his clear blue gaze. Now those same eyes were shining brightly with the excitement of a child who was about to set off on some new adventure. Krystal could not speak, so she merely nodded. She would never again allow herself to forget that this blond, blue-eyed boy with a face that was almost too perfect, was also the most dangerous man she ever hoped to encounter. If he wanted to walk to the top of the canyon, she would not deny him. If he told her to jump from the top of the canyon wall, she would not hesitate.

He did not seem to notice how horrendously she

was shaking as she placed her hand against his outstretched fingers. She had to walk swiftly to keep up with his fast steps. Once she tripped over her own feet as the heel of one of her high-topped boots hung up on the thick sagebrush, but she quickly regained her footing, fearful that Sidewinder would become irritated with her hindering gait.

She did not notice the exquisite beauty of the canyon as they hiked up the step-like ledges which were carved artistically out of the rock. Nor did she notice the shimmering sea of calm water, so clear and green that it resembled ancient glass, as it flowed peacefully into the Gates of Lodore and then turned into a vicious tumult of slashing, frothing rapids as it cut through the heart of the canyon and disappeared through the narrow exit like an angry brigade of warriors.

They stood at the very top of creation, or so it seemed. But Krystal was still too numb with fear to care. Her mind continued to paint vivid pictures of guns blazing and the lethal odor of gunpowder and blood. She wanted to go home . . . to Drake, wherever he may be by now. She wanted to be with him, to feel his strong arms around her, to gaze into his handsome face, and to hear his soothing voice telling her this had all been some horrible nightmare and that she would soon forget it.

But reality was not so sweet. Her mind was seized back to the present by the roar of gunfire once again. Krystal was sure her heart had finally reached it's limit. She closed her eyes, hoping she could just die and be released from this madness. Sidewinder's nervous chuckle reached her eyes. Good Lord, did he have to laugh when he killed someone?

"Rattlesnakes! I hate those slimy things, don't you?"

Krystal slowly allowed her eyes to open. Thank

God it had only been a rattlesnake that had met with one of Sidewinder's bullets. She tried to breathe in a normal manner, but her heart was still thrashing too wildly in her breast and she felt as though she was being smothered. Sidewinder picked up a long branch and slid it under the limp form of the grayish black snake.

"He didn't even have time to rattle." He laughed louder. "They call me Sidewinder, cause I strike without warning, too." He tossed the snake over the embankment and watched as the reptile floated down to the waiting clutches of the river. "Did you know that a rattler does not die completely until the sun goes down?"

"No . . . I — I didn't know that," she answered as she began to back away from him. "I — I'm feeling faint, could I sit down for a minute?" Her legs seemed to turn to jelly. If she didn't sit down, she was sure she would fall down. As Sidewinder helped her descend to a nearby rock, she was struck by the most helpless feeling she had ever known. She could not bluff her way out of this, nor could she hope to use her feminine persuasion, even if she wanted to do so. Sidewinder was too crafty, and too heartless to try to trick with insolent games. The afternoon sun beat down without mercy on her tender skin as the young killer knelt before her with a deep look of concern upon his face. The temperature was topping one hundred degrees today, and it was no wonder, Krystal thought as she met the intense blue of Sidewinder's eyes, she had just entered the realm of Hell.

Chapter Twenty-seven

The two shots made Drake's blood race like icy daggers of steel through his veins. The shots had to be coming from Creed or the men who were riding with him, because they were only a mile or so ahead of Drake. From one of the cedar ridges, he had watched the three horses and their riders travel down to the river. One horse carried two riders . . . Creed Ward and Krystal.

Once Drake left the seclusion of the tree feathered ridge, he had not been able to see the activity around the cabin. Now, as he inched his way down to the river, he heard the second shot. A feeling of evil seared a burning path across his chest as he spurred his horse in the sides, but the animal was still not fast enough. A gripping feeling of doom overcame him as he approached the old cabin and the silence which sheltered the peaceful canyon from the outside world engulfed him like a shroud.

He saw movement around the cabin or down by the river, and only one horse was tied to the hitching post.

Drake recognized the horse as the animal that belonged to Sidewinder. Krystal had been riding on Creed Ward's horse when Drake had watched them ride into this valley, so where had Creed ridden off to, and was Krystal still with him? The second shot had come from the top of the canyon, but it was treacherous and foolish to take a horse up that rocky trail. A man did better to climb to the top on foot. He glanced towards the towering walls of the Gates of Lodore. Had Krystal attempted to run away, and had she headed up the steep banks of the canyon?

He jumped from his horse and dropped the reins to the ground. His feet moved to the base of the rock ledge, but he did not pause to check the terrain. Slipping when his sharp-toed boot missed a footing, he ignored the pain when his body scraped against the jagged stones. There was only one thought in his mind. He knew she was up there; he could sense her presence, and the pounding terror in his heart told him that she needed him. But his steps came to a sudden halt at the edge of the rugged terrain when he spotted her sitting on a rock at the top of the cliff.

Drake's love for Krystal flooded through his body and temporarily claimed his mind as his eyes strained to make out every detail of her beautiful image. A strange sensation passed through Drake. The scene before him seemed so normal, and yet, so unnatural. He did not have time to analyze the situation, or to notice how Sidewinder and Krystal both seemed to be so out of character. He was heedless of anything except his relief in knowing that she was still alive. Without caution he charged across the top of the canyon wall. But Krystal and Sidewinder did not even look up until he had stopped only several yards away from them. It was his tall unmoving form which caught their eye.

Krystal saw his shadow from the corner of her eye, but she was afraid to turn around. Abrupt waves of nausea swept over her, making her feel weak and dizzy. A thought—just an instant of hope—taunted her apprehensive mind into thinking that Drake might be the man who belonged to the hovering dark shadow. But her eyes were frozen to Sidewinder's face. She could not bear the disappointment if it were anyone other than Drake DeGanahl who towered above them like a silent sentry.

Sidewinder turned his head slowly. Recognition lit up his face and danced through his blue eyes. Krystal watched his face, her heart bursting with a dire prayer. Please, please let it be. . . ?

"Drake," she said as her head turned with a tortured effort. Oh Lord, it really was him. Her long lashes fluttered as her face ascended to meet the burning fire encompassed in his expression. His eyes, shaded by the brim of his chocolate-brown hat, had never looked so dark green as they did when they touched upon her face. They were like the deepest depths of the enchanted sea and they bespoke of all the love he felt for her. In this stilled moment of love-laden agony, she tried to memorize every inch of his features: The strong jaw which was the perfect frame for his crooked, suggestive grin, and the soft brown curls that wound around his ears and peeked over the collar of his shirt at the base of his neck. When she had first spotted him standing above them, she had felt as though it was the first time she had ever looked upon him, now she realized with horror, it might also be the last. A sharp pain pierced her heart and tore through her chest as she realized her mind wanted to paint a picture of him that would last forever.

She reached out and grabbed hold of Sidewinder's arm as he began to raise up to a standing position.

377

He pulled her up with him while his eyes fastened on to the other man.

"Please Sidewinder, please don't kill him." The choked plea echoed across the canyon wall and disappeared with the feathery touch of the soft breeze which whistled across the stone peaks of the canyon. Her death-like grip on Sidewinder's arm grew tighter and she heard him inhale sharply.

Drake had not moved, but his arms ached to reach out to her. He did not know Sidewinder's connection in her kidnapping. Just the fact that Sidewinder was riding with Creed Ward was enough for Drake. His arm crooked at the elbow and cautiously slid back, a movement so slight it would not be noticeable to the untrained eye. The material of his vest wrinkled, barely no more than a fraction at his breast with the small gesture, and the noonday sun which clothed the top of the canyon with a kaleidoscope of golden rays, caught the light from the tip of the silver star that was pinned beneath the brown vest. A single, blinding beam flashed across the rock plateau, emitting from the reflection of the undeniable emblem.

Krystal released her hold on Sidewinder's arm and turned toward Drake with a look of anxiety upon her face. For a second, she was not sure where the brilliant light had come from, but all at once she understood. She searched his face, desperate to see the look of love in his eyes again. Had she only imagined the trembling of his lips, or the soft twinkle in his eyes when their gazes had reached across the rocky peak of Lodore Canyon? Or had that look been something else? Had the faceted lights in his pupils been the glimmer of victory . . . the victory he felt as a lawman who had just cornered his prey?

She had the urge to run to him and to beg him to love her as much as she loved him, but his eyes were locked with Sidewinder's solemn gaze. The two opposing forces stood less than twenty feet away from one another, and their expressions were both the same—steady and full of calculation. Krystal was strangling on her fear. Drake was fast . . . she had known how skilled he was with a gun since the night he had shot Joe Preece. But Sidewinder's speed was phenomenal. Drake would not have a chance. She stepped in front of Sidewinder and tilted her face upward as he pretended not to be aware of her presence.

It took every ounce of willpower not to lower his eyes, but Sidewinder knew that he couldn't look at her. He would see his sister's face again. And he would remember the first time he had strapped a gun on his hip and faced another man in a gunfight. And his suffering mind would recall how his sister had run into the street to protect him. She was sixteen and beautiful . . . Sidewinder was fourteen and filled with outrage.

Krystal did not back down and Sidewinder could feel the pressure of her body touching his. He could hear the desperation in her voice. "Please?" she said again. He hesitated before his blue eyes blinked and lowered. A mistake he realized immediately and one he could not undo. He swung out and pushed her to the side, but it was already too late.

Drake took advantage of the boy's indecision and lunged forward. He reached him just as Krystal tumbled out of the way. His body hit Sidewinder full force and they both toppled to the ground. Drake was taller and stronger than Sidewinder, but Sidewinder was as slippery as his namesake. Like a deadly rattler, he squirmed out from Drake's grip and grabbed at one of his guns.

Krystal screamed, though she was not aware of the shrill sound that flew from her mouth. She saw

379

Sidewinder's hand grip the pearl handle of his gun at the same instant that Drake reached out and knocked Sidewinder back against the rocks. The sound of their bodies crashing against the stone sounded heavy and strange. She watched through a mist of terror as they both rolled towards the edge of the cliff. From the ground where she had landed when Sidewinder had shoved her out of the way, her eyes tried to grasp the reality of what she was seeing, but the sight was beyond her mind's comprehension.

Drake and Sidewinder both rose up to their feet, still locked in a death-like clench. But they were too close to the edge, and the rocks were worn smooth from thousands of years of wind and erosion, and too slick for the leather bottoms of their tall boots. The two figures were silhouetted against the vast blue of the flawless sky by a searing gold frame which was created by the midday sun. One was a profile of a man fighting for his life and the woman he loved with a vehemence that would never end. And one was the outline of a boy whose battle cry was not yet that of a man, but equally as intense. And then they were both gone.

A scream stopped short in Krystal's throat as she raised up from the ground on wobbly legs that resisted her weak attempt to walk. She tried to imagine that this was not happening, and that at any time now, both men would reappear. She told herself that they had not disappeared over the edge of the rock wall of the canyon. Her mind must have finally snapped, or maybe in her panic, she had made up the whole thing. Maybe Drake had not really been here, and maybe she would soon discover that she had only created him in her dreams. Perhaps everything that had happened in the past few weeks had only been a figment of her imagination? Soon, maybe, she would

380

wake up and be back in Boston, and it would be time to go to work in the little brick school house. Her mother would be downstairs rehearsing for an upcoming play, and the smell of lilacs would greet her as she descended the wide staircase. Maybe . . .

Unconsciously, she moved to the edge of the cliff. She paused before reaching the spot where the two men had just been fighting. A feeling of disbelieving horror attacked her numb body and froze her to the spot. Did she really want to look over that cliff? But the round rocks beckoned to her until she knew that she had no other choice but to continue. Her vision blurred with the fear of what she might see when she peeked over that rocky ledge, yet some unknown force pushed her onward. She closed her eyes and said a silent prayer that somehow her mind had only been playing tricks on her.

At the edge, she fell to her knees and leaned over the smooth rounded slope of the deep canyon wall. Below her was a hundred foot drop into the river bed. An incoherent cry escaped from her lips. The Green River answered her strangled plea with a roar of the rapids as they angrily pushed over the obtrusive rocks which decorated the bed of the river. Her eyes frantically searched the white foaming tides and scanned the slashing whirlpools, but she saw nothing but the water and the steep red walls of the canyon. She collapsed down upon the hard mattress of stone and stared into the wide expanse of water, until the river and all within her gaze was one conglomerated blur. And then she felt the swell of tears in her eyes, but only briefly before they came rushing down her cheeks. She cried until her face felt chapped from the wetness. But she couldn't stop crying and she couldn't bear the thought of Drake falling over that edge. If tears were blood, today she would have bled herself dry.

The setting of the sun was signalled by long shadows of gloom upon the walls of the canyon and the brilliance of orange intermingled with yellow and gold resting lightly on the crest of this haven of stone. How long Krystal laid at the edge of the cliff, she was not sure. Through her tears she had watched the rushing water making demonic illusions out of the waves and thinking how easy it would be to slip from this ledge and be swallowed up by one of the swirls which reminded her of hellish jaws and gnashing teeth.

"Miss Colbert?"

The sound of the man's voice nearly caused Krystal to fall from the ledge. She bolted up and swung around to the source of the sound. The lines in Austin's face deepened as he stopped his approach. Krystal could tell he thought that she was going to fall, and for a second she had wondered the same thing. A pulse was beating in frantic succession in her temple and her heart felt like it had just attached itself to her windpipe. She staggered back away from the edge as Austin moved closer in a slow cautious walk. She looked like a terrified little animal that had been backed into a corner and was contemplating the easy way out.

Austin stopped when he was standing between her and the edge. He exhaled the breath he had been holding, secure that she could not fling herself over the edge without getting past him first. His eyes moved over her as he noted her swollen, puffy eyes and red face. It appeared she had been crying for hours. His first thought was that Sidewinder had done something to her and he felt the anger explode in his chest. He stepped closer and peered down into her face. He was sure she was in a state of shock by the way she was staring at him with such a blank expression on her face. He glanced around with confusion. "Where's Sidewinder?"

An expression of disbelief rushed across her face as the vivid memory consumed her mind once again. She opened her mouth, but nothing came out. Her wide eyes moved past Austin and fluttered downward. When she looked back up at Austin, his look was also filled with incredulity.

"Did Sidewinder—" Austin looked over his shoulder at the rapids as a shudder shook his lean frame.

"And Drake. . ."

Austin stared down at her, what was she saying? "Drake?" he repeated.

Her slender hand raised up and one shaking finger pointed down towards the base of the river. "They fought, and they—they—"

"Drake and Sidewinder? Is that what you're trying to tell me?" He grabbed her by the shoulders and peered down into her face. "Did Drake and Sidewinder fall into the river?"

Her head moved up and down as though it was in slow motion while the reality of what had happened began to sink in to her resistant mind. Another sob shook her body.

"But he's not de—dead." Her voice was quivering as badly as her small frame.

Austin pulled her further away from the edge. He shook his head with doubt. "It's a long way down to the bottom, Miss Colbert."

He began to pull her away from the cliff. She allowed him to lead her to the decline, but she abruptly stopped as they started down. A light flickered with golden hues through the center of her brown pupils as her eyes grew wide with hope. "Drake is still alive. I know he is."

Austin's shoulders slumped as his head once again gestured with a negative response. "It would be unlikely. There's a big rapid on the other side of the canyon. Disaster Falls it's called, and for a mighty good reason."

The corner of her eyes cradled large teardrops as she tried to fathom the idea of Drake being dead. Her mother . . . her father, and now Drake. No, she would not permit him to fall into the river and escape their marriage so easily. She straightened to a brave stance, though her hands still trembled and for a moment she almost felt like she was going to faint, but she refused to give into the lightheadedness that caused her to stagger slightly.

Austin grasped her around the waist when he noticed her unsteady steps. "You need to rest. You've had a bad shock. In the morning you'll feel better."

"In the morning we're going to follow the river downstream," she said in a quivering voice. "He will have to swim ashore somewhere, and he'll need me when he does."

Austin sighed as he helped her tiny form tread down the rock ledges. He was at a loss for words. Surely she didn't believe that anyone could fall into the rapids and then swim ashore as though they had been taking a leisurely bath? He led her to the base of the incline while he tried to think of something to say that would discourage her from the disappointment of such a useless journey.

"Miss Colbert?" he began. "You would be wasting your time."

She stopped and looked up at him. "My name is not Colbert anymore. It's Mrs. DeGanahl." Mrs. DeGanahl . . . that sounded good. *'Mi mujer, mi esposa, mi destino . . . hoy yo donar de mi nombre, de ya poseer mi corazon.'* Drake's marriage vow traveled softly through

384

the trails of her aching mind. She still had to ask him the meaning of those words. That would be the first thing she would do when she found him. She stopped beside the small log cabin and held her hand up to shade her eyes from the last rays of the setting sun. In another twenty minutes it would be dark.

"It would be foolish to leave tonight, wouldn't it?" She did not give Austin a chance to answer her before she rushed on. "We'll rest tonight, so that we can leave first thing in the morning. Damn! We should've left hours ago."

Austin was astounded at this little gal's spirit. Up there on the ledge, he had been certain that she was ready to do herself in for good. Now, she was issuing orders like a brigade general. It was obvious that nothing he said would convince her not to ride down the river to look for her husband. When did she become Mrs. DeGanahl? he wondered. He thought of asking her, but was too much of a gentleman to make the inquiry. He drew in a deep breath and sighed heavily. They had a long ride tomorrow, over some mighty rough terrain, and he wasn't a young fella anymore. He shook his head with sadness. Krystal DeGanahl was setting herself up for a big disappointment and he was going to have to be there to pick up the pieces when she realized what she was likely to find on the banks of the Green River.

Austin was packing their gear for the trip and he refused to let Krystal help. In fact he seemed to be in a very sour mood and acted as though she was a hinderance that he could do without. She sighed and retreated to the front door of the cabin so that she would be out of his way. The last thing she wanted to do was to anger him so that he would refuse to help her look for Drake. Her eyes kept being drawn in the direction of the canyon. In the light of the new day, the shadowed portal was a beckoning tunnel of awe-inspiring loveliness. Krystal found it amazing that the river could be so serene and smooth as it entered the sheer walls of Lodore, and then exit the stronghold in such a violent manner. She glanced around at the surrounding countryside. It was no wonder this area was a haven for men who were always looking back over their shoulder.

From what Austin had told her last night, Brown's Hole presented the ideal location for rustlers and other assorted lawbreakers since it was located within the boundaries of three different states. There were only three trails leading into the hole, known only to those men who found it a necessity to use them since they could easily be ambushed on any of the dangerous trails. Although the valley had been populated by a few legitimate homesteaders, the area was still avoided by lawmen. It would be a useless venture for an officer of the law to attempt to chase a rustler into the hole. Cattle could be driven from one state and back into another in a matter of an hour or less. Since no taxes were paid by any of the three states, Brown's Hole was virtually a forgotten locale. Austin remarked that some old timers liked to say that Brown's Hole was where the devil had taken over when God had done His work.

Krystal broke out in a rash of goosebumps as she remembered that her thoughts had been running along similar lines yesterday when she and Sidewinder had been at the top of the canyon wall. She shook off the ghastly feeling and tried to concentrate on the quiet beauty of the area instead. Sometime during the night, a light drizzle had fallen, and now it accompanied the dawn with a fresh exhilarating odor that filled Krystal's lungs with a sweet smell of hope. She glanced at Austin. He was as slow as molasses and less than enthusiastic about this quest. But Krystal refused to let his morbid opinions affect her optimism.

"I'll be back shortly," she said over her shoulder as she headed off toward the canyon. Austin cautioned her to be careful, but she merely shrugged her shoulders. All through the endless night, she had debated and wrestled with her conscience, and now she was certain that what she was about to do was the right thing.

The climb was harder this morning than it had been yesterday, because the rain, combined with the early morning dew had coated the smooth rocks with a dangerous layer of slippery wetness. Several times Krystal had to resort to crawling up the embankment instead of trying to walk over the steep ledges. A moment of panic engulfed her when she approached the spot of yesterday's tragedy, and as she fought back the urge to flee from this gateway to Hell. For Drake's sake she had to be strong.

With this thought foremost in her mind, Krystal reached down and took ahold of the little black bag which was still hanging around her neck . . . The link with the past and the key to her future. She unbuttoned the satin hook and opened the flap. Her nervous fingers carefully pulled the faded photograph from the bag and held it up to the increasing sunlight. A faint smile curved her lips as she studied the two people in the photo and she wished that she had known them when they had been together.

She replaced the old photograph back within the safety of the purse and grasped ahold of the diamond brooch. Her hand began to tremble, but not as badly as her quaking insides. It had been the discovery of the brooch which had started her mind doubting her

387

mother, and it had been because of the brooch that Drake had begun to doubt her innocence. With the existence of the brooch was also the possibility that someday Krystal would be forced to learn that her worst fears about her mother were true. Without it, she would no longer feel the consuming urge to find out why it had been hidden in her mother's lingerie drawer, instead of in the safe with all the rest of her expensive jewels.

Krystal turned the ornamental pin over and closely observed it. It was the most exquisite piece of jewelry she had ever seen and she was sure that the rows of diamonds and antique gold setting made it priceless. Why had it been in that little velvet box? There was only one person whom she trusted enough to hear the truth from, but the time had come to put Rebecca Colbert to rest in the manner Krystal felt such a grand woman should be remembered. Krystal knew she would understand.

With a show of dramatics that would have even impressed the actress in Rebecca, her daughter stood on the brink of the great stone wall while her arm slowly extended outward. The large pin was perched in the center of Krystal's outstretched hand for a minute longer, but no indecision entered into her mind as she jerked her arm up slightly and sent the circle of diamonds into the air above her head. It descended past her face and continued down into the bowels of the ageless river.

Krystal leaned forward in an effort to see the brooch when it hit the water, but it was already gone. A chill raced down her spine as she stared into the foaming rapids. The river was merciless as it hurried through the exit of the canyon walls and Austin said Disaster Falls was even more treacherous. But she would find Drake, she decided as she inched back from the edge of the towering wall, and in spite of Austin's prediction of doom, he would be alive. When they were reunited, they would go someplace where all of their misery and sorrow would be only a collection of faded memories like the weathered old photo which was contained in the little black bag that she was clutching against her breast. And they would have a family of their own, and they. . . . The beautiful picture abruptly blurred as she remembered the blinding flash of the silver star which Drake had been wearing on his chest yesterday. Perhaps the groundwork for his future had already been laid a long time ago, and maybe it did not include any of the dreams she yearned to make into a reality?

Chapter Twenty-eight

The shock of hitting the icy clutches of the river was almost enough to cause Drake's heart to stop beating, but the water which filled his lungs with an acute rush of strangling fluid convinced him that he was about to meet his Maker. He felt an indescribable pain rip through his body when he crashed against the rocks, and his senses deserted him with the dizziness that had overcome him when he had been hurled through the swirls like a limp rag doll. Giving into the madness of the wild waves and to the pain in his body, he hadn't thought of surviving, only of how soon he would die and be set free from this agony.

Even now as he fought to stay awake, he was not sure if he was still alive or if he had passed on into another existence. He felt as though his waning mind was detached from his body, because he could not feel anything below the unbearable pain in his lungs which was a result of his unconscious attempt to hold his breath during this brutal ordeal. He was floating in a sea of calm, brownish-green water, but he was too weak to try to swim for the shore.

His foggy eyesight struggled to see beyond the murky vision which clouded his pupils and the pounding of the water in his ears was enough to drive him insane. He was past the point of comprehension, past caring whether he would ever leave this death-trap. Somewhere amidst the swells of the river, he closed his eyes and drifted away to a peaceful place where nothing seemed important anymore.

He would have been content to stay in that quiet place forever, but reality was insisting that he return. Drake groaned with reluctance. He didn't want to open his eyes to the harsh light and he didn't want to acknowledge the terrible pain that pulsed through his body. He heard the murmur of voices. Krystal? Her name rested on his tongue, though he was too groggy to speak.

"Well, he's not dead," a strange voice said when he moaned. "Was he just floating down the river?"

"Yep! Just floatin' along, and then I waded out and hooked on to him with that long stick over there."

The woman smiled at her son. It was obvious how proud he was at himself for fishing the near-dead man out of the water by the way his dark eyes were glistening with excitement. "Well, I suppose we should try to load him up on Clementine so we can get him back to the house."

The youngster shook his head with an exaggerated amount of vigor and hurried off to drag Clementine down to the river's edge. The old brown mare followed the boy at a leisurely pace, inspite of the boy's insistent tugging on her lead rope.

"This won't be easy," the woman said as she studied the distance between the ground and the back of the tall horse. She was not sure if she and Bobby could lift the man up on the animal's back by themselves. First

391

things first, though, she thought with a sigh of resolve. He was laying face down in the mud and the least she could do was roll the poor man over.

She grabbed ahold of his broad shoulders and pulled until the mud released him and he rotated over onto his back. She pulled her long checkered apron off and dipped the corner in the water. As she began to wipe the thick dark mud from his face she got the eeriest feeling that somehow she knew this man. But that was not possible, she told herself while trying to fight against the nervous flutter in her breast. She raised up and flung the long ponytail of flaxen hair back over her shoulder.

"Come on, Bobby. If we don't get him up to the house, it's gonna get dark on us."

Bobby was a stout lad for his nine years and his determination to prove himself whenever possible was in their favor as they struggled to lift the injured man onto the back of the horse. With the woman under one of the man's arms and the boy pushing under his other arm, they were able to hoist him up and over the back of the mare.

The woman wiped away a stream of perspiration from her brow and began to pull on the lead rope while her son held onto the man and tried to keep his limp form from toppling off of the horse's back. The house was only a half a mile or so away and it was no time at all before they reached the old farm house and had deposited their precious cargo in the soft grass that grew in wild patches in front of the house.

Drake was bolted back to life when he hit the ground. He gasped for breath, and nearly choked when his lungs accepted the air. His eyelids quivered as they fought to open, but they felt like someone was pinching them together. He became aware of every ache and pain, big and small. Damn! Why couldn't he just die? He groaned again, and a name escaped his swollen blue lips.

"Krystal?"

"What'd he say, Ma?" Bobby asked, his young eyes wide and timid.

The woman shrugged. "Sounded like somebody's name. Well—" she placed her hands upon her hips and sighed. "Let's get him into the house." She did not relish the idea of having a strange man in her home again, but she had grown used to it over the years. Living this close to areas such as Brown's Hole and Robber's Roost, she had on more than one occasion patched up a gunshot wound or fed a meal to a man who ate with his six-shooter in one hand and a fork in the other. Sometimes she wondered if it was good for Bobby to grow up in such a wild part of the country. But then she reminded herself why she had chosen such a remote location to put down roots and her indecision was quickly cleared away.

Drake was coming out of the haze of his water-logged brain. He could see the outlines of the faces which hovered above him, and their voices were audible to his ears. When the woman pulled him up and attempted to drag him into the house by his arms, he vehemently protested. "Damn!" he said with a growl. He saw the flash of white teeth when she smiled, and he made a feeble attempt to frown through the dirt that was caked around his mouth.

"He's goin' be all right, ain't he, ma?"

Drake slowly turned his head at the sound of the small voice. The boy's face was shining with his joy. Drake blinked, a difficult gesture because of the thick mud which curtained his lashes.

"Not ain't, Bobby," the woman reprimanded. "Well—can you walk?" She asked turning back to Drake with a curious tilt of her blond head.

Drake stared at her through the veil of dirt. He knew this woman from somewhere. But . . . where? He searched his mind, however, nothing was very clear to him right now.

"With your help," he answered in reply to her question pushing the confusing thought out of his mind for now.

Getting him into the house was much easier than lifting him onto the horse since he was able to help a little bit. But his legs were so wobbly that he had to lean heavily on the woman and the little boy. Once they were inside, the first thing that greeted him was the delicious odor of fresh-baked rubarb pie.

"He can have my bed," Bobby said, smiling proudly. This was the first man he had ever saved, and there was something special about this man that made Bobby want the man to like him.

The woman shook her head and began to lead Drake to the bunk which was by the rock fireplace. He sank down onto the mattress and rubbed a mud-caked hand across his forehead. From the pain in his head, he decided that he must have struck most of the rocks in the river head-on. The woman was already kneeling before him with a bucket of water and a washrag.

Drake glanced back at the boy. "Did you fish me out of the river?"

Bobby's smile broadened until it was stretching clear across his cherub face. "Yep. Lucky for you that I was fishing, instead of doing what I was supposed to be doing." His smile faded when he realized that he had just admitted that he had not been gathering the firewood that his mother had instructed him to do.

"Bobby!" she said sharply, then succumbed to a smile when she met the grin on the man's face. "Guess he's right. You are lucky he was fishing instead of cutting wood."

Drake looked over the top of the woman's pale blond head and his eyes met the boy's wide-eyed gaze. They both began to smile with the understanding that only two men can have when they realize that they've outwitted a female.

Bobby's mother tried to pretend she didn't notice the smug exchange between the man and her son as she began to wipe the dirt off of his face with short strokes of the washrag. "You must have ten pounds of mud on you. Why you'll probably be good as new just as soon as I scrub that dirt off your skin." Her face ascended and her big brown eyes met with his curious gaze. She felt herself blush and immediately turned her head away. Now why would she suddenly feel so giddy around this man? she wondered as anger began to grow within her breast. No doubt, he was just another outlaw who had chosen to ford the river rather than face the guns of a posse. She raised the washrag up to his face again and tried to avoid looking directly at him, but her hand froze against his face with his next words.

"Jennifer Holt?"

Her wide eyes flew back up to his face. No one in this area knew her by that name. She had not been Jennifer Holt since she had fled from Green River, Wyoming, almost ten years ago. Then she saw it . . . the twinkle in the dark green eyes and lower, beneath the grime, the crooked grin that used to make the girls of Sweetwater County giggle with sly inuenduo.

"Dra—is it—Drake DeGanahl?"

Drake couldn't help the dry chuckle that emitted from his mouth. Running into Jennifer Holt after all that he had recently learned about her and Devon was ironic. "Everyone thought you were dead, even your father?"

395

She glanced nervously in that direction of the boy. "Bobby go fetch some more water from the well. This bucket will be dirty in no time. And go pull some carrots from the garden for the stew tonight."

The boy screwed up his face, and opened his mouth to protest. He clamped his lips together after a second thought and stomped through the door. He didn't want to get yelled at in front of the stranger.

Jennifer turned back to face Drake. At times, she had really believed that she had escaped the past. But deep down she had always known that eventually it would catch up to her. She thought of lying to Drake DeGanahl, that would be the easiest way out. But . . . there were other times when she had prayed that something like this would happen and she would be forced to go back home.

"Well," she said with a sigh, "As you can see, I'm not dead." The tiny lines around her large eyes crinkled slightly as she smiled with the bittersweet memories of the past which had unexpectedly flooded through her mind. She did not particularly want to remember what her life had been like in Green River. For ten years she had been trying to live it down.

She placed the wet rag against Drake's face and began to wipe the dirt away, but he grabbed her hand. A tremor shot through her body and caused her to gasp. The DeGanahl boys—both of them—had always had that kind of effect on her. She pulled her hand from his tight hold as she stood up and begin to back away. So much had happened to her since she had been that wild young daughter of Preacher Holt. Was she ready to face up to the past and everything that it would mean to her and Bobby's lives?

Unconsciously, she ran her fingers through the hair that tumbled over one shoulder in a long wheat-colored mane. He continued to stare at her, making her more nervous with each passing second. Did she look that different to him? Or was he just remembering what type of a girl she had been when they were young? And perhaps he was wondering if she had grown up to be a loose woman, too?

"Why did you let everyone believe that you were dead?"

She looked toward the window, not wanting to look into his eyes again. "At the time it was the best solution for all who were involved."

Drake stood up on his shaky legs. He wanted to see her face clearly when she spoke to him. "Who was involved, and in what?" He was beginning to suspect that there was a lot from those long ago days that he did not not know about.

"Oh," her voice cracked slightly. "My father, me, you and Devon . . . everybody." She brushed away a tear which had appeared in the corner of her eye. Her mind groped for the right words. She had went over this speech a thousand times, every time she got the crazy urge to run back home to Green River and beg for forgiveness. Now that she was forced to confront her past, her mind was a blank.

Drake raised his arms up in confusion and let them drop against his sides. "I don't understand?" She obviously was holding something back, but he couldn't figure out what it could be. He tried to recall all the memories he could summon up about their youthful lives in Green River, but there was not much information for him to go on. He had been busy with his career as a lawman, even back then. He was only eighteen when he had pinned his first badge on his chest, and from that day on, he had not had much involvement in his brother's life. All he could recollect about Jennifer Holt was that she was wild and easy with her affections, and that she had tried her feminine wiles on him the night before she had disappeared.

Jennifer wrung her hands together and began to pace the floor. Where should she begin? "Well, I reckon you recall what a rebellious girl I was when I was in my teens?" Drake nodded, that was an understatement. Her cheeks flushed a deep shade of red when she read his thoughts in his expression. "I was more than rebellious, wasn't I?"

She drew in a deep breath and continued, not waiting for him to answer her. "If the truth be known, Reverend Holt's daughter was a slut. I granted favors to more than one young man back in those days."

Drake's shoulders heaved with aggravation. He didn't want to hear about her adventures in the haystacks of Sweetwater County. "Does any of this have anything to do with the reason you left Green River?" Her elusive answers were more than his aching mind could take right now. His eyes darkened with anger as he stepped closer to her.

"Damnit! My brother has hated me for the past ten years because he thinks that I was the one who was to blame for your disappearance.

"Oh no!" Jennifer cried out as she reached out to touch him. He backed away as though her touch would burn. She drew her hand back and clutched it to her breast. "Oh Drake, I'm so sorry. I didn't mean for that to happen." She covered her face with her hands for a second and then faced him with a defeated expression upon her pretty face. "Please sit back down, Drake. It's time I told someone the whole story."

Drake remained rigid for a moment while he wondered if her explanation was worth hearing. But then he realized that he had to hear her story no matter how much he wanted to get out of here, and away from her. If she could tell him something that would help him to understand why Devon had spent the past ten years building a wall of hate between them, then Drake knew he had to hear her out. He sank back down onto the cot. His weary legs thanked him although he was too furious to notice.

"All right, let's hear it."

She smiled weakly, and in spite of his anger, he couldn't help but to notice how the years had not dimmed her beauty. Her large brown eyes were still the focal point of her face as they blinked back a teardrop, and her oval face was framed by that long straight hair that had always made him think of a wheat field just before the harvest. It was no wonder she had been such a popular young lady back in Green River. Her appearance had only enhanced her free spirit when it came to enticing the young boys. If Drake had not been so busy helping his father at the jail, he, too, would probably have jumped on the bandwagon.

Pulling a chair out from under the table which stood in the center of the room, she slid it across the floor and sat down in front of him. Now they were on eye level with one another and Drake could see the turmoil in her brown eyes and the pain written across her face. What could have happened to make her feel the need to flee from her home and even to lead her own father to believe that she had died?

Jennifer twisted the material of her cotton skirt around her forefinger. How was she going to explain how it felt to wake up one day and realize what a mess she had made of her life and how she couldn't turn to anyone for help because there was no one to blame but herself?

"Well—" she smoothed her skirt down with one hand and straightened up in the chair. "I guess I'll just start at the beginning." Drake leaned back against the wall. He ached all over and he knew he should clean up before he allowed himself to relax, but he was too intrigued with Jennifer Holt's story to take the time.

"I was never worthy of being a Reverend's daughter, especially one of such a kind and gentle man like my father was." She said the words in the passive because she had learned of her father's death a couple years ago. "Oh, but I was a hellion ever since I was old enough to walk. Did you know my mother died when I was born." Drake shook his head and frowned. She was beating around the bush and it aggravated him.

"Well, she did. And my father let me do anything that I pleased as a result. By the time I was fourteen, the only thing that pleased me was the company of some young gentlemen, and I certainly wasn't the shy type." She felt her cheeks grow hot when Drake shook his head in agreement. "By the time I got around to seeing your brother Devon, I was very experienced and still very stupid."

She wiped away another teardrop. The passing years had made her realize how much she did care about Devon but it had been much too late. "I knew how deeply Devon cared about me, but I just wasn't ready to settle down with one boy, or so I thought. When he proposed to me at the church social, I just panicked. The only thing I could think of was how there was still one young man in Green River that I had not been able to monopolize with my looks and my—well—" She paused, her eyes full of tears that she could no longer hold back. "Oh, it sounds so horrible to actually say those words out loud." Her hands flew up to her face as the tears began to spill down her face.

Drake leaned forward and touched her arm with his hand. He wanted to comfort her, but the realization

400

of what she was trying to tell him made him almost despise her. "I was that one young man, wasn't I?"

"Yes," she said as she nodded weakly. She sensed his withdrawal and was not surprised. She had hated herself for ten years, how could she expect anything else from him? She choked back another sob and continued. "I wanted both of you. I knew I had Devon — he had already told me how much he loved me. But you . . . you always played so hard to get. I was determined to give it one more try to crack through your tough exterior, even though —" she drew in a deep breath and stopped. Her moist eyes rose to meet his hard look of disdain. She thought of how he had looked that night when she had cornered him behind the old barn, almost ten years ago. He had worn the same look on his handsome face back then, too. His expression of contempt made her wish that she could just crawl into a hole and die. Everyday for a decade now, she had prayed for forgiveness, and she had worked extra hard to be a good mother to Bobby, but none of that could wipe out the terrible sins of her past.

Drake grunted as he stood up from the bunk. He was disgusted with this woman and with himself. He had been blind not to have seen what she was up to all those years ago and it had cost him all hope of ever having any kind of a close relationship with his brother. He had to get away from this woman before he lost what was left of his control.

"Drake, please? That's not the worst of it," she said in a rush of sobs that shook her whole body as she rose up to follow him.

A crooked smirk cracked the mud around his mouth. "There's more? I think I've heard about all that I care to hear from you." He started towards the door but was stopped by the boy rushing back into the house.

"I've got the water and the—" he held up the bucket in one hand and a bunch of carrots in the other hand. But the minute he looked at his mother, he fell silent.

"Bobby, please wait outside for a few more minutes?" Jennifer felt her heart break at the sight of her little boy's terrified face.

He shook his head which was topped by a thick mass of light brown hair. "Did he hurt you, Ma?" His black eyes flashed with protectiveness toward his mother. He dropped the bucket and threw the carrots on the floor as his small fists drew into two tight balls.

A smile tipped Drake's lips as he looked down at the lad with admiration. The little guy had real spunk if he thought he could defend his mother with his mite strength. Drake's affection for the boy grew. He was proud of Jennifer's son for his devotion toward his mother even if Drake himself, could not stomach to be in the same room with her a moment longer.

"Bobby!" Jennifer cried. "No, he didn't hurt me. But I have to talk to him. Now wait outside." Her voice crescendoed and she could see the surprise filter into her son's eyes.

He backed up towards the door, hesitantly. She did not usually raise her voice to him unless he had done something awful bad . . . such as sticking a live snake in the drawer with her cooking utensils. It usually took a lot to make her mad enough to yell at him, especially in front of someone else. He could tell something serious was going on between her and the man by the odd expressions on both of their faces and he didn't want to go outside, but he knew he had no other choice. He nodded slowly and turned to leave, but not before he cast a look of warning at the tall stranger once more.

Drake nodded back at him, still smiling slightly. No

402

matter how he felt about Jennifer, he would never take out his feelings on her son. And besides, he owed Bobby for his life. He swung back around, even more angry than before. "Tell me the rest, and hurry. He shouldn't have to stay out there wondering what going on in here and at the same time being scared to death!"

A meloncholy smile captured her face as she stared at the closed door where her son had just exited. "Don't you recognize him, Drake? He's the spittin' image of his father." Her eyes drifted back to his face as she watched him grasp on to the truth that no one could dispute.

Drake thought of the boy, his eyes, black as midnight, and his thick brown wavy hair and square stubborn-looking jaw. Krystal's favorite expression hovered on his lips . . . Good Lord! But all he managed to mutter was one word. "Devon?"

Chapter Twenty-nine

Krystal had never felt so guilty. And if she went through with her scheme she would have to be crazy also. She set her plate down carefully on the ground and stood up. It might be easier to talk if she was not trying to balance a plate of food in her lap. She was wrong . . . it was still difficult to propose a plan that would make her as guilty as the wanted posters accused her of being.

"I've been thinking—" she cleared her throat again. Austin and Sidewinder looked mildly interested, though the food on their plates seemed of more importance to them at this moment. "Well," she continued, "As you both know, I do not intend to give up my search for my husband." Neither man showed any surprise at her declaration, since she had made that statement on more than one occasion during the last few days since they had found Sidewinder, and not Drake, washed up on the sandy banks of the Green River.

"And since both of you have decided not to aid me

any further, I'm am going to break Devon out of jail in exchange for his help."

Sidewinder nearly choked on a piece of meat which hung up in his tight throat, while Austin retorted by dumping his plate and its contents on the ground. They had been worried about her frame of mind all the way back to Green River and now it appeared their fears had been warranted.

"You what?" Austin asked with an incredulous tone as he slowly rose up to his feet. He had agreed to bring her back to Green River so that she could be with Angelina DeGanahl, not so that she could conduct a jailbreak.

"I'm going to break Devon out of jail if he'll agree to help me look for Drake." Her chin tilted up stubbornly while she flashed her tawny eyes in Austin's direction. She had contemplated a solution for several days while they rode back to Green River and she was sure that Devon was the only person she could turn to for help.

Sidewinder coughed and managed to swallow the food which had been lodged in his windpipe. "And just how do you propose to break Devon outta jail?" A childish smirk sauntered across his bruised face and made his clear blue eyes glaze over with mirth.

"I have a plan all worked out," she rushed on. "If you and Austin will agree to help me, it should not be too difficult. If you don't," she shrugged with indifference, "Well, I'll just do it by myself."

Austin turned to Sidewinder with a look of disbelief on his aging face. Sidewinder's expression of mirth had increased, and as he pushed the brim of his hat up to the top of his forehead, a roar of laughter escaped from his mouth.

Krystal's spine stiffened. She had not expected them to laugh at her. "What is so humorous?" she demanded with another defiant toss of her head. "I thought outlaws were always breaking each other out of jail and such?"

Another round of laughter emitted from Sidewinder and this time he was joined by a low chuckle from Austin. "If you don't mind me saying so, Mrs. De-Ganahl?" Austin said, trying to sound serious. "I think you've been reading a might too many of them dime store novels about the Wild West. I heard Easterners were real fond of them little books."

Her hands angrily clenched into two tight fists at her sides. "Indeed!" she twirled around to cast her deadly glare at Sidewinder's mocking face. "Well, I'll show you both how many dime store novels I've read and how much knowledge I've gained from them." She stomped towards her horse and swung up into the saddle with ease. For a moment she was even surprised at how expertly she had mounted the animal.

More confident than ever, she looked down at the startled men and said, "Perhaps the two of you should read a few of those books yourselves so that you will know what is expected of the bad men of the Wild West!" She pulled herself up straight in the saddle, adding, "I'll have you know that the Pinkerton National Detective Agency has issued a wanted poster out on me and I am probably more of a desperado than either of you two combined!" Oh, Good Lord! She had just boasted about her criminal status. She really had lost her mind, Krystal decided with an inward groan.

Austin and Sidewinder did not move as she gave the reins a hard tug and swung the horse around in a cloud of dust. She left both outlaws within the haze of the swirling dirt with their mouths gaping open, too shocked to do anything else. She had never been so mad! They could shoot down another man without a pang of conscience, yet they refused to help her break their comrade out of jail? Well fine, she thought with another surge of rage, she didn't need their help. She could break Devon out of that jail without any help from either of them. But first, she had to devise a real plan since she had lied when she told them that she already had a plan worked out.

Glancing back over her shoulder, Krystal noticed that they were not attempting to follow her. Evidently, they had both decided that she was definitely crazy and they were probably glad to be rid of her.

In the late afternoon sunlight, she could see the towering rock formation of Castle Rock glistening in a style of grandiose above the town of Green River. Within minutes she would be on the outskirts of the town and she had no idea what she was going to do when she got there.

Krystal realized that she had little choice in the matter. Since she only knew one person in the whole town, she had to rely on Angelina DeGanahl for help. Skirting the little town with caution, Krystal headed toward the house which was located beneath the eroded cliffs. When she reached the house she rode around to the back in hopes of not arousing any unnecessary attention. She tied the mare to the fence-post and walked up to the back door on shaky limbs. How was she ever going to explain her plan to this woman? She would be lucky if the woman didn't throw her out into the street after she heard what Krystal had in mind. She drew in a deep breath and knocked on the back door. There was no answer, even when Krystal knocked a second time. It had not occurred to her that no one would be home, now she was more confused than ever. Time was awasting and Krystal felt a rush of panic. Jailbreaks had to be conducted under the cover of darkness, didn't they?

She reached out a trembling hand, and just as her fingertips touched the knob, the door swung open and Angelina's smiling face greeted her. Her dark eyes began to twinkle as she looked past Krystal, but then her gaze came back to the girl's face with a hint of confusion. "Where's Drake?" she asked with a curious tilt of her head.

Krystal tried to control the quivering in her voice as she answered the woman's question. "I'm not sure, Mrs. DeGanahl." The worried look on Angelina De-Ganhal's face was Krystal's undoing. All at once everything was too much for her to handle alone and she began to sob and gasp out the details of all the things which had happened to her since she had left Boston. She was vaguely aware of being led into the kitchen and of sitting down in a chair, but she could not ignore the comfort of Angelina's arms as she confided in the woman about everything; About her mother and the brooch. And of her marriage to Drake, the shooting of her father and even about the jail break she was planning.

Angelina remained quiet for a few minutes when she realized that Krystal was finally through with her story. She dabbed at Krystal's eyes with a lace hanker-chief and wiped away her own tears of heartbreak that she felt for the sorrow in this young woman's troubled life. It didn't seem fair for one small girl to have so much burden upon her slender shoulders, and so much pain in her young heart. Angelina was grateful that she could help to ease one portion of Krystal's misery. "Come upstairs with me," she said quietly.

Krystal sniffed loudly as the woman pulled her to her feet and began to pull her through the house. This woman's behavior constantly confused her. The only response she had given Krystal through her whole confession was how she strongly agreed with her belief that Drake was not dead. The idea of having a new daughter-in-law did not seem to phase her in the least and neither did the rest of Krystal's wild tale.

After climbing the stairs to the second floor, Angelina led Krystal into the room where she had stayed when Drake had brought her here the first time. Krystal was about to protest, thinking that the woman was going to suggest that she rest and forget about breaking Devon out of jail when her eyes caught sight of someone laying in the bed. Her eyes filled with tears again and her insides began to tremble with relief. Good Lord, she had been so afraid that Creed Ward had killed him.

John's teary gaze met his daughter's for a moment before she was in his arms. Even John was at a loss for words for a minute. His fear at what had happened to her at the hands of Creed Ward had been as great as hers had been over his fate from the gunshot wound. "Don't cry, chéri. You should've known there was no way to kill a varmint as ornery as me."

Krystal managed to laugh through her tears. Finding her father alive, and here with Drake's mother, was the last thing she had been expecting. It didn't matter how he had gotten here, only that he was safe. She glanced back up at Angelina. "Thank you," she said quietly.

Angelina nodded and continued to smile at the sight of the father and daughter reunion. She had brought John to her house to recuperate from his surgery after Drake had explained the situation to her before he had headed out for Brown's Hole to look for Krystal. She thought of the possibility of Drake being dead and immediately reinforced her opinion on that thought. "Drake is still alive, too. I can feel it."

Krystal rose up from the bed slowly and stared at

409

the other woman. She realized that Angelina felt the same as she did. Ever since Drake had fallen from that canyon wall, Krystal had sensed that he was not dead and now his mother was saying that she had the same premonition. "Then you understand why I'm going to do what I must do?" Krystal asked in a tenative voice.

Angelina turned away from the pleading look on the girl's face for a brief time. She was faced with a decision that could affect the lives of everyone she cared about. If she condoned Krystal's dangerous plan to break Devon out of jail, they would all be involved. But something told her that Krystal was going through with her scheme no matter what anyone said to try to discourage her.

"What in tarnation are you two womanfolk talking about?" John demanded.

Angelina looked back at her daughter-in-law and then glanced toward John. "I'll tell you about it later. Right now, Krystal and I have some business to attend to."

Krystal exhaled the breath she had been holding. If Angelina had told her father what she was planning, he would have never allowed her to leave this room again. She leaned down and gave her father a tender kiss on the cheek before she followed Angelina out of the room, ignoring the pouting expression on his whiskered face. As the two woman exited, Krystal could hear her father's voice complaining about being left alone when he was on his deathbed, but she did not return to him. Now that she knew he was safe, she had to concentrate on finding Drake and the next step she had to take in that direction.

"You're going through with it, aren't you?" Angelina asked in a low tone of voice.

"Nothing you can say will change my mind,"

Krystal said with a defiant tilt of her chin.

Angelina covered her face with her hands and sighed. She already knew that, but she was still hoping there would be another way. She wanted both of her sons to be safe and right now they were both in danger. If Drake was injured and in need of help somewhere along the treacherous banks of the Green River, Angelina knew that Krystal's idea was not that farfetched. Devon knew that outlaw territory like the back of his hand and if his brother was out there somewhere, Devon was the man who could find him. But if something happened to Krystal in the process, Angelina was not sure if she could live with the guilt.

Krystal saw the confusion filter into the older woman's face and she sensed that Angelina was not going to help her in spite of her firm belief that Drake was still alive. She understood Angelina's feelings of confusion, but she was not going to back out now, especially since she knew that her father was still alive. Seeing him had renewed her faith in finding Drake and in the future which they were going to share. "I'm going to do it, Mrs. DeGanahl," Krystal said in a strong tone of voice as she swung around and began to stomp down the stairs.

Angelina watched the small form of the girl as she began to descend and felt like she was being torn in two. She could not allow Drake's wife to leave her home without knowing that she had her support, no matter what. "Krystal?" she cried out.

Krystal stopped and turned back to look up at the other woman who still stood at the top of the stairs. She did not want to leave like this, but she could not waste anymore time here. The jailbreak had to be done tonight and the day was already beginning to turn into evening. Immediately, Krystal saw the change in Angelina's expression. It seemed that all she did was cry these days, and once again the tears began to fill her eyes as she began to walk back up the steps. As Angelina embraced her, Krystal knew she had found an ally in Angelina DeGanahl, and she returned the compassionate hug with a new feeling of determination and hope.

Since Drake had already provided her with a man's shirt and pants the only thing she needed to complete her assemble was the long black duster that Angelina had dug out of Drake's closet. Krystal stretched her arms out as far as possible and pushed the long sleeves up so that her fingertips reached beneath the heavy material of the coat. The hem of the coat nearly dragged on the ground but it would have to do. Angelina had even found an old hat which appeared to have been kept around for sentimental reasons, since it was long beyond any semblance of dignity, but it was the perfect accompaniment for Krystal's disguise.

Krystal stood back and observed herself proudly in the mirror when she had the last tendril of unruly hair tucked up neatly under the dilapidated old hat. Perfect — the whole outfit was perfect. Drake's mother had even supplied her with an old pair of pointed-toed boots to wear on her feet, although she was not sure how she would ever keep them on. Thanks to her small size, she looked just like a young wrangler fresh off the range, and when she smudged her face with dirt, no one would ever be able to detect who was hidden beneath the rugged mode of clothing.

There was only one thing she still needed, but it was invaluable. A gun was the necessary tool that all outlaws needed for their line of work and Krystal knew she would need a gun to pull off this job. "Oh Lord, I'm even starting to think and talk in desperado lingo," she said outloud as she exited the bedroom and started back down the stairs. She glanced towards the closed door where her father was and smiled to herself. If everything went as she was praying it would, they would all be together again soon.

The shadows of the fading daylight were beginning to settle in around the house and the rooms looked hazy with the light which was filtering through the lace curtains. She realized that the sun would be setting in a very short while. She thought briefly of the dime store novels she had taken from her students when they had hidden the pamphlets in the centers of their textbooks and she also recalled a play that her mother had once starred in . . . *The Final Showdown* was the appropriate title of the play which ironically was about the demise of a band of outlaws. A vivid picture of the last scene flashed into Krystal's mind — good against evil, and guns blazing in the orange glow of the setting sun.

Sunset and high noon, they were always the backdrop for the big gunfight. In her mother's play, and in most of the cheap magazines, the outlaws were glorified by a society which felt they had dealt them a grave injustice as they were turned into undeserving heros in a time of anti-heros. She trembled with the memory of Creed Ward and the fate she had escaped with his brutal death. A feeling of doom chilled her blood as she recalled the victorious look on Sidewinders young face when he had shot Creed in the stomach, a man who was his friend and partner, over some trivial matter of riding into town for supplies. The quiet and deceiving manner of Joe Preece reclaimed her thoughts, followed by the recollection of Drake firing into the darkness and ending Joe Preece's life in less than a blink of an eye. Every nerve in her body seemed to twitch with fear as she wondered if she was strong enough to tackle the job she had taken upon herself.

At the end of her mother's performance, and on the final page of every ten cent paperback, the hero always rode off into the sunset with the lady. Would she be reunited with Drake? and would they ride off in a blaze of glory like the colorful tales of the Wild West? she asked herself as she paused at the door of the parlor. Drake's mother had already done much more for her than Krystal had ever dared to hope for, but she had to ask Angelina for one more favor.

Krystal shook her head in disbelief as she spotted Angelina standing in front of the big oak guncabinet. It seemed that their thoughts continually ran along the same paths. Neither woman spoke as Krystal reached out and took hold of the same Colt .45 pistol that Drake had tried to teach her to use that beautiful evening when the sound of desire had taken the place of gunfire in this land of violence. As she tucked the gun down into the waistband of her trousers she glanced through the delicate lace of the curtains again. The long fingers of the declining sun were casting shimmering copper rays along the top of Castle Rock.

Chapter Thirty

The jailhouse was directly in the center of town, hardly in an inconspicuous location, but Krystal was feeling more confident with each step she took. The man at the livery stable did not even blink an eye when she had bought a horse from him and she could tell by the way he acted towards her that he believed she was just a young boy.

She curled her toes tightly in the oversized boots in an effort to keep them on her feet as she trudged out of the alley where she had just hidden the newly acquired horse along with the mare which Drake had obtained for her to ride from Odgen. Her plan was to take the marshal by surprise when she pulled the gun on him. She was counting on Devon to figure the rest of the escape out once they had locked the lawman in Devon's cell and exited from the jail.

"Oh, excuse me," Krystal said in a faked voice several octaves lower than her normal tone. Since her thoughts were jumbled with the jailbreak she was in the mist of conceiving, and the man who had stepped

415

out of the jail seemed preoccupied himself, it was inevitable that they would collide. She pulled the wide brim of the old hat down low on her forehead, but when her gaze ascended, she could not hide her shock. "Good Lord!" she gasped, forgetting to use her disguised tone of voice.

The man's breath exhaled loudly as he leaned forward. His eyes narrowed while he stared down at the dirty young cowboy before him. The big eyes, a tawny shade of brown and glazed with tears, were the only things he recognized about her appearance. But he only knew of one person who said 'Good Lord' as the normal course of conversation.

"Krystal?" he asked in a whisper.

She wanted to throw herself into his arms, and allow him to protect her like he always had in the past. But her life was not so simple anymore and the stunned expression on Les Macrea's face was proof that she could not unburden all her problems on him this time. From the end of the oversized sleeves of the duster, she motioned for him to step away from the front of the jail as she quickly retreated from the doorway. He followed her obediently until they were sheltered between the outer walls of the jailhouse and the building which stood next to it. She wiped away another teardrop that was trailing down her filthy face with an angry swipe of her hand. She had cried enough tears in the past few weeks to fill an ocean.

"Krystal? What in the world are you doing here, and why are you in that getup?" Les drew her tiny form up against his chest. He smelled of shaving lotion and cigars, odors which reminded her of her life in Boston. She buried her face into the soft material of his expensive wool suit and wished she

416

never had to let go of him again.

"I've been searching for you for almost a month. I was beginning to think that you had disappeared from the face of the earth."

She stepped back, leaving long brown streaks of dirt down the front of his finely tailored suit from the dirt she had purposely rubbed on her face and clothes. "Oh, Les, you will never believe all that has happened to me since I left Boston."

His fatherly grin curved up the corners of his mouth as he shook his head in a knowing gesture. "Well, I've been hearing some awfully strange tales about you since I arrived out West, so I don't think I'll be too terribly shocked."

"Do you know about Drake?" she asked in a timid tone which was accompanied by a bright red blush that was concealed by the layer of dirt upon her face.

He nodded again. "I know about everything, except why you felt the need to leave Boston so abruptly?" The longer he watched her, the more curious he was becoming. Ever since he had left Boston with the Pinkerton detective, the mystery surrounding Krystal and her mother had deepened. At first, no one could have convinced him that Krystal was involved with her mother's illegal jewel dealings, but now he was not so sure.

Krystal studied his face for an instant. She had known this man for all of her life, but how much could she trust him? "I had to look for my father," she replied as she glanced down at the large boots she was wearing on her feet.

Les could tell she was holding something back and it hurt him to know that she did not feel she could confide in him after all these years. "But I told you

417

that I would come out here with you. Why did you just take off without telling me?"

"Because —," she sighed with resignation, she couldn't avoid it any longer. "Because of the diamond brooch I found in my mother's bureau drawer."

Les felt the muscles around his heart grow taut. The Pinkerton detective had been looking for a diamond brooch ever since Rebecca's murder. The brooch was the reason her European partner in the smuggling ring had killed her. Rebecca had grown greedy and had refused to share the profit they were going to receive from the priceless piece of jewelry. Now the theory the detective agency was working on was that Rebecca's daughter had fled with the brooch because she was also affiliated with the illegal business. Les had been so sure they were wrong, but now he was terrified that they could be right.

"Do — do you have the — brooch with you?" Les said hesitantly.

An indifferent shrug lifted the broad shoulders of her oversized jacket. "Not anymore. I couldn't bear the idea that my mother might have stolen it, so I threw it into the river from the top of Lodore Canyon."

Les coughed and grabbed at his throat. That brooch could never be replaced. Rebecca had stolen it from a collection of antiques the last time she had been in Europe. All at once, Les realized that if the pin no longer existed, it would be easy to prove to the Pinkerton man that Krystal had not been involved with her mother's thievery. The brooch was the only incriminating evidence the agency had to go on. He grabbed her by the shoulders of her heavy duster. "Did anyone else see that brooch while it was in your possession? It's imperative that I know."

Krystal blinked with surprise at his sudden outburst. He was acting as panicked over the brooch as she had when she had fled from Boston. "No," she began, then remembered the day she had fought with Devon after he had whisked her purse out of her hands. "Oh wait! Devon DeGanahl knows about the brooch."

Les groaned as he shook his head in a defeated gesture. Devon DeGanahl! He had just met Devon DeGanahl in the jail a few minutes before he had run into Krystal, and he had never encountered such a resentful man in his life. Devon didn't care what happened to himself or anybody else, and especially to anyone who was associated with his brother, Drake. The outlaw, Devon DeGanahl, could be Krystal's downfall, regardless of her innocence.

He observed Krystal for a time before he sighed with frustration. "You still haven't told me why you're dressed like that?"

"I'm going to break Devon DeGanahl out of jail in return for his help in finding Drake."

Les coughed, his eyes widened and he was certain that the Colbert women were bound to be the death of him yet. Krystal had said that she was going to break Devon out of jail so casually that Les started to wonder if the person beneath those baggy clothes and all that grime was really Krystal Colbert! The prim schoolteacher whom he had known for the past twenty years would have been aghast at the idea of aiding a known criminal . . . unless she was one herself? Les silently cursed at himself for thinking those foolish thoughts. He was sure she was not involved with her mother's life of crime, but he was hoping that she was

419

not serious about her last statement.

"I—I must have misunderstood you. Surely you are not contemplating a jailbreak?"

A determined look entered her eyes as she tossed her head back. The old floppy hat fell down across her brows and she quickly pushed it up again. "I am! And no one is going to stop me." She explained to Les in one breathless phrase what her reasoning was behind the plan and then peered up at him from beneath the hat like an innocent child who did not understand the meaning of right or wrong.

Les reminded himself that she was not a child and that she knew exactly what she was getting herself into. "Your mother was a jewel thief, Krystal. And if you go through with this preposterous plan, you will be just as guilty as she was."

His words stunned Krystal into silence. Oh Lord! Why did he have to confirm it? She did not ever want to hear those words spoken out loud. She backed up against the wall of the building and swallowed back the tears which always seemed too eager to emerge. But she would not permit herself to cry again. His admission about her mother only fueled her desire to be reunited with Drake. Nothing was going to stand in her way. She raised her frame to its full extent and took a deep breath. "Everyone already believes that I am a criminal anyway, and it doesn't matter anymore. Finding my husband is the only important thing now, and I will do anything to pursue that quest."

Her voice had grown distant and haughty. Les was reminded of how much he loved her—as much as if she had been his own daughter. And he would have given his life if her mother had loved him as passion-

420

ately as he had loved her. But his fate had decided that he would never be any more than Rebecca's friend and advisor. He had known for years that Rebecca was dealing in something unlawful, he had turned his head the other way and made himself blind to any of her faults. There was nothing he would not do for Rebecca Colbert, and now, he would do the same for her daughter.

"Do you love this Drake DeGanahl that much?"

Her lower lip began to tremble and gold highlighted the pupils of her brown eyes at the mention of his name. Her devotion and love for her husband were written in visible emotion across her dirty face. Les drew in a struggling breath. "Well, let's get this show on the road then."

"Is that man botherin' you, boy?"

Krystal did not have time to reply to Les' statement as she swung around to the source of the familiar voice. Her hands instinctively flew up to the sides of her face. The elderly outlaw was leaning casually against the building with his hand resting on the top of his worn six-shooter. Austin smiled when her startled eyes met his gaze. He had followed her from Angelina's house and it looked as though this stranger was interrupting with their plans. A weak smile claimed Krystal's lips.

She shook her head. "No—no. Actually, he's been quite helpful." The two men observed one another in the waning light of the day. They understood Krystal's answer and they each nodded in acknowledgement. Krystal pushed the big hat up on her forehead again as she began to walk out from between the two buildings. The golden glow of the impending sunset hit her smack in the face. She closed her eyes for a

421

second and drew on the strength the two men had just given to her with their support.

"There's something real peculiar goin' on over at the First National Bank," Austin said in a slow drawl. He smiled again when he saw the question forming on her lips. "You should go inform the Marshal that his presence is needed over in that vicinity."

Krystal tilted her head in a confused manner, but Austin motioned for her to go towards the jail. She had no idea what was about to happen as she fought back the panic rising in her breast. She glanced back at Les, but his expression was as fearful as her own. Her leaden feet began to move in the direction of the jail, the heavy boots felt almost attached to the ground with each step she took. As she reached the doorway, she turned to look at Austin again, but only the darkening street met her worried gaze. She looked up at Les and he motioned with a toss of his head for her to proceed.

Her hand slipped with the perspiration that coated the knob from her sweating palms when she tried to open the door. Les moved in behind her and covered her small hand with his and together they opened the heavy door and entered the jailhouse. Marshal Reed looked up from his desk with a mild look of surprise on his face. He barely took note of the grubby-looking boy who was standing in front of the other man.

"Somethin' the matter?" he asked the other man, thinking that this little vagabond had probably tried to rob the prestigious eastern lawyer.

Les pushed Krystal into the center of the room. "This young lad and I were just passing by The First National Bank and saw something that looked suspicious. Perhaps you should go over and make sure

422

everything is all right?" Krystal turned her face up to him in amazement. His voice had been so calm and definite that she found it hard to believe that he was lying. She realized that she would not have been able to handle this on her own if she had not run into him. Her voice was lost somewhere amid the fear that had possessed her whole being.

Cameron rose up to his feet with a skeptical look upon his face. "Suspicious?" His reputation as a ruthless marshal had kept his town clear of most troublemakers, let alone bank robbers. He opened his mouth to voice his doubts when a large explosion shook the small town by its very foundation.

"What the—" Cameron did not take time to finish the sentence as he grabbed his rifle and bolted around his desk. At the doorway, he paused and turned to Les Macrea. "Do you have a gun?" Les gave his head an emphatic shake. Cameron ran to the far wall and pulled a key ring from the back pocket of his jeans. His movements were swift as he unlocked the gun-cabinet which was built into the wall and removed a .44 rifle from the interior. He tossed the gun to Les as he pushed the keys into his back pocket again. Krystal and Les both were observing his actions regarding the important set of keys, but it was apparent that Cameron Reed was not going to part with the ring as he rushed toward the front door again. There was not time for him to ponder over whether or not Les Macrea was trustworthy because there was no one else in the building for him to rely on for help. The boy who accompanied the lawyer did not even enter into Cameron's distracted mind. "Stay here and guard that prisoner. I'll send someone over to help you if I get detained at the bank."

Les gave him a lame nod of his head. For a moment after he departed neither Krystal nor Les attempted to move. It was too ironic that Cameron Reed had entrusted Devon to the two people who were planning to break him out of the jail. Finally Les began to come to his senses and motioned to Krystal. "I'll watch the door, you look for another set of keys to unlock Devon's cell."

She did not hesitate as she charged into the cell block, she had no intention of taking the time to look for the keys. The enormous boots nearly caused her to fall on her face as she skidded to a halt while her eyes adjusted to the dim light in the narrow hallway. The commotion brought Devon to the front of his cell. He had already been pacing the confines of his cell as he wondered what had caused the loud explosion. Thoughts of a lynching party breaking into the jail and stringing him up to the nearest post were foremost in his mind as his eyes followed the small figure who was charging towards his cell.

Krystal threw herself up against the bars. "I'm breaking you out of here, but first you have to promise that you will help me to find Drake in Brown's Hole."

Devon clasped hold of the bars and opened his mouth, but nothing came out. He was left speechless for an instant. He leaned down and studied the face beneath the big hat and the heavy layer of dirt. "Krystal? Is that you?"

She did not have time to grant him an answer to that obvious question. "Drake disappeared in the rapids of the Green River. Will you promise to take me to Brown's Hole to search for him if I get you out of here?" she demanded one more time.

424

Devon stared at her for a few seconds longer before he shrugged precariously. He had no idea what she was talking about, but he would do anything to get out of this cell. His only other prospect was to exit from this jail to a hangman's gallows or the four walls of the Wyoming State Prison, and neither of those choices were as appealing as escaping with Krystal Colbert.

"I'll take you anywhere you want to go, sugar." He thought of the fancy dressed man who had been asking questions about her a short time ago. Having Miss Colbert as his companion might provide to be an advantage he could profit from after she helped him to get out of this cell. He started to ask her how she proposed to break him out of the jail when she produced a gun from somewhere beneath her huge jacket. All of a sudden Devon realized that the old hat she was wearing belonged to Drake. It was his brother's favorite hat when they had been youngsters, and he had always fought their mother vehemently each time she had threatened to throw it away.

She stood back and clasped the gun in her shaking hands. "Move away from the door, I'm going to shoot off the lock."

Devon was too shocked to disagree as he stumbled backward. He had definitely misjudged this little lady. She was one hell of a brave gal to attempt a jailbreak in Cameron Reed's jail and he was not going to stand in her way. The sound of the gunshot echoed through the narrow space and for a second they were both deafened by the loud noise. Les Macrea rushed into the cell block and stopped short when he saw the reason for the shot. The last thing he had suspected was for Krystal to have a gun concealed on her person, but she still had the weapon clutched tightly in her hands as the broken latch swung back and forth from the bars of the cell door.

Devon pushed through the door and reached for the gun which she had just fired. He grabbed the .45 from Krystal's unsuspecting hands and lowered it at Les Macrea's heart. Krystal gasped in horror as she grabbed ahold of his arm. "No Devon, he my friend. I would have never been able to get in here if it hadn't been for his help."

Devon's stance remained rigid as he continued to hold the gun on the other man for a moment longer. He had no other choice but to believe Krystal because there was no time for indecision. The distrustful look in his dark eyes did not diminish as a reluctant shrug lifted his shoulders. He motioned for Krystal and Les to lead the way as they moved into the main room of the jail. Devon steps halted as his eyes lowered and fixed on the gun in his hand. This was his father's gun!

A strange feeling passed through his body as he glanced back up and met Krystal's terrified face. "How did you get my father's gun?"

Krystal paused. "Your mother gave it to me."

A chill ran down the length of his whole body. He had not held his father's side-iron in his hand for a long time! . . . The last time had been the day of his father's funeral when he had placed it in the big oak guncabinet for safekeeping. Holding the weapon now was like grasping his whole existence within the boundaries of his clammy palms. He sensed that all his years of self-destruction had been leading up to this one moment. On the other side of that door, his fate was waiting to uncoil, and he was not sure if he

426

was ready to face his own destiny yet. It surprised him that he suddenly was wishing that he could have another chance to do his life all over again. While he stood in front of the doorway and lovingly fingered the worn handle of his father's colt .45, he began to realize how many things about his life he would like to do differently.

Jennifer Holt's pretty face floated from the hidden canyons of his mind, and his father's strong voice echoed through his head. He thought of his feud with Drake which seemed so insignificant now. He felt a hand on his arm and he thought of his mother. If he could just see her one more time? He would apologize to her for all the hurt he had caused her through the years. She had always stood by him and he had never been there for her when she needed him. He glanced down, half expecting to see the understanding face of his long-suffering mother. Instead, he saw Krystal's dirt-streaked face, and her expression was filled with pain and fear, too. It was her small hand that rested on his arm. He realized that she was also facing her own fate tonight and there was no turning back for either of them.

Chapter Thirty-one

Devon understood this strange sense of doom he was experiencing about departing from the jailhouse, he always had this eerie feeling of the unknown every time he was about to walk through a doorway. But he had never had this sensation as strongly as he did tonight and it made him hesitate longer than he should have.

Krystal and Les watched him expectantly, it was his next move which would determine the outcome of this whole charade. Devon began to glance around the room as though he was in doubt of what he should do next. His eyes fixed on the gun cabinet as he realized that his father's gun was not sufficient to hold off an ambush if there should be one waiting on the other side of the door. Krystal cringed as she watched him break the glass on the front of the cabinet and begin to unload the artillery. He turned and held out a pistol to her.

"I—I don't—."

"You're goin' to need it, sugar," he said as he shoved

the weapon into her hand. Devon's gaze moved to Les and then back to Krystal again. "We don't need him."

"Oh Lord, you won't shoot him after he just helped you to escape?" Krystal said, her horror at the prospect making her feel sick to her stomach.

Devon did not reply. He grabbed a lasso from a hook on the wall and motioned for Les Macrea to sit in the chair behind the desk. Les stumbled into the chair and did not offer any resistance while Devon began to tie him securely to the chair. Krystal exhaled the breath she had been afraid to release.

"Now, Mr. Lawyer, you just tell the marshal how that little cowpoke over there," Devon motioned towards Krystal, "pulled a gun on you and held you captive until I was out of the cell and tied you up in this chair." Devon glanced back at Krystal and noticed the immense look of relief on her face. If they escaped from here tonight, he would owe her quite a few more favors, he decided as he pointed towards the door and began to move in that direction.

Krystal followed him in a numb stupor. She was glad that Les would not be involved in the jailbreak any further, but she was getting in deeper all the time. Les' remark kept ringing in her ears. Now she was as guilty as her mother. Devon grabbed hold of her arm and she knew this was the beginning of something she could never reverse.

"Are there horses out there?" Devon asked in a voice that sounded shaky.

The uncertainty in his tone was unnerving to Krystal. She only nodded her head weakly. What had she gotten them into? She glanced back at Les one more time as she heard Devon open the door. Les moved his head slightly, and from above the scarf which Devon had shoved into his mouth, his eyes blinked several times. Krystal wished she had time to tell him how much she loved him, but there was no more time. She could tell he understood.

The street was nearly dark, but the tops of the buildings were still outlined by the fiery tones of the orange and red sunset. An uninvited wind had whipped up and was playing havoc with the loose dirt in the street as miniature swirls of dust twisted in random along the empty roadway. The chaos from the explosion of the bank building had left this section of the street deserted, but before the people had left they had barred all the shutters on the windows and bolted every door.

Devon pushed Krystal out onto the crooked boards of the sidewalk and paused as the wind began to howl in a ruthless manner. Devon was struck with the thought of how it seemed that he was always riding head on into the wind. "Where are the horses," he demanded while trying to concentrate on something other than his unfortunate chain of events.

"The—they're in the alley at the end of the street." Krystal could hear the tension in his voice, and she could feel the cold shadow which hovered over their lives.

Devon cursed and grabbed her more roughly than he had planned. They had to go another five hundred yards or more before they would reach the ally and they were out in plain sight until then. He pulled her along beside him as Krystal fought to keep the huge boots on her feet, while at the same time, she struggled to keep astride with him.

"That's far enough, Devon." The voice which floated across the street was clear and controlled. It caused

Krystal's heart to lurch into her throat and the last of her bravery to fly out of her terrified body like the tumblewoods which rolled with the wind across the barren street. She twirled around to the source of the voice and glimpsed his face for just a split second before she was shoved to the ground. As her face thudded against the dirt, her mind grasped at the sight she had just seen, but it was too unbelievable for her to comprehend. Above her, she heard the roar of Devon's gun and she felt the repercussion of the blast, but her vision was blurred by the gunsmoke that hung heavy in the air as the sound of firearms exploded from both sides of the street.

The fall had caused the big hat to fall over her eyes and she was afraid to move even enough to push it back up so that she could see what was happening. She had never known such an overbearing fear and she was sure that she had only been imagining that it had been Drake who had called out the chilling warning a second ago. Her terror, however, was not powerful enough to hold back the urge to look up again. Her arm began to inch up to the brim of the hat, and as she lifted her head just enough to look out upon the scene before her horror-filled gaze, she was forced to face the inevitable.

She had failed, and because of her, men would die from the judgment that would be passed tonight by the demons which rode in the holsters upon their hips. And in the midst of it all, Drake was standing like a quiet sentry, watching her. He was only several hundred feet away, but he was on the opposite side of the street . . . on the other side of her crumbling world. She began to feel the choking dust and the lead-filled air as they closed up her throat. Had a flying bullet struck her or was it the look on Drake's face that had taken away the last beat of her broken heart?

Drake had stood out in the street longer than any sensible man would have. He had been praying that Krystal would make some sort of movement, but she remained face down in the dirt. If she had been hit, his brother would never live long enough to take another whiff of the foul air which always seemed to follow his worthless soul. But now that he had seen her move and knew that she was alive, he suddenly became aware of his own deadly position. He fell to the ground and rolled beneath an abandoned wagon as he tried to assess the situation. Drake was so filled with relief that Krystal was not dead that it took a few seconds for his mind to function again. Everything that was happening was too uncanny. If he had rode into town ten minutes sooner, he could have stopped her before she broke Devon out of jail, and if he had been five minutes later, she would have already been gone. It was as though it was destined that they should not be together, yet he knew that they were meant to never be apart.

When he took Jennifer and Bobby to his mother's house, his mother told him what was about to take place at the jailhouse in a rush of hysterical emotion. Drake had thought he would be able to reach the jail in time, but Lady Luck had been against him again. He arrived at the same time that Krystal and Devon were exiting from the jail, and just as Sidewinder and Austin were returning from the bank where they had just set off the explosion. But Drake did not have to face the whole band of outlaws alone, because Cameron Reed had figured out that the explosion at the

432

bank was only a distraction and he was already headed back to the jail, too. Now the descending nightfall was ablaze with flashes of gunfire and the deafening sounds in accompaniment. Drake did not know who had fired the first shot and he had never known such indecision. He was wearing a badge on his chest, but if he fought on this side of the street, he would be firing at his own wife. He was shocked that he could understand why Krystal and his mother had felt the need to break Devon out of jail, but now Krystal's life was in dire trouble because of it.

Krystal felt herself being pulled up from the ground, though she was not aware of who was dragging her out of the street. She searched through the smoke and dust for one more glimpse of Drake, but there was too much confusion. She regained control of her own footing and saw that it was Sidewinder who was dragging her from the crossfire of exploding shells. He pushed her in front of him and shoved her behind a stack of hay bales for protection. He was about to swing back around to the direction of the battle when he suddenly stopped and looked down at Krystal with the most unusual look upon his young face.

Krystal's brows drew together with a questioning frown while she tried to decipher the strange glint in his sky-blue gaze. Several townsmen had now joined in the battle and it was impossible to tell where the gunfire was coming from in the waning light of the dusk. Krystal started to tell Sidewinder to duck behind the hay bales with her, but he suddenly toppled forward, and the odd look was still upon his cherub face. She screamed and crawled out to where he was laying face down in the dirt. As she rolled him over,

433

she realized that he had been shot in the back and when she saw his unnatural pallor, she knew that his violent young life would end before the last ray of the disappearing sun fell behind the far horizon.

Sidewinder's lids fluttered for an instant and his eyes opened to narrow slits as he gazed up at Krystal's face. He could feel her arms cradling his head and feel the wetness of her tears upon his face, but he could not speak. He had never thought that someone would cry for him, and now he felt the urge to cry, too.

"Oh Lord," Krystal sobbed. "I'm so sorry Sidewinder. This is all my fault. I never should have asked you to help me break Devon out of jail. I'll never forgive myself." She dropped her head down and laid her face against his soft cheek as her body continued to shudder with her tears.

Sidewinder wished he could talk. He didn't want her to blame herself for his death. He had dealt with darkness all of his life and he felt like it was an honor to die for a lady as grand as Krystal DeGanahl. To leave his wicked existence on this earth with her arms wrapped around him was more than he could ever have hoped to have in his final moments. He tried to raise his arm up so that he could touch her soft face once more, but it was not to be.

Krystal heard him inhale sharply and she felt the last of his breath strike against her cheek. She knew he was gone even before she looked at his youthful face. The despair that racked her body was cut off abruptly as she was yanked to her feet again. The action was so sudden that she did not have time to protest as Devon began to drag her towards the alley where the horses were tied. As he pulled her around

434

the corner of the building, she glanced at the still form of Sidewinder one last time. She would never forget that he had given his life for her and she would always remember the good that she had found in his tortured soul.

"We gotta head north. Austin said there's a barricade at the south end of town," Devon shouted as he grabbed the horse she had tied to a fence post in the narrow alley behind the building.

Krystal climbed up into the saddle but she was hardly aware of what she was doing as Devon led her horse toward the north end of town. It was not until she saw Angelina's house in the facing light below Castle Rock that her senses snapped back to reality. She grabbed hold of the reins and yanked them from Devon. He swung around in his saddle and glared at her with a flash of his ebony eyes.

"I'm not going with you," she said in breathless gasp. "Drake is here and I'm not leaving him again."

Devon threw his hands up in the air and a snide chuckle emitted from his mouth. She was always issuing him orders. "Sugar, at this point I don't think you have much choice." He reached out to grab hold of her reins again, but she pulled back and swung her little mare around. The sun was completely gone now and the only direction she could think to go in was towards Angelina DeGanhal's house. She had no idea what she would do when she got there, she was as much of a criminal as Devon, but she could not allow him to take her away from Drake again.

Devon watched her retreat into the darkness. He was not going to go after her and chance being captured again. He kicked his horse in the sides and began to head out of town. He had told Austin that he

435

would meet him up north in the Lost Cabin area. But as he hit the edge of town he realized that he could not leave Krystal to face her punishment alone. She had almost conducted the whole jailbreak single-handedly, he owed that little lady, and he always repaid his debts.

The street was quiet down by the jail. Devon knew that to go after Krystal was sheer foolishness, but it was something he had to do. She had not even bothered to hide her horse, he noticed with aggravation as he rode up to the front gate. The gray mare Krystal had been riding was standing in plain sight in front of his mother's house. Krystal would be helpless against his righteous brother's wrath. Devon decided that he must be loco to even care.

He grabbed the mare's reins and led the horse around to the back of the house. It was too quiet. Devon slid from his horse and pulled his father's pistol out of the waistband of his jeans as he approached the back door. He wondered where his mother was, he did not want to involve her in this dangerous situation. His thoughts switched to Drake, and just as he was about to turn the knob on the back door his brother's voice bellowed through the night.

"Don't even think about goin' into that house." Drake said as he stood at the edge of the back yard, his wide-legged stance ready and poised for Devon's next move.

Devon turned slowly and faced his brother. There was only a half moon beginning to surface above Castle Rock, but there was just enough reflection to cast a light sheen across the expanse of the yard. Devon felt a trembling in his chest. He had been waiting for this chance to outdraw his brother for the

436

better part of his life and now it had finally arrived. How strange that the location where they would have their last round of gunplay, would also be the same place where their father had taught them how to shoot when they were young.

"I've come for Krystal," Devon said as a sly grin curled his lips. He wanted Drake to suffer just a little bit more.

Drake began to shake his head, but no other part of his body moved with his slight gesture. "No Devon, my wife won't be going anywhere with you."

Devon's composure crumbled slightly. His wife? "You're lying. Krystal Colbert is not your wife."

"Yes, I am," Krystal said in a small voice as she moved from the shadows of the house. She had not entered the house when she arrived because she knew Devon had followed her and she was afraid that her father would try to help her in spite of his fragile condition. So she had retreated to the shelter of the bushes beside the house until she had heard her husband's voice. Now she moved out into the middle of the yard and faced Devon with a renewed sense of bravery.

"I broke you out of the jail because you were the only one I thought could help me find my husband. But I didn't do it so that you could try to kill him." She twirled around and looked at Drake. There was no way to tell how he felt because the dim light of the moon was not bright enough for her to see the look in his eyes. She was sure that he probably hated her, but all that she wanted to know was that he would be safe when she had to leave him.

Drake had already made his choice before he came here tonight. He had made his decision when he had seen Krystal hit the dirt out in front of the jailhouse, and when he had asked Cameron Reed to let him come up to the house alone, he did so knowing that he was going to go against every rule and obligation the emblem he wore on his chest represented. But there were too many years of hate and resentment for him to avoid this confrontation with his brother, despite his previous resolution. His gun hand instinctively began to twitch with the impending action.

Behind Devon, the back door opened slowly and the face of Jennifer Holt appeared in the doorway. Devon was not aware of her presence, he was too intent on watching his brother's movements as he began to stalk out to the center of the yard. But Drake could not miss her, nor could he forget Bobby, the son that Devon did not know existed.

Drake saw the movement out of the corner of his eye, and his hand fell to his gun without a second thought as Devon pushed Krystal to the side, then raised their father's gun into the air. His confident look was shattered and his shot went wild as a stunned expression covered his face. The pistol fell to the ground as Devon stared down at his arm. He had always believed he would be able to outdraw his older brother, but Drake's hand had been so swift that Devon had not had time to even cock the hammer of his gun. Devon shook his head with disgust as he covered the bloody hole in his wrist with his other hand. Drake had taken the cowardly way out. His wrist would heal in no time, and then they would have to go through this same episode all over again. Devon began to curse at his brother and at everything in his path as he swung around and saw the face which had haunted his dreams for the past ten years.

438

Jennifer walked out onto the porch and met Devon's dark glare with her wide brown eyes full of fear and hope. She had seen his face every time she had looked at their son and she had prayed for a second chance with him at least a thousand times. But everything hinged on him now, and she could only say one final prayer that he would forgive her for the past which was not in her power to change. He began to walk slowly towards her, he was not sure if this was real or merely another imaginary vision from his fanatical dreams. He forgot about the pain in his wrist, and about the fact that Drake had just proven which of Franklin DeGanahl's sons was the fastest draw, because none of that was important any longer. The feeling that had overcome him earlier at the jail, returned . . . All the years of trying to outrun his fate had led him full circle, and at last he understood why he could not challenge the final showdown again.

Krystal looked up at Drake as he held out his hand to her. She had been observing Devon and the woman whom she knew had to be Jennifer Holt. There were a hundred questions in her spinning mind, but none of them were as important as the question in her eyes as she met Drake's gaze. His hand continued to reach out to her. She cautiously placed her fingers in his warm palm and allowed him to pull her back up to her feet. When Devon had pushed her out of the way, she had lost her balance in the heavy boots and she had fallen into the grass. Drake's old hat had tumbled from her head and her long strawberry blonde curls hung in wild profusion about the shoulders of the black duster she was still wearing. Her face was streaked with dirt and it was obvious that she was terrified of what Drake's feelings were towards her after all that had just taken place tonight.

Drake thought she had never been more beautiful. There was not time, however, for sentimental reunions. It seemed to him that there was never enough time for the words he wanted to say to her, or for the things which he still planned to teach her. But someday, they would find their place in this turbulent land, and when they did, they would have a lifetime to discover the extent of this limitless love which had lit an eternal flame within their reckless hearts.

Krystal allowed him to lead her to the edge of the darkened yard. She did not know if he was taking her back to the jail or if he was going to tell her to get up on her horse and ride out of his life forever. . . . She only cared about this moment when her hand was surrounded by the heat of his touch, and she wanted to savor each second that she was permitted to be this close to him.

He swung himself up into the saddle of the little gray mare. Krystal was sure that his plan was to take her down to the jail and place her under arrest. She reached up and let his strong arm pull her up into the saddle in front of his muscular form. Good Lord, she was not sure if she could tear herself away from him when they reached the jail, and she hoped that she could be strong enough to say goodbye to him without falling apart.

He did not bother to say anything to Devon as he began to lead the horse away from the house. Drake had made his last play in their long embittered contest, and from here on out, Devon would have to make his own moves. Drake wrapped his arms around Krystal and heard her sigh heavily. It was time he settled the score with her, too. As the town disappeared behind them and the moonlight caressed the red soil of the desert ground, Drake reached beneath his suede vest and unpinned the shiny star from his shirt. He held his hand out to the side with a pause as he studied the silver emblem for the last time. Franklin DeGanahl would not be smiling down from the heavens, but Drake knew his father would forgive him. His palm grew damp where the badge rested, but it was not as hard to turn loose of the past he had always thought it would. He tossed the tin star into the wind, but not before he made sure that Krystal was aware of his actions.

He heard her sigh again, but this time with relief. She turned in the saddle and looked up at him through the pale moonlight, but the stars had entered into her eyes and they laced her golden-brown gaze with a desire that could never be equaled.

"My woman, my wife, my destiny . . . today I give you my name; my heart was already in your possession."

Krystal realized that those were the same words he had spoken to her on the day of their impromptu wedding. She thought briefly about the dime store novels which told of the desperados who rode the outlaw trails of the Wild West and she began to smile to herself. Her adventures of the past few weeks could fill a dozen ten cent paperbacks, but none of them could ever have such a perfect ending.

Epilogue

Estados Unidos Mexicanos, 1900

It was a tale of destiny and desire as told through the eyes of those who had lived it with the passion and zest of the declining era. And it told of romantic rendezvous among the purpled hollows of the gentle desert swales and golden sunsets ablaze with the rapture of boundless love. It was the beginning of the end and the start of a lifetime.

Krystal closed the pages of the journal in which she was writing her memoirs of that brief span in time when her life had been balanced between lawlessness and justice. She sighed with contentment and leaned back against the rail of the veranda. At last they were in a place where they could all live in harmony, and most importantly, each of them had learned how to accept the mistakes of their impetuous past. The night was alive with sweet scents of orchids and begonias which climbed the wrought iron posts of the balcony. The lulling sound of crickets and the distant wail of a hungry puma accompanied the stillness of the night.

The vast hacienda was silent also.

Devon and Jennifer had taken Bobby into Mexico City for the weekend and the rest of the family—Angelina and her father, Migel Rameriz, were visiting a neighbor until later tonight. It was difficult to predict when they would see John again, since the elder Colbert had developed quite a weakness for the senoritas at the local cantina. Krystal and Drake were alone, except for the two little girls who were sleeping in the next room, but they did not pose a problem.

She watched as he approached the vine-infested porch from the other side of the lush garden. She knew the look which was contained within his olive-green gaze before he was even close enough for her to make out his expression. His features were masked with soft unspoken words of the impending rite which was about to take place, and even before he had touched her, Krystal felt the fingers of desire reaching out to her. Like smoke from an early morning camp-fire, she uncurled herself from the chair she was sitting in and leaned over rail to kiss his upturned face when he was within her reach. She was like ice and he was a raging fire which melted her soul with consuming longings.

A crooked smile curled up the corner of his mouth and his left eye narrowed with the tempting promises which her jewel-toned eyes beheld. He had an overwhelming urge to make love to her beneath the curious eye of the moon and the timid twinkling of the endless star-studded sky. Tonight nothing could prevent him from fulfilling that wish. Krystal returned his suggestive smile with her own teasing grin. She knew exactly what her husband was pondering as she reached over the black wrought-iron rail of the balcony and extended her arms.

Drake's smile deepened as he swung his legs over the rail. In the darkness, his white shirt and the glistening of his white teeth seemed startling against his tan skin. Krystal grew drunk on his nearness, she could never have enough of his intoxicating kisses. She pulled him closer as she tugged on the front of his open shirt which trailed down beneath the waistband of his jeans into a deep V. Their mouths dismissed the rest of the distance as they united with a hunger which only intensified with each breath they took.

Drake allowed her only enough time to push the shirt back from his broad shoulders, but as her slender fingers began to trail through the dense curls along his chest, past his waistband, and into the warmth of his jeans, he grew too eager to prolong this enchanting agony. With hands that yearned to caress her soft skin, he took the time to unbutton the brass enclosures of his pants so that she could continue her seductive descent. Her lips began to nip and taunt their way down this trail of beckoning brown curls as her delicate hands continued a devouring assault of blissful delight upon his pulsating masculinity.

When he had reached the limit of this indescribable pleasure, he retaliated by sliding down next to her and together they reclined back upon the thick carpet of the veranda floor. Krystal could feel the throbbing of his sensual shank against her thigh as his nimble fingers became intertwined within the honeycomb moistness of her womanly retreat and as he raised her enflamed body to a summit of unreachable heights with his proficiency.

Impatient to move on to even sweeter temptations, Drake pushed away her thin gown — the only garment

444

she was wearing — and began an onslaught of delicious osculation upon her whole body until neither of them could hold back the course of the night.

His virile saber became immersed within the beckoning hollow between her satiny thighs as their amorous junction became rampant with ravishment. Repetition had perfected each movement, but each time they indulged in this exquisite alliance it was like exploring new and unchartered horizons. And when they reached the highest peak, and there was no other direction to go but back to the place from where they had ascended, Drake drove himself against her arching hips and released the ambrosia of this ecstasy with one last lustful lunge.

Krystal clasped her arms tighter around his perspiring body and held him until she grew weak from her tight embrace. Everyday — with every passing minute — she cherished him more, and each time their wanton eyes touched, she loved a lifetime in his gaze.

Drake felt his heartbeat begin to slow down and it seemed that his breathing might reach a normal keel again. But it was always a distinct possibility that he would be overtaken by her enticing essence again and it would start all over. He sighed, not even Shangri-la was as tempting as his tawny-eyed wife.

"Well, darlin'," he began as a mischievous grin taunted the corners of his mouth. "I've been thinking that it's about time that I have a son."

Krystal smiled, they had been through this conversation twice before, three years ago with Becky and two years ago when she had became pregnant with Angie. "Oh really?" she said in a haughty tone. "But I still haven't forgiven you for that remark about —"

"I know," he interrupted. "That little remark about

445

how no man should have to put up with more than one woman like you in his lifetime?"

She tried to hide her amusement, but it was difficult. Becky and Angie were the miniature copies of their mother and poor Drake did not have a chance against the three females. Krystal sighed. "Well? Perhaps someday I might consider giving you a son. But in the meantime?" She rolled over and covered his long frame with her small but extremely competent body, "Could you make love to me just one more time?"

His roguish smile broadened. He never could deny this woman anything. And who knows . . . maybe someday?